DEAR DAUGHTER

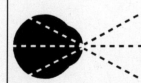

DEAR DAUGHTER

ELIZABETH LITTLE

THORNDIKE PRESS
A part of Gale, Cengage Learning

GALE
CENGAGE Learning·

Farmington Hills, Mich • San Francisco • New York • Waterville, Maine
Meriden, Conn • Mason, Ohio • Chicago

GALE
CENGAGE Learning®

LIBRARY OF CONGRESS CATALOGING-IN-PUBLICATION DATA

Little, Elizabeth, 1981–
    Dear daughter / Elizabeth Little. — Large print edition.
        pages cm — (Thorndike press large print basic)
        ISBN 978-1-4104-7467-4 (hardback) — ISBN 1-4104-7467-4 (hardcover)
    1. Single women—Fiction. 2. Women prisoners—Fiction. 3. Judicial error—Fiction. 4. Mothers—Crimes against—Fiction. 5. Murder—Investigation—Fiction. 6. Large type books. I. Title.
PS3612.I8755D43 2014b
813'.6—dc23   2014034923

Published in 2014 by arrangement with Viking, a member of Penguin Group (USA) LLC, a Penguin Random House Company

Printed in Mexico
3 4 5 6 7 18 17 16 15

For Kate and Sara

Some girls are just born with glitter in their veins.

— *Paris Hilton*

From: CNN Breaking News
   <BreakingNews@mail.cnn.com>
Subject: CNN Breaking News
Date: Sept 17, 2013 10:43:01 AM EDT
To: textbreakingnews@ema3lsv06.turner
   .com

A California judge has overturned the first-degree murder conviction of Jane Jenkins as part of the ongoing investigation into the mismanagement of evidence by the Los Angeles County Crime Lab from 2001 to 2005.

Jenkins, 26, was convicted in 2003 of killing her mother, Swiss-American socialite and philanthropist Marion Elsinger.

Jenkins made her first public appearance in ten years when she was escorted into this morning's proceedings in Sacramento. Reporters were barred from the hearing.

Jenkins is scheduled to be released later today. When her lawyer, Noah Washington, was asked outside the courthouse about Jenkins's plans for the future, he offered no comment.

CHAPTER ONE

As soon as they processed my release, Noah and I hit the ground running. A change of clothes. A wig. An inconspicuous sedan. We doubled back once, twice, then drove south when we were headed east. In San Francisco we had a girl who looked like me board a plane to Hawaii.

Oh, I thought I was so clever.

But you probably already know that I'm not.

I mean, come on, you didn't really think I was just going to *disappear,* did you? That I would skulk off and live in the shadows? That maybe I would find a distant island, a plastic surgeon, a white ceramic half mask and a Punjab lasso? Get real.

But I never meant for it to come to this. There's attention and then there's *attention,* and sure, the latter gets you fame and money and free designer shoes, but I'm not

Lindsay Lohan. I understand the concept of declining marginal returns. It was the not knowing — that's what I couldn't stand. That's why I'm here.

Did you know that the more you remember, the more you expand your perception of personal time? No, really. There's, like, studies and shit. Even though we can't outrun death, if we muscle up our memories the race, at least, will seem a little longer. That is, we'll still die, but we'll have lived more. Kind of comforting, right?

Unless, of course, you're me.

Imagine how it would feel if, out of the blue, someone were to hand you a gold medal and tell you it was yours. *Oh my god,* you'd think. *I am so super awesome! I won the Olympics. But, wait — what did I win? When did I win it? When did I train? Shouldn't my biceps be full-on Madonna? How could I possibly forget the defining moment of my life?*

And what does it mean that I did?

Now imagine that instead of a gold medal you were given a murder conviction, and you'll have some sense of how it is for me.

When I think back on the night my mother died, it's like trying to adjust a pair of rabbit ears to pick up a distant broadcast signal. Every so often something comes into focus, but mostly I just get the scrape-sound of static, an impenetrable wall of snow. Sometimes there isn't even a picture. Sometimes there isn't even a TV. Maybe if I'd had a moment to stop and think that morning I might've had the chance to imprint a useful detail or two, but the police hustled me out of the house and into a cruiser and over to the station before I could even think to worry about what I was wearing, much less what I might have done. By lunchtime I was in an interview room picking dried blood out from under my fingernails while two detectives explained what they wanted me to write in my confession.

Not that I blame them. I was always going to be the best story.

Next was the trial, which didn't have anything to do with what I knew but rather with what other people had decided I knew, and soon enough I lost the ability to tell the difference between them. And now I'm stuck with a mess of a memory, a hodge-podge of angry testimony, sanctimonious magazine profiles, made-for-TV movies — less linear narrative than *True Hollywood Story* highlight reel. I don't know what's mine anymore.

And then there's the evidence. The only fingerprints in my mother's room: mine. The only DNA under my mother's nails:

probably mine. The only name written in blood next to my mother's body: definitely mine.

(That's right. You probably didn't know that part, did you?)

It's hard enough to maintain your innocence when so many people are so sure you're not. It's impossible when you're not sure of anything at all — other than the awful, inescapable fact that you hadn't particularly liked your own mother.

The uncertainty ate at me, maggots mashing the already-decaying corpse of my brain. And in jail, isolated from any real means of investigation, all I could do was wonder. I began to treat every action of every day like an omen, a crystal ball, a goat's intestines. How would a killer brush her teeth? How would a killer brush her hair? Would she take sugar in her coffee? Milk in her tea? Would she knot her shoelaces once? Twice?

Totally kidding. Like they would have given me shoelaces.

Of all the challenges of incarceration, this was perhaps the worst: I was a fundamentally rational creature reduced to rudimentary divination. I promised myself that if I ever got out I'd try to find out what really happened, to find out what I really was.

I ignored the voice that said killing again was the only way I'd ever know for sure.

Tuesday 5:14 PM

Testing. Is the new phone
working? Did you get this?
(It's Noah.)

What the fuck is this

It's called text messaging.

*I know what it is I just don't
know why we're doing it*

I need to make sure I can
reach you.

*What people don't actually
talk anymore*

Welcome to the future.

Can I go back to jail now

Adapt or die, Jane.
:)

CHAPTER TWO

Six weeks after I got out, the last Tuesday in October, I was standing in front of a mirror in a hotel in Sacramento. I'd been there for what felt like hours, playing with my hair like a preteen twat while I worked up the courage to cut it off and color it.

In prison my hair was all I had, the last thing that made me *me.* Such a pain in the ass to take care of, too — I mean, for ages the only personal care items I was allowed were these packets of watery shampoo no bigger than the things of ketchup they give you at McDonald's. Other girls dreamed of sex or drugs or cigarettes; I'd've given my left kidney for some motherfucking Pantene. I could've saved myself so much trouble if I'd shaved it, cut it, burned it, but I didn't, even though my vanity was already my most conspicuous vulnerability.

It's an amateur move, giving a shit. I just couldn't help myself.

I combed the hair out with my fingers. After all the trouble I'd gone to, it still had the texture of something a cat had coughed up. Matted. Glutinous. It fell to my waist in a glop of coarse strands and split ends. I smeared my sweaty palm over my reflection like I was the late Liz Taylor greasing up a camera lens. It didn't help. I turned away.

Noah hadn't wanted me to feel hemmed in, so he'd found me a suite at one of those executive extended-stay places. Two hundred square feet of beige on beige cluttered up with "modern" furniture and pamphlets that trumpeted the hotel's amenities. Internet! Cable! Cutlery! It was far and away the nicest place I'd been in years.

(And I hated it. Too much space. Too many windows. Too many pillows. The bathtub was the only place I could sleep, not that I was doing much of that. The close quarters were as comforting as a hug — or maybe I mean a straitjacket.)

I waded through an awkward cluster of knock-off Noguchi side tables and flopped on the couch to catch up on the news. I hadn't turned off the TV since I'd arrived — at the top of each hour I'd flip to HLN before cycling through MSNBC, CNN, Fox. If I was feeling masochistic I'd hop over to E!. More than a month in, most of the coverage was less investigative than speculative, but it was speculation I was looking for. Nothing kills a well-laid plan like dumb luck. I propped my feet on the coffee table.

It was the middle of the night, and the networks had given up pretending they were interested in anything important; I was the top story. The host had aggressively symmetrical features and a grim expression at odds with her beauty-pageant posture. Despite the frown, her forehead was as smooth as glycerin soap. She was at least two years younger than me.

I rubbed at my brow and thought about Botox.

The woman's fish mouth was moving. I turned up the volume. "Jane Jenkins, sentenced to life in prison ten years ago for the murder of her mother, was released six weeks ago today, when a judge overturned her conviction and eight others as a result of the ongoing investigation into the deliberate mishandling of evidence by LAPD crime lab technicians from 2001 to 2005. Despite the ruling, the American public is still overwhelmingly convinced of Jenkins's guilt: A McClure Post/ABC News poll conducted last week shows that 87 percent of respondents 'strongly believe' that Jenkins is responsible for her mother's murder."

A crocodile Birkin says the other 13 percent "*really* strongly believe" I'm guilty.

"It comes as no surprise, then, that since her release Jenkins has yet to make a public appearance — or even give any indication as to her whereabouts. If Jenkins hopes for a fresh start, however, she may be disappointed: Today crime blogger Trace Kessler, who has been covering the case since 2003, announced a reward of fifty thousand dollars for information leading to the discovery of Jenkins's location —"

I fished behind the television and pulled the plug, wishing I could do the same for the Internet. I tapped a chewed-up nail against my reflection on the darkened screen.

Trace Kessler. Less a thorn in my side than a noose around my neck. I knew he wouldn't hesitate for a second if he got the chance to tug that rope tight.

Stop it. Enough stalling.

I went to the kitchenette, where I'd stashed the three-pack of All-Purpose Value Scissors Noah had brought over the last time he'd dropped by the hotel. The scissors were as sharp as a midmorning drunk: When I tested them on the inside of my arm they left nothing more than a dry, piggy-pink line. I caught myself grinding my teeth. I tried to tell myself that Noah likely considered this a compromise. Knowing him, I was lucky he hadn't stuck me with safety scissors.

When I first told him I wanted to cut my own hair, he went so still even the blue-bruised skin under his eyes seized up, as if I'd expressed an interest in weapons-grade uranium or hybrid zombie honey bees. "I'm not sure that's a good idea," he said, because at the end of the day Noah Washington was just a big old drama queen.

I rolled my eyes. "I'm not asking for a razor blade."

"You'd never do that. Too obvious."

"Too forgettable," I corrected — because at the end of the day I was just a big old drama queen, too.

In one of the kitchenette cabinets I found a coffee mug, which I flipped over so I could sharpen the scissors on the unglazed ring on the bottom, a trick I'd picked up in the prison library's wildly malapropos outdoor life section. I dragged the blade back and forth across the off-white ceramic and felt my pique subside, gentled by the repetition, the reverberation, by the soft, sweet rasp of the blade.

I took the scissors back to the bathroom,

grabbed a hank of hair, and pulled it taut. My hair was finally starting to dry, curling up and frizzing out, something that used to drive my mother crazy. She always tried to get me to wear it up — a ponytail, a bun, a chignon. "You could be so elegant if you just tried," she said once, in a rare moment of maternal optimism. As I stared at the mirror, my hands swept up the whole mass of my hair and coiled it on top of my head. It made my neck look longer, my jaw sharper, my eyes brighter, and even in the gruesome light of a hotel bathroom, I could see that she'd been right. Maybe I had some pretty left after all.

Fuck it. It's just hair.

The following Saturday, Noah arrived just before 5:00 in the morning, as promised. He bolted the door behind him before giving me a queer look. "I suppose that's one way to discourage photographers," he said.

"Flatterer."

He thrust a bag of donuts at me. "The best I could do at this ungodly hour."

I took it reluctantly. I'd been trying to put on as much weight as possible, but I couldn't exactly run out for a burger and fries, and delivery was out of the question. So I'd been living on supermarket ramen —

chicken ramen, creamy chicken ramen, spicy chili chicken ramen — and what I lacked in heft I'd begun to offset with bloat. If I sat very still I imagined I could feel the saline bubbling up under my skin. What I would have given for a nice light salad or an emetic.

Noah watched me force the last donut down, casting a critical eye over my knobby elbows and protruding collarbones. He couldn't even see the worst of it, the sunken sternum, the knife-blade hipbones. The stuff of physiological liminality, of premature birth and imminent death. And of prison food. "You're still too thin," he said.

"You're still too bossy."

His gaze darted to the side, a characteristic evasion. I liked to pretend that he did this with all his clients, that he was maintaining a professional distance, making sure he didn't see the answers to questions he'd never meant to ask. But this was an evasion of its own: It was really me he didn't want having the answers.

Noah was my seventh lawyer — or maybe the eighth? God, another thing I can't remember. I know I was represented first by one of my ex-stepfather's poker-faced lawyers, but he cut me loose when he began to comprehend the extent of the evidence against me. Next was a press-savvy Hollywood lawyer, but I dumped him when I realized he owned candy-striped dress shirts. Then there was a series of increasingly disreputable ambulance chasers, some of whom were after the money I stood to inherit if we managed to sidestep a statute or two, some of whom just wanted the fame.

Noah, on the other hand, wanted nothing to do with money or fame or even power — which was, of course, why I wanted him. As my lawyer, I mean.

We'd been together since 2006, which was the year I finally came back to myself enough to care about an appeal. He's — well — how to describe Noah? Tall, handsome, apologetic. Rumpled brown hair that bleaches blond in the summer. An accent out of a Tennessee Williams play and a genetic inclination for a farmer's tan. He grew up in some asshole of a town in Mississippi, shit poor and hungry for everything but daddy issues, but his optimism remained improbably intact. I bet he still goes home every year for Thanksgiving thinking that *this* time he'll finally talk the family into getting over *Brown v. Board of Education*.

I was given Noah's name by one of the few guards who didn't have the stomach for what enforced isolation did to those of us in the Secure Housing Unit, and as soon as I earned pencil-and-paper privileges, I began writing him. It took seventeen letters to convince him to come see me, because I knew seeing me was key. If he had assessed my case on its intangible merits — or me on mine — he never would've taken me on as a client.

But I had him as soon as he set eyes on me. I wasn't at my worst, but I was close to it: skin and bones and half catatonic. I didn't even believe he was really there until twenty minutes into our interview. He was my first visitor in years.

As I'd anticipated, his compassion was as immediate as it was ill considered. There aren't many upsides to seven weeks in solitary, but inciting humanitarian sympathy sure is one of them.

This is one of the things you need to know about Noah: No matter what you may have heard, he really did want to make a difference, to fight for the huddled masses or whatever (I mean, the guy probably potty trained at a year so he could do his part for the environment). He redeemed me by mere association. The Tourvel to my Valmont. The Hillary to my Bill. The Cindy Lou Who to my Grinch Who Stole Christmas.

If I'd been a better person I would've cut

him loose years ago.

That morning in the hotel suite Noah looked like he'd been up all night, and he probably had, what with everything I'd asked him to do. His hair had been tugged and tufted, and his usual hangdog look had gone from basset hound to bloodhound. When he sat down opposite me, his eyes flickered shut before he wrenched them open again.

He pulled a bulging folder from the stained and battered briefcase he loved to lug around to offset his good looks.

"Your papers," he said.

He held on to the folder a second longer than he needed to.

I opened the file. On top was a driver license. I held it up to the light so I could examine the picture. An uneven bowl cut and homely bangs. Discount wire-rimmed glasses that magnified contacts the color of wet cardboard. My hair was the same shade. I looked like the kind of person who doesn't know what masturbation is.

I had no idea how Noah had managed to get the license made so quickly. He must've called in a hell of a favor.

Noah was watching me as he tried to make himself comfortable on a Bauhaus club chair the color of something you'd find in a Dickensian orphanage.

"There's plenty of room over here on the couch," I said, still looking at the license.

"That thing's made of rocks," he said. "Tell me why I booked this place again?"

"Because this is the first chance you've had to spoil me." I held up the next sheet of paper. "No problem with the name change?"

"No. It's legit — well, legit enough. You planning to go by Becca or Becky?"

"Call me Becky and I'm telling *People* magazine your favorite book's *The Fountainhead.*"

If I'd been free to pick any name in the world, I would have gone for something diaphanous and fanciful, like Coralie or Delphine, the kind of name a *grande dame* gives a *petit chien.* Because no one — no one — daydreams about pretty names more than girls called Jane. And with good reason, you know? I mean, even our most illustrious Janes are world-class sticks-in-the-mud. Austen, Eyre, Doe? Spinster, sucker, corpse. It's a wonder I managed as well as I did.

(Although at least Jane is reasonably dignified. When I was arrested the tabloids decided to call me *Janie,* and ever since everyone else has followed suit. Like I needed another reason to hate Aerosmith.)

But there was no place for whimsy in my world — not that there ever was — so I picked the kind of name a person could trust . . . and forget immediately thereafter. Rebecca Parker was such a perfect choice, I worried I might forget it too.

Noah cleared his throat. "Still with me?"

I rustled about in the folder, reminding myself to — what did that damn counselor call it again? — stay in the moment. "Social security?" I asked.

"It's there," he said. "Took me the better part of the last two weeks, too, most of it in line or on hold. It was a perfect opportunity to think about my illustrious career and wonder where it all went wrong."

"You should've followed my lead," I said. "Twenty-six, fabulously wealthy, and I never even finished high school."

"Yeah, you know what my mom says when I talk to her? 'Noah,' she says, 'Why can't you be more like that nice girl Janie Jenkins?' "

"She's not the only one."

It was a tired shtick, but it still made me smile. Noah reached for my hand and managed to glance his fingertips across my knuckles before I pulled away.

"What about the money?" I asked.

After a moment he nudged a manila

envelope across the coffee table. I opened it and found records of accounts and transfers and investments — and a roll of bills. The hold on my mother's estate had been lifted, but for all practical purposes I was a fugitive, and I needed to avoid traceable transactions. Although carrying that much cash was almost as risky.

I began to count out the bills, but when I lost track for the third time I gave up. I put my head in my hands and closed my eyes. There was a noise, a low thrum from the other room — I'd left the bathroom fan on. Down the hall, a door slammed.

I started to say I don't even know what, but Noah leaned forward and cut me off with a look on his face I knew all too well. "Now," he said, "you're a grown woman, you can do what you want —"

(Has a sentence starting with "now" ever gone well for the person on the other side?)

I blew out a breath. "You're seriously going to do this?"

"I just think you need to consider the possibility that you might not be able to disappear."

"Of course I can. That nice judge said I could."

"Every single cable news network has been rerunning footage of the trial."

"Good — then everyone will expect me to look like I used to."

"Jane, they made a *movie* about you."

"Even better! Then everyone will expect me to look like what's-her-face." I frowned. "How is what's-her-face, by the way? Still doing that kid from that wizard movie?"

"Can you be serious for a moment?"

"I'll be *fine,* Noah. I'm not an idiot."

"Not usually."

"Not ever."

"I'm not sure that's necessarily a good thing." He paused, regrouped, grabbed at his hair again. "You can still change your mind, you know. You can still live a public life. Frankly, the more you try to hide, the more they'll try to find you, and there's only so much I can do from my end."

I tried not to think too hard about what I had to say next.

"Yeah, about that — I was thinking it's time to tie that end up."

"I'm sorry?"

"Don't get me wrong, I'm *crazy* grateful for everything you've done, but from here on out —"

His jaw tightened. "You're saying I've outlived my usefulness?"

"Assuming the Fifth Amendment hasn't changed in the past few weeks, yeah."

"So that's just — it? I should've known you'd do something like this."

"Don't take it personally. It's not like we're lovers."

(I'm not given to kindness, but mercy, maybe, is another matter.)

Noah slammed his briefcase on the table and snapped it open. Seconds later a plastic bag landed on my lap.

"I thought you might like to have this," he said.

I looked down and fought the urge to cover my eyes. In the bag were all the things I'd brought with me to the police station that morning — and the only personal property I'd retrieved upon my release. I saw a tube of lipstick oozing pink melt, a jumble of eye shadows shattered loose. A bronzer that had separated, two parts fatty slick to one part fecal shimmer. A matchbook, a set of keys, melatonin supplements. Too many credit cards.

"I thought I told you to get rid of this shit," I said.

"You don't even know what's in there."

"I don't want it."

"At least look."

"I don't want it."

"Jane —"

As soon as his hand settled on my shoulder, I knew what was coming, but I was too tired to fight. So I just sat back and turned toward the window, letting him spout a bunch of crap best left to needlepoint pillows and Christmas cards. He ended the same way he always did: "You didn't do it. I wish you'd believe me."

And I ended the same way I always did: "But I do believe you."

This is the other thing you need to know about Noah. He thought believing something could make it true.

JANE JENKINS

Jane Jenkins (born November 22, 1986) is an American socialite, heiress, and convicted murderer.

Early Life [edit]

Due to her extended family's long-standing refusal to engage with the press and to documented inconsistencies in Jenkins's own accounts of her childhood, confirmed details of Jane Jenkins's early childhood are scarce. The basic facts are known, however: She is the daughter of socialite Marion Elsinger (née Jenkins) and Swiss industrialist Emmerich von Mises, who died shortly after her birth. Jenkins grew up largely in Switzerland and the surrounding areas, and she moved to Los Angeles with her mother and stepfather in August 2001.

Breakthrough [edit]

Jenkins first rose to prominence with a rumored attachment to troubled British singer Oliver Lawson. Though they never publicly acknowledged their relationship, it was Jenkins who was with Lawson when he was rushed to the hospital after a heroin overdose. Though the couple was never again seen together, Jenkins, with her affinity for adventurous fashion and adventurous men, remained in the public eye and soon became a regular presence in gossip columns and tabloids.

Unusually in Hollywood, Jenkins eschewed TV and film work despite her rising star, preferring, she said in 2002, to dedicate her time to "things that didn't suck."

Personal Life [edit]
Rumored to have been romantically linked to Tobey Maguire, Joshua Jackson, Oliver Lawson, and Jim Adkins of Jimmy Eat World. Had a Lhasa apso named Fuckface.

Arrest and Conviction [edit]
In the summer of 2003, Jenkins's mother was found dead in her Beverly Hills home. Jenkins, who had never made a secret of her tumultuous relationship with her mother, was arrested later that day. After a three-month trial and two weeks of jury deliberations, Jenkins — who was tried as an adult — was convicted of first-degree

murder and sentenced to life in prison. She wore Alexander McQueen to her sentencing hearing.

In September 2013, Jenkins was released from prison as a result of the investigations into the manipulation of evidence by the Los Angeles County Crime Lab. Her current whereabouts are unknown.

CHAPTER THREE

I moved swiftly through the hotel room, ignoring the inconvenient rattle in my chest of something I was unwilling to admit to. I needed to focus: on cleaning and clearing and wiping down doorknobs and counters and handles and pulling up the plastic wrap in the bathroom, which I shoved into my suitcase to dispose of later. I dumped all my old crap into my purse and mixed it in with all the new crap in my purse, hoping I'd soon forget the distinction. When I finished I was foolish enough to catch my breath — and in the silence between one task and the next, my equanimity lost its forward momentum.

I eyed the chair Noah had been sitting in. I was under no illusions about the nature of our relationship. For seven years he'd been the linchpin of my life, and not because he kept me sane, but because together we gave rise to an insanity that was entirely our own.

Now my *folie à deux* had become a *folie à une.*

I pressed a hand to my solar plexus.

Understand that this is how it works with people like me. Self-pity is the sun around which we orbit, the great gravitational force that rules those of us for whom Things Didn't Quite Turn Out. If we're lucky, purpose (vengeance, absolution, cookies, not in that order) can keep us from falling in, from burning up, but we're fooling ourselves if we ever think we're going to break free.

But that's why God created Xanax. I slipped half a tab under my tongue and headed for the door. I had a train to catch.

The way I saw it, I figured I had about two weeks before Trace Kessler and the rest of the press tracked me down — and one week before Noah figured it out.

Oh, yes: I was lying to Noah, too.

This, at least, was a relatively recent development. The first time Noah asked me, still idly, where I'd go if I got out, I told him the truth:

"The middle."

He looked up to the sky at my response, a reflex he refused to shake despite years spent righting wrongs that could have been easily remedied if God weren't so super lame. " 'The middle,' as you say, is a pretty big part of the country. Tell me, California Girl, you thinking about any place in particular?" He held up a hand. "And no, you're not allowed to say 'one of those big square states.' "

"What about one of those small square states?"

"Janie," he said, because he knew it would annoy me.

I frowned into the distance as if I didn't already spend half my day thinking about all the places I'd rather be. "Well," I said, "a small town would be best, I think."

"Small towns get CNN, too —"

"Like anyone will expect me to be that far from a Fred Segal."

"— and news moves fast in a small town. Gossip faster."

"Not if it's boring," I said.

"You couldn't be boring if you tried."

"A girl can dream."

He came to visit two hours after the news broke about the crime lab and all the cases that were going to get thrown out. Within days we'd devised a plan: If I was released, I would go to a town in Wisconsin, close enough to Chicago for Noah to be able to check in on me when he was in town, but far enough away that no one of consequence lived nearby. I would stay in a duplex with vertical blinds, favorably located within walking distance of a Pick 'n Save and a Hobby Lobby. I'd change my name and change my hair and order everything I needed on Amazon. Maybe I'd even go to church, because who'd look for me there?

The hardest part — or so Noah thought — would be getting there.

I knew immediately that I would have to take the train. Noah thought this was a stupid idea, but I pointed out that I wouldn't have to stop for gas or show ID. That I wouldn't have to go through security or file a flight plan. That I wouldn't have to share a toilet. That most people probably didn't know you even *could* take a train anymore.

But really I wanted to take the train so I could hide in a compartment before hopping off halfway to Chicago without anyone being the wiser. Then I'd pick up a car Noah knew nothing about and drive to a town he'd never heard of. Which is to say, I had absolutely no intention of going to Wisconsin.

Christ, can you even imagine?

Rebecca Parker, I'd decided, was the kind

of person whose personality was such a big black hole her entire body was being sucked into it, so before I stepped out into the hallway I pulled myself into what I thought of as Queen Wallflower pose: rolled-in shoulders, downcast eyes, pigeoned toes. I pulled my hair in front of my face and let a strand or two stick to my lips.

I opened the door and stepped out.

Showti—

I slapped a hand over my mouth and spun around. I made it to the bathroom just in time to throw up all four donuts and the undigested remnants of the previous night's salsa picante chicken noodles.

Strangers. I was going to have to see strangers. And any one of them could be paparazzi. Any one of them could be Trace Kessler. Any one of them might want me dead.

This is another thing I kept from Noah: the death threats.

When I was in prison I received Himalayan mountains of mail, and because there were times when I wasn't allowed to have anything else to read, I remember many of the letters by heart. There were a few from the fans:

Dear Janie,
   I know you didn't do it!

There were a few from the haters:

Dear Janie,
   I know you did do it!

But mostly there were a hundred thousand variations on:

Dear Janie,
   Wanna fuck?

Then there were the not-so-nice ones, the ones that described just how much I deserved to be punished for what I had done, that described in loving detail how I'd scream when my throat was slit/face pummeled/body violated — letters that shouldn't have even been delivered to me, but I guess I had some haters in the mail room, too. Even one of these letters would have been too much, but I got about eight or nine a month. Trace Kessler sent one each week, without fail. I'll give him this, though: He was the best speller of the bunch.

So you see, the paparazzi was far from the greatest of my worries. At least the press wanted my mouth for what it could say.

I wiped my eyes and nose with my sleeve, grabbed my suitcase, and headed for the door.

On my fourth attempt, I actually managed to make it out of the hotel.

It was a mild day, and the walk to the train station took just fifteen minutes, but by the time I arrived my chest was heaving and my hands were so cold they didn't even register on the ticketing kiosk's touch screen. My pulse didn't settle into a regular rhythm until I opened the door to my compartment — something called a superliner bedroom, which sounds much grander than it was. The room smelled of carpet cleaner and was drowning in branded royal blue, but I liked the little den. It was admirably nimble, going from living room to dining room to bedroom with the press of a switch, the tug of a strap. I wished I were half as versatile.

I sat down and ran a hand over an armrest. The upholstery was so rough it could've doubled as a loofah. Silver linings.

The train pulled past the city limits and began to pick up speed. I looked out the window, to the southeast, and squinted, wondering if I could see Folsom Prison from this distance. I'd heard it wasn't so bad these days — they were even opening up a women's facility sometime soon. I would've loved to have been transferred to a place like that, to a place with some *history*, but I hadn't been eligible then. Minimum- and medium-security only, ladies.

I propped up my chin with my hand. *If I committed a minor felony right now, is that where I'd get to go?*

The train jolted forward; behind me, the compartment door crashed open. My head spun around, my hand dropped and curled into a fist, but the hall was empty. I waited a moment, ears perked. Nothing. I reached over to close the door — but it just slid open again. *Dammit:* The latch was broken. I pushed the door shut and tried to jiggle the latch back into place.

Someone knocked. I froze.

"Hello?" A man's voice, the jolly resonance of the hospitality industry. The porter, if I had to guess.

"Yes?" I said, bracing my legs behind me to secure the door.

There was a pause, then, "I was wondering if you want —"

"Nope."

"But —"

"I'm good, thanks."

Another pause. "Well, you let me know if there's anything you need."

Fat chance. "Will do!"

I pressed my ear against the door until I was sure he was gone. Then I pulled the cuffs of my cardigan over my hands and wiped down the handle as best I could.

I gave the door a dirty look before retreating to the forward-facing seat. It was another eighteen hours to Omaha, but no matter how tired I was I couldn't let myself fall asleep, not when I was so exposed. I reached into my bag to grab the only book I had — a Bible I'd taken, perversely, from the hotel nightstand. But then I changed my mind and drew back. The Old Testament was too familiar; the New Testament just got me down.

And so the only thing left to do was toss about, folding and refolding my legs under me as we crossed the mountains. We stopped briefly in Reno before venturing into the bleak expanse of northern Nevada. With each passing mile the landscape shed vegetation and elevation until it was reduced to little more than dust and bristle and the distant, mocking silhouette of more compelling terrain.

The Lady Vanishes

CELEBRITY NEWS
November 2, 2013 at 3:05 PM
By Us Weekly Staff

In the weeks since notorious accused murderer Janie Jenkins's release, one question has been on everyone's minds: Just where in the world has she gone? Sightings and tips have been pouring in to online gossip sites, and cable news networks are reporting new developments practically by the minute. But the leads are proving as elusive as Jenkins herself.

Speculation of late has centered on the exclusive Hawaiian island of Lanai, as several sources close to the case have hinted that Jenkins has traveled to her late mother's secluded villa there. But despite the legions of paparazzi that have descended on the remote island, no one has been able to uncover any sign of Jenkins.

At least not yet.

Jenkins, now 26, was convicted in 2003 of the brutal murder of her mother, Marion Elsinger (née Jenkins), the enigmatic ex-wife of a number of prominent European businessmen, most recently Jakob El-singer of Zurich.

Elsinger was discovered the morning of July 15, 2003, when police were called to the Elsinger house by Janie, who reported the crime with what the emergency responder later called an "eerie calm." When the police arrived they were shocked not only by the physical trauma that had been inflicted on Elsinger's body but also at what appeared to be a brazen attempt on Janie's part to destroy key forensic evidence.

Although it's clear that the DNA evidence in Jenkins's case was indeed mishandled by the Los Angeles County Crime Lab, it seems that most Americans still believe Jenkins is guilty. While there are those who have cautioned against vigilantism, others, such as Trace Kessler of the crime blog "Without a Trace," have embraced it. Kessler has been particularly pro-active in his pursuit of Jenkins, even going so far as to offer a reward to anyone with information that might point to Janie's location.

In the end, whatever the information or misinformation might be, one thing is clear:

Guilty or not, wherever Janie Jenkins plans to go, she has a treacherous road ahead of her.

CHAPTER FOUR

When I woke up Sunday night it was dark and smelled of something sweet, and so it took me too long to remember where I was — it was dark and smelled of something sweet when I found her, too. But this was a different dark, an unremitting dark, not one softened by cut-velvet curtains. And it didn't smell of curdled blood, it smelled of oranges. Antiseptic oranges.

Lysol, I realized. I was in the bathroom. *Again.*

I pressed the heels of my hands against my temples and squeezed my brain awake.

I remembered then. I'd started nodding off early Sunday evening — somewhere near Denver — but that stupid door kept slamming open, startling me awake, admitting the unsettling chatter of passersby, alerting me again and again to my inadequate defenses. I tried to stay awake by dwelling on the thought that exhaustion must feel a lot like dying, but even that wasn't enough. It had been three days since I'd slept.

Finally, deliriously, I'd given up and locked myself in the bathroom.

The rest of me rebooted, and my senses kicked in one by one. I identified first no fewer than seventeen knots in my lower back. Second, a set of dim outlines: of the toilet, the showerhead, the drain in the floor, and the crazy space phone Noah had given me. It was buzzing.

The last phone I had was a clunky green Nokia with a screen the size of a postage stamp; this phone was sleek and white and didn't even have a keypad. It didn't even look like a phone — but then, I didn't need it for talking. I just needed it to keep tabs on Trace Kessler.

I pulled up his latest post.

Are we just going to let her get away with this? Will she never be held accountable for her actions? No. We will NOT. This will not stand. There is a MURDERER on the loose. It's time for those of us who believe in justice to track Janie Jenkins down.

I shoved the phone into my back pocket. *God,* what was his damage?

I fumbled for the door handle and pushed

my way out into the compartment — and swallowed a curse. I wasn't alone: The porter I'd managed to avoid the night before, an older man with more-salt-than-pepper hair and a face that belonged on a box of Quaker Oats, was in the process of turning down the bed. The blankets had been snapped tight, and he'd just placed a foil-wrapped chunk of chocolate on the pillow. He'd been there for some time.

He looked up. "Sorry to disturb you, Ma'am," he said, uncertainty nipping at the edges of an otherwise Rockwellian smile. "I didn't realize you were in here."

I skimmed the sour off my expression and reached for my social graces.

"You, too," popped out.

I winced.

"I mean," I went on, "I didn't realize *you* were in here, either. Obviously. So . . ." I reached for my glasses and nudged them up my nose to give my hands something to do.

Just then, the train came to a bridge and slowed. I reached for the compartment door, knowing what was coming, but I was too late. When the train sped up again, the door rolled open. I glanced over; in the hallway two women with mom-of-four-kids hair walked past.

"So I read Janie Jenkins has, like, disappeared," one bellowed.

I sucked in a grotesquely audible breath. The porter's eyes locked on mine. And then at least twenty seconds passed as I wondered if it would be too conspicuous if I just shut myself back in the bathroom.

I decided to try to draw the porter's attention to the window and away from my face. "The scenery here is so lovely, don't you think?"

He frowned.

("Wasn't she in Hawaii?" the other woman brayed.)

"How about this weather?" I asked.

("I heard she's on her way to Chicago."

"What? You mean where *we're* going?"

"Oh my god, Mary, what if she's on our train?")

The porter was starting to look nervous, fiddling with the toiletries that were balanced precariously on the edge of the tiny sink that was set into the compartment wall next to the bed. Shampoo. Conditioner. Shower Gel. Face Lotion. A travel-sized soap.

"How 'bout them Bears?" I tried.

From the hallway there was a guttural noise of disgust, and then the first woman spoke up again: "If I saw Janie Jenkins I'd spit in her face."

51

The second woman didn't hesitate. "I'd run."

I rubbed my forehead. The porter was turning the little bottles again and again. His hands — were they shaking? Had he recognized me? No, surely not. This was a man who saw hundreds of people a day. He'd take no more notice of me than a greengrocer would a head of lettuce, right? Even if it was a head of lettuce that had been hiding in a bathroom, small talked like someone just off the psych ward, and was heading for a city suspected to be the destination of a notorious suspected murderer. . . .

I took the smallest, slightest experimental step toward the porter, and he flinched, knocking the entire collection of toiletries onto the floor.

"Well, shit," I said.

His gaze cut to the hallway and back. "I should really —"

I'd like to say that what I did next was a conscious decision, but in truth it was out of my control, the rubber band of my true character snapping back into place.

I sidled forward, reaching around the porter to pull the door shut. This time, miraculously, it latched. *Everything* latched.

The porter tried to inch away; I didn't let him.

"Before you go," I said, "I do have one question."

He swallowed. "Yes, Ma'am?"

I took another step forward and flicked a finger at his name tag. "Mr. Shelton, is it?"

"Yes."

"Well, I was wondering if you happen to have a first name."

His breath caught, held.

Almost reflexively, my right hand slipped into my purse. "Of course, I don't suppose it would be too difficult to track down myself, what with duty rosters and all. In fact, I bet everything's online these days. Names, numbers — addresses." I found the sharpened scissors, wrapped my fingers around the handle. "Privacy just isn't what it used to be, is it?"

"I won't say anything," he croaked out.

I smiled. "Say anything about what?"

He shook his head helplessly.

I let the scissors fall back to the bottom of my bag. "Right answer," I said. I stepped back and opened the door. "See that you don't forget it."

He dashed out without a backward glance, bless his heart.

My eyes tracked back to the toiletries, and

I caught sight of myself in the mirror. Unsurprisingly, my smile wasn't warm. It was forced and terrible, a carnival caricature.

Was that how a killer smiled?

I relaxed my cheeks and eyelids and jaw until my expression approximated something like amiability.

God, that's even worse.

I grunted and bent down to retrieve the bottles from the floor. No reason to leave perfectly acceptable shampoo and conditioner behind.

No one who knew Janie Jenkins would have believed she was capable of murder.

"I never would've guessed," said Grant Collins, one of Janie's classmates. "I mean, why would she do it? She was already famous." He paused. "And smokin'."

Ainsley Butler, eighteen, was one of Janie's closest friends and originally one of Janie's staunchest supporters. "It isn't true," she told me over a cocktail (that the waiter at Soho House hadn't thought twice about serving her). "I've known Jane since she moved here," she said. "I mean, I'm basically her best friend. She borrowed clothes from me all the time. She would never do anything like this."

When I asked Ainsley to comment on the reports of Janie's fractious relationship with her mother, she was less forthcoming. "I don't know anything about that," she said, tight-lipped.

When I spoke with Ainsley shortly before the trial, however, her demeanor was markedly different. I asked her if she thought of her friend differently now that she knew the details of the crime. "I'm so appalled and disgusted," she said. "But now? Looking back? I'm totally not surprised. And I just feel so blessed that she's facing the consequences for her actions, because I am 100 percent positive I would have been next."

— Alexis Papadopoulos,
And the Devil Did Grin:
The Janie Jenkins Story

CHAPTER FIVE

A few minutes before midnight, the train ground to a halt in front of a stout brick building. I grabbed my stuff and poked my head out into the hall before hustling over to the space between my car and the next. I propped my suitcase up with my knee and struggled into my coat and gloves, letting the syncopated rumble of the train urge my thoughts out of the rut they'd fallen into.

I'd never make it to Omaha, not now — scare tactics like the ones I'd just used are only effective in confined spaces. As soon as the porter's terror dissipated he would realize how empty my threats had been, and before long he'd be on the phone to his wife or daughter or Trace. And I'd be damned if I let the first photograph of me in ten years be taken on fucking *Amtrak*. I mean, the lighting alone.

No, I had to get off this train *now*.

I tucked my chin to my chest, shoved open

the door, and hopped off, dragging my suitcase behind me. I let out a breath when it became clear that I was the only passenger to disembark. The town — McCook, that's what the sign said — clearly wasn't much of a tourist destination, but given my luck so far, I wouldn't have been particularly shocked to discover that it was hosting the Nebraska State Fair or county sheriffs' convention.

I charged forward like I knew where I was going, and I managed to make it out of the station and down the street before the train departed. As soon as it was out of sight, I stopped to take a breath and get my bearings. I was heading west, that much I could tell, but whether I was heading into or out of town I couldn't say. McCook defied such distinctions, a town of scattered ashes without a gravestone.

I walked on. The air smelled of burnt autumn leaves even though there weren't any trees that I could see — but then, there weren't any streetlights either, so who could say what was or wasn't out there? The only noise was the clatter and roll of my suitcase on the uneven pavement, the fleshy slap of my shoes against the concrete. I kept looking over my shoulder.

I pulled up my coat collar to warm away

58

the goose bumps.

Then, *there,* two blocks over: a motel, a mom-and-pop kind of place with a hand-stenciled sign and a rusty blue truck parked off to the side. I cased it from across the street, drumming my fingers against my lips. Through the lobby window I could see hardwood floors and bearskin rugs, a tidy display of brochures, framed pictures of fat cattle. A young woman leaned on the front desk, staring intently at the cellphone in her hands.

Perfect — except, *shit,* for the security camera in the back corner.

I looked down the street, but I couldn't see anything else, not even in the distance. I was cold, I was tired, and I knew I was in for a nasty crash the moment my stomach processed that last sick slosh of adrenaline from the train. I needed privacy more than anything at that moment.

I closed my eyes and ran some lines. *Hi! I don't have a reservation, but I was wondering if you might have a room for the night? A single, please. Yes, it's just me. Oh, my name's Rebecca — Rebecca Parker. Yes, I'm from California. Oh my gosh! You're right! So observant! The weather is much nicer there. I know, the sunshine, am I right? Can I just say that I'm stunned that someone with such wit and acumen is stuck behind the desk of a motel in a town no one except you has ever heard of —*

I pinched the bridge of my nose. No. Try again.

Hi! I don't have a reservation, but I was wondering if you might have a room for the night? A single, please. Yes, it's just me. Oh, my name's Rebecca — Rebecca Parker. Yes, I'm from California. It is lovely there. You should visit some day! And can I just say that I love what you've done with your hair?

Better. I pulled a fuzzy knit cap from my bag, tugged it low over my ears, and walked in. I stepped up to the desk and clasped my hands together to keep them from trembling. "Hi, I —"

"Welcome to the Country Inn," the woman said, lifting her head without lifting her eyes from her phone. "Registration's on the left."

"I don't have a reservation, but —"

"It's Sunday night. Neither does anyone else." She dropped her cellphone into the purse hanging from the back of her chair. "It'll be sixty bucks — well, actually, it's really like fifty-nine forty-five because of tax and everything, but I don't have any change."

"Don't you want to know what kind of

room I want?"

"Yeah, we've only got one kind." She looked me over, frowned. "Unless you want the handicap one?"

I turned my face to the side. "The regular one's fine."

"Cool."

I slid the money toward her and wrote a name in the registration book. She didn't even glance at it.

She couldn't have been more than twenty years old; her hair was shoulder-length and slicked straight back from her forehead. It might've been brown, might've been blond, who could tell through all that product. She was trimmed with an unwieldy jumble of accessories, bangles and feathers and scarves and bells — a cat toy in knock-off Hermès.

Her name, according to the tag pinned to her chest, was Kayla.

Top-to-bottom train wreck.

Although — I was one to talk. I'd approached my new look like a bomb squad would a suspicious package: There would be no uncontrolled explosions of desirability on my watch. Beneath my lumpy, oversized coat I was wearing a twin set and pleated trousers, ballet flats with bows on them. The shoes were too small — a reminder to dowd down my natural gait — and had soles so thin I could feel the grout lines on the lobby's tile floor. My underwear came up to my navel.

I felt my eyes soften as I let myself indulge, just for a moment, in the memory of more fashionable days. I regretted it almost immediately. The first image that came to mind was of the last truly hot thing I ever wore: a pair of boots I stole from my mother's closet on the night she died.

I did that a lot back then, stealing my mom's shit. Not because I was a psychopath or a sociopath or whatever-other-kind-of-path the prosecution argued I was. I did it because I was a teenager, and — my god, people, how many times do I have to say this? — that's what teenagers do. (Unless you're the kind of kid who wants to be a DA, I guess.)

But if it matters, I wasn't actually planning on stealing those boots: I was planning on stealing some money. Two weeks earlier my mother had taken away all my credit and debit cards in retaliation for a photo shoot I'd done for *W,* and since I'd decided I needed to get fucked up, I needed cash.

Which meant it was time to hunt for buried treasure.

Despite being almost exclusively attracted to financiers (or perhaps because of it), my mother harbored a profound distrust of banks, and she kept her valuables — cash, letters, jewelry, keys — hidden all over the house. In empty wine bottles, in the pockets of fur coats, in hardcover copies of books she thought I'd never read. She used decoys and misdirection; she hid useless items in obvious places so you wouldn't look for the useful items that were inevitably right nearby. She used what I liked to think of as Jane Repellent: sachets of lavender and white rose, my mother's favorite scents. She used to scatter the things everywhere. Once I asked her if maybe they were multiplying and should we perhaps call an exterminator before our noses rotted off in protest. She just gave me her favorite look — *Jesus Christ, Jane* — and walked away.

The house was swarming with staff that night, so I had to be careful about my search. (My mother was throwing some event for whatever charity she was pretending to care about. Special-needs dolphins or unattractive children or whatever, I don't know. I was never deemed fit to attend her parties.) But it was easy enough to lift a walkie-talkie from one of the party planner's minions and track my mother's movements that way — even if it meant I had to listen to their delusional twitterings about

63

the sublime stylish charming lovely Mrs. "No please call me Marion" Elsinger.

As soon as I heard she was sampling gougères in the kitchen, I headed for her closet.

In no time at all I uncovered all sorts of crap (a ruby stick pin, a set of keys, an erotic letter from stepfather number three), but it took me a while to find the roll of twenties in the hollowed-out heel of a Tory Burch wedge. I was just pulling out the cash when I saw the boots peeking out from behind a rack of clothes from Chloé's frankly forgettable 2002 spring collection. I'd never seen the boots before, but *oh,* they were luscious — above-the-knee black leather, an elegant toe. They were the perfect height, too: just shy of *Pretty Woman.* I tossed the walkie-talkie aside, dropped to the floor, and grabbed for them. I slipped the left one on and tugged at the zipper. It caught on my calf.

"Skinny bitch," I muttered.

I braced my leg against the wall and pulled.

A noise from the bedroom. The rap of high heels on hardwood. My mother.

I scooped up the walkie-talkie, the other boot, and everything else I'd strewn on the floor and began hopping toward the connecting door to the bathroom, but the sound of low, angry voices stopped me short. There was someone in there with her. *Who the hell was that?* I held on to a nearby shelf for balance and put my ear to the wall.

"I don't owe you shit," my mother was saying. I reared back. I'd thought she reserved that tone for me.

Whoever else was in there spoke next. It was a man. "You think you're so much smarter than everyone else, don't you?" he said.

"Smarter than you doesn't mean much," she said.

"Should've slapped that mouth off years ago."

They moved away from the door, and their voices grew faint. I pressed the entire length of my body against the wall, but even like this I could only catch fragments of what they said next.

"— you think I won't —"

"Fuck you —"

"What you did —"

"— get away with anything —"

"No one will —"

"I never —"

"— Tessa —"

"— Adeline —"

"Jane."

"Hello?"

I gave a start. Kayla was watching me, her forehead crumpled in annoyance.

I blinked. "I'm sorry?"

"I asked if there's anything else you need," she said.

I stared at her. "No?"

"So . . . like I said, your room's on the second floor."

"Great. Thanks."

"And, again, the stairs are just over there."

I nodded. Right. *Right.*

"Right," I said. I drew in a breath. "I guess I'll just need my key, then!"

Her next words were slow and very deliberate: "It's in your hand."

I glanced down. "Oh."

For Christ's sake. Get it together, Jane.

"Hey," Kayla said abruptly. "Do I know you from somewhere?"

"No," I said again. But this time it wasn't a question.

She squinted. "Are you sure?"

My own eyes narrowed. "Way sure."

"Well, okay," she said after a moment. "I hope you enjoy your stay or whatever." She shook her head and reached into her bag for her phone. The jangle of a key chain reminded me of something — the blue truck out front. My shoulders settled. I smiled.

Boots and cash aren't the only things I know how to steal.

My legs had just enough juice left in them to get me to my room. Once inside, I bolted and chained the door behind me. I checked the windows and closed the drapes. I unplugged the phone. I pulled back the faded floral-print bedspread and the beige thermal blanket. Then I went into the bathroom, turned on the light, and locked that door, too, before climbing into the bathtub and pulling the shower curtain closed and waiting for my heart to return to a regular rhythm instead of thumping clumsily against my ribs.

I'm sure there are those for whom getting out of prison is a whole, like, Beethoven's Ninth sort of thing. Rousing, joyous, accompanied by a choir. But for me — for most of us, I'd guess — it was more like Beethoven's Fifth. We're too busy being taken aback by the sheer size and scope of things to do anything but lose our minds a little, like the first time you go to a grocery store and realize there's more than one kind of Wheat Thin.

I'd braced myself for the disorientation — it wasn't the first time I'd been released into the wild, after all — but I hadn't anticipated the brute force of it. I mean, sure, I'd known I was out of practice with people. Who wouldn't be after the last ten years? Even when I wasn't in isolation, I'd been relegated to the bottom rungs of prison society, the status reserved for snitches, psychopaths, and slobs, and my conversations had been largely limited to terse exchanges with guards and counselors, none of whom were particularly interested in small talk — if they were interested in talk at all. Before Noah, months would go by with no more than a hundred words drooling out of me, 90 percent of them yes or no.

But even so, *Jesus.*

I stretched out in the tub, rolling some of the tension out of my ankles. My feet just barely reached the wall above the faucet. I kicked, scuffing black swirls on the pale pink tile.

Jane wuz here.

I scrubbed the marks off with the elbow of my cardigan. My name looked a lot better in blood.

I toed off my shoes and hugged my knees to my chest. *Enough.* I had more important things to think about. Like a car. I had one waiting for me in Omaha, a generic late-model sedan I'd picked up on Craigslist because I figured late-model sedans were what all the best criminals drove, but now I'd have to improvise, and I hate improvisation. It's lazy, the last recourse of myopics and fools, and I didn't want to admit to being either.

Plus, unless I was very much mistaken, in this particular case improvisation meant stealing Kayla's truck. Which meant I'd have to wake up hella early.

I pulled off my glasses and rubbed the lenses with the hem of my sweater. God, what was I even doing? Conducting an *investigation*? Pursuing a *lead*? No, I was following a *hunch,* a hunch based on a fragmented memory of a conversation I'd barely heard.

Tessa, Adeline, Jane.

I told the cops all about the conversation I'd overheard in my mother's closet, but they were so sure I was full of shit from the get-go. It didn't help that when they begrudgingly allowed me to listen to a few audio samples in an effort to identify something — anything — about that mystery man's voice, all I could provide were a few flimsy adjectives. The voice was brusque and mean, that's all I knew, I said. The homicide detective actually rolled his eyes at me when I told him this.

It also didn't help that there wasn't any

evidence anyone else had been in her room. Nor was there any evidence my mother knew anyone named Tessa or Adeline. For a moment I felt a flicker of hope when I learned that one of the servers who worked the party was named Adel*aide,* but the only remotely suspicious thing about her was a boyfriend who worked at Abercrombie & Fitch.

Eventually I began to doubt myself, too, particularly when I considered how strange it was that she'd have a man in her bedroom: Even when my mother was married her room was off-limits to anyone but her. Then there was the fact that her voice had been raspy and angry and full of four-letter words. The more I thought back on it, the more those words sounded like something *I* would have said.

The longer we went without finding anything to go on, the deeper I descended into One-Armed Man territory. Not even *Noah* thought it could lead anywhere.

After all: If there was really something to find, wouldn't Noah have found it?

Then again, it was the only thing I had.

As soon as I was considered sane enough to spend time in the prison library, I began the slow and agonizing process of combing through the shelves. Legal texts. Popular fiction. European history. Menippean satire. Early American literature. Self-help. You name it, I read it. And as I did I slowly but surely compiled a list of Adelines.

Adeline the cyclone.

Adeline the blood parasite.

Adeline the record label.

For a while there it wasn't looking good, and the people in charge of administering my Seroquel sure as hell knew it. But then I found Adeline, Illinois, a pinky-toe town roughly equidistant from Madison, Chicago, and Cedar Rapids, not far from where John Deere fabricated his first steel plow. That I was so excited about its discovery is a testament to just how desperate I was, because as far as I knew my mother had never set a French-pedicured foot anywhere in the area between Los Angeles and New York. But there were straws to be grasped at, too: Adeline's relative proximity to Peoria, where one of my stepfathers had apparently owned a factory; the record rainfall the year my mother died; the fact that I had once heard her say the word "Dubuque."

Noah, finally, agreed to look into it, though he was careful to lead-line my balloon. Whenever he updated me on his progress, he would open with something like "Please remember we need to manage our expectations." But I was so frantic for good news that I took as encouragement the mere suggestion I should have expectations left to be managed. Without context, even the feeblest hopes loom large and beguiling.

Then, one day, his visit began a little differently, with a question he'd shied away from the entire time we'd known each other.

"How are you?" he asked, fiddling with one of the shitty ballpoint pens he preferred.

I didn't know how to answer, so I consulted my Magic 8 Ball of Social Interaction. It settled, as usual, on Act the Stone-Cold Bitch.

I slouched in my seat and lit a cigarette. "Peachy."

"Good."

"Is this when I'm supposed to ask how you are?"

He tapped his pen against his legal pad. "If you'd like."

"No offense, Noah, but I've had better conversations in solitary."

"We can't all be Dorothy Parker."

"I'll settle for Dorothy Gale."

He tossed the pen on the table. "I'm not here to entertain you."

I yanked on my chains. "And yet it's the only thing you've managed to do for me so far."

He wet his lips; my concentration flickered. Then he nodded, clearly coming to some sort of decision. "There's something I have to tell you," he said. "About Adeline."

My head jolted up so abruptly my neck cracked. "Yeah?" I said. "What?"

His hands moved toward mine. When the guard in the corner opened his mouth to object, I drew back reflexively, but Noah kept reaching out anyway, until he was cradling my wrists like they were newborn kittens. The guard took a step forward; Noah stopped him.

"Please," he said.

That's when I knew he'd come to tell me that he'd come up empty, that he was giving up on Adeline.

There was a screech of a sound that I supposed came from my throat.

Noah's hands tightened on mine. "Jane—"

My eyes rolled back; just before they closed, I saw the guard looming over my shoulder. What did he think was going to happen, I wondered, almost dreamily. I was five foot two. I weighed about seven pounds. I was *shackled*. There was nothing I could do, absolutely nothing.

No, wait — there was one thing. I opened my eyes. A mean, mulish expression settled

73

on my face.

I looked at Noah's stupid soft go-wherever-they-wanted hands and pressed my sawtooth nails into the tender underside of his arms, digging slow and steady and hard like I was trying to get purchase on an orange peel. I felt the skin split; warmth welled up. I squeezed and squeezed and squeezed until, finally, I felt him start to fight back.

Over in the corner the guard was muttering things like *crazy* and *bitch* while calling for backup on his radio, and as soon as I heard the door open I released Noah and schooled my features into a more acceptably blank stare — less like a mule, I told myself, more like a cow. But who was I trying to fool, really? Seconds later the guards had me up by my elbows, and before I could think *in for a penny* I was kicking and screaming and spitting because why not, I was fucked regardless.

I'll never forget the expression on Noah's face as he watched them drag me away. Like Mother Teresa ministering to the poor. Like *he* had been the one to let me down.

That's why I never told him when I found the other Adeline. He never would have forgiven himself for not finding it first.

I folded a towel under my head and

turned on my side, trying to ignore the way my bones pestled into the bottom of the tub.

It was late and it was Sunday, but I knew Noah would still be working by not nearly enough light, mapping out a strategy for whatever sad-sack case had been dropped on his desk. I could imagine what his office looked like: cluttered and crumpled and smelling of Chinese food — although I'd never actually seen him eat, had I, so what did I know? What did I know about him at all, really? It doesn't mean much to say a person's your whole world when your whole world consists of an hour every other week.

As I fell into what counted for sleep, I wondered if he still had my marks on his arms.

Kayla @kaylaplayah
Good morning Nebraska!!!
11:12 AM — 3 Nov 2013

Kayla @kaylaplayah
"If you believe in yourself anything is possible" <3 <3 <3
4:19 PM — 3 Nov 2013

Kayla @kaylaplayah
Graveyard shift at work tonight ugggh
10:34 PM — 3 Nov 2013

Kayla @kaylaplayah
RT @MileyCyrus Space ballllllllllz
10:35 PM — 3 Nov 2013

Kayla @kaylaplayah
You guys the weirdest chick just came in I think she was a bag lady lol
12:42 AM — 4 Nov 2013

Kayla @kaylaplayah
Who wants pancakes
5:03 AM — 4 Nov 2013

Kayla @kaylaplayah
SOMEONE STOLE MY CAR FML
9:38 AM — 4 Nov 2013

CHAPTER SIX

Sunrise is such a sudden thing out on the prairie, a razor's edge of cold light that slices all at once from the horizon, across the empty land, and straight into my freaking eyes. Its radiance hurt like a hangover.

Strange, but I actually wished I *was* hungover. Because when you're so busy thinking about how awful you feel you forget for a moment how awful you are. Because pain can be its own relief. Because throwing up is a super-effective way to stay a size 0. If I'd been hungover, maybe I wouldn't have had to cling instead to my unease, buttressing back one kind of anxiety with another.

It was just past eight on Monday morning. Hours and hours to go, even though as the crow flies, my destination was just three hundred or so miles north of McCook, but once I'd seen the size of the truck's gas tanks, I'd decided to stick to state highways and county roads as much as possible, and each one, from 83 to 80 to 61 to 4A, would be a little shittier, a little slower than the last. Plus, I'd lost time when I stopped at an all-night laundromat outside North Platte so I could swap Kayla's license plates with those from a similar-looking truck in the parking lot.

(Thank god for my Swiss Army Knife. Multi-tools are like insults, girls — you should always have one on hand.)

The grasses swayed in the breeze. My hands tightened on the steering wheel. I felt like I was heading out into a great green ocean in the run-up to a summer storm, and the water was getting deeper and the currents were pressing me places I didn't necessarily want to go and at any moment the swells might break into —

Jesus Christ. I swear, sometimes I open my mouth and a high school lit mag falls out. The point is, I was scared.

Eight hours later, about twenty miles north of Chadron — just across the South Dakota border and approaching the Black Hills, on an unnamed road that didn't appear to have been repaved since the Eisenhower administration — the check engine light came on.

I glanced out the window, then at the map

on the passenger seat. *Shit.* I was literally in the middle of nowhere, and not even the banality of prison life had been able to convince me to take auto repair. If the engine died now, I was fucked.

I pushed my greasy bangs to the side and tried to get ahold of myself. I knew from experience that if I wasn't careful my panic would melt me down until I wasn't even myself anymore, until I was just a barely sentient bag of churned-up guts. The moment I found my mother's body, my wires got rerouted; these days, cascade failure is perpetually imminent.

Hollow reed, I told myself. *I am a hollow reed, and trouble blows through me like the wind.*

Nope. Nothing.

My vision started to go dark around the edges.

Okay, let's try some of that Tibetan breathing shit.

Nada.

My vision started to go dark in the middle.

"Oh fuck —"

I slammed on my brakes just as my front right wheel spun off the shoulder of the road, kicking up a flurry of dust and gravel, but I knew that it wasn't going to be enough. I dimly recalled something from the one day of driver's ed I hadn't skipped —

I threw the wheel to the left.

The truck fishtailed. I couldn't turn into the skid, so I clenched the wheel, squeezed shut my eyes, and steeled my stomach. The truck whipped around in a circle; I gagged once, twice, and then the back wheels caught on some gravel on the far side of the road.

The truck gasped and shuddered to a stop.

I sat there for a minute, perfectly still. I restarted the car. The engine *sounded* fine.

I removed the key, pulled the hood release, and climbed out of the truck, holding on to the open door to support my gelatinized legs. Once I'd steadied myself I went around front to peer at the truck's — I don't know, guts? Whatever you call the stuff under the hood. The engine smelled like burnt coffee and looked . . . enginey.

I leaned against the truck's bumper and pulled out my phone. There was no service. I took reluctant stock of my surroundings, finding nothing but barbed wire and utility poles. I looked toward Chadron, toward Hot Springs. A half hour in either direction — provided the engine held out.

A crackle of gravel, the grumble of an engine.

Something sour erupted in the back of my throat, as if I'd just had a sip of milk when I'd expected orange juice.

I peeked around the raised hood. A car was pulling up behind me.

No, strike that — a *police car* was pulling up behind me. It might've been unmarked, but I knew what it was: Ten years in prison had given me a near-infallible nose for authoritarian stink.

I straightened my glasses and put on my best these-aren't-the-droids-you're-looking-for face.

There were two men in the car, and even through the windshield I could see they were engaged in the kind of forcefully gesticulated discussion that characterizes serious business. I lowered the hood and edged around to the driver's side door. I pulled it open.

The men climbed out, and I didn't know whether to be relieved by or wary of the fact that neither was in uniform. Either they were off duty or detectives — if they even had detectives in South Dakota.

My eyes went first to the driver. He was a long, lazy kind of lean, dark enough that Hollywood could happily have cast him as eighty different ethnicities. Messy-haired, dressed in faded jeans and a Jethro Tull

81

T-shirt. Mirrored aviator sunglasses, which meant he either watched too much TV or no TV at all. What I could see beneath those glasses might've been pretty apart from the upkeep: chapped lips and a scarred nose, the sort of patchy beard beloved by seventeen-year-old guitar players.

The other man was heavy and white-blond, his Cro-Magnon brow paired disconcertingly with a long, patrician nose. His eyes were more socket than ball, dark hollows shadowed by a massive forehead that cast so much shade the man had probably never needed sunglasses in his life. After a moment I realized he was pointing in my direction.

I eased into the driver's seat and slipped the key into the ignition. I couldn't run, but maybe I could talk them into leaving. And as soon as they did, I'd drive the other way.

I checked the rearview mirror. Slim was muttering something I couldn't make out. Shady threw up his hands before stalking off and propping himself against a fence post. He pulled a cigarette from his shirt pocket and stared off into the distance. I didn't notice Slim's approach until he was right next to me.

I smiled, cheerful dismissal at the ready.

"She dead?" he asked.

This is when each and every nerve ending in my body went completely numb.

Just numb.

Everyone always asks what my first thought was, when I found her. But it wasn't like that. I didn't have any thoughts at all until much later. I was mixed up before I even opened my eyes, still reeling from the previous night's dire combination of blended whiskey, prescription painkillers, and agonizingly fatuous conversation. And anyway, thought was beside the point — when I walked into my mother's room part of me already knew. Whether that was because I sensed that something was wrong or because I myself had already done that wrong something, well: that's the 16.5-million-dollar question.

Then, before I realized what I was doing, I was down on the floor with my face next to what was left of hers, shouting in one bloodied ear while scooping up tissue and viscera and bone, trying to spackle her over like she was a bucket and I was Dear Liza. Of course, by that point it wasn't of any use.

This was the last time I saw her. If only they'd let me come to the morgue — the neat stitches of a pathologist would have been a welcome relief — but I wasn't allowed the privilege, such as it was. So instead my retinas are forever burned with the image of a stranger, a woman whose curated beauty had been splattered across a room. It was hardly even a body; it was a spill.

I wish I'd been able to look away, but just then sight was the kindest of my senses, a hug and a hot toddy compared to the stench, the swamp, the silence. I found myself mesmerized by all the parts of her she'd tried never to let anyone see: a beige blotch of sun damage on her décolletage, a purple-veined calf. I hadn't known that her lip liner was tattooed on or that she had a bald patch in the middle of her left eyebrow. One of her implants had collapsed, punctured by a bullet. For a second I could see what she had looked like before, when I was little, before the surgeries and injectables and miracle creams made from monkey come.

She had never been more dear to me than she was in that moment.

Then I saw what she'd written on the floor:

JANE

This is when, finally, I had my first conscious thought:

I can't let anyone else see this.

(And I didn't.)

No matter what my clownishly optimistic therapists and social workers have tried to tell me, that morning isn't something I'll ever be able to "get over" or "process" or "come to terms with." A person can't stumble on their murdered mother and expect to be fine and dandy the day or the year or the decade after. Nope, lucky me, I get to hold on to this particular experience for the rest of my life. It's like that house-guest who leaves his dirty underwear in your bathroom and open cans of tuna in the kitchen — or, worse, the other way around — and no matter how nicely you ask refuses to leave.

But I'm not lying when I say that it *is* better than it used to be, less a crippling terror than a sustained cognitive dissonance. Something I'm so used to that I can almost forget it's there . . . unless I make the mistake of thinking about it. Then it's impossible to think of anything else. Like: blinking, breathing, the feel of your tongue in your mouth. But instead of your tongue it's your fingers, and instead of your mouth it's your mother's blood.

The cop was right the fuck up in my face. He was grabbing me by one shoulder and shaking me. "Hey, lady, you in there?"

I reared up like the snake I was, ready to strike, but my sense reasserted itself just in time. I retreated, nearly impaling myself on the gearshift in the process. An inconvenient memory surfaced of the last time I'd had sex.

I shifted self-consciously. "I'm sorry, I was thinking of something else." My words were wooly, cumbersome, just like the rest of me. I ran my tongue over the sharpest points of my teeth to wake it up.

The cop took off his sunglasses and positioned himself in front of the open door. His eyes were the color of wet tar.

"Your truck," he said. "I asked you if your truck is dead."

"Just a false alarm. See?" I turned the key in the ignition and hoped the growl of the engine was convincing enough.

He leaned down and examined the dash, saw the warning light. "It's a long way to a mechanic," he said. "Pop the hood, I'll take a look."

"Oh, no, really, you don't have to —"

He walked around to the front of the car. My foot tapped twice on the gas, consideringly. Then I turned off the car and went to join him. He was fiddling about with some sort of belt-type thing like he knew what he was doing. His hands were sure; his arms looked strong.

I became aware all at once of the bitter wind. I wrapped my coat around me.

He glanced up, caught my shiver. "You're not from around here, are you?"

I jerked my chin at the desolate landscape. "No one's from around here."

Stop it, Jane. Now is not the time for personality.

He shook his head and returned to the engine. I indulged in a little fantasy: that the hood would crash down on the back of his skull.

"Is it busted?" I asked.

He lowered the hood. "Can't tell — I need to check one more thing."

He had just rounded the front of the car when the wind stirred again, carrying toward us a distinctive skunky smell. My gaze snapped to Shady: He was leaning against the fence, and he wasn't smoking a cigarette — he was smoking a joint.

"What the hell kind of cops are you?" I asked Slim, unable to repress a throb of repulsion at the very word.

He took a step back at this, and one hand went to where his hip holster would have been.

My body moved itself into its own defensive position, nails at the ready.

"What makes you think we're cops?" His words were as easy as his stance wasn't.

"You're *obviously* cops," I said — but were they? No badges. No sirens. No guns that anyone could see. Just a white Crown Vic they could've picked up anywhere.

I glanced back at Shady. He was scratching lazily at his side, looking noticeably more relaxed. He had one of those skinny-legged bodies in which 95 percent of his body mass was concentrated in his stomach. It hung over his belt like a water balloon. I stared at it, wondering how it would feel to pop it open.

I'd read him wrong, I knew. He was no cop.

But Slim — he was a different story: He was leaning against the truck with the sort of studied indifference you learn to recognize once you've spent enough time in an interrogation room. I told myself to tread lightly, but my jaw still wanted to snap at the man.

"So where you headed?" he asked.

I adopted a breezy expression to hide my momentary inability to remember which meaningless states went where. "Montana."

I realized this was the wrong thing to say a second too late.

"There's an actual highway that can get you there, you know."

"I like the scenic route."

His expression was plainly skeptical. Why was he asking? Why did he care? What the fuck was wrong with him? What the fuck was wrong with *me*?

I came perilously close to sniff-checking my armpit.

"So what sort of business you have in Montana?" he asked.

"What sort of business you have *here*?"

Another wrong thing to say. He crossed his arms, watching me.

"Come on, man, we're late!" Shady shouted, shattering what I realized then had been a prolonged silence. I broke eye contact with Slim. I had to resist the urge to draw a circle in the dirt with my toe.

"Leo! The time!"

"Jesus Christ, Walt, I'm coming." With a grunt of annoyance, Slim stalked around to the side of the truck and flicked open the front fuel door. He looked back at me. "Figures," he said.

"What?"

"Next time you fill up, maybe think about putting the gas cap back on." He made an ostentatious show of tightening the cap and clicking the little fuel door shut.

I clenched my teeth to keep myself from blurting out that it wasn't my fault, that I wasn't that stupid. *Goddamn Kayla.*

"Thanks," I managed. I didn't smile or shake his hand, even though I knew that would have been the normal thing to do — but then again I noticed he didn't exactly reach for my hand, either.

"Well," he said, finally, "I suppose now's the time I tell you to have a nice day."

"It's a bit late for that," I said, louder than I would have liked.

Strike three. The speculative glint in his eye crystallized into suspicion. As soon as he turned to walk away, I climbed back into the truck and locked the door behind me. I turned on the car; sure enough, the check engine light flicked off.

Moments later, the cop and his friend sped off, their car kicking up a cumulus cloud of dust. By the time it settled they had disappeared, leaving me with the impression that maybe I'd just fallen prey to some kind of deep prairie mirage.

Later, of course, I'd wish I had.

Jane Jenkins
Santa Bonita Women's Center
April 24, 2004

Sweet Jane,
I almost didn't write you this week. Part of me worries that these letters are gifts, glimpses of the outside world, maybe even a kind of companionship. And you deserve none of those things, of course.

Do they let you read letters in solitary? I heard that's where you are. You just get into trouble wherever you go, don't you?

I still think you should have gotten the death penalty, but I suppose solitary confinement is a reasonable compromise. I hear the hallucinations can start as early as 72 hours in. Is that true, Jane?

What do you see when you hallucinate? Do you see your mother? Does she talk to you? Does she tell you what she really thought of you?

Do you see me?

I see you, Jane. I see you on the ground, just as broken and bloody and debased as your mother was. I see your blood dripping through my fingers.

But that's not a hallucination, that's a dream.

Trace

CHAPTER SEVEN

Eighteen months ago, on a day I can't describe for you because, *hello,* I was in a high-security prison where nothing ever changed, I finally found what I thought of as "my" Adeline — in the geology section, of all places. There, on the 527th page of a never-checked-out survey of twentieth-century metallurgical technology (donated by a well-meaning sedimentologist whose daughter got busted for intent to distribute), I came across this passage:

> A number of mines in the southern Black Hills were abandoned in the late nineteenth century when more substantial deposits of gold were discovered to the north.[5] In the next decades, however, many of these early sites would prove to be tremendously lucrative sources of tin, and would be reclaimed by the same prospectors who had initially abandoned them.

And this footnote:

5 This kind of rash paranoia is characteristic of this time period, when prospectors regularly relocated at the first and slightest sign of better opportunities elsewhere. Nowhere was this phenomenon more manifest than in Ardelle and its long-forgotten sister city, Adeline, two settlements that were never fully populated simultaneously, their residents instead choosing to move back and forth depending on where the mineral wealth was thought to be that year. The towns' population settled more or less permanently in Ardelle after 1901, when the Chicago, Burlington, and Quincy Railroad built a spur line to Ardelle but was unable to traverse the mountain pass to Adeline.

Such a little thing! Hardly even a reference! It would have been so easy to miss were it not for my increasingly manic attention to detail. But, in my mind, the very unlikelihood of the discovery and of its relevance gave it credence — what is knowledge anyway but a series of wild improbabilities sigmaed up into inevitability?

On the days when I still let myself think that I might eventually get out, I began to plan my visit to Ardelle. First, I knew, I'd need a disguise. The physical part, as always, was easiest. I initially entertained a brief fantasy of transforming myself into a femme fatale: dark, finger-waved hair, stilettos, barbed innuendo delivered in a throaty European accent. But I knew that my compulsive need to look hot — and yes, I can admit that it's a compulsion — was one of my greatest weaknesses, which meant that hotness was the first thing that had to go.

Hence the hair.

(By the way, don't think I can't hear you now: "Your hair! We get it! Jesus!" But honestly? If you're really thinking that it's only because you've never known what it's like to have legitimately rad hair.)

My new persona, I knew, would be trickier. Not only would I need to throw off the press and anyone I met in Ardelle, but I would also need to be the kind of person who could ask questions without triggering questions in return, the kind of person in whom eccentricities and social awkwardness would be tolerated, even indulged. After long hours of consideration I came to a dispiriting conclusion: I'd have to make myself into a nerd.

Fortunately, I had some experience with

this particular species. For the first fifteen years of my life I had been shuffled from tutor to tutor, learning all the things my mother thought ladies (or bastard children of petty nobility) should know — which as far as I can tell were gleaned directly from an Edith Wharton novel. I studied etiquette, music, antique furniture, napkin folding. I can spot a fake Picasso at a thousand paces; I dance the gavotte; I'm adept with a lemon fork, a butter pick, and a piccalilli spoon. My education was then rounded out with perfunctory attention to the more usual subjects, which were taught largely by mediocre or disgraced academics who were unwilling to cry uncle and find another field.

These are the seeds from which Rebecca Parker was born. It was a perfect disguise, really, something that no one but Noah would ever expect me to be: smart.

And smart in a way that served my particular purpose.

Rebecca Parker, I decided, received her B.A. in Old Stuff About America from the University of A State That Grows Corn. Her undergraduate thesis, "Something Something Gold Rush: Something Something Nineteenth Century," won the departmental thesis prize. Her work has been published in impressive journals no layperson would have heard of, like *Tedious Details About the Dakotas* and *Undersexed Antisocial Nerds Discuss Cowboys.* She has frequently presented at major conventions hosted by associations with "history" in their names. Her current research interests include pioneer somethings and American Indian something elses. Ask her about any of this and you will be so crazy bored that you would rather self-lobotomize than ask a follow-up.

(But I made a few flashcards and wrote a short paper on nineteenth-century settlement patterns just in case you're not.)

Then I was released, and all my ifs turned to whens. I sent Noah running around California putting together my new identity and ordering my new wardrobe, and while he was otherwise occupied, I planned my trip to Ardelle, mapping my route and booking a room at the only local inn that had a website. Here I caught a break: When I called to make my reservation, I spoke to the inn's sweetly enthusiastic proprietress, a woman named Cora Kanty.

"You can't come then!" she said when I asked about availability.

For a moment, I was nonplussed — *Other people wanted to visit this place?* — but I recovered quickly. "In that case, is there another hotel you can recommend?"

"Oh, no, that's not what I meant! It's just that if you can wait until November, you can join us for Gold Rush Days, our yearly festival! It's great fun, especially if you're a history buff like me."

I thought through the possibilities. A festival would provide the perfect cover. There would be crowds to hide in, events to attend. If there was anyone named Tessa in Ardelle, I'd be sure to run into her. All I needed was a good reason to be nosy — which was where Rebecca Parker came in.

"November it is, then," I said. "Because as it turns out, I'm absolutely *fascinated* by history."

By the time Kayla's shitty truck and I got to Ardelle, the sun was setting, and my immediate impression on arrival was that things would probably look a lot better once it was pitch dark.

I hadn't been able to find very much information about Ardelle, so I didn't quite know what to expect. I knew the town was classified as a "census-designated place," as kindly a euphemism as I can imagine for "one-horse Podunk shit hole." I also knew its per capita income ($35,835), racial breakdown (White, 98.6 percent, American

Indian and Alaska Native, 1.4 percent), median age (47.2), and primary industries (logging, mining, tourism). Even so, I had never imagined I'd find nothing more than a few dozen buildings hashed into twelve blocks by a grid of five streets.

I found it helpful to think of the town's layout in terms of the buttons on a telephone, like so:

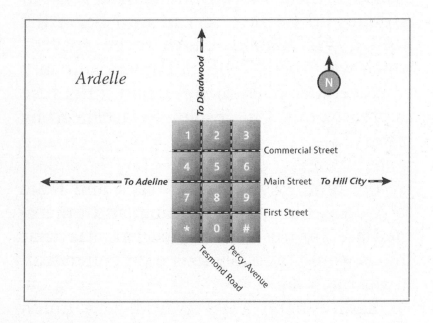

(For gas, press 6.)
(For groceries, press 2.)
(For city hall, press 5.)
(To speak to an operator — well, sorry, you're shit out of luck, because anyone with that kind of vaguely marketable skill prob-

ably left town long ago.)

Most of the businesses I passed as I rattled down Main Street were already closed for the day — if, indeed, they had ever bothered to open at all. I parked the truck in the darkest corner of a lot off Percy, just past the inn. I checked my reflection in the rearview mirror. My eyes were wide and red-rimmed: I wasn't used to wearing contacts, or that's what I told myself.

I stepped out of the truck, walked to the street corner, and turned in a slow circle. According to my map, the town was built into a couloir — the eastern approach to the pass to Adeline, I guessed — with Main Street running the length of its nadir and transitioning from state highway to county road. If I squinted, I could see where Main Street then narrowed into a single lane of jagged asphalt and disappeared abruptly into the trees. The gully was sufficiently flat-bottomed to seat the town comfortably, but the mountain slopes rose so precipitously on three sides that it was impossible not to imagine the forest was about to fold in on you.

Just one house was set high in the hills. A Romanesque revival. Pretty. Incongruous.

When I looked down Main Street, I could see a dry cleaner, a hardware store, and a pool hall. Across the street was a single-screen movie theater playing a superhero movie even I knew had been released the previous spring. A few teenagers were milling about in front, disconsolately. I walked down to the inn, a dusky blue Queen Anne with a shingled roof and a wide front porch. Next to it was a church, a hulking and charmless pile of red brick that blocked out what was left of the sun, shadowing the inn in its own little wedge of premature twilight.

A gust of wind blew through the pass and slammed into me. My hand automatically came up to keep my hair out of my eyes, but my hair had been sweat-dried solid. An unexpected benefit of a stressful day.

I shivered. I'm no stranger to cold weather, of course, but things were different here. No sable muffs. No châteaux. No après-ski.

No mother.

I pulled my bulky blue jacket closed and tightened my gray fleece scarf. It smelled of plastic bag.

Something was wilting in the vicinity of my chest. I mean, seriously? *This* place? What connection could my mother possibly have to a town like this? She was as fastidious with her surroundings as she was with her attire, because she knew that even a D-flawless diamond looks like crap in a 10K setting. She had even considered *Beverly Hills* to be beneath her.

I turned and headed toward the inn. One thing made sense, at least: If my mother had known someone who lived here, no way would she have ever admitted it.

Ardelle, for those who haven't had the pleasure of making its acquaintance, is nestled deep in the Black Hills, thirty or so miles from Mt. Rushmore, on the eastern slopes of Odakota Mountain. As we Ardellians know, our stunningly beautiful hometown was once little more than a gristly clutch of prospectors, founded in 1885 by J. Tesmond Percy's Mining and Manufacturing Company and named, along with nearby sister-city Adeline, for Percy's twin daughters. The population swelled in 1888 after Percy's claim yielded three veins of gold, and by the 1890s Ardelle was a respectably sized town, with one church and three bars.

When the gold in Ardelle began to run low, the town sent a contingent west to the by-then-abandoned camp in Adeline to see if anything might be salvaged. Much to their surprise, a rich lode was found soon after! When the prospectors relocated, the shopkeepers went with them, and soon Ardelle became a town in name only.

Of course, the gold eventually ran out in Adeline, too.

But the rhythm of life in Adeline and Ardelle was set, as both towns were blessed with silver, tungsten, zinc, and tin.

Over the next twenty years the local population moved from one side of the mountain to the other, depending on where the most lucrative mines of the moment were. These relocations happened so often that some families even built identical houses in each town to make things easier! Eventually, however, Ardelle's comparative accessibility drew more and more of the local population, and today there are no full-time residents of Adeline. Even so, no one in Ardelle would call it abandoned. Adeline, they say, is simply waiting to be reborn.

— Cora Kanty,
Ardelle Women's Historical Society Newsletter, vol. 1, iss. 1, January 10, 2011

Chapter Eight

When I stepped into the Prospect Inn I nearly tripped on my tongue. Now here was a room my mother would have approved of: It was neat, elegant, and dripping with money.

I wiped my shoes on the doormat before crossing what appeared to be the kind of antique Turkish rug that absolutely cannot stand up to foot traffic, which meant that it had been replaced no more than six months prior. To my left was the salon — well, you might call it the sitting room, but in my opinion any room that contains a recamier can only be called a salon — and to my right was the reception area. There, at a Hepplewhite desk, sat a slender girl with a paperback book, one delicate white hand floating over the corner of a page with the preternatural calm born of the knowledge that the world spun for her alone. She wasn't waiting to turn the page. She was waiting with supreme confidence for the page to come to her.

I used to know what that felt like.

When she looked up, her hair caught the light of the lamp behind her, and I was momentarily incapacitated by the alteration it effected. Her strawberry-blond hair turned incandescent — like Greek fire, I thought. I scratched at the back of my own scalp, hoping it might urge the poetry out of my head. It isn't easy to recalibrate after ten years of ugliness.

"Hello," she was saying, "how can I help you?" Even her words were a power play, so painstakingly soft that I had to lean in to hear her. I was just like the page of her book: bending to her will.

I tamped down my first, second, and third through eighth responses, reminding myself that Rebecca Parker had probably never uttered a mean-spirited word in her whole boring life. "I have a reservation?" I said instead. "Last name Parker?"

She opened up a card file and picked through it. "You're a day early."

"I just couldn't wait, I suppose."

"Really." She tilted her head to the side and then back, as if deciding how best to frame a photo. "You know, we have a girl in town who's just magic with hair. I'm sure she could fit you in while you're here."

"That's so sweet of you to offer," I said, because it would've been a damn shame to come all that way only to get thrown in jail for strangling a bratty kid. And if I was going to get thrown in jail, it was going to be for a damn good reason.

"Well, that's why I'm here. I'm Rue — I'll be making sure you have everything you need while you're with us."

In that case, could you tell me if you happen to know someone named Tessa? Or you could just tell me if you happen to know if I'm a murderer — either way!

I shuffled to the side and made a show of scanning the room while I gathered my thoughts. To my left was a table laid with yellow cakes and a silver tea set. To my right was an oil painting that looked an awful lot like a Manet. In front of me was Rue's book.

Her eyes were still trained on me.

Time to act normal.

"What are you reading?" I asked.

She lifted her eyebrows — which were golden and winged and looked like they'd never needed to be plucked in her life, damn her — but she answered me anyway. "*Jane Eyre.*"

"One of my favorites," I lied.

She smiled. "Of course it is."

I forced my hands to relax, when all I wanted to do was grab her by the neck and pitch her to the ground. You have to cut girls like Rue off at the knees if you don't want them to eat your face off. I know that better than anyone.

The night my mother was killed, I went to a party at this girl Ainsley Butler's house.

Ainsley's parents were out of town that week — Cabo, probably; like their daughter, they had no imagination — and she'd promised an "epic" throw-down, which I'd decided to go to even though the only things that are consistently epic are bores, failures, and poems, insofar as those are separate entities. Later people would say I was there for the alibi. But honestly I just couldn't bear the thought of another night at a club filled with actors and models and boys who weren't embarrassed to be DJs.

Ainsley came from oil money — but not, like, Rockefeller oil. Upstart oil. Likes Louis Vuitton oil. Loves Showing Off oil. And so when Princess Ainsley decided she wanted to be the next Tori Spelling, her daddy up and moved the whole family into a faux Tudor monstrosity in Bel-Air. The desperate throngs of teenagers there that night, hurtling drunkenly against each other in the hope of stumbling into what would best-case scenario be a thoroughly mediocre orgasm, were a perfect complement to the décor.

When I arrived I crept around the edges of the party as inconspicuously as possible until I found my way to a room that might have been called a study had anyone in that house been capable of complex thought. In the back corner, beneath a reproduction Holbein, was what I was looking for: the sideboard. I poured myself a generous serving of something expensive and smooth and was nearly halfway through when I heard a snuffling behind me.

I turned to find a huddle of girls in front of the room's staggeringly large sofa. They were young — twelve or thirteen — and tiny, hardly formed, that awkward stage between eft and newt. Soon enough they'd start buying big breasts and bigger bags of coke, and before long they wouldn't dream of sitting in a circle unless it involved some kind of a jerk, but that night they were still little girls, and for a fleeting moment I wanted to gather them up in a bear hug and spirit them away someplace simple and straightforward, like — I don't know, Glendale or Encino.

A chubby redhead mustered up her courage and stood. "Hi, Jane," she said. She had the willfully cheerful voice of a preschool teacher. Her skirt wasn't quite long enough to hide her dimpled knees.

I climbed onto a massively proportioned chair and pulled a pack of cigarettes out of my purse. As the girls awaited my response, they crowded together, expectantly, baby penguins angling for regurgitated fish.

"Mind if I smoke?" I asked, not that I cared. Back then I didn't ask questions; I collected data.

They shook their heads emphatically. The redhead half raised her hand, requesting permission — actually requesting permission — to speak.

I nodded, enjoying myself.

She gestured toward my cigarettes. "Could I —"

"No."

She shrank back and I lit up, holding the smoke in my lungs until I felt the fizzy tingle in the back of my head that always accompanies the first smoke in a chain. The party promptly became more bearable.

"What's your name?" I asked the girl.

"Maggie," she said, "Maggie O'Malley."

"Jesus. Your parents Boston beat cops or something?"

"I'm sorry?"

"Forget it." I looked her over. A skirt that didn't quite fit; a halter whose neckline she kept picking at. Along her jawline, a constellation of plump whiteheads she'd tried to cover with concealer. Her red plastic cup clearly hadn't been touched. "What're you drinking?"

She hesitated. "Vodka cranberry?"

I plucked the cup from her hand and took a sip; it was strong enough to make my lips curl around my teeth. I set it on a side table. "Are you trying to get laid or something?"

"What? Oh my god, no. Gross."

"Then don't accept mystery drinks from strangers. If you're going to be stupid, be stupid on purpose."

Maggie pushed back her hair and lifted her chin, and I wondered with some horror if she might be about to ask me to the seventh-grade prom.

"Are you really dating Tobey Maguire?" she asked instead.

The rest of the girls found their voices all at once. "No way," one said. "I heard she's with Pacey —"

"— that guy from that movie —"

"— Leonardo DiCaprio —"

"Leo totally only dates models." This from Maggie, who shot me an abashed look immediately thereafter. But I didn't take offense. I just sipped my whiskey and admired my boots and let them speculate. They'd come up with taller tales than I ever could.

I had long since stopped following the conversation when I realized a guilty silence had fallen over the group. I opened my mouth to say something, but then I caught sight of a blond weave and enough body glitter to blow a pupil. Ainsley. I stretched my way to the sideboard for a refill.

Ainsley's hand was wrapped around the bicep of a guy with the oily good looks of a serial adulterer. She was wearing an outfit so relentlessly hideous I refuse to describe it.

She stood just outside the door to the study, examining the girls and toeing the threshold like it was quarantine tape. "I didn't realize we were throwing a charity ball," she said. She turned to her escort with a plump smile (p.s., her lip liner was a blue-based red that was totally inappropriate for her skin tone). "Remind me which charity we're benefiting again — is it Save the Children? Or Special Olympics?"

The girls drew in on themselves, chins caving in. Maggie hugged her purse, a vintage Kelly bag that had seen better days. I had a sudden, unwanted vision: Mrs. O'Malley pulling the purse from the depths of her closet — a look on her face I'd heard about but never seen — and placing it in Maggie's waiting arms, all in honor of her having been invited to a real teenage party even though she was ginger and fat. They'd probably taken pictures.

I swirled my drink, thinking. Then I settled back in my chair and lit another cigarette. At the strike of my match, Ainsley spun around, her sneer shifting to something toothier when she recognized me.

"Jane! I didn't think you were coming."

I puffed three very deliberate circles of smoke. "*Touched by an Angel*'s in reruns."

She had the same look on her face she always had whenever she tried to sit down in a miniskirt. It made me smile. Ainsley was desperate to convince the world we were BFFs. She probably thought it could help her acting career.

"Why don't you come outside?" she asked. "The crowd there is more *our* kind of people."

"Friends of yours?"

"Of course —"

"Not interested."

Her face paled under her bronzer. "But —"

I crooked my finger at the arm candy. "You. What's your name?"

He looked at Ainsley with a panicked expression, because even a dog can sense danger. "I don't think —"

"Grant's with me," Ainsley said.

I hummed and recrossed my legs.

"Why don't you just come outside with us?" she asked again, with a whiny undertone and an artless pout.

"Because," I said, "I've no interest in idiots unless I'm fucking them." I turned to Grant with a smile that was not, I'm sorry to say, particularly nice. "So, *Grant* — what do you say?"

When, not sixty seconds later, I left the room with Grant trailing obediently behind me, such a happy, astonished smile broke over Maggie O'Malley's face that I almost forgot to dig out my Clé de Peau concealer and toss it her way.

"For the freckles," I said.

But of course the joke was on me. Three months later each and every person in that room testified against me.

My mouth opened to tell Rue exactly what I thought about her —

"Rue? Are you in here?"

I turned. An auburn-haired woman with Rue's face was standing in the front hall, kid-leather-clad hands on her hips. A strand of fat black pearls peeked out from beneath her scarf, which, unless I am very much mistaken, was cashmere.

So this is the money. Or, at least, someone close to the money.

I told my heart to settle down. Just because she was rich didn't mean she'd known my mother.

When she saw Rue, the woman threw up her hands. "I've been looking all over for you!"

"Well, congratulations," Rue said, "you've found me."

"I thought Shandra was working tonight."

"Yeah, me too."

"Why didn't you call? We're about to sit down to dinner — you know it's our last dinner party before the festival starts. We've been expecting you."

"If you wanted me to be at your beck and call, then you shouldn't have forced me to take this stupid job in the first place." The older woman primmed her lips and made to hold up a finger, but Rue spoke first. "But that's beside the point, Mother, *dearest,* because in case you haven't noticed, we have a guest."

If I hadn't already been watching the woman, I might not have caught the near mechanical efficiency with which she modulated her expression, a child prodigy manipulating a Rubik's Cube. "Oh, you must be Miss Parker! You're early!" Her voice dripped with an unfamiliar, syrupy sweetness I eventually translated as pleasure. A memory clicked into place. This wasn't Tessa. This was the inn's owner.

"Ms. Kanty?" I asked.

She waved her hand. "Call me Cora." Her eyes crow's-footed at the corners when she smiled; had they not, I might have believed that she was still in her late twenties. Her hair was in a charming little braid, a bit wispy and pinned in a coronet to the top of her head. The style should have been too young on her, but it complemented her ruddy cheeks, which were flushed not from cosmetics or the cold but from what appeared to be — high spirits?

Second-generation rich, I decided. Conditioned to her privilege but still delighted by it.

"— is going to be particularly special this year," Cora was saying, "and I really think you'll —"

"Is anyone else joining you?" Rue asked.

I started. "I beg your pardon?"

"Do you have a boyfriend?"

"Really, Rue," Cora said, sharply.

"What?" Rue said. "I just need to know

how many chocolates to put on the pillows. I mean — I can probably guess, but I just thought I'd check."

"Rue, that's enough." Cora twisted her smile back into place before turning to me. "Teenagers," she said. I nodded sympathetically, even as part of me spat and scrubbed its tongue at the realization that I was siding with someone's mom.

Cora grabbed me by the elbow and led me into the foyer, away from Rue's little smirk, and my body's focus narrowed down to the ten or so square inches of contact between us. Even through three layers of clothing it felt like she was running a bristle brush over a half-healed burn. It took all my concentration not to pull away.

"We have nothing planned tonight for the festival, I'm afraid," Cora said, "but if you'd like, we'd love to have you join us for dinner."

I'd rather fuck a Christmas tree.

"I'd love to."

She clapped her hands. "Wonderful! Now why don't you let Rue show you to your room, and then we'll all head over together." She reached over and tucked my hair behind my ear. "And don't mind Rue. So what if you're single? Who knows — maybe you'll meet someone here."

Rue was already halfway up the stairs by the time I started after her. She looked back at me over her shoulder with a vulpine twinkle. "You'll be up in the attic," she called down cheerfully. "Just like Bertha Mason!"

1 MS. BUTLER: I DIDN'T EVEN INVITE HER, FOR ONE THING. SHE JUST
2 SHOWED UP.
3
4 MR. THOMPKINS: AND HOW DID YOU KNOW THE DEFENDANT?
5
6 MS. BUTLER: WE WENT TO SCHOOL TOGETHER. WHEN SHE BOTHERED
7 TO SHOW UP, THAT IS.
8
9 MR. THOMPKINS: AND DID YOU SEE HER THAT NIGHT?
10
11 MS. BUTLER: I DID.
12
13 MR. THOMPKINS: CAN YOU SAY AT WHAT TIME?
14
15 MS. BUTLER: TEN OR TEN-THIRTY, I THINK.
16
17 MR. THOMPKINS: DID YOU SPEAK TO HER?
18

19 MS. BUTLER: YES, AND IT WAS VERY UNPLEASANT. SHE WAS

20 ANGRY AND AGGRESSIVE AND VER-BALLY ABUSIVE AND I FEARED

21 FOR MY SAFETY.

22

23 MR. THOMPKINS: WERE YOU SUR-PRISED BY HER BEHAVIOR?

24

25 MS. BUTLER: NO. SHE WAS A BITCH, ASK ANYONE.

1 MR. THOMPKINS: MS. O'MALLEY, HOW WOULD YOU DESCRIBE THE
2 DEFENDANT'S STATE OF MIND ON THE NIGHT OF JULY 14TH?
3
4 MS. O'MALLEY: SHE HAD BEEN DRINKING.
5
6 MR. THOMPKINS: COULD YOU GUESS HOW MUCH SHE HAD BEEN
7 DRINKING?
8
9 MS. O'MALLEY: MY IMPRESSION WAS THAT SHE WAS VERY DRUNK.
10
11 MR. THOMPKINS: DID YOU ACTU-ALLY SEE HER DRINKING?
12
13 MS. O'MALLEY: YES.
14
15 MR. THOMPKINS: HOW MANY DRINKS?
16
17 MS. O'MALLEY: JUST ONE, ACTU-ALLY.

18

19 MR. THOMPKINS: THEN WHY WOULD YOU SAY SHE WAS
20 "VERY DRUNK"?

21

22 MS. O'MALLEY: BECAUSE SHE WAS ACTING SO WEIRD.

23

24 MR. THOMPKINS: IN WHAT WAY?

25

1 MS. O'MALLEY: LIKE SHE KEPT STAR-ING AT THE FLOOR OR AT THE
2 WALL, AND THEN WHEN AINSLEY CAME IN, SHE WOULDN'T LOOK AT
3 HER AT ALL.

4

5 MR. THOMPKINS: IS IT POSSIBLE MS. JENKINS WAS UNDER THE
6 INFLUENCE OF A NARCOTIC?

7

8 MS. O'MALLEY: I DON'T KNOW. I THINK MAYBE SHE WAS JUST —

9

10 MR. THOMPKINS: YES, MS. O'MALLEY?

11

12 MS. O'MALLEY: NO, YOU'RE RIGHT, SHE WAS PROBABLY TOTALLY ON
13 DRUGS.

CHAPTER NINE

We left the inn in the care of the elusive Shandra, a petulant twenty-something who arrived in a huff after receiving a terse call from Cora.

"Thanks for nothing," Shandra said, picking at the corner of one eye where her lashes had come unglued. "I was on a date."

Rue smiled thinly. "Don't worry. The backseat of Xander Pierson's Chevy Corsica will still be there when you get out."

"Rue." Cora was holding the door open. "If we leave your father alone with the food, we'll be stuck with nothing but last night's coffee cake."

"We should be so lucky," Rue said under her breath as she swept past me.

The Kantys lived on the very edge of town, in the westernmost house on Main Street. It was another Victorian — in shades of lavender, as far as I could tell from the porch

122

light — and it was as postcard pretty as the inn, with a neat little fence and hedges trimmed just so. I would have bet good money that the handsome handmade autumnal wreath on the front door was worth at least half as much as Kayla's truck.

A scarecrow was seated on the porch swing, legs crossed and arms stretched out along the back of the bench and pinned in place, a grotesque parody of insouciance.

"Rebecca?"

The bench swayed back and forth, the scarecrow's face moving in and out of the shadow of the broad brim of its hat. At its apogee the porch light spotlit the red slash of its mouth.

"Rebecca."

I jumped. *That's your name now, moron.*

Cora was looking at me. "Are you okay?"

Get a goddamned grip. This is easy — it's dinner en famille, *not a state banquet.*

(But then again — what did I know of *famille*? I only ever ate with my mother when there was no one else for her to eat with.)

I stammered out a smile. "I was just admiring — the door." I looked at it and cataloged everything I could that might interest someone like Cora. "The hardware," I said with some relief. "Is that P&F

Corbin?"

Cora's face cleared. "It is! And original, too — took me *ages* to track down." She tucked her arm into mine conspiratorially. "Let me tell you, Rebecca, you wouldn't believe the state of this place when I first bought it back —"

She pulled me inside. Rue flounced on ahead, and Cora chattered on about the renovations and period detail and various bits of decorative arcana, pointing out the design of the foyer, the vintage grate on the radiator, the wallpaper that had been salvaged from some nineteenth-century mansion. We came to a set of antique oak double doors, which Cora didn't need to draw my attention to. They were lovely, inlaid with pink and green stained glass. A botanical design: tendrils of foliage and a five-petaled flower. I reached out to touch it —

"Everybody," Cora said, "I'd like you to meet Rebecca Parker."

I turned to find Cora presenting me like I was a girl she'd pulled out of a hat. And then my mouth went desert dry: In front of me I counted seven serving dishes, three kinds of forks, a ham the size of a first-grader, and four faces I didn't know.

I lifted my hand. "Hi?"

■ ■ ■ ■

One of my tutors back in Switzerland was this stickly ex-classics don who'd left his post at King's College after being caught with two of his students in a position so compromising Catullus himself would have blushed. Nigel was cheerfully unrepentant about the whole thing, as evidenced by the fact that he was as comfortable telling me about it as he was elucidating the finer points of Homeric Greek. His second-favorite story, though, was about this poet — his name was Simonides — who was performing one night for a bunch of rich guys when, *boom,* the banquet hall collapsed and crushed everyone inside.

Everyone, that is, except for Simonides, who had, serendipitously, stepped outside just moments before the accident.

The bodies of the dinner guests were so fucked up that when it came time to arrange for the burials no one could figure out who was who. But Simonides was known for his great big brain, and so the families turned to him for assistance. "Help us," they begged him. "Help us identify our loved ones so that we might put them to rest with their ancestors! Please, sir, tell us anything you can remember!" What happened next, as Nigel told me, was that Simonides closed his eyes, took a deep breath, and then proceeded to recite the names of each and every guest in the exact order of their placement at the table.

Simonides: proof that poets can actually be good at parties.

Ever since, when confronted with a group of unknown people — and when I estimate the level of mortal peril to be reasonably high (which in Beverly Hills was always) — I try to channel my inner Simonides. Which is to say that I look each person in the eye, listen to their name, and then make up a really lame rhyme so I won't forget it even if the roof caves in.

I took a deep breath and surveyed the Kantys' dining room. Six people were staring at me: Rue, Cora, and the four others I was going to have to meet.

Two were women. Could one of them be Tessa? I didn't think so — they were closer to my age than to my mother's, and pretty. My mother, ever an expert in the sorcery of aesthetic relativity, preferred only to know people who were less attractive than her.

So, where to start?

No, that wasn't a rhetorical question, it was a test. Because the answer is always this:

You start with the most powerful person in the room. He or she is inevitably the one you'll have to win over or throw over in order to get what you want.

In this case the man in question was easy enough to pick out — he was the handsome older one at the far end of the table. He had slate-gray hair and the sort of face that exudes intelligence, with sharp cheekbones and thoughtful blue eyes and a serious nose. He was sipping at a gold-rimmed teacup, his little finger curved gracefully. It was that finger as much as anything else that convinced me of his status. It was a *Yeah, so I'm a man in South Dakota who drinks tea like Lizzy Bennet, what of it?* sort of finger.

I stepped forward and held out my hand. "You must be Cora's husband," I said.

The crowd, as they say, went wild. To my dismay, my ears stung with a blush.

When the laughter had died down, Cora, wiping a tear from the corner of her eye, said, "No, dear, this is Stanton Percy."

I sighed. "As in Percy Avenue?"

Cora nodded and gave my arm a reassuring squeeze.

"I do hope you won't hold that against me," said Stanton smoothly. "I promise there's no metaphorical significance to the potholes." His voice was surprisingly rough and deep for such a neat, elegant man. It was the kind of voice you'd expect from a blacksmith, not from a man who starched his shirts. I tried to imagine it filtered through insulation and drywall.

You think you're so much smarter than everyone else, don't you?

I shook my head. I couldn't tell if he was the man I'd heard that night.

"I beg your pardon, Mr. Percy —"

"Stanton, please."

"Stanton," I repeated.

Stanton, Stanton, a man of . . . high standin'.

Cora put her hand on the shoulder of the man at the other end of the table. "And *this* is Eli — my husband."

I smiled over at him. Eli had the ruthlessly disciplined build of a long-distance runner or a military man, someone who wasn't just fit but who had been so fit for so long that his body didn't even allow for the possibility of outward expansion. We were made of wet clay; he'd spent time in a kiln. And he knew it.

His expression was polite but unenthusiastic, clearly a husband who would exhibit the precise level of excitement his wife required of him and no more. Under the table, his foot tapped impatiently.

Eli, Eli, he . . . wants to make a . . . beeline?

"A pleasure," he said, begrudgingly — a less than helpful vocal sample size.

Cora pointed at one of the two women on the far side of the table.

"Then this is Kelley," she said.

The woman who waved in response was small and dark-haired, with heavy black glasses. Her skin might have naturally been a healthy golden brown were it not for a wan overlay that screamed too many hours spent indoors. Her fingernail polish was black and chipped, and she was smiling so broadly I could see the flash of a tongue stud.

"It's so nice to meet you," she said, and my god I think she meant it.

Kelley, Kelley, as sweet as . . . apple jelly.

"And this is Renee." The second woman was farm-girl beautiful, a Teutonic blonde who looked like she knew her way around a compound thresher. Her hair was long and loose and the sort of natural gold that inspires agricultural simile — it looked like flax or corn or winter wheat. (At least I'm assuming it did. I don't actually know what flax or corn or winter wheat look like.)

She was dressed in tight jeans and a flannel button-down that gaped slightly over her chest. I tried not to tug at my own pants, which were too big in the hip and too small in the thigh, so the ass was just sort of pooling around the tops of my legs like maybe I was wearing a diaper underneath.

Renee, Renee, she . . . something something something.

"Hey," she said.

Ah: *Renee, Renee, whose hair's like hay.*

An expectant silence. Oh, shit, it was my turn to talk — "Thank you all so much for having me." My voice broke on the last word. I put my hand to my throat. Being nice required a much higher register than I was used to.

Cora put her hands on me again, directing me to the one empty chair with a firm press on my shoulders. "Just make yourself at home," she said. I promptly tried to calculate how much I needed to slump to appear at ease without appearing impolite. Across the table, the two women exchanged a look.

Cora poured me a glass of water before sitting down on the opposite side of the table between Eli and Renee. "You know," Cora said, "Kelley and Renee are two of Ardelle's most successful businesswomen."

"High praise indeed," Renee muttered.

"Kelley runs the bookstore down on

Percy," Cora continued, "and Renee owns the most gorgeous gallery just a few blocks down. You should see what she has on display — there's sculpture, textiles, photos —"

"Cora, as always, is too generous," Renee said. "The stuff I sell is more on the crafts side of the arts-crafts spectrum, if you know what I mean. But this is my home, so I've got to make do. We don't exactly have a huge demand for postminimalist earth art, you know?"

"Not yet, anyway!" Cora nudged her with a friendly elbow. Renee seemed deeply uncomfortable — she kept fussing with the cuffs of her shirt — but whether this was due to Cora's optimism or affection, I couldn't tell.

I wished I had something to futz with too, but when I'd changed for dinner I'd picked a shirt with the least-flattering sleeves possible (i.e., three-quarter length). I tried to fold my hands in my lap but decided that was too formal, so I took my left hand and laid it on the edge of the table in what I hoped was a negligent manner. I adjusted my ring finger slightly until it looked right. There.

"Eli, no."

I looked up. Eli was spooning potatoes

onto his plate. Cora placed her hand on his. "We're not all here," she said.

"Rue!" Eli called out. "Sit down! Now."

His words were as precise as his bearing, with a bite that brooked no argument.

Should've slapped that mouth off years ago. My eyes narrowed.

Eli waited until Rue was seated before he lifted his spoon toward Cora. "*Now* may I?"

"No, because we're *still* not all here." She looked at the table and frowned. "Oh, shoot, and now we're short a place setting — Rue, honey, would you get another chair, please?" Cora bustled back to the kitchen and returned with an armload of china and silver.

"Cora," Kelley said. "Who else is coming?"

Cora shooed me to the right and Rue to the left and began to lay the dishes and cutlery between us. "Well —" she said.

Renee groaned. "Oh, Cora, no."

Cora straightened. "Look, he's all alone in that ramshackle house of his. God only knows what he's eating."

"Some skank from Sturgis, probably."

Kelley gagged.

Stanton snapped his fingers. "Children, please." Everyone quieted. I moved my right heel to put my foot in parallel with the other.

Stanton watched me over his teacup.

"You'd be here for the festival, I imagine."

"I wouldn't miss it!" I said. "I'm a historian, you see, and I specialize in the demographic and socioeconomic ramifications of nineteenth-century —"

"Cora," he cut in swiftly, eyes already glazing over, "remind me what the first event is . . . ?"

"The Bean and Cornbread Breakfast." Cora turned to me. "We use only authentic recipes from the 1880s."

"I don't think that word means what you think it means," Renee said.

"Authentic?" Cora said.

Renee eyed the ham suspiciously. "Recipes."

Eli sat up in his chair, catching sight of something through the window. "There he is."

Renee barely had time to fashion another scowl before the He in question walked in. When I saw him my stomach dropped so hard and so fast I'm pretty sure it landed somewhere in the Earth's outer core.

"And this," Cora said, unnecessarily, "is Leo La Plante — Kelley's brother and Ardelle's finest."

I sank low in my seat. *Leo, Leo, the cop I totally met earlier today when I was acting nothing like a virginal historian and everything like a bitchy ex-con, oh man am I screwed.*

What? They don't all have to rhyme.

"You're late," Renee said to Leo by way of greeting.

"Fuck you too, Renee." Leo dropped a kiss on Cora's cheek before peeling a can off a six-pack and dropping the rest in front of Eli, who grunted in appreciation.

He very nearly succeeded in making me think he hadn't seen me.

"You're not even going to apologize for being late?" Renee said.

Cora found something of great interest at the bottom of her wineglass, and Kelley rubbed her eyes as if hoping she could make them see something else. Stanton yawned.

"What would you know about apologies?" Leo asked.

Cora shot Kelley a beseeching look, which Kelley didn't see, because she was rubbing her eyes again.

"I know when they're called for, for one thing — hey!" Renee whirled around: Kelley had pinched her upper arm. "That hurt!"

"Dude," Kelley said. "Chill."

Renee gave Leo the finger; he returned it before sitting down in the empty chair that was, of course, right next to me. He turned to me and smiled. I hated that I noticed he'd shaved.

"It's so nice to see a new face here in town," he said. "What did you say your name was?"

I weighed the importance of getting to know the prominent citizens of Ardelle against the importance of getting the fuck away from this guy.

No, he's just a cop, I told myself. *And probably not even a very good one.*

"I'm Rebecca," I said.

He tilted his head. "Really. I wouldn't have guessed it."

Or maybe he is *a good one.*

"My mother named me after a character in her favorite book," I said.

"*Vanity Fair?*"

I smiled at the table. "The Bible."

Leo sat back in his chair and stretched out his legs. My knee skittered away from his like roaches from a light. He nodded, as if double-checking an answer and having it come up right.

He wasn't trying to threaten me. He was trying to test me.

But why?

Well, I'd just have to test him right back.

"You know," I said, "you seem really familiar. Is there any chance we've met before?"

His eyes narrowed. "Depends. Ever been in police custody?"

I relaxed. If he didn't want the table to know that I'd seen him on the side of the road, then I must have seen something he didn't want shared. I had some leverage, then.

"Cora," Eli said, with a dark look at Leo, "please tell me we can eat already."

Cora's hands fluttered up in dismay. "Oh, of course — go ahead."

We served ourselves and began to eat. While the meal was not precisely, as Cora had claimed at the inn, "nothing fancy," it certainly was trying to be. I scooped up asparagus with a broken hollandaise and fingerling potatoes that were crisped nearly black. The ham I left alone. I kept a running count in my head — *one-Mississippi, two-Mississippi, three-Jesus-God-why-isn't-there-a-state-name-longer-than-Mississippi* — to remind myself to take a bite every time I got to sixty.

At *forty-Mississippi* Leo spoke up again. "So what brings you out this way, *Rebecca?*"

"The festival, *obviously*," said Rue.

Leo ignored this. "How'd you hear about it, if you don't mind my asking? Not too many people manage to, you know, and I'm sure Cora would love to know how her outreach is working."

I caught myself pulling at the collar of my turtleneck. "Cora told me about it herself," I said. "When I called to book a room."

Rue's eyes were wide with disbelief. "You mean you wanted to come here before you knew about the festival?"

I shoved a potato into my mouth, and I took my time chewing it. I took even longer swallowing it, but that wasn't because I was thinking, it was because the potato had the texture of talcum powder. "I'm a historian," I said once I'd choked the thing down. "I go where the history is."

"But where did you come *from*?" Leo asked.

Kelley pulled her napkin from her face. "Geez Louise, Leo, this isn't an interrogation."

"At least he's not talking about Pink Floyd," Renee said.

Leo waved his fork at her. "You're only insulting yourself, darlin'."

Kelley caught my eye and shook her head, her finger moving in a looney-tunes circle next to her many-pierced ear. One of her earrings was a yellow smiley face. Another was a heart.

"Speaking of history," Cora said, neatly

changing the subject, "you're looking at four fifths of the Ardelle Women's Historical Society — the 'women's' part, of course, is a bit outdated now, but Stanton refuses to let us change the name."

"Wait, who's the fifth member?" Renee asked.

"Nora Freeman," Kelley said.

"I thought she quit?"

"She can't quit. We have to have a Freeman on the board. Abiah wrote it into the charter."

Stanton grunted. "Just about the only time my grandmother got something wrong."

"But we get an annuity from her trust as long as we keep her on the membership roll," Kelley pointed out.

Renee thought about this for a moment. "You mean she pays for our donuts?"

"Yes, she pays for our donuts."

Renee raised her glass. "In that case: to Nora Freeman!" When no one else raised their glass, she rolled her eyes, swept her hair back with one hand, and downed the rest of her wine.

"I have to know," Cora said to me, leaning forward. "Are you planning on writing something about Ardelle or Adeline? I've always thought it's such a tragedy that we're so underrepresented in the literature, and

138

I'd love to ask you about —"

I'm not here for you *to ask* me *questions, lady.*

"Of course I hope to write something," I said. "I just haven't figured out quite what. I suppose you could call this a scouting expedition."

Cora nodded eagerly. "There are some wonderful old letters written by Stanton's grandmother —"

"I was thinking I might look into the town's more recent history as well —"

Eli's fork screeched across his plate. No one seemed surprised by the sound. I tucked his reaction away in the mental file I'd just marked "What the fuck is up with this dude Eli?"

"You know what you should do?" Cora said. "You should head over to Kelley's. Ever since city hall had that termite problem, she's been keeping most of the town archives in the back of the bookstore."

"Don't expect anything too sophisticated," Kelley said. "It's mostly just high school yearbooks and historical society newsletters and moldy copies of the *Daily Nugget.*"

"That's a newspaper?" I asked.

"Not anymore," Cora said. "It stopped publishing — when was it, honey, 1980-something?" When Eli didn't answer immediately she poked him in the shoulder with her fork.

"Eighty-nine," he said. He served himself another slice of ham. His third. My stomach twisted.

Speaking of, I was behind on my bites. I spooned up a bit of the hollandaise.

"Has your family lived here long, Eli?" I asked when I could speak again.

"His great-grandfather moved here in 1885," Cora said. "Same as Stanton's family."

"Everyone had gold fever," Stanton said.

"But the gold ran out, right? So why did everyone stay?"

"They thought the gold was going to come back."

"Were they right?"

Stanton took a sip of his water. "That's the thing about gold fever — there's no cure, just remission."

Eli reached for another piece of ham.

"Does anyone still live in Adeline?" I asked.

Kelley shook her head. "Not since the late eighties."

"But not so long ago that most of the houses aren't still reasonably intact," Cora said. "Like the old house Eli grew up in — it's just like this one, did you know? The two towns are basically mirror images of each other." As she warmed to the subject, her voice took on the confident singsong of a practiced salesman. "Adeline is such a unique site, you'll see that for yourself, I'm sure. It's charming, it's historic, it's —"

"In ruins," said Renee.

Cora dropped her fork on her plate. "It doesn't matter how it looks now. It just matters how it'll look when I'm done with it."

Renee huffed. "But Cora, the cost of restoration alone —"

"And there's hardly anything left —" Kelley said.

"You really think we can compete with Deadwood?" Leo asked.

"That place is just too fucking creepy, if you ask me."

We fell silent and looked at Rue. She was pushing a limp spear of asparagus from one side of her plate to the other.

"Language, honey," Cora said, weakly.

"What? It is."

I sighed and tuned them all out, tapping my knife and fork against my plate so at least it would sound like I was eating. But really I was spiraling. I'd suffered through an entire dinner, and all I'd managed to do so far was collect a few scanty observations. Adeline was creepy. Cora was perky. Eli

141

liked to eat. But so what? None of them was Tessa — and my gut told me that until I found Tessa I couldn't go any further. I simply didn't have enough information. I mean, I couldn't exactly just bust out with, like, "Yeah, hi, I know we just met and all, but did any of you by any chance kill my mom? Chilly Hitchcock blonde? Real pretty? Boobs out to here? Hey, no worries if you did — seriously, I thought about it plenty of times myself. It'll be something we have in common!"

But I was never going to find Tessa if I just waited for the information to fall into my lap. So where did I go from here? If she'd had something to do with my mother's murder, I had to be discreet. Otherwise she would hear I was looking for her, and I might scare her off. My only lead would vanish.

The cop. I could ask the cop. Maybe I could even get away with asking a blunt question or two. After all, he was the only person in town I had any leverage on.

Too bad he was also the only person in town who had any leverage on me.

I set down my fork. I folded my napkin. And I let the conversation at the table wash over me while I thought about how best to approach Leo — and steadfastly refused to consider the possibility that the real reason I might not find Tessa was because she didn't actually exist.

JANIE JENKINS

CAT AND MOUSE

Jane Jenkins, the notorious ex-party girl
who was convicted of the brutal murder of
her mother . . . and who has been fever-
ishly sought by the press . . . spent the
first weeks after her release in a hotel in
Sacramento, California, TMZ has learned.

We're told the California Executive Suites
hosted a guest who never left her room
and who requested that housekeeping
services be suspended for the length of
her stay. After this guest checked out, the
housekeeping staff found a suspiciously
clean room . . . and a pile of $20 bills —
$400 in total — on the nightstand.

The suite showed no signs of having been
occupied, but when a curious housekeeper
(who has requested anonymity) searched
more thoroughly, she discovered a
crumpled piece of paper under a chair
cushion with the number of a local cab
company. TMZ called the number and

144

confirmed that the company received a request from a guest at the hotel named "Zelda Zonk," an alias famously used by Marilyn Monroe. But when the driver arrived at the designated pickup time, no one was there to meet him.

Multiple sources report that a man bearing a resemblance to Janie's lawyer was seen entering and leaving the building several times, and further TMZ investigations have revealed that at 3:40 a.m. on October 17th, a guest at the hotel used the hotel's business center to book a flight departing on November 2nd from Sacramento to Anchorage, Alaska . . . but sources at the airline report the ticket was never used.

Is Janie trying to throw us off the scent? Or did something come between her and that flight? The murder of Janie's mother isn't the only mystery here.

CHAPTER TEN

Kelley cornered me while everyone was busy clearing the table.

"Come have a drink with us after," she said.

I stole a glance at Leo. Cora was trying to say something to him, but he was watching me. And listening. I thought back to my earliest etiquette classes. It had been a long time since I'd bothered caring about whether or not my nos were polite.

"I appreciate the invitation," I said, "but I'm not sure if it's a —"

"It's a fucking great idea," Renee said as she walked by with an armful of glasses.

In another life I would've flicked a cigarette at Kelley's feet and walked away, no matter how nice she might be. But in this life, I just said, "Um, okay?"

"We can scrounge up something to eat, too," Kelley said before turning back to the table and gathering up the dirty forks and knives with a grin that made her look even less like her brother. There was such buoyancy in her expression — it made me think of the bounce of a little girl's corkscrew curls as she skipped down a garden path.

Leo's face, on the other hand, was tight and controlled. If he wanted to smile he probably filed the appropriate paperwork ahead of time. In triplicate. I almost couldn't believe they were related.

But then, I of all people should know that blood ties don't always show on the surface.

Across the table, Leo was reaching for my glass —

I moved to intercept him. "I'll get that," I said.

A deliberate I-know-that-you-know-that-I-know twitch of his lips. "Oh, it's no problem," he said.

"I wouldn't want it to get lost on the way to the dishwasher." I grabbed the glass, along with my cutlery and plate, and started toward the kitchen.

He leaned in and whispered in my ear: "If you're trying to put me off, you're doing a pretty bad job of it."

I turned back and took my napkin, too, for good measure.

Ten minutes later I was walking down Main

Street with Kelley and Renee, sidestepping potholes and hugging myself against the cold. It couldn't have been much more than twenty degrees out, but you wouldn't have known it to look at them. Renee was wearing a puffy thing of ruthless practicality; Kelley's coat was a patchwork of black-and-white tweeds and safety pins that shouldn't have kept a fire warm, but she seemed perfectly cozy nevertheless. I felt like the runt of the litter left out on a cliff to die.

I looked to the south, to the house on the hill.

"Who lives there?" I asked.

"Stanton, obviously," Renee said.

"Nice place," I said.

"If you like that sort of thing."

I rubbed my hands together and forced myself to keep moving.

Kelley's hand wrapped around my wrist and tugged me forward so I was sheltered between them. "Not used to the cold?" she asked.

"It's been a while."

Renee sniffed. "If you think it's cold now, just wait until tomorrow."

I pulled my hand free and stuffed it in my pocket, hoping I didn't look as awkward as I felt. For someone who had spent ten years in a women's prison, I sure was uncomfortable around women. But, then, I hadn't exactly grown up with them: My mother had never been comfortable with women either, and apart from the occasional maid or cook, our staff was always exclusively male. From time to time one of my stepfathers would remark upon the matter, typically with more than a hint of jealousy. My mother would always respond with something along the lines of, "It's not that I prefer men, darling. I simply know what to expect with them."

When she said this, she was usually looking at me.

We stopped in front of a building that, had its windows not been painted over, would have looked like one of those chain restaurants that advertise all-you-can-eat bread sticks. This was the Coyote Hole, the only place worth drinking at in Ardelle, or so Kelley and Renee told me. Apparently it had for many years been an underperforming restaurant even by Ardelle's standards, but when the owner passed away she left the place to her nephew, a man named Tanner Boyce. He managed to reverse the Coyote Hole's fortunes in short order by installing half a dozen TVs and shelling out for satellite sports coverage.

"Don't get too close to Tanner," Renee

told me. "He's catching."

Inside it was hot and damp and vaguely morose, like a locker room after a loss. Athletic accouterments aside, Tanner hadn't done much to convert the Coyote Hole from family restaurant to twenty-one-and-up bar. The booths along the west wall were still upholstered in red vinyl; the tables were still covered in gingham-patterned plastic. There was a stack of high chairs and booster seats in one corner, and just to the right of the door was a small arcade with skee-ball, Galaga, Ms. PacMan, and a vending machine shaped like a chicken.

"Margie used to give the kids a token at the end of the meal," Kelley said as we passed. "You'd put the token in there and the chicken would give you a prize in a plastic egg."

"Tanner uses it as a condom dispenser," said Renee.

We moved through the pool players and dart throwers and squeezed ourselves up against the bar, which was littered with chartreuse popcorn. Renee grabbed a handful from a red plastic basket. She let out a sound of pleasure. "God, after eating at Cora's this stuff is like ambrosia."

I frowned. They'd all seemed perfectly happy at dinner. "But you all cleared your

150

plates —"

"Yeah, into our napkins. Kelley and I paid Rue five bucks each to sneak our leftover food into the Dumpster."

The bartender came our way, and even if I hadn't seen Renee's shoulders tense I would've known I was looking at Tanner. He was just shy of handsome, but not so far off that I couldn't imagine a potential appeal under certain circumstances, in the same way that even a gross old bag of Cheetos can manage to look good three bowls into a dime bag. His arms were lean and muscled and covered in a thicket of tattoos he'd probably copied from a mixed-martial-arts magazine.

He smirked as he approached, and I noticed that his eyes weren't just undressing Renee. They were recording her with night-vision video and posting it on the Internet.

He boxed Renee in between his elbows and leaned forward until his face was almost touching hers. "I don't get off until two," he said. "But I always say life's not worth living if you just get off once a night."

She shoved him back. "Dream on, Tanner."

"Every night, Renee." He ran his tongue over his teeth when he smiled, and he smelled of something that probably had "breeze" in its name.

"What're you drinking?" he asked me without taking his eyes off Renee.

I studied the collection of bottles behind the bar. Bottom-shelf all the way — not that I should be thinking about drinking anything from any kind of shelf. "Club soda with lime," I said.

"Right. One Bride of Christ, coming up."

I pushed my glasses up on my face so I could get a better look at him when I delivered the set-down he deserved — like "Yep, that's me, just another girl who'd rather fuck a dead guy than you" — but *goddammit,* the only thing Rebecca could do was show a watery smile. He shoved the drink at me and didn't apologize when it spilled all over my hand.

"Ignore him," Kelley said. "Renee wouldn't go out with him in high school and he's been taking it out on all of us ever since."

I raised my eyebrows.

"Surprised I turned him down?" Renee asked.

"Surprised he went to high school."

"Well, only in the loosest possible sense." She threw back her head and drained her beer. "So you're probably wondering why we asked you here."

"It's not for the food?"

Kelley and Renee exchanged a look.

"Not quite," Kelley said.

"We thought we should warn you," Renee said.

I busied myself with my glass, taking a moment to identify the tightness in my chest as expectation. "Warn me? About what?"

"About Ardelle," she said.

I looked up. "I'm sorry?"

"It's not that people haven't tried to write about it, you know. It's just that once they get here they never end up finding anything worth writing about. Yeah, sure, it's a little weird how we keep moving back and forth and everything, but that's not really interesting — it's stubborn. I just don't want you to waste your time."

I slid a finger down the side of my glass and wiped off the condensation on a cocktail napkin. Why would two businesswomen in a struggling town be warning off a potential customer? "But the festival —"

"The festival sucks," Kelley said.

"Hard," Renee said.

"Even *we* really only put up with it for Cora's sake."

"And because we like the free food," Renee said. "But there will probably be like twelve or so people who aren't from Ardelle, and everyone else will be drunk. It'll be like attending a high school reunion as a significant other, except the reunion is five days long. And on the last night we have to wear costumes."

Expectation sharpened into suspicion. What game were they playing? Did they do this with everyone who came to town — or had I said something that triggered a warning bell? I decided to play along.

"I don't know," I said, not even having to fake my bewilderment. "I'm kind of into costumes."

Renee patted me on the shoulder. "That's just because you haven't smelled them."

I tried my drink and frowned. Tanner hadn't given me soda water; he'd given me tonic water. It was turning into that kind of night.

"Are you trying to get rid of me?" I asked, trying for a light tone.

Kelley laughed. "Of course not. We just don't want you to expect, like —"

"Something good," Renee said.

"But —"

"Shit," Renee said. "Speaking of sucking hard . . ."

I followed her gaze; Leo was approaching. "Ladies," he said. "Renee." He reached over the bar and grabbed a bottle of beer, which he opened with the heel of his hand. Once he'd settled on the stool next to Renee, he pulled out a pack of cigarettes, tapped one out, and held it to his mouth.

Tanner appeared just in time to swat it out of his hand. "Take it outside, Leo."

Leo shook his head. "It's colder than a polar bear's tit out there."

"Come on, man. It's the law."

"What's my line again?" Leo tapped a finger against his temple. "Oh yeah, I know: 'I am the law.' "

"Some of us'd rather not get cancer, Leo," Renee said.

"You live here cancer'd be a blessing."

"Only if you're the one to get it."

Leo ruffled Renee's hair before wedging a new cigarette in the corner of his mouth and lighting it. Tanner threw up his hands and walked away. Renee snatched the second cigarette and tossed it over the bar.

"I'm happy to wait while you pick that up," he said.

"And I'm happy to watch you wait."

I tugged on Kelley's sleeve. "What's their deal?" I asked, keeping my voice low.

"Oh, nothing much," she said. "They just used to be married." She looked at them and frowned. "Well, technically they still are."

"Why haven't they made it official?"

Kelley shrugged. "They say there's no reason to rush. They're already separated. Although even when they were living together they were always kind of separated — if that makes any sense."

"You'd be surprised," I said.

I sipped my tonic. It really needed gin.

Renee and Leo's discussion had escalated: She was hissing and poking his shoulder with increasing force. When she pulled back a fist, Kelley intervened, grabbing Renee's arm and putting a hand on Leo's chest.

"Change of subject!" she said, and from the look that passed between Leo and Renee I could tell that this was a favorite tactic of Kelley's. "Leo, let's start with you: I heard you were out looking for Walt Freeman today."

Walt? Where had I heard that name before? And why was Leo watching me so closely?

"It was no big deal," Leo said. "The guys over at Pine Ridge just told me he'd been spotted down there."

"Who's Walt Freeman?" I asked.

Renee snorted. "Oh, just the closest thing Ardelle has to a master criminal. We're *super* grateful to have Leo here to protect us from the big bad pot dealer."

"We actually should be," Kelley said. "His weed is crap."

Leo let his head fall back. "Seriously, Kelley, I'm right here."

I set down my drink. Oh. *That* Walt — the pot-smoking Neanderthal. This was even better than I'd hoped.

I widened my eyes and let my mouth open slightly. "Is Walt very dangerous?" I asked.

"He's less a Moriarty than a Joker," Kelley said. "But, like, Cesar Romero, not Heath Ledger."

Renee put her hand on mine. "Just pretend you know what that means," she said. "That's what I always do."

I nodded absentmindedly. So Leo had been hanging out on the side of the road with a known criminal — or, a criminal known for more than just smoking weed, anyway. And now he was lying about it. This wasn't just leverage: This was proper blackmail material. Finally, something I knew how to work with.

When I looked at Leo, he tossed a piece of popcorn in the air and caught it neatly in his mouth. Ah — the practiced nonchalance of a player caught in a bluff. If he changed the subject now, I'd know for sure I was onto something.

"So what were you guys talking about when I got here?" he asked. "Looked serious."

(I hid my smile.)

"Nothing much," Renee said. "We were just trying to put Rebecca here out of her misery."

"Seriously," Kelley said. "I mean, Deadwood's really nice, and I can recommend a great hotel up there."

"I've heard of worse ideas," Leo muttered.

I shook my head. "It's so thoughtful of you to think of me, but Deadwood really doesn't interest me. It's the town twinning I'm curious about. And anyway, I like it here."

"Why would you like it here?" all three asked simultaneously.

"But — you all seem to. Or is this another food-in-the-napkin thing?"

"What food-in-the-napkin thing?" asked Leo. "Wait, were you guys —"

Renee clamped her hand over his mouth. "Look," she said, "if it'll help make my case I'll tell you everything interesting that has ever happened in Ardelle." She waved at Tanner — "Another Coors!" — and turned back to me. "I bet I can tell you all there is to know before he comes back with my beer."

I held out my hands in surrender. "Okay, fine," I said, "tell me."

She took a breath. "So. In 1885 some old white dudes came and found some gold. It ran out. Then they found some tin. It ran out. Then they started cutting down trees. Those ran out, too. The end."

I smothered a noise of impatience. "There has to be more to it than that," I said. "You just described the history of . . . Earth."

"Other major events include: the winter of '34, when my granny Moore lost two chairs and a cat to a kitchen fire; the spring of '72, when Kelley's aunt crashed her brand-new Firebird into a telephone pole over on Route 61; the summer of '85, when Eli's little sister ran off with a bank robber; and the spring of '97, when Walt was kicked out of MIT and came back home to build a better bong. Does that cover it, Kel?"

Kelley shrugged apologetically. "Yup, just about."

"Don't forget the time you were caught drunk-skinny-dipping in the Obermeyers' kiddie pool," Leo said.

"Oh right," Renee said. "And that. Thanks, Leo."

I picked through the ice at the bottom of

my glass with my straw. I didn't believe for a second that Kelley and Renee were just acting out of the goodness of their hearts — or that nothing else had ever happened here. But I sensed that it was time for a strategic retreat. The guards in prison had always known that I was at my most biddable when I was about to be at my most dangerous, but no one would think such a thing of Rebecca Parker.

Well — Kelley and Renee wouldn't, anyway. Leo would require more finesse. I was going to have to risk getting him alone. Which I was pretty sure I knew how to do.

I stood up and fished around in my bag for some cash. "Thanks so much for keeping me company, everyone, but I should get going — Cora told me they lock up at ten."

"Oh, don't worry about that," Kelley said. "Cora keeps a key under the stone angel in the front yard."

"If I don't get to bed soon, I'll never wake up in time for breakfast." I pulled out a few dollar bills and paused. "Cora doesn't cook the breakfast, does she?"

"Would that change your mind about leaving?" Leo asked.

I turned my back to Kelley and Renee so I could give him the smile I always used in the past on women who thought they were prettier than me. "Be careful what you say, or I might start to think you don't like me."

And on that note, I walked out, sure that Leo wouldn't be far behind. Men like him always have to get the last word.

As soon as I stepped outside, my phone buzzed. Another post from Trace.

Forget Hawaii, forget Thailand, forget whatever glamorous foreign locale you think Janie Jenkins might have fled to. She NEVER even left Sacramento . . . until recently, at least. The bitch is up to something. Whatever it is, readers: DON'T let her get away with it. Find her, and that money could be YOURS.

I read the post three times over. I'd figured I'd have at least three or four weeks before the press managed to track me down, but I'd forgotten to factor in the accelerant that was Trace's insatiable loathing. Yet another reason not to dawdle.

Well, good. It's not like I wanted to stay, anyway. The faster I got out of this shit hole, the better. I'd find Tessa, find out where she'd met my mom, and then get myself wherever that was ASAP.

The strike of a match; the scent of smoke;

a voice: "Whatchya reading?"

I didn't need to look up to know who it was. "My horoscope. It says, 'You will meet a tall dark asshole.' "

Leo took a drag. "Psychics just aren't what they used to be. I'm not all that tall."

I straightened and made a show of jamming my phone angrily into my pocket. "Well, this was fun. Now if you'll excuse me —" He blocked my path, as I'd hoped. My performance was practically perfect — except I couldn't keep my eyes from darting to his cigarette.

He noticed and shook out another from his pack. "Want one?"

I quit smoking the day before my last hearing, just in case the gods needed a last sacrifice before finally condescending to throw me a bone, which meant — and I'd been trying really hard not to do this math — that it had been forty-eight days since my last cigarette.

That's 1,152 hours.
69,120 minutes.
4,147,200 seconds.
At least five eternities.

I leaned ever so slightly toward Leo's cigarette, a flower yearning for its carcinogenic sun. "I don't smoke," I croaked out.

"Sure you don't." He exhaled in my direction and watched the smoke dissipate, a predatory look on his face that made me take a step back. "I ran your plates, you know."

Oh shit.

I forced myself to smile sweetly. "So you *can* do actual police work."

"Did you know it's registered under another name? A name that is *not* Rebecca Parker?"

"I just bought it; the transfer hasn't gone through."

"You bought that thing by choice?"

"Haven't we established I don't know anything about cars?"

He rolled his cigarette back and forth between his thumb and forefinger. "I don't think we've established much of anything at all."

The door to the bar flew open and a drunk couple staggered out, holding on to each other to keep from falling over. We watched them shuffle down the street until they vanished into the darkness.

"So why are you really here?" Leo asked.

"How many times am I going to have to answer that question?"

"Yeah, well, if I remember correctly, you

originally said you were on your way to Montana."

"I don't exactly give my number out to men I've just met. I'm not that kind of girl."

"Hm." He took another drag. "I guess we'll see about that, won't we?" He smiled, and in the warm glow of the cigarette he wasn't half as ugly as I'd thought he was.

Something flared behind my ribs.

I wasn't really surprised.

Like most affectations, my dismal taste in men has become a habit. The last guy I slept with was this dude Kristof (you didn't think I'd actually have sex with that gross Grant guy, did you?), and his name alone probably tells you all you need to know. I remember Kristof as being literally from Transylvania, but of course I don't actually remember for sure. He was certainly from somewhere in Eastern Europe. Slovenia, maybe? Slovakia? Some country whose language gave the court interpreters major trouble, anyway.

Kristof had been in L.A. for a year or so when I saw him for the first time, cutting a line of coke in a club on Melrose like he was Michelangelo with a cube of baby laxative–laced Carrara. When Kristof wasn't pursuing me he was pursuing some career I never bothered asking about — modeling, probably, because he was almost too pretty: finely boned and smooth-cheeked, with a soft, labial mouth. A cherub who'd discovered Pilates and porn. Had I been twelve years old I would have believed him to be the most exquisite thing I'd ever seen. At seventeen, though, I knew him to be uncanny, and even as I finally let him at my dress and my neck and my thighs, I wondered if kissing him would be like kissing a carcass or kissing an alien. I already knew it wouldn't be like kissing a man.

Not that I particularly cared.

It was Kristof I was with the night of the murder — I met him just after I'd stolen my mom's boots, an hour or so before I left for Ainsley's party. We'd arranged to meet in the billiard room, which my mother had meticulously designed to evoke a sense of Old World grandeur, a time when men were men and women were chattel. There was wood paneling and framed portraits and expensive brandy, a walk-in humidor and a twelve-gauge Winchester on the wall. (Not that I need to remind you of that.) It smelled of leather and lemon Pledge.

I don't think my mother could possibly have spent more time decorating any other room in the house, and yet it was far and away the room she frequented least. Which made it the room I frequented most.

When Kristof arrived I offered him a drink, a cursory nod to something like respectability, but he took the glass from my hand before I could fill it. Moments later I was busy dealing with the flurry of his advance. I can report that in the end he was more alien than carcass, which is to say that it could have been worse. I was mildly diverted, anyway. Enough so that by the time I registered the sound of footsteps in the hallway, we'd already been walked in on.

There were four of them standing in the doorway — all men, presumably guests looking to enjoy a cigar — and when none of them apologized for the intrusion, something uneasy slithered through me. When Kristof swore at them in whatever it was language he spoke, three of them scuttled off, but the fourth lingered in the doorway. I hooked one leg around Kristof's hip for balance and reached over for the shotgun — my mother always kept it loaded. I hefted it to my shoulder and leveled it at the intruder's face. He stared at me for a long moment before stepping back and letting the door swing closed. I didn't lower the gun until I was sure he was gone.

Then I hiked up my skirt and let Kristof

fuck me against the Louis XV credenza.

There are those for whom recklessness is a state of abandon. Of thoughtlessness. Of a conscious decision to ignore repercussions and eventualities. And I bet it's liberating for them, like spinning in circles and falling to the ground. But that's not me. My recklessness was a demonstration of restraint. I spun in circles to prove I could walk a straight line after.

Kristof talked enough during that he never noticed I didn't talk at all, and though I shuddered when his fingers brushed my bare skin, like all the men before he mistook distaste for desire. A few minutes later he threw back his head and bleated a series of meaningless adverbs while I thought about all the things you can make another person's body do.

Monday 9:34 PM

Are you there?

Monday 9:47 PM

Answer me please.

I need to talk to you. It's important.

Monday 10:04 PM

Jane. I know why you said what you said. I don't care.

Don't worry this isn't some fucking love letter.

Monday 10:13 PM

Goddammit write back.

Monday 10:37 PM

WHERE ARE YOU

CHAPTER ELEVEN

I considered Leo. He looked nothing like Kristof except in the way that one bad idea looks like another.

"What?" he asked.

"Take me back to your place."

He coughed up a cloud of smoke. "You're unpredictable, I'll give you that."

"It's not like that. I just want to talk," I said.

"I can't tell if you're joking."

"Not into it? No worries, that's cool. I'm happy to have a chat with the state police about how I saw you with Master Criminal Walt Freeman this afternoon."

"Not joking, then." He ran a hand through his hair, scratching at the nape of his neck. "Serves me right for being a Good Samaritan."

"I always thought the Good Samaritan was a smug son of a bitch." I pulled at his arm. "Come on, Officer, let's go."

He stubbed out his cigarette. "It's Chief, actually."

"Of course it is," I muttered.

We walked in silence the rest of the way, turning south on Percy then west on First Street, passing another series of bricked-and boarded-up businesses. It wasn't late, but there wasn't anyone on the street. There wasn't anywhere for anyone to go.

He set a brisk pace, and I was out of breath by the time we got to his house, a run-down Italianate chipped in gray and topped by a cupola that tilted left at a seventy-degree angle. A real Boo Radley special. The front yard was fenced in by the kind of brutish chain link you'd expect to see at a junkyard. In the driveway, two rusty motorcycle skeletons were propped up against a cinder-block wall, partially hidden by the white Crown Victoria. When we walked up the front steps we passed a sign with a picture of a Bichon Frise and the words "Shave and a Haircut — Two Biscuits!"

It wasn't until I absently cataloged the sign as Not Something a Killer Would Have that I realized I'd never stopped to wonder if Leo had been the man I'd heard in my mother's closet that night.

When he opened the door, I hesitated.

Then a ball of white fluff ran at us, and I forgot to be wary.

Dogs: my other weakness.

Leo bent over and scooped up a puppy that could've fit in a Marc Jacobs hobo bag, pinning it under his arm and muzzling it with his free hand. "This is Bones, and, yes, he bites. You two will get along just fine."

I scratched Bones behind his ears before I could stop myself.

Leo gave me a bemused look and carried the dog into the back of the house, leaving me in the front hall. I heard the rustle of a bag followed by the metallic clatter of kibble being poured into a bowl.

I wandered into the living room. A pair of blue chintz sofas sat on a thick pile rug; the walnut coffee table was stacked high with what appeared to be gardening magazines. A philodendron sat in one corner.

I frowned. A philodendron was *definitely* not something a killer would have. Or a dirty cop, for that matter.

"Are you sure this is your house?" I asked when he returned.

"It's my parents' house. They moved about ten years ago to a place Cora's folks found them in Florida. They love it. My dad found a D&D meet-up and my mom has time for her orchids."

"Haven't gotten around to redecorating, huh?"

"I like it like this."

He crossed his arms, waiting for my next move.

But because suddenly I wasn't sure what my next move was, I walked over to the fireplace to look at the framed photos on the mantel.

Leo and Kelley as children, splashing in a lake. A man and a woman in formal dress, standing outside a church.

"Your parents?" I asked.

He nodded.

Leo in a soccer uniform, a ball balanced on his toe. Kelley, wearing a tutu and a bored expression.

"Are you going to tell me what you want?" he asked.

"In a minute," I said, thinking furiously. I'd thought I had Leo's number, but maybe I didn't understand him at all. What kind of a person kept so many family photos?

What kind of a person kept *any* family photos?

Leo's high school graduation. Kelley's college graduation. Leo's police academy graduation. Family trips to San Francisco, Seattle, the Grand Canyon.

I came to the last photograph. It was a

group shot, with a dozen or so people standing in a ragged line. Leo looked to be in junior high. Kelley was just a little girl.

"What's this?" I asked.

Leo came up behind me to get a closer look.

"That's from the town's hundredth anniversary," he said. "There was a whole thing." He pointed to a blond teenager who had the gaunt look of either a recent growth spurt or not enough food. "See, that's Eli."

"Who's that next to him?"

"His sister."

"Pretty," I said.

He made a noise of agreement.

I sucked in a breath and rolled my next question around in my mouth, trying to feel out whether or not it was the right thing to ask.

I asked it anyway:

"What's her name?"

"Tessa," he said.

In a show of superhuman restraint, I kept my face from betraying any signs of the firestorm of absolute incomprehension that raged through me.

"You know what?" I said after a long moment. "I changed my mind. My questions can wait." I took a shaky step back. "But I think I'll take that cigarette after all."

■ ■ ■ ■

I won't say I ran out of Leo's house, but I didn't exactly walk out of it, either. As soon as I turned onto Main Street the wind whipped up, knocking me off balance. It took tremendous effort to keep my feet under me, but I refused to slow down until I spotted a corner I could duck behind. I stopped and put the cigarette Leo'd given me between my lips.

My hands patted down my pockets reflexively, but — *shit.* I didn't have a lighter. I dug around the bottom of my bag, fingers skidding . . . *Yes!* I pulled out a matchbook, plucked a match, and struck it. A flare of light, a butterfly kiss of heat. I was just about to touch the flame to the cigarette when I saw it.

The cigarette fell from my lips. I didn't move to catch it.

I'd forgotten about the matchbook.

I was the one who called the cops, you know — after I found my mother. After I found my voice. But I'd had a cigarette first. I'd backed away from the body and the blood and rifled through my things for a light, as frenzied as if it had been 4,147,200 seconds since my last cigarette then, too.

Finally I'd found this matchbook. It was nothing fancy. Just the plain white cardboard kind you get at a gas station. The perfect size for a single, bloody thumbprint.

Through the flicker of the flame, I saw my mother's face as it had been that morning, slack and juicy, a tomato crushed underfoot.

The wind blew again, extinguishing the match. I tossed it to the ground and lit another.

My mother, earlier that same night, plucked and polished and poised, except — was that a spark of anxiety in her eyes?

I lit another.

My mother, when I was very young, her nose still too tipped-up, her lips too thin.

Then I pulled out the photo I'd stolen from Leo — and lit one last match.

I let out a breath. In the picture, Eli's appearance was so different: His shoulders sagged, and his clothes looked like they'd never wash clean. Tessa wasn't much better. Her clavicles jutted up beneath her skin. Her hands hung limply at her sides. Her smile was cruel, but she was so young and pretty that had anyone else found the picture they would have been hard-pressed not to smile back.

Not me, though.

Nope.

Because Tessa was my mother.

The match burned down to my fingertips.

I didn't feel a thing.

FROM THE DIARY OF TESSA KANTY

August 15, 1985

Fuck this place.

CHAPTER TWELVE

When I woke up the next morning — in my room's impeccably restored claw-foot bathtub — the photo was still clutched in my hand. I peeled my eyes open so I could look at it for the eightieth or so time. Apart from Tessa and Eli, there were four families in the shot: Kelley and Leo's; Renee's; Walt's; Stanton's. The slim, silver-haired woman with her arm around Leo was his and Kelley's mother; the round-shouldered man with the sunny smile was their father. The old women whose face was wrinkled through with good humor must have been their grandmother.

Renee and her mother were equally blond, equally hard-edged.

All five members of Walt's family wore Vikings jerseys.

Stanton's wife and son looked like they wanted to be absolutely anywhere else in the world.

But it was Tessa and Eli my eyes returned to again and again. They were alone: no parents, no grandparents, no nothing. And they were standing so close to one another that it seemed impossible that they wouldn't somehow be touching. But they weren't.

I tapped my mother's face. Why had she run? I mean — apart from the obvious. Even I couldn't fault her for not wanting to stay in Ardelle.

Did you hate everyone in your family, or was it just me?

My mother never talked about her family. This hadn't struck me as particularly un-usual when I was younger. In our circles the subject of family was a delicate one. If, on the one hand, you came from money or beauty or power, you wanted people to know it. On the other hand, having to advertise those connections was an admission of their inadequacy — no one's ever needed to ask Nat Rothschild about his genetic provenance. I could see now how well this had worked in my mother's favor.

Marion Jenkins, as I've been told, came to Zurich in the fall of 1985 in a swirl of silky hair and Yves Saint Laurent, the estranged daughter (she said) of a wealthy American family that was whispered to be connected with the Chernyshev-Besobrazovs of New

179

York. She was in Switzerland as part of a rebelliously old-fashioned Grand Tour, but once she came, she never left, and within weeks of her arrival she had won over the finer people of Zurich with her gentle manners and good heart. To this day the city's hostesses still refer to her as *Seelewärmerli:* "little soul warmer."

I'm not even fucking kidding.

She met my father at a New Year's Eve something-or-other in St. Moritz. She was the only one of her party who couldn't ski (didn't know how), and he was the only one of his who couldn't (older than dirt). While everyone else was tackling the slopes of Corviglia, she kept him company and made him laugh and snuck him all the brandy his grandchildren told him he shouldn't be drinking. The next morning he whisked her away to his château outside Sion, where they lived together until his death the following Christmas, barely a month after they had me.

My mother maintained to her dying day that she never, *ever* would have guessed that dear sweet Emmerich was actually a minor member of the house of Hapsburg-Lorraine.

. . . Yeah, his family didn't buy it, either.

And so my father's family would have nothing to do with either of us, and since my parents had never married, there was no reason they had to. But they couldn't keep her from inheriting a piece of his estate — my mother was good at picking lawyers too — and after that she didn't ever have to worry again about the inconvenient opinions of petty nobility. She set herself up in Geneva, established a foundation or two, and soon enough even my illegitimacy was considered part of her charm.

Like she always said, "You can get away with anything if you wear great clothes, throw great parties, and give money to kids with cleft palates."

She would have made a great pope.

So no, my mother didn't talk about her family, and if anyone else did, they never said anything to me. Sometimes, though, I let myself wonder — usually about her parents. Mémé and Pépère, I called them. I liked to picture them sipping scotch and scowling at Dominican nannies from the window of their Upper East Side classic six. But really, I knew my grandparents were dead. Whenever anyone else talked about their own parents, my mother got this lazy, supercilious look on her face, like a newly-wed playing wingman for a sadly single friend. She knew she'd never have to suffer through that stage of her life again.

I always imagined I'd feel the same way.

When you look into your family's future, it's loss you anticipate, not gain.

And yet, here I was, newly possessed of an uncle and a cousin. Twice as many blood relatives as I'd ever had. Would I recognize something of myself in them — of them in myself?

Would they recognize me?

What the fuck have I gotten myself into?

It took me ten minutes to convince myself to set the picture aside and crawl out of the bathtub. A slather of soap and the raw scrub of a washcloth later and I was ready to defile myself again with polyester blend — this time a sweater I'd ordered from a maternity catalog and a pair of pleated-front slacks. (That's right: motherfucking *slacks*.)

I cinched a belt around the too loose waist and walked to the pretty little escritoire by the window (which if you craned your neck just so afforded a glimpse of the road that led out of town). I ran a finger along its edge. It was an elegant enough piece of furniture that when I first saw it I'd wished, however briefly, that I had correspondence to complete so that I might put it to good use. Gentle communications to a devoted older sister, maybe, or a response to an invitation to an upcoming ball.

182

My mother would have laughed herself sick at the very thought. I knew exactly what she would say: *You're no English Rose, Jane — you're an American Aphid.*

My phone vibrated on the bedside table and I grabbed for it, grateful for the distraction. I checked the display: another text message from Noah.

I'm going to try this one last time.

I sank down on the bed. I knew it was a terrible idea to write back. I always gave too much away when it came to Noah, no matter what form the communication. And he was probably pissed I'd ignored him the night before — which was precisely why I'd ignored him. If he was angry, maybe he wouldn't come after me.

No, I couldn't text back. Complete radio silence. It was the only way. I tossed the phone on the bed.

It vibrated again.

Oh, fuck it. I snatched up the phone.

Are you alive?

      I'm not dead anyway

How's Wisconsin?

My thumbs stilled. Had he already figured

out I wasn't there?

Fine

You should know they've
tracked you to Sacramento.

I heard
How

Sounds like housekeeping.

Guess I should've tipped
more

His next text took nearly a minute to
come through.

Not the response I ex-
pected.

What did you expect
Where the fuck is the
punctuation
Oh
What did you expect?
Concern?
Urgency?
Irritation?

:(

:o

:<

Better?

Not really.

Tough

This time he didn't text back. Mission accomplished. I guess. I rubbed at my nose. The skin had begun to chap.

I trudged out of my room, trying to think happy *We Can Do It!* thoughts. Maybe this wouldn't be so bad. Breakfast used to be my favorite meal, you know, and not just because my mother was never awake for it. Downstairs the festivities were in full swing. Nearly eighty people had crowded around the ten or so tables, and the room was gurgling with overindulged digestive systems. More than one person had his hand resting on his stomach. Kelley waved at me from one table; next to her, Rue scowled. I ignored them as politely as I could as I studied the room. I counted three dozen men who were old enough to have been in my mother's bedroom that night. One was Stanton. One was Leo.

But Eli was the one I was heading for.

No — *my uncle* was the one I was heading for.

God, I should've brought some stronger drugs.

Eli barely looked up when I approached. I took a seat between him and another guest, a dark-haired man with a square jaw and over-it eyes who was nursing a cup of coffee, his glower deeper than could be explained away by mere morning crankiness. When I sat down, I accidentally kicked the stranger's chair.

"Pardon me," I murmured.

"Uh huh," he said. He was dressed indifferently, in jeans and a rumpled gray Henley. The hatband on his blue and orange cap was stained white with sweat. He lifted his chin to facilitate the largest possible yawn.

I kicked his chair again, on purpose this time.

I watched Eli out of the corner of my eye. He was shoveling away at a plate of beans that could've fed an entire mining camp. Cora sat down next to him and scooped another mound onto his plate.

Maybe he killed my mother for her food?

"Good morning," I said.

Eli mumbled something around his fork.

"Did you sleep well?" Cora asked.

"Like the dead!"

I smiled at Eli and opened my mouth.

Speaking of the dead —

The door to the kitchen banged open and a plump woman with the sparse fuzzy hair of a newborn emerged with a tray, her fleshy chin wobbling as she walked toward us. She dropped two plates of eggs and cornbread in front of the sullen-mouthed man and me. "Out of beans," she grunted. Cora's lips thinned as she watched her leave.

The man looked at his food like a death-row prisoner who'd just been delivered the wrong last meal.

I turned back to Eli —

"I was hoping to have the chance to introduce you," Cora said to me, drawing the nameless man closer. "You two are the only ones here by yourselves, and I thought that, in case you wanted company, it might be . . ." She trailed off at the man's blank expression, then rallied. "Rebecca, this is Peter! Peter, Rebecca. Rebecca's a historian."

She faltered again when he made no move to shake my hand. "Peter," she continued, too brightly, "is a writer with a *magazine,* and he's covering the festival for them — isn't that exciting?"

Peter waved his hand in front of his face

187

as if clearing a stench. "I'm thrilled to be here."

I gave him the least attractive smile I could muster. "Likewise," I said.

Next to Cora, Eli was eating furiously. Better to hold off on conversation with him until his mouth isn't otherwise occupied.

I smoothed my napkin over my lap and examined my own food. My knife was mislaid. I flipped it blade side in. I wondered if it might make things easier if I just went ahead and stabbed myself in the side of my neck and was done with it. A reporter. Christ.

An even more blood-curdling thought: *What if he wasn't the only one?*

I eyed the other guests at the table. There were two couples and a family of four. One couple ate with their heads bent close together, their motorcycle jackets slung over the backs of their chairs. The woman was reaching for another piece of cornbread, and the tendril of a tattoo peeked out from under her sleeve. I cringed. Tattoos — one of the few things my mother and I agreed on: We both thought them vulgar. Of course, my mother's reasons were cosmetic, whereas mine were tactical. You should never saddle yourself with something so hard to change.

The other couple was quite young, just

out of college, maybe, and shabbily dressed. On a budget holiday, I'd guess. The family, meanwhile, was uncannily proper: They had matching white shirts and perfect posture and didn't even look at their forks as they raised them to their mouths.

They were all clearly from out of town — no one was eating much.

I let out a breath. Harmless, the lot of them. I was sure.

"Will anyone else be arriving today?" I asked Cora.

"No, this is it. But of course you never know who's going to decide to stop by on the spur of the moment." She stirred cream into her coffee. "Though I tend to think these things are so much nicer when they're cozy like this, when we can all really get to know each other."

"Well, it suits me perfectly," I said. "I love meeting new people."

Cora smiled — and I did, too. Mostly because I was pleased to discover she was so susceptible to praise.

I looked back at Eli, and then at Peter. *Who should I tackle first?* I took a long sip of water, because as Sun Tzu said, the general who loses a battle makes but few calculations beforehand, and also the general who hydrates has a nicer complexion.

The cook dropped another plate in front of Eli and he set to work, deciding things for me. I turned to Peter.

"So, you're a writer?" I asked.

"A journalist."

"What's the distinction?"

"Journalists don't get to choose their assignments." He turned to look out the window, missing the reflexive pitch of my eyes toward the ceiling.

"Well, who knows?" I said. "Maybe you'll get more of a story than you bargained for."

His shrug was so impressively Gallic in its contempt that I couldn't quite figure out if he was a threat or a joke. Either way, I suspected he'd need more coffee to be of any use to me.

I turned back to Cora. "So what do we have to look forward to today?"

She picked up a yellow brochure from a pile next to her plate and handed it to me. "Here's a schedule. The tour of Adeline is up next, and the shuttle leaves from the inn at ten-thirty. But in the meantime, I think you might like to swing by Kelley's bookstore. She knows even more about Ardelle and Adeline than I do — plus you can take a look at the museum and the town archives."

"So Kelley was born here?" I asked.

Cora laughed. "*Everyone* was born here."

"Except you," I guessed.

For a moment her perpetual smile wasn't really a smile at all. "I guess I've always wanted to live in a place with some history," she said. "The closest we have to a cultural monument in Panama City is the Bon Temps bingo hall."

"That's where you met Eli?" I asked. "In Panama City?"

Eli waved his fork; Cora nodded. "Eli was stationed there," she said. "One night he walked into a bar I was at — and, well, you know what they say about men in uniform."

"Panama City's a long way away. Do you get to go home to see your family very often?"

"Not as much as I'd like. There's just so much to do here, what with the inn and the restoration and the festival — I don't have much free time."

Eli finished the last of his cornbread. I pounced.

"And what about you, Eli?"

"I don't have much free time either," he said.

"I mean, do you get to see your family often? Or do they all live in town?"

He set down his mug and looked me in

the eye. "Everyone in my family is in this room."

I started — did that mean that he knew his sister was dead or just that she was dead to him? Or was he pretending he never even had a sister to begin with?

He pushed up from the table before I could ask anything further. "Excuse me," he said.

We watched him go — Peter included, I noticed.

"That was abrupt," Peter said lightly.

Cora managed a laugh. "Like I said, there's just so much to do!"

I straightened my glasses to get a better look at the worry lines on Cora's face. If I was reading things right, she was mortified, and whatever bad impression Eli might have given, she would try to correct. She was showing me her tender underbelly; I decided to take a swipe.

I moved closer to her, careful to lean in and prop my chin up, because that's what people who give a shit do. "I can tell that you love it here," I said, "but Eli — why did he decide to come back?"

She sighed. "To tell you the truth, I don't really know. Eli doesn't even seem to like it here sometimes. I can't understand why not."

"It's only natural," I said.

"How do you mean?"

"It doesn't sound like you liked Panama City, either."

"Well, that place is the pits."

"So's every place when you're a kid. You could grow up in a Swiss chalet and you'd just learn to hate hot cocoa."

Peter was only half listening, intent as he was on smashing his eggs with the back of his fork. Every so often his eyes would dart to another corner of the room before returning to his plate, disappointed, having found nothing of interest. *He could be dangerous,* I thought — but he could also be useful. If he had a story he cared about, he could ask all the tough questions. I just had to make sure he found the right story — and that I was in earshot.

I smiled, getting into the idea. He could be my very own Renfield. If he did a good job, maybe I'd even give him a spider or two.

I threw out my first lure: "Didn't I hear that Ardelle had its fair share of trouble back in the day?"

"Where did you hear that?" asked Cora.

"What kind of trouble?" asked Peter. His eyes fully focused on the two of us for the first time all morning. *Bingo.*

Cora's spine snapped straight. "I'm sure I don't know what you're talking about."

"What kind of trouble?" Peter repeated. When Cora didn't immediately respond, he put his hand on hers and smiled. "It could be great background for the piece."

"Well, I suppose —"

"Great," Peter said, pulling out his notebook and pen.

"You have to understand," she said, twisting her napkin, "that when Eli was a kid it wasn't a happy time. Economically, I mean. The tin was running out, and people were losing their jobs, their houses. The Percys, obviously, made it through just fine, but for the rest of us — the rest of *them,* I mean — it was really rough. Particularly for Eli. His mom passed away when he was just a kid, and then his dad died of a heart attack when Eli was just a couple years out of high school. And he didn't leave Eli much more than a mortgage and some worthless land up on the mountain. Eli tried to get work in town, but it wasn't enough. Eventually he had to sell the house in Adeline."

I rocked back in my seat. My mother had grown up *poor*? And yet she still thought it was okay to spend so much on shoes?

"Who'd he sell to?" Peter asked.

Cora hesitated. "Stanton. Stanton owns

194

most of Adeline now, actually." She firmed up her expression. "And it's a good thing, too — there's a man who appreciates history."

"But that must have been hard for Eli, losing the house," I said.

"It really was. Especially right after his sister —"

"His sister?" I said, very carefully.

"Oh, it's nothing," she said. "She just left town, that's all."

Peter was watching her, a speculative gleam in his eye. "But before — he said all his family was here today. Why didn't he mention a sister from out of town?"

"It's not something we really like to talk about."

"Where is she now?" Peter asked.

Cora piled her cutlery on her plate and set down her napkin. "You'd know as well as I," she said.

ARDELLE VISITORS GUIDE

Attractions

Mining Museum, 238 Percy Ave.

Visitor Center, 205 Main St.

Oglala Sioux Interpretive Exhibit, 238 Percy Ave.

Events

Gold Dust Days. First week of November. Schedules available at the Ardelle Visitor Center (located in the Prospect Inn).

Lodging

The Prospect Inn, 205 Main St. This impeccably restored historical building treats visitors to modern-day service in a nineteenth-century setting. Twelve beautifully furnished private rooms with double beds and *en suite* bath. Internet. Showtime. Breakfast and afternoon tea.

Dining

The Coyote Hole, 300 First St. Full bar, satellite TV. Half-price drinks on Game Day.

VFW Post #919, 124 Tesmond Ave.

MacLean's General Store, 398 Main St. Buffalo sticks/jerky, homemade jams and jellies, kuchen.

Shopping
Odakota Gallery and Gifts, 142 Main St.
La Plante's Booksellers, 238 Percy Ave.
Hill Creek Outfitters, 140 Main St.
Rita's Consignment Shop, 155 Commercial St.

Campgrounds
A campground/RV park can be found three miles west of Ardelle, on the other side of the pass. Pull-thrus, full hook-ups, 20/30/50 amp, dump station. Picnic table, horseshoes.

CHAPTER THIRTEEN

Peter was doing such a good job so far that I decided to dangle another spider in front of him.

"Seems a little suspicious, doesn't it," I said.

"What does?"

"That whole thing about Eli's sister."

Peter nodded hesitantly, not quite convinced.

"I wonder . . ." I said, trailing off deliberately.

"What?"

"If that bookstore owner knows so much about the town, maybe she'd know something about Eli's sister, too."

"That's a good idea, actually." He stood up. "I guess I know where I'm heading next."

I threw out my hand. "Wait," I said.

How was I going to convince him to let me tag along? I ran through my options.

Men like Peter exist to have their egos flattered, so one strategy was to play the hopeless girl with a crush. But what does a hopeless crush look like? Was I supposed to flirt ineffectually? Should I flush and look away? I wasn't sure. I've had just a handful of crushes in my life — if something's attainable you can't exactly long for it, and the men of my acquaintance weren't exactly known for their reticence.

Then there were my clothes to consider.

No, if I was going to convince Peter to keep me in the loop, it obviously wasn't going to be for my sexual allure.

Okay, then, hero worship it is!

"Why don't I come with you?" I said. "I don't know if Cora mentioned, but I'm a historian — maybe I could help out? This sounds like a story with potential, and I'd love to watch you work. I always had dreams of being a reporter, you know. Just like Lois Lane!"

He sighed. "Oh, hell, why not? All anyone else in this town wants to talk about are the hors d'oeuvres they're serving at Saturday's ball. Come on — let's go."

Even though the bookstore was a short walk away — just four blocks — it was wet and cold enough that by the time Peter and I found the place I felt like a soggy bathroom sponge. A bell rang when we entered.

The front room was crowded with merchandise — souvenirs, mostly — and smelled of rawhide. I drifted from display to display, examining pottery and textiles and unattractively self-published local histories. Cora, I noticed, had authored one of the books: *Gold Rush Gothic Revival: Decorative Art and Architecture in the Boomtowns of the Black Hills.* My eyelids drooped just looking at it.

The next volume, though, was more promising. *The Founding Families of Odakota's Twin Cities* — written by one Kelley La Plante. I slid it out. It was separated into five sections:

The Percys
The Kantys
The Freemans
The Fullers
The La Plantes

I pulled the photo out of my bag and counted. Yup, five families.

"What's that?" Peter asked over my shoulder. I shoved the photo into the back of the book.

"Nineteenth-century history," I said. "It's

fascinating — I'm reading about the representational politics of ethnic minorities as it relates to the construction of the transcontinental railway. Would you like to see it?"

He paled. "Maybe later."

I let out a breath and opened the book again. I flipped past the foreword — and found a Kanty family tree.

No mention of Tessa.

But the family tree wasn't totally useless: Now I knew I was related to Renee too. Second cousins. *God, bitch really must be in my blood.*

I turned to the first page of the Kanty history.

Albert Kanty, the area's first European settler, arrived in 1881 from the Prussian province of Posen (now part of the Greater Poland Voivodeship) in the company of his young wife, Casimera, and her sister, Agnieszka. Kanty's was the largest claim in the area, more extensive even than the claim that would be staked eight months later by Tesmond Percy. It was Percy's claim that proved to be the more lucrative of the two, however, and once Kanty had exhausted his own reserves, he took a job with Percy's fledgling mining company. Even so, until his death in 1897, Kanty

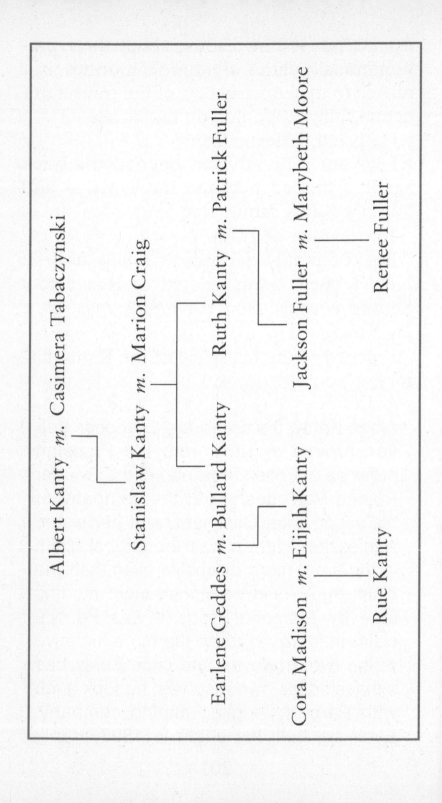

continued to search his own land in the hopes of finding another lode.

"I should have known it wouldn't take you long to uncover my secret."

My heart stuttered. Kelley had snuck up on me. Her hair was in pigtails today, and she was wearing a black shirt printed with a motto I didn't recognize.

I steadied my breathing. "Your secret?"

She nodded at the book. "That I'm a geek *and* a nerd," she said.

It took me a split second to regain my mental footing, and there was something in Kelley's steady gaze that made me think she'd noticed.

"It's very well written," I said.

"You should take it — on the house. It's not often I meet someone who actually wants to read the thing."

"Thanks," I said, meaning it. "It's a great place you've got here." (I didn't mean that.)

"I guess." She combed through a display of feather necklaces. "I'm not crazy about the merchandise, but I can't really afford to get rid of it."

"They're not that —" I started, but Kelley shot me a look. "Okay, they're pretty bad."

"This used to be just a bookstore — a real one — and even then people would come in and see me and be all '*How,* little squaw. I'll take a pair of your best moccasins and a bag of buffalo jerky.' So when I took over from my dad — well, I started stocking moccasins and buffalo jerky."

"Why don't you just move somewhere where people actually buy books?"

She smiled. "I tell myself that conning them into buying overpriced crap is the best revenge."

"But where's the museum?"

"The *museum*?"

"Cora said this was also a museum."

Kelley rolled her eyes. "Classic Cora. Calling what we have a museum is a gross exaggeration. We barely even have an exhibit. But you're more than welcome to take a look if you want — it's just over here." She led me through a door to our left, to a display that was little more than a series of cases containing vintage mining tools of deeply questionable historical consequence. There was a row of pictures along one wall, each identified by an unevenly typewritten label. Several showed Cora's inn, and I had to hand it to her — her restorations were spot-on. The only difference I could see was in the signage. The modern-day Prospect Inn was marked with a routed cedar sign, but back in the 1890s things were much simpler, just a crudely lettered board that read "Rooms." In one picture you could see a blowsy, petticoated woman slipping in through a side door.

Kelley nudged me forward. "Coffee's through there."

I stepped into the kind of room you can feel in your nose hair. Books were stacked on books; shelves were stacked on shelves; dust was stacked on dust. I moved to the nearest bookshelf, tilting my head to read the titles before pulling one out. On the cover a green-skinned woman embraced a tiger-tailed man. I actually thought for a second about buying it. I hadn't read for fun in years — ten years, in fact. Solitary confinement and obsessive investigation kind of gets in the way of that.

"And this," Kelley said, "is what Cora likes to call the Oglala Sioux Interpretive Exhibit." She was fighting a smile.

"I don't follow."

"Each of these volumes is an artifact of great cultural importance to Ardelle's Oglala Sioux community — which is to say, my dad."

"Sounds like Cora could've had a career in advertising." I put the book back. "He didn't take his books with him to Florida?" I asked. Only when Kelley failed to respond did I realize what I'd given away. "I ran into your brother again on my way back to the inn last night," I said lightly. "He mentioned that your folks had retired."

She watched me, her face teetering on the edge of so many different expressions all at once, I couldn't even begin to guess what she was thinking.

"I was hoping you'd be halfway to some-place nicer by now."

Over Kelley's shoulder I saw Renee, barefoot and cradling a mug of coffee, standing at the bottom of a staircase I hadn't even seen. I looked her over anew, wondering if I'd see her any differently now that I knew she was my second cousin, and I couldn't resist searching her face for something, anything, that reminded her of me. I wasn't exactly counting on it, though: Any similarities between me and my mother had always been conspicuously absent. I'm blowsy blond, fox-faced, built like a bal-lerina but lacking the grace. My mother, on the other hand, looked like Marilyn Monroe — but carried herself like Grace Kelly. I wasn't just the apple that had fallen far from the tree. I was the apple that had been eaten up by worms, too.

It was only because I was watching Renee so closely that I noticed it. When she came over to stand next to us, Kelley brushed her knuckles against Renee's hip in a way that made me think she wasn't even aware she was doing it. The side of my mouth quirked up. They may as well have been carrying matching copies of *Rubyfruit Jungle.*

For the first time in I don't know how long, I let out an honest, full-throated laugh. It was an awful, rusty sound, like a screw being stripped by a drill, but it was, I admit, a relief to know it was still there.

They both turned to me, Renee stepping slightly in front of Kelley, unifying their front. The softness that had snuck into their smiles was replaced by a grim watchfulness.

My own smile sagged, and I tugged it wearily back into place.

Secrets are my stock in trade, but damn if they're not a pain in the ass.

There are three ways to approach secrets, you know. The first is what you find on soap operas and in poorly executed middle-school maneuvers. First you uncover a piece of incriminating information, and then you use it to force a steady stream of favors or payment or behavior. The problem here is that, if extended indefinitely, the expected cost of compliance eventually outweighs the cost of exposure. Moreover, the probability that you'll lose your monopoly on your information increases with each passing day. Never, ever assume that you're the only person digging for dirt, especially in Los Angeles. Vipers are measured by the pitful for a reason.

The second approach is more effective: You make one, single, very carefully chosen demand. And you give your mark just one chance. This was my usual MO. If the mark doesn't do as you ask, when you ask, you leak their secret. No excuses. No mercy. Brutal consistency is the key to credibility. Mothers, dog trainers, Israel — you know what I'm talking about.

But there's also a radical third approach: You reveal that you know the secret . . . and then you keep it under wraps. Do that, and they're not just going to tell you other secrets, they might even keep yours in return. And they'll think they're doing it of their own free will when what you've really done is painstakingly aligned your incentives. That's all trust is, really. Some people are just incentivized by virtue.

That's why I decided on the third approach. *It might be just what I need to win them over.*

"What's so funny?" Renee said, breaking the silence.

"Does Leo know?" I asked.

They exchanged a look.

"Know what?" Kelley asked.

I decided to see how they'd react if I let a little Jane show through: "That his wife is doing his sister."

Kelley stifled a giggle. Renee rolled her eyes. Success.

"Come on," Kelley said. "You have to admit that when you put it like that it *is* pretty funny." She wrapped an arm around Renee and dropped kisses on the curve of her neck until Renee relaxed. Then she pointed at me. "I take back what I said about you needing to leave town. I think we're going to keep you."

I let my shoulders settle.

Footsteps sounded in the neighboring room; Kelley and Renee pulled apart. Seconds later the reporter wandered in. I retreated to one of the corner bookshelves.

"Hey," Peter said to Kelley and Renee, clearly uninterested in preamble. "Are these the archives?"

Renee gave him a disdainful onceover, lingering on his navy-blue espadrilles. "Yeah, sure, have at 'em." She jerked her thumb toward a pyramid of sagging cardboard boxes in another corner of the room.

The look on Peter's face was reminiscent

of a nightgowned virgin in a vampire film.

"It's on microfiche, too," Kelley said apologetically, "but the reader's been broken since June."

Peter went over and, with two fingers, lifted a box flap. The cardboard was limp and green, with the texture of a cracker that had been left too long in chicken soup. "If you have any questions," Renee said, "you're probably better off asking Hermione Granger here."

Kelley raised her hand. "That's me," she said. "But I also go by Kelley."

Peter took a step toward her. "I'm Peter Strickland, and I'm writing a piece on Ardelle —"

"Oof, what'd you do to deserve that?" asked Renee. Kelley elbowed her in the ribs.

"— and I was wondering if I could ask you a few questions."

"Sure, I'd be happy to help," Kelley said. She settled herself on the room's plump green sofa and patted the cushion next to her, sending up a chalky puff of dust. Peter squinted at the sofa in distaste before settling down next to her.

Renee leaned against the wall next to Peter, not realizing, I didn't think, quite how protective her posture was. I kept my distance, stroking the spines of the books, pretending to be engrossed in my explorations. Giving myself a reason for being there.

"I was wondering what you could tell me about the Kantys," Peter was saying.

Dance, monkey, dance.

I took a deliberate step away — but not so far away that I couldn't hear Kelley's answer.

"Well," she said, "Albert Kanty was the first to stake a claim out here, of course, so they've been in Ardelle even longer than the Percys."

"But it was the Percys who founded Ardelle."

Kelley shrugged. "It wasn't a very good claim."

"That must have generated some resentment."

Renee laughed. "The Kantys hold grudges like you wouldn't believe. I don't think I ever even heard Eli say two words to Stanton until Cora came along."

Well, *that* sure sounded like my mother. She always kept a running log of everything I'd ever done wrong, a Santa Claus with a chip on his shoulder. Like the time I was five and made her miss a flight to Turks and Caicos because I'd decided my nanny was a ghost that only I could see. The time I was eight and ruined a dinner party because I was looking for a secret passage in the coat closet and sent a decrepit archduchess into a dead faint when she came in to find her mink. The time I let that photographer for *W* into our house. Everything I ever did was unforgivable — irrevocable. In the court of my mother, running a red light was the same as capital murder.

I moved to another shelf, pulling out a book here, a book there.

"What can you tell me about Tessa Kanty?" Peter asked.

"Not much," Kelley said. "I haven't seen Tessa since I was a kid."

"Were she and her brother close?"

"I really couldn't say."

Now why did I think she was lying?

"And what was her relationship with, uh" — he pulled out his notepad and checked it — "with Jared Vincent?"

I froze. *Who the fuck is Jared Vincent?*

"That's your angle?" Renee asked. " '85 Bonnie and Clyde? There's no story there."

Peter's lips thinned. "Jared Vincent stole thirteen thousand dollars that was never recovered around the same time that his eighteen-year-old girlfriend disappeared. Sounds like a story to me."

A hardcover fell to the floor.

. . . the summer of '85, when Eli's little sister

ran off with a bank robber.

How hadn't I made the connection?

Wait — my mother had only been eighteen?

Renee thumped her mug on the table, startling me out of my haze.

"If it's a story, it's short," she said. "Just one word, in fact: coincidence."

Kelley, good cop as ever, put her hand on Peter's arm. "Don't mind her," she said. "Tessa and Renee — they're family. It's a touchy subject. But she's right. There's nothing particularly scandalous about it. Tessa just had terrible taste in men."

"Not so terrible if it made her more than ten grand."

"No one thinks Tessa took that money," Kelley said. "If she had, she'd've given it straight to her brother — they lost their house in Adeline that same year. That money could've saved it."

"That's hardly —"

Renee shut him down. "It's not that people haven't tried to write about Ardelle. But once they get here they never end up finding anything worth writing about. We're not interesting; we're stubborn. Don't waste your time."

Oh, for Pete's sake. That whole bit was a *stump speech.* Renee's eyes met mine, and she shrugged apologetically.

213

"But if you really want to know more," Kelley said, soothingly, "why don't you come with us to Adeline? You can see the old Kanty house for yourself, get a feel for the family or whatever. It's more interesting than the archives, I promise."

He crossed his arms. "I'd rather stay here, if you don't mind. I'm not particularly interested in architecture."

"You might be surprised," Kelley said. "But sure, go ahead — make yourself at home. I just hope you brought some Claritin."

Peter wasted no time making his way over to the boxes, which he pulled down and arranged in a methodical line, shifting a few here and there after peeking inside each. He muttered something incomprehensible.

I whirled back around and stared blindly at the books in front of me. My mother had thought matching your shoes with your purse was morally questionable. And she'd been involved with a *bank robber*?

"If we don't hurry up, we're going to miss the shuttle."

I looked up. Kelley and Renee were standing by the door, waiting. For me, I realized.

"Nothing worth writing about?" I muttered.

Renee shrugged. "Like Kelley said —
we're family."

CHAPTER FOURTEEN

The drive to Adeline was rough going. The road hadn't been properly maintained for years and was potholed and buckled, the trees pushing their roots up through the pavement, eager to reclaim their land. The hired shuttle bus wasn't equipped for the terrain, and it jolted us unpredictably up into the air and then back down on the hard rubber seats. It didn't feel so different from that time I fucked a heavy-metal drummer. I certainly felt just as queasy.

I tried to focus on Cora, who was at the front of the bus giving us a history lesson.

"The first documented commercial gold mine in the United States was discovered in 1799 —"

Ugh. No.

"So," Renee said from behind me, her voice low enough that only Kelley and I could hear it, "I hear you've been making time with Leo."

"Not like you're making it sound," I said. "We just happened to leave the bar at the same time."

"And he 'just happened' to tell you his life story along the way?"

I put one hand to the cold glass of the window, then pressed it against my cheek. "It was small talk, nothing more."

"We passed Leo's on our way home, you know," Renee said. "We saw you leaving."

"I even waved," Kelley added. "Guess you didn't see me."

I closed my eyes. "No," I said. "I definitely didn't see you."

Renee patted me on the shoulder. "It's okay. I get it. He's got a real sexy-ugly thing going on."

"Say it runs in the family and I'll punch you," Kelley said.

Renee stretched an arm around me over to Kelley, tapping her shoulder twice with her fingertips before settling them on the seat back. Even in plaid flannel her arms were lissome and lovely.

The bus was climbing through the pass, and the trees were edging closer. My ears tried to pop but couldn't; a bulge of air pressed hard against my left eardrum. Renee was saying something else, but I could hardly hear her, and so heedless of what my

217

mother would have called impropriety, like applying lipstick at the table or emailing thank-you notes, I pinched my nose and tried to equalize the pressure in my head. When my ears cleared everything was so loud I wondered if I'd needed to pop them ever since I'd arrived in Ardelle.

"I'm not interested in Leo," I said. "I'm just here for the history."

"So you've said," Renee murmured. "And yet you're not paying Cora much mind, are you?"

I turned to look at her, to determine whether the gleam I knew would be in her eyes was amusement or suspicion.

"I got momentarily distracted," I said. "But I'm not interested in him — not like that."

Renee sat back. "Well, I suppose I'm not one to talk."

I jostled along with the rattle and give of the shuttle's suspension. Cora was saying something about Custer.

"How long has it been since you lived in Adeline?" I asked Kelley.

"Not long enough," said Renee.

"We left in eighty-five," Kelley said, "when I was ten and Renee was twelve. That's how we met, actually — me and Leo and Renee. The not-entirely-white-trash from the

218

wrong side of the pass."

"Don't forget Walt —" Renee said.

"Like he would let us."

"And what about Eli?" I asked.

Kelley tilted her head to the side. "Yeah," she said after a moment. "Eli was there, too. We didn't see much of him — or Tessa. They were a few years older than the rest of us. After their dad passed they each had to work like six jobs — Renee, remember when she used to work at MacLean's?"

"Oh man, that was the best; she'd give us fleischkuekle with ketchup whenever that old bat was being a bitch."

"We got a lot of fleischkuekle," Kelley said.

"What about the kids from the *right* side of the pass?" I asked.

Renee stuck out her tongue. "That would be Mitch Percy's crowd. How he found Lacoste in rural South Dakota, I'll never know."

"That's Mitch Percy of *those* Percys," Kelley said. "Stanton's son."

Cora's voice intruded: "— to the southwest is the acreage purchased by Energy Innovation Corp during the uranium bubble of oh-seven, and to the northwest we have the Odakota Nature Preserve, which is a wonderful place to visit if any of you happen to enjoy hiking —"

I turned back to Kelley and Renee. "Stanton seemed nice enough," I said.

"He is, mostly," Renee said. "No clue how he spawned such a colossal fuckup asshole."

"Genes," I said, "are a son of a bitch."

I looked out the window again. I could see a clearing in the distance. We were almost there — to the place that had made my mother. I knotted my scarf and pulled it tight enough to hurt.

Adeline may once have been laid out in Ardelle's mirror image, but the resemblance now was less striking than sad, as if someone had taken Ardelle and given it a tanning bed and fifty cigarettes a day. I stepped out of the shuttle bus directly onto a lump of something fetid and brown.

"Guess the burros are back," Renee said. "Welcome to beautiful downtown Adeline!"

I scraped my boot off on the shuttle's front bumper before heading to join the others in front of a weathered greige house. The supports on the front porch had begun to give way, and the overhang sagged on either side, the architectural equivalent of a pair of aging tits. It was a house, I thought, that had given up on Adeline long before Adeline had given up on it.

"This," Cora was saying, "is the childhood

home of my dear husband, Eli, and you may recognize the similarities to our current home, which we passed as we were leaving Ardelle. It was built in the eighteen —"

"How long did they live here?" I asked Renee.

"Eli sold the house when he enlisted, back in eighty-five — the same time most of the rest of us left."

Eventful year.

"— we soon hope to return the buildings to their prior glory." Cora took a breath to puff out her chest in pride, and I seized the opportunity to raise my hand.

"Can we go inside?" I asked.

Cora looked back at the house and scratched the side of her head. "I wouldn't feel comfortable," she said. "I really don't think it's safe. But maybe you could come back when we're finished with the restoration! We plan on fixing up not only the old Kanty house, but also the old post office and city hall, which are just a half mile away — so if you'll come with me, we'll get this tour started!" She led the herd forward, the visitors following docilely behind, Rue trailing off to the side like a distracted toddler. I walked with the group for a hundred yards or so, just until we rounded a corner and I saw Kelley and Renee turn their attention to one another.

I doubled back to the Kanty house and examined the porch. What was Cora going on about? It might not look too good, but it certainly seemed sturdy enough. But I held on to a wood column for balance and prodded the boards of the porch with the toe of my boot, just in case.

See? Fine.

I stepped forward and pushed open the front door — which promptly fell off its hinges. I caught it just as it hit the floor, the crack of wood on wood echoing through the hall. I went still and silent and waited. For the sound of footsteps. For the sound of voices. But, thank god, no one came.

I replaced the door as best I could and peered around. Your standard foyer, with two large rooms on either side. I had stirred up dust with my graceless entry, and for a brief moment the sun refracted through motes so profuse the air glittered like a fairy glen. But then the dust settled, and the room took on the hue of the water at the bottom of a tub after you plunge up a muck of soap-scummed hair.

I smelled cigarettes and spilled beer; vermin scuttled in the distance.

To my left was what had once been a living room. Some of the furniture had been abandoned along with the house: There was a stained couch, a maple coffee table marked with a set of three long scratches, a set of TV trays stacked in a corner. The floor was scattered with footprints, some tiny (mice, I hoped) and some larger (skunk, I feared). At least one set was human.

I headed up a staircase that was carpeted in something that once had probably been a pale yellow but years of neglect had muddied to the color of desert camouflage. Beneath that was wood so rickety I felt as if I were walking on popsicle sticks. On the walls were whitish squares where family pictures must once have hung.

I mean, that's where family pictures are always hung in movies, right? I wouldn't know otherwise. My mother never hung family photos in public areas.

(Or private areas, for that matter.)

At the top of the stairs were four doors; I opened the nearest one. I could hardly see inside the room — I couldn't tell if there were heavy drapes, or maybe if there weren't any windows at all. I took a single step forward and was waiting for my eyes to adjust when I felt the stale air shift. Something ran at me. I threw myself to the side and it raced past me down the hall, where it was joined by a second, larger, creature. The things were mostly gray, with white faces and rat tails. One showed a sharp-toothed snarl. They were possums. And they rather reminded me of Ainsley.

I took a step back; they tracked me with oil-slick eyes.

After a tense moment (for me, anyway), they dodged left and scurried through an open door. I darted forward and slammed it shut behind them. I caught my breath and hoped that room didn't contain any clues, because I sure as fuck didn't want to go in.

I went back to that first, dark room and stepped inside. I felt along the wall until I found a spindly chair, which I swung in front of me in swooping arcs like it was a torch in a cave as I moved toward what I hoped was a window. It was. I threw open the musty velvet curtains, receiving a spray of dust in my face for my efforts. When my vision cleared I saw that I hadn't done much to brighten things up. The window was encrusted with dirt, and the light barely shone through it. I wiped the panes clean with the cuff of my coat, but most of the dirt was on the outside. I tried to lift the sash, but it wouldn't budge.

I examined the room insofar as I could. Unlike the rooms downstairs, this one still had all of its furniture. There was a bare mattress on a box spring, a particle-board bureau, a low bookshelf that held three dozen paperback classics with unbroken spines. A nightstand with a missing leg and an empty drawer. There weren't any posters or pictures or knickknacks or even indications that there had ever been posters or pictures or knickknacks. Instead there was a sense of deliberate absence that didn't fit with the rest of the house. This room hadn't been abandoned; it had never really been lived in to begin with.

I looked at the nightstand again. It was cheap furniture trying to look expensive, with wood stained so dark you couldn't see its imperfect grain and an alloy bail pull that was a clumsy copy of a Chippendale design. I pulled the drawer back open, examining the insides. I frowned. The proportions were wrong.

Wait, I'd seen this before — in every house I'd ever lived in.

I tapped one corner of the bottom of the drawer until the opposite corner popped up. Beneath the plywood was a manila envelope marked with a girlish roller-coaster scrawl: "Confidential!" I ran a finger across the letters before opening the envelope and upending it.

Something heavy slipped out and fell to

the mattress. I looked at it, then smiled.

Playgirl, April 1985. *Tom Selleck: A Bachelor in Paradise. Tim Hutton: Sex Symbol with a Conscience. Yuppies: Nude.*

That's when I knew absolutely and without question that this room had been my mother's.

MARION ELSINGER

Marion Jenkins Elsinger (1957–2003) was a Swiss American philanthropist. In 2003 she was murdered in Beverly Hills, California. Her daughter, Jane Jenkins, was initially convicted and is still suspected of having been responsible for her death.

Early Life [edit]

Marion Elsinger, born Marion Jenkins, lived in Switzerland from 1985 to 2001. She was married four times (most recently to Jakob Elsinger) and had a well-documented relationship with Swiss industrialist Emmerich von Mises, with whom she had her daughter, Jane. She lived in Los Angeles, California, from August 2001 until her death.

Philanthropy [edit]

A dedicated patron of the fine and decorative arts, Elsinger was an active supporter of several prominent museums throughout Europe, including the Österreichische Galerie Belvedere, the Fondation Beyeler, and the Kunstmuseum Basel and Museum für Gegenwartskunst.

She was also known for her charitable work, frequently raising money for the Midwest Food Bank, Hunger Relief International, Orphan Grain Train, and the Cleft Lip and Palate Association.

Death [edit]

On July 15, 2003, Elsinger was found dead in her home in Beverly Hills. Her daughter, Jane Jenkins, who was allegedly seeking control of Elsinger's fortune, was arrested and convicted of her murder.

In 2013, Jenkins was released. The case, however, remains closed.

CHAPTER FIFTEEN

I sat down on the bed and flipped through the magazine, looking less at the pictures than for traces of its owner — a dog-eared page, maybe, or the sweaty print of a titillated finger — but as far as I could tell the magazine was in mint condition. She had never even looked at it.

Which made perfect sense. The magazine was another of her red herrings. A salacious morsel meant to keep you from looking for more.

So where's the good stuff?

I stood and lifted the mattress off the box spring but found nothing, so I got down on my back and inched my way under the bed frame. On the far side of the bed I could just barely make out a flap that had been cut into the fabric lining the bottom of the box spring. I reached in and withdrew a bright pink diary with a heart-shaped lock.

Another red herring, no doubt. It was also

entirely too obvious. I picked open the lock with the aglet of a bootlace and turned to the first page.

Fucking fuck off, Eli.

Love,
Tessa

The rest of the pages were blank. It wasn't really a diary, after all — it was a warning to her brother. But to me it was another clear sign that there was something else left to find.

I reached in my mind for my catalog of all my mother's favorite hidey-holes. It took a moment to work my brain back there, and I squinted a little, as if slightly sharper vision might somehow sharpen my memory, too. *The books,* I remembered. She liked to hide things in books she thought no one around her would ever read, never realizing, of course, that I would read everything, because when had she ever credited me with anything other than disloyalty.

I examined the bookshelf. Thirty years ago my mother lived alone with her brother, so what would she have least expected *him* to read? *A Tale of Two Cities.* Too fun. *The Count of Monte Cristo.* Too swashbuckling. *Women in Love.* Too intriguing. *The Hunch-*

back of Notre Dame. Too smoking-hot gypsy. *Crime and Punishment.* Yahtzee.

I pulled it out and rifled through the pages. Nothing, nothing, a million pages of nothing. I was about to exchange it for another title when finally something caught my eye, a sentence scrawled in the same loopy hand: *This book sucks.*

I shoved the book back on the shelf. That little hypocrite. The last time I used "sucks" in her presence she had looked at me, taken a sip of her bourbon, and then said to my stepfather with a lazy wave of her hand, "Don't say I didn't warn you."

I checked the rest of the books. Nothing there, either.

I wiped the sweat off my neck. Fortunately there was still one last place left to look — my mother always did love her closets.

As soon as I stepped up to the door I knew I was in the right place. I could smell the sachets.

Sure enough, the closet wasn't empty: There were three bulky garment bags hanging from the closet rod. I unzipped one and pulled out a dress. Size 2, basic black, a high neck and low back. Donna Karan. I kept looking. A wrap dress, Calvin Klein pants, something off-the-shoulder. No way were these my mother's clothes. These were clothes bought by someone who thinks Nordstrom sells high fashion. Plus, they were too new. I leaned in, and beneath the lavender and rose I caught the clean-slate smell of fresh dry cleaning. I groped about until I found a claim tag — they had been taken to a dry cleaner in Rapid City, and recently.

Why was someone storing clothes in this nasty old room?

A noise outside caught my attention. I looked out the window and managed to make out the fuzzy shape of the tour group rounding a building at the other end of the block.

I stuffed the dresses back into the bag and jammed it on the far side of the closet. I moved my hands briskly over the closet walls and shelves, feeling for indentations, for soft spots, for the telltale sliver of a panel that hadn't quite been wedged fully into place. I tugged on the light cord without thinking, but of course the electricity had long since been shut off. When I let go, the chain at the top of the fixture tapped the pointless lightbulb once, twice, three times. The cord swung back and forth in front of my eyes. Back and forth.

I blinked. Maybe it wasn't a pointless lightbulb after all.

I hurried back into the bedroom and

retrieved the chair, climbing up on it so I could reach the light and unscrew the bulb. I slipped the fixture from its casing and shoved a hand up into the ceiling cavity, hoping to god there weren't any animals up in the joists. My fingers glanced across — something.

The porch boards creaked.

I tugged harder and felt the something give. I grabbed it, barely registering the blue-veined blur of a business envelope as I tossed it into my bag.

Downstairs, the front door opened.

I replaced the chair, squared the mattress on the box spring, and tiptoed out into the hall.

"Hello?" a voice called. "Is someone here?"

I looked left, then right, but the stairs were the only way out.

"I can hear you up there," the voice said. It was a woman — no, a girl. *Rue.*

I backed down the hall, out of sight of the top of the staircase.

"Whoever you are, you're not supposed to be in here," she said.

Rue was climbing the stairs. One, two, three, four — halfway up now. I held my breath and commanded my heart to settle down, because soon she'd be close enough to hear it. And there was nowhere for me to go.

Then, a scratch and a low growl from the other side of the door at my back. Just as I saw the pointed tip of a boot emerge from behind the corner, I pulled the door open, shielding myself behind it as the possums flew out and down the hall. There was a shriek and then a squeal, and one of the possums hit the wall with a thud just before I heard Rue thunder back down the stairs. The other possum checked in briefly with its compatriot, and the two of them ran after her together.

I sent up a prayer of thanks — and also a promise to give twenty thousand dollars to a possum sanctuary the moment I got myself out of this mess.

Once I caught my breath, I reached inside my purse, groping around until I felt the rough edges of the envelope I'd found in my mother's closet. I withdrew it, opened it — and felt my shoulders slump.

It was nothing special. Just cash. Five twenties.

Well, I guess it's better than four twenties.

I pulled out the bills and tucked them in my wallet — it was technically my money, after all — and I was just about to crumple up the envelope when I saw the business card inside. On it was an address:

2130 Metzger St., #5
Rapid City, SD
55701

I closed my eyes and leaned against the wall. Finally. A clue.

I crept downstairs, putting as much of my weight as possible on the banister to quiet my steps. I checked to make sure the tour group was still out of sight before stepping out onto the porch and blinking into the sunlight.

A hand came down on my shoulder, and I'm very sorry to say that I was a total damselly cliché about it: I screamed.

A low laugh sounded in my ear, and I caught Renee's Ivory soapy scent.

"You scared the crap out of me," I muttered.

"No kidding," she said. She looked past me into the house. "Place still full of possum?"

I brushed the dust from my pants with rough strokes. "How would you know?"

"We used to come here back in high school — it's why the place went to shit so fast. Nothing like drunk teenagers to fuck with a building's structural integrity."

"Some parts of the house aren't in bad shape," I said.

"I find that hard to believe —"

"Like Eli's sister's room, for instance."

Renee's lips rounded on one word before settling on another. "And which room was that?" she asked.

"Upstairs, first door on the left."

"How do you know it was hers?"

"Someone's been using it," I said, as if I hadn't heard her question. "And not just to party."

Renee's gaze flickered off into the distance, and whatever she saw deepened the lines on either side of her mouth. "They'll be coming back soon," she said. "If anyone asks, I took you to the brothel. Cora refuses to include it on her tour."

She led me around the side of the house and in between two low brick buildings. We caught up with the tour group just as Cora was wrapping up her presentation of a small steepled church. "This, naturally, was the very first building to be abandoned," Renee whispered as we rejoined the group.

"A fun fact about Ardelle," Cora was saying, "is that once St. Barb's closed, most Catholics began attending First Lutheran in Ardelle, because it was too difficult in winter to make it to the next closest church, which is — is it in Custer? Rue, honey, is that right?"

"Sure," Rue said.

"But no one goes there anymore," Cora said.

"Actually," Rue said, "Joey Macarelli's mom used to make him go Tuesdays and Sundays."

Renee grinned at me, then shouted out, "Tell them why she stopped, Rue!"

Rue snorted. " 'Cause Joey knocked up Colleen Obermeyer. And if church twice a week couldn't keep him from sleeping around, she figured she might as well save on gas."

Cora pinched the bridge of her nose. The stiff-faced mom and dad gave each other a smug *that'll-never-happen-to-us* look.

"What?" Rue said, hands on her hips. "You should be *happy* that I know. You can't keep from getting knocked up if you don't know what knocking-up is. Jesus." She stalked away, her magnificent hair tossing in her wake.

For a moment Cora looked genuinely thrown, but then she firmed up her enthusiasm and clapped her hands. "Well, enough of that!" she said, "We'll all be seeing the other church tonight — that's First Lutheran — as they'll be hosting our potluck dinner! But now it's time for our picnic lunch over at the campground. I hope you'll join us all there — it's a wonderful opportunity to meet the town's residents, and I hear that Suzy MacLean will be bringing her famous *fleischkuekle* — that's a meat pie, for those of you who haven't had the pleasure."

"Try it with ketchup!" Kelley said.

CHAPTER SIXTEEN

"Didn't everyone just eat a huge breakfast?" I whispered to Kelley.

Kelley swallowed a bite of fleischkuekle. "Five years ago, at the first Gold Rush Days, only a quarter of the town showed up to only a quarter of the events. Then Cora started bringing in pies from some fancy place in Rapid City. It kind of grew from there." We were standing on the edge of the Adeline campground picnic area, holding paper plates that were limp with fry oil, shivering along with most of the rest of the town — with the notable exceptions of Renee and Stanton, who were playing horseshoes and were already flushed with competitive spirit. From the sharp-tongued profanities that cut through the general din of mastication, I gathered Renee was losing.

I couldn't find Eli anywhere. I bit into my own fleischkuekle, hoping a bit of food would settle my stomach. All this stress eating would make me Middle American–sized in no time.

Cora came over, mouth pinched with disapproval. "Rebecca, I didn't see you on the tour — I hope you weren't —"

"I was with Renee," I said.

Kelley shot me a look, but Cora didn't notice. "She took you to the brothel, didn't she?" she said on a sigh. "Well, I guess that's better than Eli's old house. At least its roof isn't about to fall in."

"I'm sorry," I said. "Was it off limits too?"

"Oh, don't worry about it. I just hate for people to get the wrong idea. It wasn't really such a rough-and-tumble place, you know — the Percys made sure of that." Cora looked at her watch. "Oh crumbs, I've got to get going. Eli's already setting up over at the church, and if I'm not there to oversee things, we'll all end up sitting on the floor. I'll see you there?"

Unfortunately.

"Absolutely!"

Kelley and I wandered over to watch the horseshoe match. Renee was getting absolutely destroyed.

I waited a minute before speaking up. It's never good to seem too eager.

"What did Cora mean?" I asked. "About the Percys 'making sure of that'?"

"Well, this was a company town, you know? And Tesmond wanted it to be a reflection of his own character — all moral and upright and whatever. So he tried to boot out the prostitutes by zoning against residences that housed single women." She smiled. "The prostitutes figured out a way around that pretty quickly, though."

"What did they do?"

"They married the employees. The men were more than happy to oblige, as I understand."

I took another bite of my pie. Stanton had just thrown a horseshoe within an inch of the stake. Renee threw hers to the ground in frustration. "How long is this match going to take?" I asked.

Kelley waved a hand. "They'll play for hours. Renee never likes to end on a loss — but she also never wins. She won't stop until she can't see the stakes. Stanton's the same way. This is sort of a perfect storm."

"What time is the potluck again?"

"Starts at five."

A clang and a cheer from the crowd. Renee had finally scored a point. I applauded distractedly as I contemplated my next move.

I knew without a doubt that Tessa Kanty and Marion Elsinger were the same woman.

The photographic resemblance was one thing — the behavioral resemblance, though, was even more striking. Mom and her secrets. "A lady never lets on," that's what she always said.

And now, I had an address. But I hadn't exactly learned anything that might lead me to the identity of the man I'd heard in her room that night — other than the fact that she seemed to treat her brother like . . . her brother. All siblings tried to read each other's diaries, right?

"Hey, Kelley?" I asked.

She looked away from the game. "Yeah?"

"What does Eli do?"

"Oh, he's retired."

"Already?"

"He used to be in the air force, but — once he married Cora . . ."

She didn't need to finish the sentence.

"I mean, don't get me wrong," she said, "he still has plenty to do around here. I think he was talking about getting a geology degree or something — he's always been a little bit crazy about that stuff. When he was a kid he'd do things like save up his allowance so he could buy a metal detector. He used to spend hours out on the mountain."

"That sounds like — fun."

"Not if you never find anything."

I thought back to my years in the prison library. "I know the feeling."

But I don't intend on feeling it again.

I finished off my pie and licked my fingers. "When is the shuttle heading back to Ardelle?"

"Three-thirty," she said. "Why?"

"I just wanted to make sure I had time to change before dinner."

And also to break into my second Kanty house in a single day.

God, déjà vu sure is a shitty feeling.

I looked up at the Kanty house in Ardelle and shuddered. It really was identical to the house in Adeline, in every way but its upkeep. In the light of day it was as pretty as ever — even the scarecrow on the porch somehow seemed welcoming — but I didn't trust any of it, not anymore. The Kantys were related to me, which meant lying was in their blood.

I scanned the front of the house for a way in. The doors looked solid, and the windows were closed against the cold. Maybe I could climb up to the second-floor balcony — that door looked jimmy-able. But then, *no, wait,* a better idea: I remembered what Kelley had said about the spare key Cora kept at the inn. I checked to make sure the road was clear, then I crept through the garden, pushing aside branches and needles until I found a bronze statue of an angel hidden under a hedge. I lifted it up and retrieved the key from under it.

If foolish consistency was the hobgoblin of little minds — well, thank god for hobgoblins.

I let myself in and moved briskly through the foyer, ignoring the vintage radiator grate and the salvaged wallpaper and the stained-glass doors. The family rooms, I knew, would be on the second floor. At the top of the stairs, I stopped. The door to my left — *Tessa's room,* I thought — was cracked open. I peeked inside, losing interest as soon as I saw the purple bedspread and a well-loved stuffed dog. Rue's room. Whatever.

The next room was a guest room: Venetian blue walls, a sturdy mahogany bedroom set — was that a George Bullock side table? Nice. I searched the room quickly, checking under the bed and in the dresser drawers, but all I found were fresh sheets and towels and an unopened two-pack of extra-soft toothbrushes. Apart from a terry-cloth robe in a protective plastic bag, the closet was empty. Cora really did take hospitality seriously.

Then there was the master bedroom. It

was comparatively modern, with bare floors and simple furniture. Cora's nightstand — at least, I assumed it was Cora's — held a small pot of flowers and a book about some world's fair. Eli's was empty. Apart from the neatly creased bedclothes and perfectly polished dress shoes peeking out from under the dust ruffle, there was no other sign of his presence in the room.

The last room, though — the last room was his study. I stepped inside. The walls to either side were lined with bookshelves; in front of me was a metal drafting table covered in large, thick sheets of paper that curled up at the corners. I swung the task lamp so I could examine them.

It took me a moment to figure out what I was looking at — it had been a long time since I'd seen a topographical map outside of a geology book. I flipped through them and found a survey that dated back to 1885. Everyone's land was outlined: the Percys, the Kantys, the La Plantes, the Fullers, the Freemans. The Kantys and Percys had ten times as much land as the other three families combined. I traced the property lines of the Kanty claim, then turned to the next map: 1897. Their claim was smaller now. 1908: smaller again. The most recent map was from 1992, and it showed the now *very* small Kanty claim divided into two sections: one marked E, the other marked T.

My mother had still owned this land in 1992? It can't have been worth anything, then. She never met a nonportable asset she could wait to unload.

I sat down in the desk chair and spun in a circle. When I came to a stop I was facing one of the bookshelves. I squinted at the titles: *The Modern Prospector's Handbook. Gold Diggers Atlas. Gold Mining in the 1980s.*

Kelley hadn't been exaggerating, then. Eli definitely still had the bug.

I spun again. This time my gaze landed on the other bookshelf. Military thrillers, historical nonfiction, and biographies on the top shelves. And on the bottom shelves, a set of thick, black-leather photo albums. I pulled the first one out — a note fell to the floor.

Eli —
I know you said you didn't want these, but trust me, one day you'll be glad to have them.

All my love,
Cora

Seemed like Eli had cared for photos as much as my mother did.

246

I opened the book: Rue's baby pictures. *Who cares?* Cora and Eli's wedding. *Double who cares?* Eli and the man who must be his father — my grandfather. I stopped. I could see a hint of Eli in the man's strong jaw, a hint of my mother in his firm mouth. But there was nothing of me.

Speaking of my mother, though, where was she?

I turned the pages faster and faster, the pictures flying by, and nowhere — not in one single picture — did I see any sign of Tessa.

Had Eli insisted on banishing all evidence of my mother's existence?

The thought was uncomfortable, even though it was something I'd wished dozens of times before. So why did it feel so wrong now? Was I the only one allowed to hate my mother?

I decided not to think too long about that.

I removed any traces of my intrusion and left, pulling the door closed behind me. I walked to the other end of the hall, pausing when I caught a glimpse of something through Rue's open door. I looked in. Like any good teenager, Rue had taped posters to her walls — there were singers, actors, bands I'd never heard of. A few of her posters, though, she'd had framed. These were landscapes. And I recognized them all.

Montreux. Appenzell. Zernez. Lucerne.

Her walls were covered with pictures of Switzerland.

Now, what were the chances that this was just what the kids were into these days?

JANIE JENKINS

STRANGERS ON A TRAIN

Last we knew, Jane Jenkins, 26, was staying in an unremarkable hotel in Sacramento, CA. Most outlets speculate that
she flew from Sacramento to another
domestic location . . . either on a private
jet or under an assumed name. But TMZ
believes that Jenkins left not by air, but by
train.

We have received an anonymous tip from
a Chicago woman who claims her father
saw Jenkins with his own two eyes. He is
reluctant to come forward, his daughter
says, due to the fact that Jenkins threatened him if he went public with his information . . . which is as clear a sign as any
that the woman he met was indeed Jane
Jenkins. Her father, our source says, was
on the Amtrak California Zephyr, which
runs from Sacramento to Chicago.

We know that Noah Washington . . .
Jenkins's *extremely* devoted counsel . . .

249

has flown frequently to Chicago in the past several months, purportedly to take depositions on a class-action lawsuit he is involved with there. Does this mean that Jenkins, too, is heading for the Upper Midwest? Only time will tell.

CHAPTER SEVENTEEN

I didn't have time to think too hard about what I had found in the Kanty house, not if I didn't want to be caught poking around where I most definitely shouldn't be. So I crept out the door, snuck the key under the bronze angel, and ran back to my room to change before heading to the potluck. As I stepped back outside, my phone vibrated. I pulled up the alerts. *Motherfucker:* TMZ had found the porter.

And, worse, Trace smelled blood.

We CANNOT ignore the fact that we have no confirmation that Jenkins took the train all the way to Chicago. We have no reason to think she would even go to Chicago. The fact that her scumbag lawyer was seen in that area should make it clear that she's NOT heading in that direction. When she was last seen the train had just crossed the Colorado-Nebraska state line, and it would be foolish to discount the possibility that Jenkins detrained at one of the stops between Denver and Chicago. If we hope to find Jenkins it is ESSENTIAL that we focus on these thirteen stops. She will have had to rent a car, buy a car, call a taxi, or catch a bus. This is where we should be looking, readers.

And for those of you who say I should let it go, that I should let her live in peace, I ask you AGAIN: if Janie Jenkins were really innocent, why would she be hiding? Face facts, people. I have a 180 IQ, and even I can't see how anyone else could have done it.

A wave of dizziness washed over me. Maybe Trace had a point. So what if my mother had said she was from New York but was really from South Dakota? So what if she'd dated a bank robber? I still didn't have any sign that someone in Ardelle might have wanted her dead — unless "she was mean to me in her diary" could be considered a strong motive.

But there had to be *something,* right? There had to be some reason why my mother had never told me anything about this place.

When I stepped down into the basement of First Lutheran I was blanketed by the rashy heat of too many bodies. I stripped off my coat, hat, and gloves and tossed them on a messy pile of outerwear that appeared to have been shed in a similar frenzy.

The room reeked of rubber soles and Right Guard; the floor was covered with that gray-flecked yellow linoleum that always looks like it's been splattered with gravy no one bothered to clean up — which come to think of it is actually probably the point. At one end of the room was a stage with a single amplifier and a drum kit I eyed with trepidation. The stage was skirted in orange fabric; a few balloons floated half-heartedly on either side.

Fold-out tables were lined up in two uneven columns, each set with harvest-gold place mats and decorative cornucopias. A few people were already eating, but most were still crowding the buffet, a crush of mismatched Tupperware and tinfoil serving pans that had been set up at the opposite side of the room.

I searched the crowd for familiar faces as I walked in, trailing my fingers along the wall.

"Raffle ticket?"

I turned. Stanton was sitting at a table I

hadn't noticed even though it was directly in front of me, his left hand on the handle of an old-fashioned bingo-ball spinner. His hair was parted neatly on the side — his scalp showed a rosy flush from the heat, a becoming shade that most women would pay a small fortune to replicate on their cheeks — and his smile was wide. At his feet a cooler was stocked with off-brand soda and Capri Sun.

I pulled out my wallet. "How much are the tickets?"

"Don't you want to know what the prize is?" he asked. "Apart from the tax deduction, that is."

"I'm sure it's for a good cause."

He spun the bingo basket with a flourish. "That it is, Miss Parker. And in that spirit, the tickets are twenty dollars apiece."

"Seriously?"

He looked to either side, then leaned forward with a conspiratorial heft of his eyebrows. He put a hand to one side of his mouth. "If you promise not to tell anybody, I'll give you one for ten."

I handed him a bill. "I guess I'll take two, then."

He tore three tickets off the sheet. "Here," he said. "My treat. Can't have a guest in our town feel anything less than welcome."

I scribbled "Rebecca Parker" on the tickets — giving myself a mental thumbs-up for remembering my own name — and slid them across the table.

Next I went over to the buffet, loaded up a plate with something gray, and fought through the mess of chairs until I came to Peter. He was sitting at a table by himself, alternately looking through a heavy white binder and scribbling in his notebook.

I wondered what he'd found for me while I was gone.

He didn't say anything when I set my plate and drink down. Guess it was my turn to break the ice.

"Have you tried the meatloaf?" I asked.

"I'm vegetarian," he said.

"You know how you can tell if someone's a vegetarian?"

"How?"

I took a beat. "They'll tell you."

He didn't laugh.

I pushed the meat back and forth on my plate, fashioning two small hills on either side of a narrow valley.

"So," I said, "did you find anything good in the archives? I bet you're already halfway to some scoop by now."

He looked up finally, then slid the binder over to me, rapping a laminated article with his knuckle. "Here," he said. "That bank robbery everyone seems not to want to talk about? It was never solved. The money was never recovered."

"Fascinating," I said. Next to the article was a mug shot of a man whose dark curly hair fell to his shoulders. "Is that the robber?" I asked, lacing my words with a maidenly tremble.

"Yeah, his name's Jared Vincent. He was arrested three days after the robbery."

"So doesn't that mean the case is closed?" I asked.

"To the police, it is. But I think he had an accomplice. If he'd had the money, he'd have turned it in. Gotten a reduced sentence."

"You think she ratted him out?"

"The way I see it, they were in on it together. She betrayed him and made a break for it; he paid the price."

That sounded as strong a motive for murder as I'd ever heard. I ran my finger down the margin of the text, trying to skim the words but having a hard time focusing on the letters.

"Is he still in jail?" I asked — meaning, of course, was he still in jail on July 14, 2003.

"I don't know. I'm still trying to get someone at the police department to talk to me — I can't find anything online. This place is Google poison."

I felt something on the back of my neck, not so much a prickle as an abrasion. I looked over my shoulder and saw Leo staring at me from across the room. My lip curled.

Jane, focus.

I shook myself and turned back to Peter. "Was this guy Jared from Ardelle, too?" I asked. "Is that why no one will talk about it?"

"I can't tell. I mean, yes, he was from Ardelle, but I don't think that's what's going on. I can't imagine they'd have any reason to protect him — sounds like a lot of people here used that bank. He might as well have been stealing straight from their pockets."

"Is the bank here in town?"

"No," he said. "It's, um . . . hold on." He pulled the binder back and spun it around to read it. He flipped to the next page, scanned it, then flipped to the page after that. "Says here it's over in Custer. The Jenkins Savings and Loan."

"Oh," I said when my tongue finally unstuck itself from the roof of my mouth. "That's a nice name."

I stabbed at my meatloaf some more. It

hadn't even occurred to me that I should worry about Peter finding out that Tessa was also Marion Elsinger née Jenkins — my mother was better than that. She would have covered her tracks.

But I hadn't expected that she might have tried to get cute.

"What about Tessa?" I asked. "Have you had any luck finding her?"

"Not even the slightest. There's no trace of her — anywhere. And no way someone who's innocent goes to that kind of trouble." Thankfully, at that moment we were interrupted by a cacophony of teenagers. Rue — and a coterie of beefy boys and mediocre beauties. Your typical adolescent cohort. One of the boys snuck a hit from a silver flask and then elbowed his buddies triumphantly, just in case he hadn't already been obvious enough. I was vaguely disappointed in Rue. I'd hoped she had vision.

A girl in stiletto-heeled Mary Janes that were probably from Payless poked Peter in the arm. "Yeah," she said, "so we're going to sit here, okay?"

The girl stood expectantly next to Peter's chair. When he didn't move, she sat down next to him with a huff. He gave her a stern, grown-up kind of look that didn't quite hide the fact that he was looking down her shirt.

Apparently even Peter could be distracted from his ambition.

The other kids scavenged chairs and squeezed in around the table; one of the boys elbowed me in the boob until I made room for Rue. It was only when she forced her chair in front of mine that I really got a good look at her.

At what she was wearing, rather.

"That's a fancy dress for a potluck," I said.

She showed absolutely no indication of having heard me.

"Donna Karan?"

The smile she turned on me had all the amiability of sulfuric acid flying at my face. "I'm surprised you recognized the brand."

"I think I've seen this dress before. Maybe on the cover of a magazine?"

Or in the bedroom of an abandoned house.

I was about to say more, but we were beginning to attract attention — the blonde was giving me a full-on *what-the-fuck* kind of look. I turned away, slouching my shoulders and breathing through my mouth. In other circumstances I might have found my situation amusing. Me, Jane Jenkins, huddling on the outskirts of a group of adolescents even more tragically delusional than the ones I'd once known. *Kids.* They still thought they knew something the rest of us didn't, the way every generation thinks they're the ones who invented sex, the way every generation thinks they're the ones who will be remembered. They still had *I'm-better-than-this* dreams, *one-day-we'll-leave-this-all-behind* aspirations. What they didn't understand is that it doesn't matter who you are or where you're from. No one ever leaves it all behind. The best you can hope for is to start off in the least horrible place. The rest of us just have to make do.

I curled myself around the growing ache in my stomach, a mousy pill bug who'd been poked.

This is how Leo found me, ten minutes later — not, of course, that he was looking at me. He was looking at the same thing Peter and everybody else was: Rue.

Typical.

"Hey, Rue," he said. "What's that you've got there?"

Rue glanced down at the silver flask that had made its way around the circle to her. Then she put it behind her back and angled her body so her pretty knees pointed at Leo.

"Leo, baby," she said.

Leo stepped back and looked up at the ceiling. "Rue — *actual* baby."

"Don't be like that," she said — and I'll give her this, she pouted magnificently.

Everything else, though, was strictly bad regional theater.

Leo sighed. "Here's what we're going to do," he said. "You're going to give me that flask, and then — because never let it be said I'm not a gentleman — I'm going to go fetch you something else to drink. And when I come back, we can forget that this ever happened. So, what do you say? Would you like a Coke — or a Diet Coke?"

Rue curled a lock of hair around one finger. "How about a bourbon. Neat."

"Don't push me, Rue."

Rue chewed a cocktail stirrer in the ostentatiously lascivious way of a girl who's just discovered blow jobs. I wanted to grab her by the shoulders and yell at her, "Play coy, already!"

"Come on," Rue said. "What my dad doesn't know won't hurt him."

Leo plucked the stirrer from her mouth and tossed it on the table. "I don't think you know your father like I do." He held out his hand. "Give it here."

"Whatever." She slapped the flask into his hand and turned back to her friends.

"Always a pleasure, Rue," he said, slipping the flask into his pocket. As his gaze slid my way, something in his expression changed, like a snake when it sheds its skin.

"What?" I said under my breath. "*I'm* legal."

"Funny you should say that," he said. He grabbed my arm and hauled me to my feet. "Walk with me."

Before I could protest, he'd pulled me halfway across the room, past Kelley's wide, searching eyes. I smiled at her as breezily as I could, as if it was a totally ordinary everyday thing to be manhandled by an officer of the law — which, of course, for me it was. Leo hustled me through a door marked *Private* and closed it firmly behind us.

"You could've just asked nicely," I said, rubbing my shoulder.

"Would that have worked?"

I turned away.

The room was cramped and windowless, lined with wood paneling that had been painted off-white in an unsuccessful attempt to brighten the place up. Most of the space was taken up by a metal desk with a laminate top. The light was the yellow-green of piss in pea soup, and it flickered irregularly. A moth was trapped between the fixture's glass globe and its bulb.

I perched on the desk and left the chair for Leo. Higher ground and all.

He twisted open the flask he'd taken from Rue and held it up. "Want some?"

"What is it?"

He took a drink and grimaced. "Strong."

"I think I'm okay."

He screwed the cap back on and set it on the desk next to me. "In case you change your mind," he said. "So what were you and Rue talking about?"

"The usual. Boys. Bras. Menstruation."

My left leg started swinging of its own accord, something I used to do to draw attention to my ankles back when I wore pencil skirts and skyscraper heels. And Leo's attention was drawn, all right. But his mouth didn't look restless with interest; it looked sour, as if he'd just sucked on a lemon — and intent, as if he knew he still had thirty lemons left to go.

I suppose there probably wasn't anything nice about my rickety old ankles anymore anyway. Not that you could really even tell under the thick cuffs of polyester. My slacks didn't have legs so much as logs.

But still, my foot banged against the desk — *thump thump thump* — until Leo's hand shot out and grabbed my leg just below my knee. I tried to pretend I was an amputee, that the feeling of his hand on my shin was just a phantom pain, not something that was actually happening. Because if it *was* actually happening, it was the first time my leg

had been touched in a long, long time —
even if his touch was as intimate as that of a
Bulgarian aesthetician applying a last layer
of wax to a client's asshole.

"I want my picture back," he said.

"What picture?"

"Don't turn dumb on me now." He adjusted his hand and something pinged all
the way down to my heel. I tried to pull
away, but he held me tight.

"Fine," I said. "I'll drop it off tomorrow."

"Good."

"Glad we've cleared that up."

"Me too."

I glanced at the door, taking some comfort
in the fact that Leo hadn't locked it, even
though I was sure he'd considered it. Thank
God Kelley had seen us on our way in. If I
died in here, at least someone would find
my body.

"So is that it? Am I free to leave?"

His fingers clenched and he drew in a
portentous breath I knew didn't bode well.
"No," he said. "You can't go until you
explain how, exactly, you came into possession of a stolen truck — with stolen plates."

I stifled a groan of dismay. Now I was going to have to find another car. And hide
the old one.

"I should also mention that knowingly

transporting stolen goods across state lines is a federal crime."

I rolled my eyes. "Only if said goods are worth more than five grand, which we both know isn't even remotely the case. But nice try."

"Luckily, I'm pretty sure grand theft auto is still in play."

I watched him closely, wondering whether whatever he'd been up to with the sunken-eyed pothead was worse than grand theft auto. The fact that he hadn't already taken me in gave me hope.

"So arrest me, then," I said.

His eyebrows went up. "That's all you have to say?"

I relaxed. He was just fishing. I was safe for now.

"No, there is one more thing," I said. "Get your fucking hand off my leg."

He did, but he didn't retreat, he didn't fall back in his chair and cross his arms in frustration like I'd hoped. Instead he stood up and put his hand flat on the desk, the tip of his thumb brushing my hip. I recognized it as an intimidation tactic — and goddammit, it was working. Anxiety was scraping the pulp from my skin.

"I'm going to ask one more time: Why are you here?"

"For the history."

"Lies." His breath smelled, not unpleasantly, of stale mouthwash and Marlboro Reds.

"Why do you care, anyway?"

"I have a rule: Never trust a pretty girl."

"Good thing I'm not pretty."

"More lies."

He leaned toward me, and I hate to say that I leaned forward, too. But then, just when I was sure his lips were about to do something to mine — and just when I was almost sure I was about to let them — his free hand came around the back of my head, seizing the hair at the base of my neck. He tilted my skull to the side, and he wasn't gentle about it. My whole head felt hot and foggy, like when your missed medication finally catches up with you.

I wrenched myself from his grasp and turned my face to his. His expression was so smooth, so even, so clear, not like ice or glass or still standing water but more like the night sky when you can't see any stars, when you find yourself swamped with desperately unproductive thoughts like *What comes after infinity?* I had no idea what I was supposed to say.

He put his mouth next to my ear. "Whatever you're doing, it's only a matter of time

266

before I figure it out." Then he gave me one last look and left the room. I stayed on the desk for some minutes after, trying to figure out if I was glad he was gone.

CHAPTER EIGHTEEN

I slipped out of the church and walked down the street to the Coyote Hole. It was time to deal with Kayla's truck. I'd seen an old barn in Adeline where I thought I could hide the thing, but I couldn't go driving there while so many people were heading home from the potluck. I didn't want to wait in my room, either: I'd spend six hours compulsively checking the locks and the light switches and the windows and the power sockets and the closet and the shower and the ever-malignant void beneath my bed until, with luck, my body finally gave out on me. And that was the best-case scenario.

The Coyote Hole was my only remaining option.

I ordered a soda water and found an empty stool between a roly-poly man in a blue plaid shirt and a woman in low-rise jeans whose meaty ass crack was visible to the entire bar. I took great pleasure in sitting there — my body felt so light as I sat between them, like I'd just landed on Venus and was enjoying the weaker gravity.

A drunken giggle as sweet as a fart in a wet swimsuit sounded in my right ear. I looked over to see the woman next to me making eyes at some guy at the other end of the bar.

"Well, if it isn't Mitchell Percy," she said.

I twisted around to look at Stanton's son. He had none of his father's old-fashioned elegance: Mitch's good looks were thoroughly nouveau riche, from his oversized dive watch to his Just for Men hair. He wore the khaki pants and polo shirt of the kind of man who'd carry your groceries out to your car before sexually assaulting you. Every time he shook someone's hand, a part of him probably mourned the fist bump that might have been.

The woman next to me straightened, hauling up another inch of marbled fat from beneath her waistband. "So what's a nice guy like you doing in a place like this?" she said. She clearly thought her tone was flirtatious, but she sounded like a little girl talking to her woobie.

Mitch smiled, his bleached teeth blue in the low light of the bar. "There's nothing

269

nice about me, sugar."

"We missed you at the potluck tonight."

"And I sure missed being there."

I reconsidered the woman. She wasn't *that* bad, I decided. Her shirt was so low cut I could see the stretch marks on the tops of her breasts, but unlike me, at least she *had* breasts. And she wasn't really fat. She was just thin enough to let you know she gave a shit, like she probably shaved her bush every once in a while, but she wasn't so thin that she could be exacting about things like coming during sex. She was a lazy man's woman. A rainy day in the dark kind of woman.

I sipped my soda water and pretended to watch the game. The one on TV, I mean.

"I made my famous peach pie," the woman was saying. "But lucky you, I've got another one waiting at home. I could heat it up in no time."

"Sorry, sweetheart," said Mitch, and another person might have believed he meant it. "The wife's on me to watch my weight."

She lifted her glass to him. "Well, if you ever change your mind, you let me know."

"You know I will."

The woman puffed out a little breath of hoppy air before squaring her shoulders and calling over another drink order to Tanner. Only I saw the disgust that bloomed through Mitch's face as soon as she turned away. It dimpled up in the soft cartilage on the end of his chin, unfurled around his mouth, tugged at his gaping nostrils. He threw a few bills on the bar and left.

The woman caught my eye out of the corner of hers and gave me a rueful smile that glimmered with far more intelligence than I would have expected. "Girl's gotta put herself out there, you know?" She held out a surprisingly delicate hand. "I'm Crystal," she said.

"Rebecca," I said.

"Here for Gold Digger Days — ? Oh, why even ask. Of course you are."

I nodded. "Nice to meet you, too."

Tanner delivered her drink, which she attacked with gusto. I took the opportunity to get a closer look at the skin on her neck, a reasonably reliable way to gauge a person's age in a world with low-cost plastic surgery. I figured she was in her early forties, give or take — how old my mother actually would have been if she were still alive.

(I still couldn't believe that my mother had pretended to be ten years *older* than she really was. That was dedication.)

I turned back to Crystal. "So what's with

you and that guy?" I asked, jerking my head toward the end of the bar.

"You mean Mitch?"

I nodded.

"Oh, nothing much. We went to high school together. I guess I've had a thing for him ever since."

"I can see why." And I guess that was true. The singles scene in Ardelle was probably pretty grim.

"I mean, he's still cute," Crystal said, "but back then, oh man. He was all freckles and muscles and hair. Like he belonged on a poster. There was a time when I thought that maybe — but, well, I guess I was with Darren already anyway, and then before I could ever do anything about it, I was having his baby." She took a long drink. "Timing never was my thing."

But there was something in the slump of Crystal's shoulders that told a different story. After almost thirty years with nothing to show for it, most people would've given up. She was genuinely disappointed, though, which made me think that once upon a time she'd been genuinely encouraged. I bet that one night she got down with Mitch Percy, and then afterward he never acknowledged it had happened. That was just the way of things with girls like her and guys like him.

And even if she wanted to shout to the world that, no, she was a different kind of girl, in fact she was the *exact opposite* kind of girl, because she was the one he'd once really wanted, what could she do? The only other party to what happened didn't care for the truth. She lived in flickering gaslight everyone around her claimed was constant.

"Well, it's his loss," I said after a moment.

Crystal turned to me, surprised. "Thanks. So . . . do you have any great teenage loves who got away?"

Like I'd love a teenager. Blech.

"Oh no," I said. "I never even went to prom."

She put her hand on my arm. "Maybe that was for the best," she said. "I went to prom with Darren, and look how that turned out."

I waved at Tanner, gesturing for another soda water, wishing desperately I was asking for something else. He caught my eye and then, very deliberately, looked the other way. Dick.

"But seriously — would it really have been *so* unlikely?" Crystal, sensing a sympathetic audience, was warming to her anger. "It's not like I had nothing going for me. Sure, he could've done better, but he *definitely* did worse, believe me. Every piece of trash in town went down on her knees just to get

273

closer to his wallet."

Her voice was rising, and people were starting to look over. I shifted uncomfortably and tucked my chin to my chest. "So you weren't after his money?"

"Hell, no, I was after his body." She burst out laughing then, shaking her head and absently rubbing the side of her face, as if her resentment was just a muscle twitch she could soothe away. "I'm sorry. It's been a long night. No — scratch that. It's been a long thirty years."

"Tell me about it."

"It's just such bullshit. I was a nice girl — I mean, too nice at times, obviously — so why didn't I get my chance? Instead I had to watch him with girls like fucking Tessa Kanty. That girl was rotten to her core, a thief and a liar and god only knows what else, and no way she wanted anything but what he could buy her — but she was beautiful, so why should he care about all that other stuff?" Crystal lifted her glass and held it unsteadily in the air. "To Tessa Kanty, the biggest bitch in the Black Hills."

At that moment I was half tempted to do something I'd never done before: give a near stranger a spontaneous hug. Finally, someone who actually got it.

"I think you've had enough." I looked up

and saw Tanner glowering over us. How long had he been standing there?

He reached out and started to pull Crystal's drink away, but she jerked it back. "Shut up, Tanner. You didn't even know her."

"Don't have to. I know Eli. He wouldn't want you talking about his sister."

"Yeah, well, he didn't know her, either. Tessa was a money-grubbing whore, nothing more, nothing less." Her eyelashes were working wildly to hold back her tears.

Tanner relinquished her glass with a sigh. "Okay, Crystal, fine. Finish up. Just keep it down, would you?"

"Thanks, *Dad*." She turned her head to swipe a hand over her eyes. I snuck her a cocktail napkin, which she dabbed at her nose. "Bet this wasn't listed on Cora's schedule," she said. " 'Come one, come all, see Crystal make an ass of herself!' " She sniffled. "God, I'm so embarrassed."

"Don't be."

"You're nice."

I swallowed back the instinctive denial.

She sipped at her drink, and in the silence, inevitably, we both found ourselves watching the game. Like everyone else in town, we were just looking for something to do that didn't involve thinking.

Too bad not thinking wasn't an option.

"Crystal," I said. "Can I ask you a question?"

"Sure."

I found another cocktail napkin and folded it into squares. "What happened to that girl you were talking about? To Tessa?"

"She ran away." Crystal looked down into her beer. "No one was sad to see her go."

I looked down into my own empty glass. It was better than telling Crystal I hadn't been sad to see her go, either.

"Do you know why she left?" I asked. "Was it Eli —"

"Oh, no, she left for the same reason girls like that always run away: 'Cause she got knocked the fuck up."

As soon as the streets seemed empty enough, I headed back to the parking lot next to the inn. I climbed into the truck and started the engine. Then I pulled out my phone.

"Contact me any time, for anything," that's what Noah had said. I hoped he'd meant it.

I put the car in gear and jammed the phone between my shoulder and ear.

No one answered.

I swerved around a pothole; the phone fell

276

to my lap. I chanced a quick glance down at it and stabbed at Noah's name again before pressing it to my ear.

"I told you to text," he said.

"I missed the sound of your voice."

This was meant to be a joke. It didn't come out that way.

I checked my rearview mirror, then snapped my eyes back to the road in front of me. It wasn't my best idea, talking while driving, but neither of these things could wait. "I need something," I said.

"Of course you do. But I don't work for you anymore, or don't you remember?"

"Well, I know how you love pro bono —"

"Jane, it's late —"

"Look — ah, shit." The truck lurched and I nearly bit my tongue off.

"Where are you?"

"Never mind that, just — I need to know if you have my birth certificate."

"Why do you need that?"

"Do you have it or what?"

"Of course I have it, I had to use it to get your name changed — you're lucky I'm still at the office."

I heard a rustling of papers.

"Okay," he said, "here it is. Now what?"

I tightened my hands on the steering wheel and made sure I was in the very center of the road. "When was I born?" I asked.

"Uh, Jane —"

"Just tell me, would you?"

"The same day you were always born — November 22, 1986. Is this your weird way to remind me to get you a present?"

"Shut up and let me think." The truck thudded over the buckled road. I pretended it was pulling my mind along with it. "Wait," I said. "What's the name of the hospital?"

"Hold on, give me a second, this is all in German —"

"And also French and Italian, surely you know one of those. Didn't they teach you anything at Yale?"

"Yeah, useful languages, like Spanish."

"Very funny — keep looking. It'll probably be the word ending in 'spital.' "

"Thanks, I never would have figured that out — no, I don't see anything."

"Are you sure?"

"Wait, could this be it? *'Hausgeburt?'* "

I pulled over to the side of the road and threw the truck into park. "What'd you say?"

"Hausgeburt."

"Spell it for me, because your German is *Scheiße.*"

"Hey, I'm helping *you* here." But he

spelled it anyway.

I rested my forehead against the steering wheel. "Are you absolutely sure that's what it says?"

"Positive."

I sat up and put the car into gear again. "Okay, great, thanks, nice chat."

"Wait, did you see that —"

I hung up.

Hausgeburt. My mother — *my mother* — had a home birth? The same woman who took Vicodin when she had a hangnail? No fucking way. Goddammit, she'd lied about *my* age, too, hadn't she? Which meant my father wasn't some decrepit dead dude from Lichtenstein — he was some loser from South Dakota.

That bitch. I'd had a father all this time.

Worse, I'd been reading the wrong horoscope for *years.*

What many people don't know — but wouldn't be surprised to hear — is that Janie Jenkins has been stirring up controversy since the moment she was born: At the time of Janie's birth, her mother was not married to her father, Swiss billionaire Emmerich von Mises. It was widely known that they had planned to marry, and Emmerich publicly acknowledged Janie as his own, but unfortunately he died in December 1986, at age eighty-six, just two months before he was to have wed Marion.

The children of Emmerich's first marriage had been opposed to the relationship with Marion from the start, suspecting her of using their father for his money. And, indeed, Emmerich left Marion a generous bequest. It was whispered, however, that she was also considering taking legal action to ensure the ongoing financial support of her daughter. However, there is no sign that she ever filed suit.

When I spoke to the von Mises family, I learned the story behind the alleged dispute. Andreas von Mises, Emmerich's son, explained their reasoning. "It is not that we wanted an innocent child to go without," Andreas said, "but the family was extremely reluctant to side with the woman who we then believed had callously manipulated our father. However, once we registered our objections and told her we would make them public if we needed to, Marion withdrew her claim. She was just looking out for her daughter, she said — and she didn't want to tarnish my father's legacy. In retrospect, I . . . regret the incident. I misjudged Marion. She was only trying to do what was best."

— Alexis Papadopoulos,
And the Devil Did Grin:
The Janie Jenkins Story

Chapter Nineteen

"You look like shit," said Peter as he slid into the chair opposite me at breakfast Wednesday morning.

Of course I looked like shit. After I'd parked the truck in the abandoned barn in Adeline it had taken me just over an hour to hike back. Even after a hot shower, the tips of my fingers were still tingling.

"I don't sleep well in strange beds," I said.

Or strange bathtubs.

And my thoughts sure hadn't helped.

Do you ever think about it, about nothingness? I do. I think about it all the time.

Because of course it's nothingness that awaits us. *Of course* it is. If it weren't, why would our hearts keep pumping any longer than they had to? Why wouldn't we all emerge into the world, pure and innocent, and then, before we had a chance to get into any trouble — before we even had a chance to take our first, oily shit — just immediately shut down our systems and head straight to the hereafter? If there were a better life after death, why bother getting fitter for survival's sake? Why would evolution even be a thing? Why fight for something second best? If death was *really* awesome, in a life-or-death situation, our bodies wouldn't muscle up with epinephrine and cortisol, our brains would hit us up instead with sloppy sleepy happy love. Hannibal Lecter would be our Mickey Mouse.

No. There's fuck-all to look forward to. Our bodies understand this. The real problem is, it's unbearable to *know* this.

So we cope. We fashion faith and magic and online personality tests, orthopedic inserts for the five-inch stiletto heel that is mortality. And you know what: We're good at it — we're really fucking good at coping. That's why I think — why I think that maybe when the end finally does come it will be easier than I fear. I think our minds all scavenge about for the closest thing to comfort, whatever that may be. The satisfaction of noble sacrifice. The pride in a job well done. The promise of a bright, white light.

Or denial. That'll be my go-to. Even as those very last seconds tick down, even as everyone else knows with absolute certainty that This Is It for me, I'm sure I'll still be expecting a miracle cure, a second wind, a call from the governor. Some sort of glitch in the self-destruct system.

Hope is asymptotic in its decline. If the past ten years have taught me anything, it's that.

But if all this is true . . . then what did that mean for my mother? The coroner said it took her *minutes* to die after she was shot. Did she try to sit up or reach for something to tie off her leg, to press against her face? Did she call 911 and ask for help? No. She scooped up a fingerful of blood from her chest and wrote my name next to her on the floor.

There was no denial there. My mother knew damn well what was coming. Otherwise, she would have tried to save herself. Instead, her last act was a fuck you.

What, then, eased my mother's way? Even I can admit that she was human, so there must have been *something*. But it sure as hell wasn't faith or sacrifice, and I can only come up with one other option: that she was in so much pain, oblivion would come as a relief.

I'm not sure how I feel about that.

I shook myself back into the present and looked down at the mess of pancakes on my plate. I wasn't really eating them. I was just kind of digging at them like they were a Mayan ruin and I didn't want to disturb whatever lay beneath. Way subtle, subconscious.

"Who was that guy you went off with last night?" Peter asked.

At that, I took a bite. I'd never realized how useful food was at buying time — and disguising alarm. It was one thing if Kelley and Renee had noticed Leo's interest in me: I could count on their discretion. But it was another thing if *everyone* noticed.

"Kelley's brother," I said after I swallowed.

"You seemed to know each other pretty well."

"Everyone in town is just really friendly. I bet that takes some getting used to for you, being from New York."

"Well, when it's coming from a cop — yeah."

"Leo's a cop? I never would have guessed."

(It sure is easy to play dumb with a guy like Peter.)

I sat up, as if I'd just had a brilliant idea. "Hey, you know what you should do? You should ask *him* about that bank robbery. He probably knows all about it."

He shook his head. "Tried. If he knows anything, he's not saying. Not to *me*, anyway." He paused. "But you — you he likes." He gave me a meaningful look, by which I mean that he rounded his eyes like a Kewpie doll. His left eyelid kept twitching, as if it couldn't quite decide if a wink would be too much.

"Would you like me to ask him for you?"

He smiled. "I'd really appreciate it."

"I'd be happy to." I paused and thought of the business card in my bag. "And is there any way you might be able to do me a favor in return?"

"Well . . . I guess?"

"I know this is kind of a weird thing to ask, but I really need to run a few errands today. For personal things." I paused. Should I just go ahead and say I needed to buy super tampons? No, better to stick with the insinuating caesura. "But my car's dead, so I was wondering if maybe I could borrow yours?"

For whatever reason, the request didn't faze him. "Are you sure you can get the cop to help out?" he asked.

Not even a little.

"Positive."

He shrugged and pulled the keys out of his pocket. "Sure, why not? The magazine's paying for mileage. Just don't flake out on me. I really need that guy's help."

"It's a deal." I held out my hand. I'd meant for him to drop the keys in my palm, but he shook it instead. His skin was warm and damp, like half-risen dough.

I was just on my way out the door when a heavy hand fell on my shoulder.

"Rebecca, right?"

I turned around and found Eli. His face was set in the same stern lines it always was. I wondered if I was supposed to salute.

"That's right," I said. "Good to see you, Eli."

His eyes darted off to the side. "I saw you sitting with that reporter guy," he said.

"Peter?"

"Yeah, that's him." He hesitated. "Look, I don't want to make you feel uncomfortable or anything, but I was wondering if you could tell me what he's working on."

I glanced at Peter. He was still engrossed in his binder.

I looked back at Eli. This would require some delicacy, but if I could get him on my side, it would be worth it. "Let's talk outside," I said.

He followed me out to the front porch. I sat on the swing; he leaned against the railing.

I folded my hands in my lap. "You're worried that he's writing about your sister," I said.

His fist clenched, then released. "Goddammit, I told Cora a reporter would be a pain in the ass."

I gave him a reassuring smile. "Is there something I can do?"

"Do you know what he's planning to write?"

"He's looking into the bank robbery, that's all I know."

"Well — I suppose I can't stop him from reading what was already in the papers," he said.

His voice was tight, but in the moment before he'd responded, I'd seen his jaw relax. Interesting.

"I'd be happy to keep an eye on him if you'd like," I said. "Make sure he's minding his manners, that sort of thing. I was planning on spending some time in the archives anyway."

He put his hands behind his back and looked out at the street. "I'd appreciate that."

I sat back and stared at Eli's profile, looking for the answer to the question I wasn't yet brave enough to ask:

Ever been to Beverly Hills?

■ ■ ■ ■

An hour later I was heading north on US-16, driving as fast as Peter's shitty rental could take me. The cloud cover that day was unsettlingly uniform, smooth and white. It looked like a perfectly clear sky whose blue had been sucked right out of it, like there'd been a fundamental molecular shift in the Earth's atmosphere since last I'd looked.

I knew I was taking a risk in going to Rapid City, but *god* it felt good to get out of town. The farther away I got, the easier I could breathe. I mean, granted, yes, Rapid City was a cosmopolitan metropolis compared to Ardelle, and each additional person I ran into would increase the odds that I'd be recognized. And then there was this address I was heading for — it could be the headquarters of the Janie Jenkins Is Crazy-Guilty Club for all I knew.

Although . . . at least then I'd be making someone's day for once.

But the risk was worth it. I had an address — *an actual real-life clue.* And even if I didn't know where I was going, I knew that the place had meant something to my mother. Otherwise she wouldn't have hid it so well.

Rapid City came into view, a dusting of buildings that from a distance looked less like structures than a scattering of people gathered for a picnic in the park. I checked the map I'd picked up at the inn and headed downtown, to the sort of historic district that was largely maintained for the purposes of weekly art fairs. I parked in front of a boxy four-story building with a western-wear outfitter on the first floor. I checked the directory listing. The lower units were all occupied by various practices — a chiropractor, a podiatrist, an accountant. Next to unit #5 it read *M. Copeland, Photographer.*

My brow furrowed. If there was one thing my mother hated, it was photographers. Could someone else have hidden the address? If I'd come all this way just to find out that Rue liked to get glamour shots, I was going to burn off her hair.

I pushed the buzzer.

"Come on up!" The voice was so clear it sang straight through the static of the intercom.

I climbed up a narrow stairwell to a door that was otherwise just like all the other doors, light green with streaks of blinding-white primer showing through where the painters had gotten sloppy. Before I had a chance to rethink my decision, the door opened.

"You must be Candace!"

The woman who greeted me was white-haired and tiny — tinier even than me — and dressed in a macramé tunic and flowing skirt. Her feet were bare, her toenails long and unpainted.

"Well, actually —"

She pulled me inside and swung me over to a chevron-patterned sofa. "I'll just make some tea, why don't I?"

I looked around me. The room was triangular and windowless; on the hypotenuse, a pass-through led to the kitchen. It was silent save the sound of running water, a kettle being filled. The clatter of mugs being removed from a too-full cabinet.

"My name's not Candace!" I said, not wanting to get caught in a useless lie.

"Oh, that's fine, too!" she called back.

I sat down. The ceiling, a grid of pin-pricked acoustic tiles and fluorescent lights, was better suited to a room full of cubicles. The overhead lights were turned off, though, the room illuminated instead by the small forest of floor lamps in one corner, as if a few rays of agreeable gold light could dress up the room's bleak pragmatism.

The woman poked her head out through the pass-through. "Are you here for engagement photos? Wedding photos? Maybe something special for your boyfriend or girlfriend?"

Special photos? That sounded even more like Rue.

I rolled my lips over my teeth, thinking through what I wanted to ask. "I'm looking for pictures of my mother," I said, swiftly, as if the sentence were a single word. "She was one of your clients, and since she passed away — well, I don't have as many photos of her as I'd like." I cast my eyes down and away, like I do when a therapist asks me a question that I need to pretend is hard to answer. "I was wondering if maybe you saved some negatives."

The woman set her elbows on the edge of the pass-through and propped her chin in her hands. Her expression went soft and loamy and sympathetic. "I'm not sure how far back my files go, but I can certainly take a look. Do you know when she would have come in?"

"Not exactly — probably eighty-four or eighty-five?"

Her eyes snapped to mine. "I'm sorry," she said, "but you must be mistaken. I've only been in business since ninety-two."

"But I found your address in her things." I dug the card out of my bag and she came around into the living room to take it.

She read it once, then turned it over and over again before handing it back.

"She kept it in a very special place," I said, "so I assumed — I thought it was something important."

"I'm sure it was."

"Can you tell me what used to be here?"

She sat down next to me. "What did you say your name was again?"

"Rebecca."

"I'm Marilyn. Are you from around here?"

I reined in my impatience, reminding myself that I wasn't some cop who could just bulldoze an interview subject. "No," I said. "I'm from California."

"Oh, lucky you. Such a lovely part of the country — I have friends up in Monterey. Glass artists. They do *fabulous* work. Maybe I should give you their information, in case you're ever up that way." She crossed her legs and pulled absently on her earlobe. "How long ago did she pass?"

I swallowed. "My mother? It's been ten years now."

"Not so long, then." The kettle whistled, and she drifted back into the kitchen to pour the tea. She emerged with two steaming mugs and a carton of cream tucked between her shoulder and her chin. She set everything down on the coffee table, rotating the mugs until their handles were aligned. "My own mother's still alive, if you can believe that," she said. "A hundred and four and still kicking like a Rockette. The heart of a horse, the doctors say — and the mind of one, too. You know, I came out here twenty years ago so I could be with her at the end, and now . . . well, I'm still here, aren't I? Seventy-four years old and just waiting for my mother to die."

I opened my mouth, but nothing came out.

This is a story you probably know. And I can't dispute its veracity.

The night of the murder, after I left Kristof in the billiard room, I ran upstairs to grab my purse before leaving for Ainsley's.

My mother was waiting for me in my room.

"Pack up whatever you want to take with you," she said. "We're leaving first thing tomorrow."

I stumbled in surprise, and when I caught my mother's disgusted look I wanted to shout, "I'm not drunk, I'm clumsy!" But in

all honesty she probably would have preferred the former. It would have meant my
gracelessness was just a temporary condition.

"What are you talking about?" I said. "I
can't leave."

"You can and you will." This, for her, was
the end of the discussion, and she turned to
go back to her room. I wasn't about to let it
end there, though. I ran ahead of her.

"But I'm finally starting to get somewhere," I said.

"As what — professional jailbait?"

I drew back. "At least I *earn* my money."

I caught a rare glimpse of that one wrinkle
between her eyebrows before she rubbed it
away. "I'm leaving whether or not you come
with me," she said.

"Is that supposed to be a threat?"

"Yes."

"What part of 'I don't need you' don't
you understand?"

She put a hand on the wall, and for a moment I thought my words were so cutting
that she'd needed to steady herself. But she
was just setting up her next volley. "You
know," she said, "when I had you I thought,
'Finally, *finally* I'll have someone on my
side.' "

"That's a terrible reason to have a child."

"Twenty-twenty hindsight."

She pushed past me, and if I'd been thinking clearly I might have let it go. I might have let her go. But I had no more control over my actions than a lit fuse does its direction, and so instead I spat out the five little words that take root in a girl's brain as soon as she grows breasts:

"I wish you were dead."

She turned, her smile a well-honed knife.

"Never forget, Jane: Wishes are for cowards."

"I suppose this isn't a particularly polite thing to ask," Marilyn was saying, "but when you've been waiting as long as I have, you have a lot of time to wonder." She laced her fingers around her mug. "Will you tell me what it was like? Losing your mother?"

I swallowed. "No one's ever asked me that before," I said.

"I'm so sorry to hear that."

"Why?"

"Because it means people only care about how they want you to feel."

I reached for my mug, ran my finger along its rim. "I'm not sure what I'm supposed to say to that."

"Was it sudden?"

I looked up. "Not sudden enough."

"I suppose it never is." Marilyn sat back, pulling a long strand of white hair between a forefinger and thumb and turning it slowly, like she was cranking her thoughts up out of a well. "May I see that card again?"

I handed it back. She looked at it. I couldn't read anything from her expression. It was as blank as that morning's sky. I dunked my teabag up and down, up and down.

"This used to be a medical practice," Marilyn said at last. "That's one of the reasons I bought it — they bricked up all the windows, so it's perfect for photography. It's like one big darkroom."

"What kind of medical practice?"

Her big toe tapped against the linoleum in time with my teabag. "It was a women's clinic." She paused. "It was empty for years before I bought it — no one else wanted it. I got a great deal."

My hand stilled. The teabag spun in a slow counterclockwise circle. "Why wouldn't they have wanted it?"

"It wasn't a clinic for just any kind of woman. It was for women who found themselves . . . in a certain kind of trouble."

"Oh," I said. I pulled the teabag out and dropped it on the table. We both looked at our mugs.

The buzzer sounded. Marilyn stood up and went to answer it, moving slowly, like she was pushing her way through waist-deep water — or maybe it just looked that way to me. I remember wondering why the buzzer was still buzzing — *Was that Candace leaning against it? Had someone else come? Was it broken?* — but no, I realized, it was just the noise in my head.

Then a switch flipped inside me, and the world lurched back into motion, me along with it, and by the time Marilyn opened the door I was right there next to her. I pushed past a startled bobbed brunette and ran out. Marilyn must have stepped out after me, because as my feet tumbled down the stairs I heard her call out, her voice echoing in the stairwell, "Sometimes it's possible to want something and not want it at the same time."

"I hope your mother lives forever," I yelled back.

By the time I got to the car my body was fizzling from the inside, as if my blood had turned to acid and had set to working away at my bones.

I climbed into the front seat and leaned my forehead against the steering wheel, flinging my thoughts around in the hopes of finding an alternate explanation. That the address card was for a friend. That it was the sort of contraband hush-voiced teenage girls passed around at slumber parties. That it was some kind of practical joke.

You have to understand: It's not that I was shocked that she'd thought about an abortion. I was a sexually active adolescent in a *Sex and the City* world, remember. No, I was shocked that she hadn't gone through with it. I was always the one thing in her life that stuck out. I couldn't believe she'd passed up the chance to smooth me over.

Maybe she hadn't been able to believe it, either.

Our fight that night hadn't ended in the hallway — if it had, maybe the looky-loo caterers who had witnessed my "threat" would've been able to testify as to what happened next.

Recognizing that I'd lost the battle, I'd retreated into the nearest bathroom, ostensibly to fix my hair. My mother followed.

"What do you think you're doing?" she asked.

"Heading out." I felt my hands go to my hips and my jaw jut out.

"But I just said —"

"Objection, your honor. Immaterial." I

turned to the mirror, examined my reflection, and reached into the neckline of my dress to adjust my boobs.

"Jane," she said.

I fluffed my hair. "What."

"Look at me."

There was something in her voice that made me obey. She was wearing pearlescent white silk that lit her skin like moonlight, transmuting her from granite into marble. Her eyes, limned by three coats of Chanel Inimitable Waterproof, were a deceptively placid blue, slicked shiny by the benzos I knew she took most nights. I fingered the hem of my skirt and took a small step back.

"One day you'll have a daughter —"

"Not if I can help it."

"One day you'll have a daughter," she said again, mildly, as if she were a waiter telling me the daily specials, "and when you do, then you'll understand what you really are."

"Let me guess — a slut? A brat? A crushing disappointment?"

"No." She reached forward and tipped up my chin. "A missed opportunity."

Silly me, I'd always thought she'd just meant I wasn't living up to my potential. But maybe what she really regretted was that I was even living to begin with.

I turned the key in the ignition and listened to the indifferent hum of the economy rental. It wasn't too late — I could still let *this* go. It would take me a little more than twelve hours to drive to the duplex in Wisconsin. A key was waiting for me there, hidden under a doormat that read "Go Away!" — Noah's idea of a joke. The duplex had two bathrooms, Noah had told me. That meant I'd have my pick of *two* places to sleep. A 100 percent improvement on what I had now.

But I might never have another chance to find out who my real father was.

I wondered if he'd look at me the same way my mother had.

I drove east on I-90 as far as the Badlands before changing my mind and turning back toward Ardelle.

Idiot.

BEVERLY HILLS POLICE DEPARTMENT

Incident No. 2938-a

NAME OF PERSON GIVING STATEMENT
Officer Michael Balmores

DATE OF STATEMENT: July 16th, 2003
TIME STARTED: 10 AM
TIME COMPLETED: 1030 am

On July 15th, 2003, Officer Gregory Tucker and I responded to a report of a possible homicide at the home of Marion Elsinger on Laurel Way. When I arrived I was met by Jane Jenkins, who had called in the report. Although Jenkins seemed to be calm and collected, her clothes, hands, and face were covered with blood.

Jenkins escorted me to an upstairs bedroom, where I found a woman of approximately middle age lying on the floor. She had bled heavily and had been inflicted with what appeared to be gunshot wounds. It was clear the victim was deceased. I secured the crime scene and alerted the coroner.

When Officer Tucker and I began to ask

Jenkins about the circumstances in which she had found the body, she was unable to provide any details. As we continued to ask, she grew increasingly agitated. I asked Jenkins to calm down, and at that point she became physically aggressive. She attempted to attack me, and Officer Tucker was forced to restrain her. As soon as additional support arrived, Officer Tucker escorted her to the station for further questioning.

CHAPTER TWENTY

When I got back to Ardelle, I stopped first at the inn to drop off Peter's keys.

Rue was sitting at reception, reading, holding herself so still I knew she had to be feeling the night before. Apparently Leo hadn't swiped the last of her moonshine.

I dropped the keys on the desk just to see her flinch. "I was wondering if you could return these to Mr. Strickland for me," I said. She looked up and blinked once, the motion exaggerated and slow, as if her eyelids were speaking English and I was a foreign tourist. Then she returned to her book.

"Still reading *Jane Eyre*?"

"Your powers of observation astound and amaze."

"Wait a second —" My hand shot out and grabbed for the book, but Rue snatched it away. "Can I see that for a second?"

"No."

"Why not?"

"I have to finish it by tonight."

The paperback book had a pristine, unbroken spine — one of a matched set. And just yesterday I'd seen the others. That was my mother's book.

Had she written anything in it?

"Can I borrow it when you're done?" I asked.

She pressed it to her chest. "I've promised it to my friend."

Behind me the front door jangled open. A pack of guests — presumably returned from whatever festival activity I'd skipped that morning — stomped away the cold, and Cora issued a jaunty invitation to afternoon tea. I didn't take my eyes off Rue.

"Are you reading that for school?" I asked.

"I'm not in school. The one here closed, and Mom doesn't want me driving all the way to Custer. So I'm getting my GED. It's faster, anyway."

Well, that answered that. Rue was lying — the GED didn't test on specific works of literature. Or at least it hadn't when I'd taken it.

I looked behind me. The guests were filtering into the salon, and Cora was rattling off a list of oolongs and rooibos and darjeelings. In a matter of moments she'd see me, and then I'd be stuck drinking more fucking tea and making more useless small talk. I'd have to come back to deal with Rue later.

I inched away from the desk, away from Rue's hungover smirk, hesitating just once more before ducking down the hall, through the kitchen, and out the back door.

It was time to return Peter's favor.

The police station was on the corner of Tesmond and Commercial, a hatbox of a building framed by two cast-iron street lamps that were on even at two in the afternoon. I paused at the foot of the stairs and tipped my face up to the sun like I was in the last shot of an antidepressant commercial. The sun wasn't particularly warm, though, and the breeze sweeping down from the pass smelled of rotting pumpkins. I dragged myself inside.

The station consisted of a single room, which was square and high-ceilinged and painted a mucilaginous shade that made my eyes itch. There were two desks — one empty, one occupied by an affable-looking man in uniform — a wall of filing cabinets, and a jail cell with a stainless-steel toilet and a cot. Two booted feet rested on the bed frame.

I stood in front of the officer on duty until

he roused himself from his paperwork. He had baby-plump cheeks and eyes so big his face projected perpetual delight, as if he were always opening a birthday present and finding exactly what he wanted inside. His nameplate read *"Officer Billy."*

He smiled. "Can I help you?"

"Is Leo in?"

"I'm sorry, Ma'am, he's gone for the day. Can I take a message?"

I clasped my hands in front of me and rocked forward on my toes. "Well, I'm not sure if he mentioned this, but Leo said I could have access to some of the old records. For research." I hunched my back and shoulders a bit like I imagined a researcher would.

"Chief La Plante told you this?"

"He did." Then, before he could keep thinking about it: "I don't need to see everything you have, of course — just whatever you have from the early eighties or thereabouts."

Before Billy could answer, the cot in the cell let out the eerie extenuated creak of a closet door that seems to be opening on its own; both Billy and I turned to look. The man inside sat up, and his deep-set eyes locked on mine. It was Walt Freeman. Master criminal. Pothead. *Shady.*

"You," he said.

Billy looked between us. "You two know each other?" he asked.

"Of course not," I managed.

Walt shook his head. "I don't have time for this." He leaned forward and threaded his arms through the bars, tapping his middle fingers against his thumbs. "Billy, dude, you've got to let me get online."

"Walt, if you want better Internet access, maybe you should stop getting thrown in jail."

"Or Leo could stop being such a cock."

I let their stupid squabble fade away. So Leo had arrested Walt after all. While I'm the first person to acknowledge my rampant narcissism, I knew it wasn't remotely unfounded to suspect that this had everything to do with me. When I'd met them on the side of the road, arresting Walt seemed to be the last thing on Leo's mind — but Walt was the only thing I had on Leo, and now that I'd come to town, he was a liability. What was Leo planning next? Was he going to arrest me? Blackmail me? Either way, I was in trouble.

"I've got things to be doing," Walt was saying.

"Yeah?" Billy said. "There a Dragon Ball Z marathon on or something?"

308

"If you're not gonna bail me out, at least let me use your ethernet cable."

Billy's mouth dropped open. "You've gotta be kidding me."

"Come on. Sharing is caring, little bro."

Walt did a sad-eye-pouty-lip sort of thing. Like a lost puppy. Who had rabies. "Pretty please?"

Billy threw up his hands. "Fine. Just don't do anything illegal, okay? If you do, I'm telling Mom, and then she'll never change her mind about posting bail."

"Sure, whatever you say." Walt turned and bent over, digging under his cot. When he stood up he had a heavy black laptop in his hands. He slid open the door and planted himself at the desk next to Billy's.

I gave Billy an incredulous look. "You don't lock the door?"

Billy flushed. "Chief La Plante has the only keys to the cell. But don't worry, he's not dangerous or anything. Except to me, maybe."

"He's your brother?"

"Unfortunately."

"Is everyone in this town related?"

"Seems that way, sometimes. Mom always says it's like a Thanksgiving dinner that never ends. Now, what were you saying you needed?"

I glanced at Walt. He didn't seem to be paying attention. "Old case files and arrest records," I said.

"I'd love to help you," Billy said, "but I wouldn't feel comfortable letting you go through our stuff without talking to Chief La Plante first."

I batted my eyelashes before remembering they were hidden under a gross greasy fringe. "It's just that I'm kind of working under a deadline," I said.

"I could give Leo a call —"

"No! I mean . . . please don't go to any trouble on my account. I'm sure I can track him down myself."

"That's probably your best bet. Doubt he'd pick up my call anyway."

"Do you have any idea where he might be?"

"Depends if Mrs. Kanty got ahold of him. If she did, he'll be at the VFW, helping her set up for tonight's event. If not, he'll be at the Coyote Hole."

"That's very helpful." (Which it was — at least now I knew how to avoid him.)

"But if you can't find him," Billy continued, "Kelley has all those old papers over at her place — they used to publish the police blotter every week. On Mondays, I think. Maybe that would help? That's what I told the last guy who came in here — uh, Paul or Patrick or —"

"Peter?"

"Yeah, that's right. He was just here a couple hours ago. Maybe you can catch him."

"You just missed him," Kelley said when I walked through her door.

"Peter?"

"Leo."

I tripped over the sill and caught myself on a rack of L'il Nugget onesies.

"He was looking for you, too," she added slyly.

"This isn't Mystery Date," I muttered.

"Could've fooled me."

God, Kelley's smiles were such a pain in the ass. I scowled, which just made her smile more.

"Was Peter in here too?" I asked.

"He came to look through the newspapers again." She led me back to the archives and pointed to the neat row of labeled plastic bins that had replaced the crumbling boxes. "He tidied up, too."

"What was he looking for, do you know?"

Kelley shook her head. "No clue. Whatever it was, though, he seemed pleased."

But a bank robbery in Custer wouldn't

have been in the Ardelle police blotter. Had Peter been looking for something else? About Tessa, maybe?

I knelt down and opened the bin marked *1982–1984.* I began to pull out the Monday papers.

Kelley sat down on the couch and propped her feet on the table, ankles crossed. "You know, I've never been much interested in anything after the turn of the century, but the way Cora keeps telling me *not* to write anything about the twentieth century makes me think I should totally write about the twentieth century."

I found the first police blotter.

February 26, 1982
10:37 pm Caller on Tesmond Road reported that someone had rung doorbell but had not been there when the door was answered.

Well, this was pretty fucking promising.

"If you don't mind my asking," I said, "why are you interested in any of it? The history stuff, that is."

Kelley leaned her head back and looked at the ceiling. "This may sound strange, but I like it here. I feel a connection to the place — and more of a connection than, like,

'This is where I grew up,' or whatever. Or maybe it's just that I don't know how to live anywhere else."

September 8, 1982
1:12 am Caller on First Street reported that neighbor kept slamming door. Officer advised her to leave a note.

"How long have you and Renee been together?"

"Hard to say. We've sort of always been together. But if you're asking how long we've been sleeping together, then I'd say it's been about three years."

"Does Leo know?"

"He's not an idiot. Plus, Renee couldn't wait to tell him."

"So why are they still married? Why were they *ever* married?"

When Kelley didn't respond, I looked up at her over the papers. She was staring off to the side, rubbing her palm against her cheek. "I can't really blame him," she said eventually. She pulled her hand away, looked at it, then set it firmly on the arm of the couch. "I mean — who *could* blame him? Renee's super hot."

Something went soft and sad inside me. "You're not so bad yourself," I said.

Kelley laughed. "I knew it. You're just using Leo to get closer to me."

"Sounds like I wouldn't be the first."

I ducked my head back toward the papers.

April 3, 1983
12:13 pm Walk-in reported driver who used his turn signal but did not turn.

"So why aren't you out?" I asked.

"It's not like we're *in,*" she said. "I just don't like making a big thing of it."

"In my experience that tends to make the thing even bigger."

March 12, 1984
6:08 pm Caller reported that there was a large bag on Commercial Street. Officer ultimately determined that the bag contained trash.

I tossed the papers in the box and sat back on my heels. I took off my glasses and shoved my bangs off my forehead. This was useless.

When I got my glasses back on I saw that Kelley was giving me a weird look.

"What?" I asked.

"Why don't you try 1985?" she said.

"Did you remember something?"

314

"No, but I have a feeling." She came over, knelt next to me, and tugged over another box. She turned it around to show me its side, which Peter had thicketed with Post-its marked with dates.

"Oh."

"He has his uses."

Together we picked through the papers until we had the relevent issues spread out in front of us. Apart from a single article about the Reagan inauguration, the lead stories were all local news: record high temperatures at Mount Rushmore; the grand opening of the Adeline campground; the First Lutheran Christmas pageant; at least three potholes (one major, two minor).

"What do you think we're going to find?" Kelley asked.

"I'm hoping Tessa Kanty's checkered past."

I opened up the first paper and began reading. "Do you have a pen?" I asked.

Kelley went back to the couch and dug under the cushions. "Red or black?"

I took the red. Twenty minutes later I'd circled seven items:

January 20, 1985
11:39 pm A 17-year-old Adeline resident was brought in for suspected petty larceny.

She was later released.

May 17, 1985
2:33 pm An 18-year-old Adeline resident was arrested for petty larceny. The charge was dropped.

May 18, 1985
12:34 am Investigated domestic disturbance on Main Street. The caller, a 21-year-old Adeline resident, reported being pushed and struck by an 18-year-old woman. Officers gave the woman a warning.

June 7, 1985
7:28 pm An 18-year-old Adeline resident was arrested for petty larceny. The charge was dropped.

June 8, 1985
1:23 am Noise disturbance reported on Main Street in Adeline. An 18-year-old woman and a 21-year-old man were cited.

July 21, 1985
12:47 am An 18-year-old resident of Adeline and her passenger, an 18-year-old resident of Ardelle, were stopped on suspicion of underage drinking and driving

under the influence of alcohol. The passenger was released; the driver was charged.

July 22, 1985
11:08 pm Caller reported concern about man and woman on Main Street in Adeline whom he could hear yelling. Officer investigated and filed report. An 18-year-old resident of Adeline and a 21-year-old resident of Adeline were each issued a warning.

I sat back. "Just so I'm sure, how many eighteen-year-old girls were living in Adeline in 1985?" I asked.

Kelley looked at me. "Just one."

"And how old would Eli have been back then?"

"About twenty-one."

I pointed to the second-to-last item. "And, here, the DUI — the eighteen-year-old companion — is there any chance that was the man who was arrested for the robbery?"

"Jared Vincent," Kelley supplied. "And yeah, that sounds right. He was from Ardelle, so I didn't know him, but I think he graduated the same year Tessa would have."

"Would have?"

She hesitated.

"I'm not Peter — you don't have to shut me down. I'm not here to write some exposé."

"Just because I like you doesn't mean I know you any better."

I studied Kelley. Today her hair was twisted into a forest of messy buns, and she had three earrings in her left ear and four in her right. Her lips were waxy with Chap-Stick. Her eyes were brown and warm. I'd never had to ask anything from someone like her — from someone who wasn't somehow icky on the inside.

I decided to try something new.

"Well, what if you did?" I said. "Know me better."

"Are you saying there's something I should know?"

"Yes."

"And will you tell me what it is if I ask?"

"Yes."

She sat in silence, thinking it over. Then she nodded to herself and lifted her head. "Deal."

I let out a breath. She hadn't needed to ask, I realized, but I'd needed to offer. It was like mutually assured destruction. Just . . . nicer.

Her smile turned wicked. "But if your

secret something is that you like ladies, too, I have to tell you: Leo's going to be super pissed."

I laughed despite myself.

She settled back against the couch. "Okay, so here's what I can tell you — it's not much, I'm afraid. All us Adeline kids actually knew Tessa pretty well. Like I said, she was the only teenage girl there, which meant she had a monopoly on the baby-sitting business. We probably saw her — oh, two or three times a week."

I tried to picture my mother as a baby-sitter. "Was she any good at it?"

"I don't know if my mother would have said so, but I thought she was. Tessa wasn't much into rules, you know? Like, whenever she watched us we'd get to stay up past our bedtimes and paint our toenails purple. Even little Billy Freeman. That's kind of what I remember best about her. That she was fun." She paused. "And that she was pretty, of course, but everyone remembers that."

"You liked her."

"Well — yes."

My brain was busy shorting out, so it took me some time to figure out what to say next.

"What was her relationship with Eli like? From those police reports it sounds like they didn't get along too well."

Kelley's gaze flickered then firmed. "You should probably take that with a grain of salt. The police were always giving Eli and Tessa trouble. 'The Kanty Curse,' Renee calls it. Until Cora came around, the family . . . well, they didn't have the best reputation. Tessa and Eli could've been fighting over the Atari and the cops would've cited them for it."

"Kelley," I said. "Again: I'm not Peter."

She sighed. "Okay, yeah, so they weren't blameless, either. Eli and Tessa had their problems. Who *wouldn't* have had problems? I mean, first their mother died, then their father died, and then they were saddled with that mortgage and Tessa had to drop out of school so she could work. And before Eli enlisted he was — different. Still really focused and driven, but he didn't know how to control his temper. Neither did Tessa, for that matter."

"Why do you think she left?"

"I don't think there was necessarily any, like, one inciting event." Kelley said. "I think she just left to . . . get out. We all know so much about each other here — and we all *think* we know so much about each other — that sometimes I think this place acts like a . . . like a funhouse mirror, you know?

None of the glass here is flat anymore. And some people can't take it."

"But not you?"

"I like the distortion."

I stacked the papers and set them aside. "Do you think she robbed that bank with Jared?"

Kelley pinched her lip between her fingers. "Look," she said, "if you tell Renee I said this, I'll scratch your face off, but yes: I absolutely think she robbed that bank. Like I said — she wasn't much into rules."

CHAPTER TWENTY-ONE

I watched as a stream of bulky-jacketed people made its way down Tesmond toward the VFW post, a chunky gray building with aluminum siding and a roof pitched at the steep angles of a Swiss chalet. **STRIP STEAK 1ST SAT,** the sign outside read. **BREAKFAST SUNDAY. REDEMPTION NEVER.**

Okay, it might not have said that last part. But it was starting to feel that way.

I took a hard right and slipped into the alley between an abandoned hardware store and an abandoned bakery. I pressed my forehead against the cool, crumbling brick. Almost five days out in the world, and what had I learned?

A) My uncle was definitely an asshole.

B) My mother was maybe a criminal.

C) My father was probably American.

Three for shitty three.

From my lips issued forth, long and low,

322

that most holy of words:

Fuuuuuuuuuuuuuuuck.

I closed my eyes. Dammit. It wouldn't be long before the press — or worse, Trace — tracked me down. And I still had so many questions.

Like about Jared: Had my mother really betrayed him? Was he still in jail? Or had he gone to L.A. ten years ago to pay her back?

Then there was Eli. Had my mother left town because of him? Had she wanted to leave L.A. because of him, too?

And who the hell was my father?

I looked back around the corner of the bakery toward the VFW. I had to go — I had to keep pushing for information. I couldn't let Leo or anyone else scare me away. I was Janie Fucking Jenkins, for shit's sake. People were supposed to be scared of *me.*

I straightened and told my legs to get moving.

Their response was a resounding, "Bitch, please."

My resolve dissipated in an instant. Janie Fucking Jenkins, indeed.

Maybe I could find my courage some-where else. I leaned back against the wall and pulled out my phone. I typed a mes-sage.

Hi Noah

It took five minutes for him to write back.

What's wrong?

> Nothing just wanted to say
> hi
> Hi

I have to go into a meeting.

I blinked. Okay, then. I tried something
else:

> I also wanted to say thank
> you

Now I know something's wrong.

Wow. Harsh.
But then the phone rang, and I smiled.
"I thought you were going into a meeting," I said.
"Is this Janie Jenkins? This is Kurt Johnson, and I'm calling from *NBC Nightly* —"
I threw the phone against the wall as hard
as I could. I told myself to breathe, but my
lungs were apparently in league with my
legs.

It rang again.

I picked the phone up and smashed the screen against the siding — twice.

It was still ringing.

I checked the screen. It wasn't even cracked.

"What the *fuck.*"

"You need to remove the SIM card."

I looked up. Leo flicked the cigarette he'd been smoking out into the street and reached for my phone. He silenced the ringer. "Do you have a paper clip?"

My mouth closed, opened, then closed again. I reached into my bag and dug into its depths. Pen, no. Tampon, no. Scissors, no. I pulled out a pair of pink steel-point tweezers. "Will these do?"

Leo took the tweezers and did something with them to the side of the phone. He popped out a chip, which he tossed on the ground and crushed with the heel of his boot.

He gave the tweezers back to me. "Handy."

"They're also good for fine and ingrown hairs," I said.

"So what was that all about? Problems with an ex-boyfriend?"

"Yeah, something like that. Thanks for your help."

"I'm not *all* bad." He dropped my phone into my bag, then reached over and tugged up my coat collar. "Why don't I walk you over to the VFW — make sure you don't get lost."

"What, you're a gentleman now?"

"If it suits my purposes."

"It's only across the street."

"Just walk with me, would you?"

His hand settled against the small of my back and sparked something across my skin, something I no longer had a name for. I was a blind man who'd forgotten which color's which.

"I heard you were looking for me," he said.

"I thought you didn't answer Billy's calls."

"Wasn't Billy who called me."

My body went cold. "Walt," I said.

"That's right, I finally caught him."

"Look at you, Eliot Ness."

He leaned in. "I don't know if I mentioned this, but the other day I was actually *this* close to catching him. Had him in my car, even. But then I stopped to get gas and he just — snuck away."

"And you were too embarrassed to tell anyone about it. Even though someone might have seen you two on the side of the road."

"That's what I was thinking. Cigarette?"

"Go fuck yourself."

We were almost at the entrance. Faint strains of classical music could be heard through the half-open door. The other stragglers were stubbing out their cigarettes and stomping their feet before heading in.

I looked at Leo. "Well, as long as we're exchanging information, I don't know if I told you *this:* My truck seems to have just up and disappeared."

Admiration teased at his lips. "What a shame. I can't imagine what could have happened to it."

"This place is just full of mysteries, isn't it?"

I reached for the door, but Leo threw out his hand to keep me from opening it fully. He didn't say anything, waiting for me to make the next move. And, even knowing better, I did.

"What if we made a deal," I said.

"I'm listening."

"I'll leave — which'll reduce your workload by, what, 50 percent?"

"What do you want in return?"

"Access to your records room."

"Not a chance."

"Access to some very specific records, then."

I'd like to say that he drew me close then,

but in truth we drew close to one another. His eyelashes, I noticed, were short and brambly, nothing that might cause a girl to wax poetic. But I stared at them nevertheless, because that way I wouldn't have to pay attention to his eyes.

I wasn't just treading on thin ice. I was stomping on it.

"Which ones?" he asked.

"Jared Vincent's arrest record. And any associated case files."

His expression didn't change, not one bit, which is how I knew I'd surprised him. He turned and pushed us through the door.

"I think I'd rather keep you where I can see you."

I slapped his hand away and then slapped his arm for good measure.

"You know," he said, "I haven't had this much fun in forever."

I hate to say this, but neither had I.

I've already told you about Kristof, so I suppose now I might as well tell you about Oliver — for the sake of context, mind you, not because I'm looking for some kind of absolution.

Oliver, you see, was my first.

(The word you're probably thinking of right now is "lover," but the word I'm thinking of is "mark.")

I'm sure you've heard a version of this story before — probably the one where he spotted me at a club in Hollywood, hanging upon the cheek of night like a jewel or whatever, and was immediately transfixed by my beauty. But the truth is, we met at this place down near the shitty end of Robertson, on a stretch the mechanics' signs still call Beverly Hills but the maps don't even bother to name.

Wait — let me back up.

The fact is, you have to start as you mean to go along. It's an easy mistake to make — to fuck up in the beginning — because of course at the start you don't have a clue how you *should* go along. I mean, just look at Paris. She was so perfect in so many ways. But if your debut is a sex tape with a nobody — I mean, some guy named *Rick*? Come *on* — it will never be forgotten that you were slumming it from the start. The stench of pussy rot will stick to you forever, no matter how much peach you put in your perfume.

But sorry, ladies, in my world the reality is that you're going to have to fuck your way out of obscurity, so if you can't have a Rick — and please, never ever have a Rick — who do you choose?

Well, in my (I don't think it's wrong to say expert) opinion, you can't start out with a tycoon or an heir or, god forbid, a hotelier, because no matter how much money these men have, they're basically just glorified butlers, always hovering attentively nearby in impeccable dress, occasionally holding your purse. You also can't choose an actor, because they're simply not human. Avoid them at all costs.

If you're really serious about doing this, what you have to do is find a musician. They have the edge, the creativity, the celebrity, the talent, and if you're lucky, they'll die young. Your best bet is to find one who's vaguely critically admired but also Top 40 material. It wouldn't hurt if he has an accent. Voilà. Instant exposure, minimal indignity.

Not that I understood any of this when I met Oliver. I just got lucky. But in retrospect he was perfect: The don't-give-a-shit attitude. The dry English wit. The alcoholic thirst of forty Russian men.

I was fifteen, and I'd just moved to L.A. We'd moved because my mother wasn't quite ready to relinquish her then-husband, Jakob Elsinger, a Swiss banker of appropriately clockwork dependability who had been drawn to Southern California's equally clockwork climate. My mother initially opposed the move — "America is so tiresome," she'd say with a languid sigh, conveniently ignoring the fact that she *was* American — but Köbi talked her into it. He had a way of doing that. He was the only one of them who ever could. I can't believe I never asked him to teach me how.

But I thought I knew everything back then.

I couldn't wait to leave Switzerland. I was sick of the endless parade of tutors, of the long, lonely hours with nothing to do and no one to see. I'd argued that I should be allowed to go away to boarding school, but my mother never seriously entertained the notion, and not even Köbi could get her to budge on that one. My mother meant to homeschool me once we got to California, too, but I exercised the nuclear option: I registered at the nearest public high school.

She agreed to let me go to one of those fancy hush-hush private schools easily enough after that.

I loved my new school. Not the actual coursework, of course, although I secretly appreciated the chance to learn something other than party manners and European decorative arts. The social side of things, though, was another matter entirely. Oh, the glorious *rapacity* of those children. They didn't have teeth; they were born with fangs (slash publicists). I can't tell you how refreshing this was, how invigorating. I'd spent a lifetime living with a pathologically discreet mother in a world where overt ambition was akin to leprosy. Los Angeles was an Irish Spring body wash of a city.

After just three weeks in the company of my classmates I had acquired more practical cultural knowledge than I had in three years with the finest tutors in Europe. *I* may not have been born with fangs, but that's where I learned to sharpen my talons. And also to apply fake lashes.

Meanwhile, my mother was floating on a cloud of charity functions and plastic-surgery consults, and Köbi could see the ocean from his twelfth-floor office. It seemed a perfect arrangement. I was almost happy.

But then my mother fucked it up. She and Köbi had been fighting for months, so it didn't come as a *total* surprise when it happened. By that point their marriage had begun to remind me of one of those African lakes that burp out poisonous gas, and every time I went to sleep I wondered if I'd suffocate in my sleep. And so I knew that eventually one day I would come home from school to find my mother having Kö-bi's things packed up. I even knew what she would say: "I suppose you'll blame me for this, too."

I didn't know that she would threaten to take me out of school.

Well, fuck that noise.

That's when I decided to go for a walk down Robertson to a bar I'd seen once when I made the mistake of letting my driver cut through Culver City.

It wasn't the nicest of places. The bar was backlit with red LEDs, which at night probably effected a sort of Eurotrashy glow, but in the middle of the day it just felt like we were all sitting under one of those heat lamps they use to keep Big Macs warm. The barstool was too hard beneath me, with a curved metal back that presumed some kind of scoliosis, and the glasses tasted like detergent.

I was three vodkas in when Oliver sat down two stools over. I barely registered his presence, much less his identity. I remember distantly noting the round-toned rumble of his voice as he ordered — "whiskey, rocks, yeah?" — but I was otherwise uninterested. *Judge Judy* was on.

"A little young for this place, aren't you?" was the first thing Oliver said to me.

I looked over. There were two of him — my eyes had already gone dopey from the booze — but I could tell that he had a runner's build, lithe and muscular. He wore jeans and a T-shirt. And not a novelty one. It was just plain blue cotton. On the bar in front of him was an inexpensive phone and a yellow pack of cigarettes. In another city this might've meant he was just a normal guy, but in L.A. it was nothing less than a masterfully conspicuous repudiation of conspicuousness. I was impressed.

"Probably," I said.

We sipped our drinks in silence. He ordered another.

"You live here?" he asked.

"For now."

I could hear the ice cubes rattle in his glass as he swirled it. When I imagine the noise a brain makes as it's cogitating, this is still the sound I think of.

"You like it?" he asked.

"What's not to like? And don't say something tedious like 'the traffic.' "

"I was going to say 'the locals.' "

When I looked at him this time I managed to ratchet my eyes into something approaching focus, and as his two images converged, they went solid where they met — a Venn diagram of a man. It was in that

334

intersection where I finally recognized not just who he was but what he was: the way I was going to keep myself in California.

In one beautiful moment, everything I'd ever learned crystallized into a perfect, glittering plan.

My mother thought she could hide me away again? Then I'd just turn myself into someone who was impossible to hide.

I sidled over to him, pulled out one of his cigarettes, rolled it between my fingers.

"Give a girl a light?"

We ended up back at his place. I was as awkward as a preschool Christmas pageant, and he was kinder than he needed to be. Holding my hand during. Talking to me after. The next morning, when we woke up together, I was warm and hungover, and I almost changed my mind.

Then he reached over and ruffled my hair. "I'm going to take a shower," he said. "It's been fun."

I went downstairs, shoes in hand. I tiptoed past the second-floor terrace and the first-and-a-halfth-floor deck and the first-floor pool, and then on through to the white-on-white kitchen he obviously never used. I leaned against the counter and let my feet fall flat to the concrete floor, soaking up the chill. I opened the refrigerator and pulled out a beer. By the time Oliver came downstairs, I was on my second.

"I thought you'd left," he said.

"Not yet."

He just stood there.

"There's coffee, if you want it."

"Uh — brilliant, thanks."

I waited until he'd filled a mug and lit a cigarette before I told him.

"You know I'm not eighteen," I said.

"Neither am I."

"I mean I'm not *yet* eighteen."

"So what?"

"Oh," I said, flattening my lips into the neither-smile-nor-frown of pitying superiority. "I forgot. It's probably different in England."

"I don't follow."

"See, in California, fucking me's a felony."

His mug crashed onto the counter. "Bullshit."

"Sorry, mate."

He rubbed his hand over the back of his head in a manner I found deeply satisfying. "But you were right there with me —"

"Doesn't matter," I said. "But don't worry, there's an easy enough way to fix this."

He eyed me warily — though that could

have just been because my mascara was all smeared to shit. "What do you want?"

"Just a little favor."

"Why does that sound too easy?"

I reached over and ran my knuckle across his cheekbone. "It's a pretty long favor."

Oliver and I were together for three months, playing off our looks, charm, and the titillating possibility that what we were doing might be illegal. He consistently encouraged rumors that our relationship was chaste, and I consistently encouraged rumors that it wasn't, earning him female fans and me male fans. It was wildly mutually beneficial, as firm a foundation for a partnership as anything.

But you have to walk away from the table eventually, and as soon as the press started reporting on Oliver's wandering eye I knew it was time. It's not that I particularly minded the acts themselves — after that first night neither one of us ever wanted to touch the other again — I just minded the indiscretion. I wasn't about to become the victim. It wasn't sympathy I was after.

Lucky for me, at that time his drug use was spiraling, because even clever Oliver couldn't sidestep every cliché. And then, wouldn't you know? I just happened to be with him the night he overdosed.

(By the way, he was never in any *real* danger of dying. I just needed him to get close enough that I could reasonably claim to have saved him. You don't really think I'd have done anything like this without having studied a toxicology textbook, do you?)

I was the one who called 911; I was also the one who called E! The next day's photos of Oliver being rolled into the ER on a gurney while I ran alongside in the five-inch Louboutins I'd picked out specially were some of my most fetching ever.

I suppose I could have stayed with Oliver. Stuck by him. Been the girl to reform him. Gotten him off the booze and the drugs. Professed my love for him to *People* magazine.

Or I could have gone out the very next night and shimmied up against a succession of chiseled-face models.

Guess which one I chose?

But it was better for us both, really.

(Plus, honestly? After he got out of rehab his music went to shit.)

After Oliver, it didn't take long to figure out how to game the system. Within a month I'd managed to trade my obscurity for burgeoning notoriety; within six I no longer had to introduce myself to strangers.

A year and a half later, just a few weeks before my mother died, I scored my first magazine cover. I didn't even have to leak a sex tape to do it. (Not that I wouldn't have.)

And the sad truth is, it wasn't even that hard. All it took was a drunk hunk and a battered copy of Clausewitz and understanding that when it comes to fame, there's no difference between being loved and being hated. One's just much easier to do. If you can stand it.

BEHIND THE MUSIC:
"OLIVER LAWSON"
Transcript, pt. 4

Narrator: Many have said that Lawson hit rock bottom when he embarked on a relationship with Janie Jenkins, the infamous Hollywood celebutante who would later be convicted of her mother's murder.

Oliver: Obviously it was quite a tempestuous relationship. She was very controlling, and I know that seems implausible given how young she was, but believe me: She never acted her age.

Yes, you said, to me
But I wasn't thinking
I wasn't seeing
Which now I know
Was exactly what you wanted

Yes, fantastically
And we moved together
And it seemed like pleasure
Which now I know
Wasn't ever what you needed

Narrator: After the split, Lawson went to rehab for drug and alcohol abuse. The first song he produced after his release was "Yes/No/Maybe," the symphonic ballad that would end up being the biggest hit of his career.

Oliver: I wrote that while I was staying in a sober-living house up in Malibu. It was a good time for me, I was really digging deep into my emotions and confronting my imperfections, and that helped me get back in touch with my music. Because I just think that's where all our great music comes from — from a place of honesty and humility. That's how we make art.

No, you said, to me
At my weakest moment
When my pride was broken
Which now I know
Was the thing you found most thrilling

No, impossibly
How I tried to take it
How I tried to fake it
Which now I know
Was the plan from the beginning

Narrator: And then, just one year later, Jenkins was arrested for the murder of her mother. Lawson proved to be a key character witness at the trial.

Oliver: The fact that I testified against her shocked some people, I think. After all, she was the one who got me to the hospital that night — I might not be here if it weren't for her. But I knew her better than anyone, and I knew that it was my responsibility to make sure that the jury heard my perspective. I always said that Jane could do anything if she put her mind to it . . . but I was always scared about what she'd decide to put her mind to.

And maybe, I said
And can't we, I said
And why not
And I can
And you can
And we can

But no, remorselessly
And you walked away then
With your heart unladen
Which now I know
Is the only thing that saved me
. . . maybe

CHAPTER TWENTY-TWO

"What kind of dinner do we get to have tonight?" I said as Leo and I fought our way into the VFW coatroom.

"Am I the only one who reads the schedule? Why does Cora even bother photocopying these things? We're not having dinner — we're dancing."

I froze. "You're fucking with me."

Leo pulled a crumpled piece of yellow paper out of his back pocket and handed it to me. "Not about this."

He hung up my coat and pulled me out into the main room, where I saw for myself that he was telling the truth. Christ. I hadn't seen so many bad dancers since I went to that Radiohead concert.

"Cora makes us all take a lesson before the big thing on Saturday," Leo explained. "The party, ball, whatever she calls it."

"And you all just — go along with this?"

He shrugged. "It makes her happy. And I

heard this year there's crème brûlée. Come on — but watch out for Cora. She insists that all the out-of-town guests take lessons. If she sees you, you'll be stuck dancing for hours. Try not to let her catch your eye."

Cora caught my eye.

She waved, and Leo backed away. "Better you than me."

I looked behind me on the off chance that Cora had been waving to somebody else.

No such luck.

I headed over. Cora was talking to Stanton, one hand placed entreatingly on his arm. "I would just be so grateful if you could help out with the lesson tonight," she was saying.

Stanton shook his head. "I'm afraid you're my only worthy partner, my dear — and you'll be too busy with the beginners."

"Now Stanton, charm won't get you out of this one."

"I'd be a miserable teacher. Where you see potential I see impossibility."

"Well, if you won't teach, at least treat Rebecca here to a dance." She reached over and pulled me forward. "We can't leave our single guests without partners."

He hesitated only briefly — his gaze snagging on my sea-green cardigan — before his manners reasserted themselves. "It would be a pleasure, of course."

I took his hand. It was solid and callused and strong, and I couldn't help but look at it in some surprise. He laughed, reading my face perfectly. "I'm not that old," he said. "Now come, child."

We moved to the center of the room. He placed his hand precisely under my left shoulder blade. I caught the hint of a frown — I was too short for his arm to be at the proper angle, and I suspected he knew it — but his brow smoothed over when I raised our joined hands to my eye level and firmed my wrists and elbows. I felt an unfamiliar flare of satisfaction. I hadn't waltzed in years, but goddammit, I still had it.

A new song started, and we began to move, from strong to long to tall step. God, I love the waltz, the way the elegance of the one-count draws your attention away from the restlessness of the two-three. And I'd forgotten how relaxing a compulsory posture could be.

"Is this Prokofiev?" Stanton asked.

"Khachaturian," I said without thinking — I had the sense that Stanton wasn't the sort of man who liked to be wrong.

"Yes, of course," he said. He kept his hand firmly on my back, settling us further into the music, into its rise and fall. For once the noises inside my head surrendered to the sounds outside it.

Briefly, anyway. I'm not going to lie, their speaker setup was pretty crap.

"You dance very nicely, Miss Parker."

"I had lessons."

"How unusual."

I turned my head toward Leo. He was standing with Eli, a bottle of beer hanging loosely from his hand.

Stanton and I whirled away.

When Leo came back into view, he was watching me. He tipped his beer in my direction. Then we whirled once more, and he was gone. I searched the room, but he'd disappeared. The faint glow of pleasure the waltz had kindled in me was snuffed out.

"I wish my son shared your interest in classical music," Stanton was saying. He maneuvered us into the corner where Mitch was sitting with a group of other mid-to-late-forty-something men and a case of Coors. I felt the distaste shudder through him. "But I suppose not all parents can be so lucky."

Mitch crushed a beer can and lobbed it toward the trash can. It missed.

"John Mitchell Percy," Stanton barked.

Mitch and his friends sat up.

"While I realize that you are beyond

humiliation," Stanton said, "at least try to pretend otherwise in my presence."

He led us to the other side of the room with a grunt of displeasure.

I felt the strangest urge to defend Mitch. "He seems very popular," I said.

"You say that as if it were some kind of achievement."

"Isn't it?"

Stanton drew me into a neat little arch turn, his movements so deft that I felt as if my hand was floating up over my head of its own accord. As I spun, the cuffs of my slacks — the closest thing I had to petticoats — rose up, and a draft blew against my exposed ankles. I looked behind me. Someone had left the door ajar.

When I was brought around to face Stanton again, his smile had waned. "There's no need to pretend you like the look of him either," he said.

"I'm hardly one to comment on a person's looks."

His arms sagged momentarily before snapping back into position. "And here I thought you were going to be interesting."

"Excuse me?"

He spun me out and back in. "I loathe self-deprecation."

"Because it's phony?"

"Because it's easy."

"And what's so bad about that?"

"If it's easy, it's not worth doing."

"Try telling that to a sixteen-year-old boy."

His eyelids flickered. "Wit, my dear, is even easier."

"So what does that leave?"

"Strength of character, of course."

The music came to a close; I pulled away two beats early. Though I'm sure no one else noticed.

Just after Stanton withdrew, a crackle of laughter from Mitch's table caught my attention. Mitch's hands were moving in huge oily swoops that could have been outlining either a woman's body or a hot-air balloon. He leaned over and whispered in his buddy's ear, eliciting a smirk, then stood up and headed to the restrooms that were located off a dark little hall. When he got to the men's room, he looked back over his shoulder — scanning the room but missing me — and stepped inside.

Moments later, Rue pushed away from her table full of teenagers. She opened the same door.

Interesting. And gross.

I mean, sure, there's something to be said for bathroom assignations. There's no awkwardness about whether or not anyone is going to stay the night. There's no room to get creative, so you don't have to worry about anything other than the bare (ha ha) minimum. Sure, you never feel too good about yourself after, but at least you get it over with.

But it isn't quite the same when the parties in question are a man in his forties and a girl in her teens.

I glanced around the room, but other than Mitch's beer-bellied friend, no one else seemed to have noticed what was happening. I kept my eye on the bathroom doors and waited for them to reemerge.

Rue returned after a few minutes, unnecessarily smoothing the ends of her hair — it was only mussed on top. A growl tried to fight its way out of my chest, but I shook it off. Rue was a big girl; she could protect herself. And right now, it was Mitch I cared about — I couldn't imagine catching him in a more vulnerable position. It was the perfect time to ask a few questions.

I slipped across the room and down the hall. When I opened the door to the men's room, Mitch was tucking in his shirt. His belt, I noticed, wasn't even undone.

"Well, hello there," he said easily.

I took a step back. Didn't he realize he'd

been caught? "I beg your pardon," I said.

He put one hand on the doorframe above my head, positioning his armpit directly in front of my face. "I do love it when they beg," he said.

I realized then that I just might have miscalculated. This man wasn't remotely vulnerable.

I glanced to my left, but my view of the dining room — and my escape route — was blocked by the open door. "I'm sorry," I said. "I thought this was the ladies' room."

His other hand shot out and grabbed my elbow. "You're the one who was dancing with my father. You sure you don't want to trade up to a newer model?"

"You sure you don't want to rethink being such a *dick*?"

The hand above me clenched, and a vein throbbed in his neck. I took a breath and another step back.

Calm the fuck down, Jane.

"Look," I said. "I just wanted to use the bathroom."

His brow furrowed.

"This *is* the bathroom, right?"

"Have I seen you somewhere before?" he asked. "I mean, before tonight."

"The other night at the bar, maybe."

"No — before that." He tilted his head,

and his eyes caught the light from above the sink. They were a familiar shade of navy blue. ("Like the blood of a horseshoe crab," Oliver once told me, and he didn't mean it as a compliment.) Crystal's words from the night before came roaring up into my mind:

Instead I had to watch him with girls like fucking Tessa Kanty.

I couldn't keep myself from saying the words: "Do you have any kids, Mitch?"

He reared back. "What? Um — yes, three. Why?"

"Any daughters?"

"One."

"Are you sure about that?"

He shook his head helplessly. "I don't understand —"

Something even uglier than usual burrowed up out of me, crowding out all the questions I should have been asking.

"What's her name? Your daughter, I mean."

"Uh — Madelyn."

"Tell me, Mitch, what would you do if you found out that Madelyn was sneaking into public restrooms to suck some middle-aged man's cock?"

He paled. "I don't know who you think you are, but —"

"You're a father," I said. "Fucking act like one."

I spun on my heel and walked away.

The Running (Wo)man
Celebrity News
November 7, 2013 at 12:14 AM
By Us Weekly Staff

Recent information has come to light regarding the whereabouts of the nation's most glamorous ex-con, Janie Jenkins. Trace Kessler, who runs the blog "Without a Trace" and is offering a substantial cash reward for information that leads directly to the discovery of her location, speculated yesterday that Jenkins could likely be tracked from one of the towns along Amtrak's California Zephyr line.

Today our reporters contacted rental car agencies and taxi dispatchers in these areas. While they found no sign of anyone fitting Jenkins's description, when they called to check at hotels within walking distance of the train stations in question, they came across a small motel in McCook, Nebraska. The same night Jenkins was seen on the California Zephyr, a single guest by the name of Coralie Jones checked into this motel just forty minutes after the train came through.

Security footage shows only a figure in a

heavy coat and a bulky hat, but according to the desk clerk on duty at the time, the guest had dark brown hair and glasses. If Jenkins was indeed the woman who checked into this motel, the search for her whereabouts may soon be coming to an end.

CHAPTER TWENTY-THREE

By the time I emerged from the bathroom, Rue was already on her way out, waving at her friends across the room with a secretive little smile designed to make them wonder where she could possibly be going. It made me wonder, too.

I had to hurry to catch up with her, and I was outside and halfway down the block before I'd even pulled my arms through my coat sleeves. I could see Rue up ahead, walking briskly. The urgency of her movements suggested she had somewhere more important to be than a party, like maybe she was a presidential aide who had to deliver a last-minute edit of the State of the Union. I ran up to her.

"Rue! Wait!" She stuttered midstep, then pivoted prettily toward me on the ball of one foot. Cora must have made her take dance lessons too.

"What?"

"I left my room key at the front desk." I held out my hands, shaking them a little, as if to say, *nothing up my sleeves!*

Her head tipped back, her arms fell limp at her sides, and she let loose an agonized groan. "Seriously?"

"Sorry."

She huffed. "Fine, whatever, let's go," she said.

She turned and headed toward the inn. I tagged after.

"Are you on your way somewhere fun?" I asked. "Like a party or something?"

She laughed. "Why, you want to come along?"

I fell silent. As we walked, I found myself admiring Rue. She had the posture of a debutante and the gait of a supermodel, all innocent shoulders and knowing hips. It was a neat trick.

Rue unlocked the door to the inn and pushed me inside. She went immediately to the front desk, surefooted even in the dark. "What room are you in again?"

"Eight." I wiped off my glasses with the sleeve of my jacket and positioned myself in the archway between the foyer and the reception desk — or, rather, between Rue and the front door.

I heard a muttered curse, and the desk

lamp came on. Rue's expression was twisting with increasing annoyance. "It's gotta be here somewhere," she muttered.

"Oh, I'm in no hurry."

She gave me a look that could have melted tungsten. I let her search for another minute or two just for that.

Then I pulled out my key and shook it. Rue looked up. "Oops," I said. "Guess I had it all along."

"What the hell?"

"Sorry," I said. "I'm sort of making this up as I go along."

"I don't understand."

"I just need a quick moment of your time." I took a step forward. "I want *Jane Eyre.*"

"If you're that desperate for a reread, the library opens at nine."

"No, I want *your* copy, please. The one you took from your father's house in Adeline."

Rue's eyes narrowed. "That was you?"

I shrugged and said the word that always came far too easily. "Guilty."

"Look, I don't — no, you know what? I'm calling my mother." She pulled out her phone and headed for the door, but I stepped in front of her before she could get too far. "What do you think you're —"

"How long have you been fucking Mitch Percy?"

Her fingers stilled.

"He's very handsome," I prompted.

She slid her phone back into her pocket. "If you like that sort of thing."

"The good-looking sort of thing?"

She flipped her hair. "The past-his-peak sort of thing. I guess he was a big deal back in the day or whatever, but he's not exactly a badge of honor now. Just another ex–prom king who still hangs out with all his buddies from high school. Now he has hair in his ears and only uses the law degree Stanton bought him as a way to pick up girls."

"Seemed to work on you well enough."

"I picked *him* up, not the other way around."

"You sure about that?"

Silence.

"Is it for his money?" I asked. "Because I have to tell you, that doesn't usually work out so well."

"I'm Cora Kanty's daughter. I don't need money."

My smile was sure and slow. "Oh, never mind — I know. Either your mother wants him or your father hates him."

"I don't have to listen to this —"

"But if that's the case, why are you still

keeping things under wraps? Wouldn't you *want* Mommy and Daddy to find out? What's your plan, Rue?"

"He has nothing to do with my plan. I'm just killing time until I can get the fuck out of here."

"So go. What's keeping you?"

"I can't just run away — I'm seventeen."

"You're scared, is what you're saying."

"I am not. I just can't do *shit* without permission."

As soon as I heard the hint of panic in her voice I knew it was time. *Go big or go home, Jane.* I took a breath.

"That didn't stop your aunt," I said.

"Yeah, but she was eight—" She cut herself off. "How do you know about my aunt?"

"Give me the book, Rue."

"Who *are* you?"

I ran the back of my thumbnail over my eyebrow. Thinking. Then I shrugged off my coat, folded it over my arm, and held my hands out for hers. "Might as well get comfortable," I said. "This might take awhile."

She followed me upstairs without another word.

When we got to my room I went to the

window and pulled the curtains closed. I poked my head in the bathroom, peeked behind the shower curtain, and shut the door. Next I hesitated, not wanting to look silly in front of Rue, but then — *fuck it* — I checked under the bed anyway.

Then I patted the bed's woven coverlet and gestured for her to sit beside me. She perched as close to the edge as she could without falling off.

"I'm not sure how to put this," I began.

"You're not some sort of psycho killer here to chop me up and eat my fingers, are you?"

"Not quite."

This didn't seem to comfort her. But then, it wasn't meant to.

"You asked who I was," I said, "and I think you deserve to know: I'm Tessa's daughter."

She shot to her feet. "Bullshit. You look nothing like her."

I sighed. "No," I said. "I never did."

"Why should I believe you?"

"You really think I'm here for the *festival*?"

Her shoulders fell. She was the last person who could fault that logic. "So where is she now?"

Forest Lawn Memorial, probably, but Rue didn't need to know that. "I'm not sure —

that's one of the reasons I'm here. To find her."

Her mouth fell open. "You don't know where she is?"

My mouth fell open, too. We must have looked like those carnival clowns you target with water guns.

"Don't tell me *that* was your plan? You were going to go *find* her? What the fuck did you think would happen? That she'd take you in? Be your new mommy? You don't know anything about her."

She lunged for her bag and withdrew *Jane Eyre,* brandishing it in my face. "I know plenty." I grabbed for the book, but that doe-eyed whippersnapper was quicker than I would have thought — and taller. She held me off with one arm and kept the book out of my reach with her other.

"Okay, so — look," she said. "I'll give this to you, but only if you promise to tell me about her." I must have appeared uncon-vinced, because she rushed on, going for the sympathy vote. "Please. My dad won't tell me anything. I just want to know what she's like."

I had a sudden image of her lying in my mother's dusty old bed, dressed up in the "fashionable" clothes she stored in my mother's old closet, reading my mother's old diary like it was a copy of *In Style,* dreaming of the glamorous life she'd soon be sharing in.

Role models. At least that's one crime I'm innocent of.

"I'm going to regret this," I said, shifting onto my back. "What do you want to know?"

Her voice, when at last she decided to use it, was almost impossibly small. "Is she very beautiful?"

I pressed the heel of my hand into my forehead. "After however many years you've been stuck on this planet, you finally, *finally* meet your long-lost cousin, the one person in the world who maybe actually knows anything about this aunt you inexplicably admire, and you have the chance to ask her *anything* — and that's what you want to know? Is she pretty?"

"I don't know, it seemed a good place to start."

"Fuck me."

She stiffened. "Look, if you don't want the book, that's fine —"

"Okay, yes, fine. My mother — when last I saw her, anyway — was very beautiful."

"What does she do?"

"Not much of anything, really —"

Rue held up the book again, waggling it

362

like a tambourine.

"Charity work," I said. "She does charity work. She really likes to give back. Like — to the earth."

She frowned. "I always thought she'd be a model or something."

"It's really not that different."

"Did she ever talk about us?"

I paused, trying to figure out whether to tell her what she wanted to hear or what I wanted her to hear. "No," I said eventually. "But . . . I'm sure you were always on her mind. That's why I came. I thought I might find her here."

"She would never come back. She hated it here."

In retrospect, it was Rue's certainty that set me off. I mean, what the fuck did she know about my mother, anyway? What the fuck did *anyone* know about her? My whole life I've been hearing shit like this, from stepfathers and staff and prosecutors and character witnesses. "You have to understand about your mother," they'd say, which really just means "I am absolutely sure you won't understand anything at all." I was the last person in the world who needed to be told anything about my mother. The irregularities in my orbit might have been the result of her gravitational pull, but I was the one who was visible to the naked eye. I was the one you had to look at to know she was there. *I* was the proof of *her* existence, not the other way around.

"She hated it everywhere," I said. "You wouldn't know it to look at her, but she *loved* hating it everywhere. She had a genius for it, really, for mining unpleasantness wherever she went so she could hate something that wasn't herself. And if she couldn't, well — that's where I came in."

"Jesus, chill, I get it — you've got issues. Tell it to your therapist."

I realized then that I'd risen to my feet and was doing something with my hand that was humiliatingly close to shaking my fist.

"Did she ever get to Switzerland?" Rue asked.

I sat down heavily. "Is that why you have all those posters?"

"You were in my room?"

I waved a hand. "I was looking for the bathroom."

"She wrote about it," she said after a moment. " 'Switzerland is a country that knows —' "

" '— how to keep its secrets.' Yeah, I've heard that one before." I caught my breath. "So I'm assuming the copy of *Jane Eyre* is her diary?"

She nodded and handed me the book. I opened it and rifled through the pages, not surprised to see strings of unreadable letters written between the lines of printed text.

"It's in code," she said.

"Thanks for the insight."

She looked at me as if she were seeing me for the first time, then reached over and put a finger next to a page number. "That's how you know the date. Page one is January first, page two is January second, and so on."

"How'd you figure that out?"

"She mentions her birthday."

"When's that?" I asked without thinking.

Rue blinked. "February eighth."

"Of course. How could I have forgotten?" I cleared my throat. "And how do you know what year it was?"

"She complained about the hundredth anniversary celebration — and *Police Academy 2*. That kind of cinched it."

"What's this code she's writing in?"

"It's, like, one of those things you find on the back of cereal boxes. It's really easy. See here — here's the last entry." She turned to page 227. "August fifteenth," she said.

ETBJ SGHR OKZBD

"Count ahead one letter."

I translated — and let out a bark of laughter. Rue gave me a tentative smile. "She's funny," she said, looking to me for confirmation.

My own smile faded. I turned back to the book and pointed at a tiny circle that had been drawn on the top right corner of the page. "What does that mean?"

She shrugged. "I don't know, but there's one on every page." She turned a few pages back to show me.

"And here I thought you'd uncovered all her secrets. Maybe it's time to go back to spy school, huh?"

"God, do you have to be such a bitch about everything?"

"Yes, actually, because that's the only way you'll listen to me."

"I'm not a child, you know."

"When you're my age you might see things differently."

She leaned forward and squinted at my face. "How old are you, anyway?"

"Twenty-six — oh, shit, no, I guess I'm twenty-seven. Fuck." I scrubbed a hand over my face. "Never mind. Just — look, does she say anything about —" I stopped myself before I said "Eli." I took a breath, changed my approach. I couldn't ask the girl about her dad. "Does she say anything about any boyfriends?" I asked instead.

"Not really," Rue said. "She just sort of wrote down when she went out with whoever it was. I don't know his name — she just called him 'J.' "

I started. "J?"

"Yeah, you might have heard of it: It's the letter that comes before K."

Enough already. I came to my feet. "You know what? We're done here. Thanks for the book, thanks for playing, don't forget to tip your waitress."

"So you can dish it out but you can't take it?"

"You know why no one will tell you anything about Tessa?" I said. "Because they're *embarrassed.* Because she got away, but she didn't win." I hesitated, felt the wisp of a thought begin to materialize, then shook it away. "If you think Tessa was so wonderful, fine, go ahead, be just like her — you've already got a great head start. And I'm sure in thirty years all the little girls will sit by their windows at night and dream of becoming you in their turn. 'Please God,' they'll say, 'Please let me grow up to be the girl who blew Mitch Percy in a bathroom stall.' "

"Already thinking you know what's best for me? Now I know you're family for sure."

She grabbed her coat and bag, then paused. "And what do you know, anyway? Who's to say your version of your mother isn't just as made up as mine?"

I would have thrown the diary at her, but she'd already closed the door.

I fell back on the bed. I breathed deeply and dragged my thumb across the edge of the book, across and across and across again, riffling the pages, letting the shush of the paper and snap of the cover gentle my thoughts and ease my mind.

Shush, snap. Shush, snap.

I took a moment to admire the plaster-work on the ceiling.

Shush, snap. Shush, snap.

I watched the pages blur by under the press of my thumb. Letters and numbers and circles flashed before my eyes.

Shush, snap. Shush —

I sat up. Circles. I opened the diary to the first page. In the upper right was a small circle. But this one was filled in. I ran my thumb along the pages again, this time as I would with a flipbook. I watched as the circles went from empty to solid to empty. Like the phases of the moon. I counted the number of pages between solids: twenty-eight, give or take.

She'd been charting her menstrual cycle. I was sure of it.

I counted back from the last entry to the last solid circle. Forty-six days. Then I flipped forward another fourteen pages or so, hoping I remembered tenth-grade biology correctly. Tessa had written only one entry around the time she would have conceived, on July thirteenth.

CNMS BGHBJDM NTS. I HR VNQSG HS. "Don't chicken out. J is worth it."

I closed the book and closed my eyes.

Mitch might not start with J— but Jared sure as hell did.

I really, really needed to get that police file.

CHAPTER TWENTY-FOUR

It was 3:00 in the morning, and Leo's lights were on. I was trying to decide if that was good or bad.

I'd been watching his windows for two hours at that point. I'd circled the house three times, clinging to the dark and the quiet, avoiding broken branches and scattered motorcycle parts and particularly crunchy-looking leaves. The first-floor curtains were open, but Leo wasn't in the living room, the dining room, or the kitchen. I didn't know the layout of the second floor, but the house was old enough that, even if I couldn't see him, surely I should have been able to hear him. If he was in there, he was asleep. Or maybe he was drunk. Or maybe he knew I was coming.

Regardless, the silence unsettled me. I guess for some people silence can be restful, or even a relief: a cry that's been soothed, an ache that's been eased, a wittle wabbit that's been cuddled up close. But for me it's just the moment before the monster comes back to life.

I picked at the bark of a denuded tree and again eyed the dog flap on the back door. The night was cold and damp, and what must have once been a rosebush was pressing into the back of my neck, but still I held off. A few thorns seemed better than the alternative. If I woke Leo up, I didn't think he would be too happy to see me.

Except the alternative also meant not having Leo's keys, and that meant I'd never get access to those police records. Short of a swingers' party, breaking into his house was the best way I could think to proceed.

Also, I guess I was kind of starting to enjoy a good breaking and entering.

I crossed the yard and knelt next to the kitchen door. I pulled up the dog flap and looked inside. The room was empty and nearly silent. All I could hear was the soft hum of the refrigerator. I let out a little nicker and waited for the clatter of tiny paws, but nothing came. Hopefully that meant the dog was asleep.

I took off my coat, balled it up, and shoved it through the flap. I peeled off the heavy cable-knit sweater I'd put on back at the inn and shoved it through, too. My hat and gloves went next. I was left with just one layer, a mock turtleneck that was two sizes too large. I winced as the chill knifed into me. The wind was calmer here than it was on Main Street, but it was still sharp enough to sting.

I examined the dog door. It was higher than it was wide, so I'd need to go through sideways. It shouldn't be too hard. I'd done an assload of yoga back in the day, and this was just a variant on four-limbed staff pose — right? I stretched my arms over my head and began to ease my way through. As soon as my shoulders were clear, I tried to lift my body up off the ground, but my arms weren't strong enough, and I couldn't find the leverage. I kicked ineffectually, the door frame digging into my side where my shirt had rucked up.

I threw out my right arm, my fingers just glancing across the leg of the kitchen table. I took a deep breath and stretched my arm out again. I groped for the leg until — finally — my fingers curled around it. I dragged myself forward. I heard something tear and felt a sting, but then I was through.

I rolled over and checked my ribs and hip. The skin was, if not an angry red, then at least a bad-tempered pink, and pinpricked with blood. There was a larger cut down near my hipbone. I rolled my shirt back down and pressed it against the wound. It wouldn't do to leave blood on Leo's floor.

I reached down, retrieved my clothes, and slipped on my gloves. Sure, they were thick winter gloves that made my hands as big and clumsy as bear paws, but you know what bear paws don't have? Fingerprints.

I put my hands on my hips and examined the room.

Now, if I were keys, where would I hide?

The first floor was decidedly lacking in hiding places. Apart from the empty picture frame on the mantel, the living room looked no different than it had before. The philodendron needed water, maybe. The dining room's sole furnishing was an area rug ghosted with the impressions of the table and chairs that had once been there. And the kitchen was stocked with little more than beer, soap, and kibble — and also a jar of peanut butter, which I grabbed and put in my pocket.

I crept upstairs, my footsteps muffled by the faded blue runner, and came to a study. If Leo spent much time in this room, he clearly didn't spend it working: The item of greatest value in the desk drawers was a loose spring from a retractable pen. The file cabinet contained folders labeled in a neat feminine hand. Recipes. Appliance manuals. Tax records. Nothing unusual. Certainly nothing that would unlock the police station.

The door to the other room was closed. I pressed my ear against it, listening for signs of life, human, canine, or otherwise. I eased the door open. The air was thick with a sweet-sour sweatiness underlaid with — bourbon? Perfume? Sometimes I mistake the two.

I peered at the bed. There were too many lumps to count. I couldn't tell if he was alone or not.

I took off a glove and opened the jar of peanut butter. I scooped out a finger-full, which I waved back and forth in front of me like a censer. Seconds later, there was movement on the bed. Two little eyes opened, two little ears came up. Bones jumped down, scurried over, and leaped up on my knees, attacking me with his wet nose and tongue. I scratched the back of his neck; he wiggled happily. I let him lick the peanut butter off my finger while I pressed my face into his fur.

Then, reluctantly, I flung a glob of peanut butter out into the hall. Bones chased after. *That should keep him busy for a while.*

I shoved my hand back in my glove and

pulled myself to my feet. My hip was throbbing and sticky with blood. I jabbed it with
a fist. I had to squeeze my eyes shut against
the pain, but when I opened them again my
vision was clearer. This time when I looked
at the bed I could tell — I let out a breath
— that Leo was alone.

I moved forward, wary, pausing each time
I felt a floorboard start to give. I pulled open
his nightstand drawer as cautiously as if I
were removing the uranium core from an
ICBM. The sheets rustled; I nearly puked
up my heart. I looked down at Leo's face,
searching for signs of awareness, but his
breathing was low and steady, and his
eyelids were undulating in some kind of a
dream. He smacked his lips, then fell silent
and still.

I looked in the drawer — nope, no keys,
just spare change, a phone, crumpled re-
ceipts, condoms. *Where else could they be?*
I let my gaze drift around the room. It
landed on Leo's feet, which were sticking
out from under the sheets. I could see the
cuffs of his pants — he'd fallen asleep with
his clothes on. *His keys must be in his pocket.*

I pulled the sheet up from the bottom, so
slowly I thought I might not manage to get
it up past his waist before sunrise, but when
I finally did I saw the bulge in his back

375

pocket. I tugged off one of my gloves with my teeth and slipped a finger and thumb into the pocket. I began to pull on the key fob — he stirred, his feet rubbing sleepily against one another. I held my breath. After a moment his legs settled, and I gave the keys another little pull. But I achieved the same result: little restless movements from Leo, a slight shallowing of his breath.

I turned at a noise from the hallway — but it was just Bones. He was lying on his back, licking his paws. If only men were as easy to handle as dogs.

Wait a second — they totally are.

I bit off my other glove and laid my bare hand on the back of Leo's neck. His skin was slick and hot with sleep, but I didn't let myself flinch back. Instead I threaded my fingers into his hair and, after a moment's hesitation, massaged them gently into his scalp. He relaxed, murmuring something I couldn't make out. I waited for him to exhale, and then I pulled the keys free.

He shook his head once, side to side, and fell still.

But I left my hand on his neck for a few moments more just to be sure.

WITHOUT A TRACE
Thursday 11.7.13

Trace here.

I never thought I'd say this, but bravo to US MEEKLY for having accidentally done some actual investigative journalism. (You shitbirds owe me a 10% commission on your ad revenues for that post, by the way.) So now we know that as of Monday, Janie Jenkins was in McCook, Nebraska. We also know, as I've been saying all along, that she is traveling in DISGUISE. Brown hair and glasses, people. Be on the lookout. We almost have her. JUSTICE will be served.

CHAPTER TWENTY-FIVE

I pressed my face against the police station window, holding my breath so I didn't fog it over. The desks inside were abandoned. The lights were out. The cell was empty — Walt's mom must've finally bailed him out. I unlocked the door and went inside, moving quickly now that I didn't have to worry about rickety floorboards or rickety cops. A few fumbles of the keys later, and I was stepping into the room marked Restricted Entry (i.e., Definitely Don't Look in Here No Seriously There's Nothing Interesting, We Swear). I slipped the keys into my pocket, closed the door behind me, and turned on the lights.

For such a small town the records room was disproportionately large, probably twenty feet by ten, with gray metal cabinets as high as my eyebrows, files stacked precariously on top. I traced the perimeter of the room until I came to Va–Vi. My fingers trembled as I picked through the files. Then I found it: Jared Vincent. I slipped the folder into my bag and headed for the door — and that's when I saw the cabinet labeled Ka–Ke.

I checked my watch. It was just before 5:00. I had plenty of time. And it was just one more folder, right?

As soon as I opened the drawer I knew which file was my mother's: the fattest one of the bunch. I had to use two hands to pull it out. Her record was on top, and it was substantial. She hadn't actually been arrested for anything, but she'd been suspected of just about everything. The items in the police blotter only covered a third of what Tessa had been brought in for — and the records didn't even begin until her eighteenth birthday.

2/08/1985 Possession of a controlled substance
2/14/1985 Traffic violation
3/01/1985 Petty theft
3/04/1985 Traffic violation
3/28/1985 Traffic violation
4/14/1985 Petty theft
4/28/1985 Solicitation

When I got to the last entry, I sucked in a

breath. "Well, fuck me," I said, none too softly.

"What're you doing?" came a singsong voice from behind me.

I swung around to find Walt watching me from the open door. I'd forgotten just how much taller he was than me.

"Where the fuck did you come from?" slipped out.

"The can," he said.

"The one in your cell broken or something?"

"If I sit on it too long it leaves a mark on my ass."

His eyes dropped to the folder. "What are you doing with that?"

I stuffed the folder in my bag. "Historical research," I said. "Now if you'll excuse me, it's past my bedtime."

He grabbed my arm. "I'm going to ask you just one more time: What are you doing with Tessa's file?"

My heart stuttered. "What do you know about Tessa?"

"That you shouldn't be asking after her."

"Hey, look, I'm not trying to cause any trouble," I said. "I'll leave the folder here with you, okay? No harm done. Just — I'd just like to ask you a few questions first, if I could." I lifted my chin and looked him in the eye as best I could. "Please."

All of a sudden, his frown resolved into something else, something fearsome, something that made me think of shadows upon shadows.

"Oh, holy fuck," he said. "You're Janie Jenkins."

When I had thought about this moment — the moment I was Found Out — I'd anticipated terror or sadness or maybe even relief. A grand emotion of some kind, anyway, the stuff of sinking stomachs and heaving bosoms and other emphatic anatomical gestures. But when it finally happened, I didn't feel anything at all. I didn't even think. I just ducked under Walt's arm and ran.

He caught me before I even made it to the door.

He hauled me up by my underarms and carried me out to the main room. He set me on Billy's desk and sat down on the chair in front of me, looking pleased with himself.

"It's actually a pretty good disguise," he said. "Props."

I made another break for it. This time I managed to get a whole foot away before he caught me and plopped me back on the desk.

"My god, you really *don't* think things through, do you?" He shook his head in disbelief. "I guess that explains why you did it the way you did it. I always figured you just couldn't think of a better way. Who would've thought I was actually giving you too much credit?"

"You're referring to my mother, I presume?"

"*Duh-doy.* I mean, a shotgun? Seriously? Hel*lo* forensics."

I squared my shoulders. "I never actually fired that gun."

"So you got the gunshot residue on your hands — how, again? Does Cover Girl put potassium nitrite in its concealer?"

"No, I had residue on my hands because —"

"Oh, right," he said, "I remember: you have a story for that one, too." He leaned closer, his face tight. "You have a story for everything, don't you?"

I let out a noise of pure, animal frustration. "Why do you even care? Is this about the reward money? Because if it is, I'll give you more. Lots more. Hell, I'll set you up with your very own grow op. . . ." I trailed off, catching sight of something over Walt's left shoulder: the cell door was open.

"I don't want your *money,*" Walt was saying. "I want the truth."

I gauged Walt's expression — and the distance between the desk and the cell door.

"Okay," I said slowly. "Truth it is."

He sat back. "I can't wait to hear this."

I took a breath for dramatic purposes. "I never planned on using the gun."

"What?"

"Pills and wine, that would've been the way to go. I thought about that one a lot. I could've just dissolved some Valium into her wine. She had a prescription for about a thousand milligrams a day, so I would have had easy access. And then — here's a neat trick — just for kicks, I could've slipped her some potassium supplements. The raised potassium levels in her vitreous fluid probably would've convinced the coroner that the time of her death was later than it was. An alibi would've been a piece of cake."

A muscle jumped in Walt's jaw. Confidence growing, I slid forward until I was teetering on the edge of the desk.

"There's also nicotine," I said. "It's one of the deadliest poisons on Earth, did you know that? You can cut up some cigarettes and distill it. It might even have been relatively undetectable in a smoker, which my mother secretly was."

I let my toes touch the floor.

"But the easiest way would have been to arrange something when I was out of town. In New York, maybe. Or I could've taken one of those creepy hosting gigs at a club in Vegas. All I would've had to do is loosen the fitting on the gas boiler before I left. At night my mother kept the house tight as a drum — no open windows, no drafty doors. She would have fallen asleep and never woken up."

"So why didn't you?"

My legs tensed.

"It would've been too kind."

Walt never saw it coming. I threw myself at him, pinning his arms and thrusting with my legs as hard as I could, rolling him and the chair back toward the cell door. By the time he realized what was happening, I had momentum on my side. I kicked the chair the rest of the way in and ran for the open door. I pulled Leo's keys from my pocket. Walt hit the back wall and bounced forward. He flew up from his seat and ran at me, one arm outstretched.

I slammed the door on him.

He snatched back his hand, giving me just enough time to shove the biggest key into the lock and send up a prayer. It turned;

the lock clicked into place. The moment I pulled out the key, Walt's other hand shot out from between the bars and grabbed onto my hair, pulling me back toward him. I wrenched myself away, howling when I felt a hank of hair rip from my scalp.

"You *suck,*" he shouted.

We looked at each other, both breathing heavily, him cradling his hand to his chest, me pressing a hand against the back of my skull. It came away wet. This was turning into a rough night.

"Yeah, well, I don't like you much either," I said. "Jesus Christ, that hurt."

"Good," he said. He sat down on the cot; his chin fell to his chest. "I think you broke my hand."

"I did not, don't be a baby."

He scowled. "I don't know what you think this is going to accomplish," he said. "Leo and Billy'll be back in the morning. I'll tell them everything."

"I know," I snapped. "And if you'd just shut up for a second I could figure out what to do."

"You're nuts."

"No *shit.*"

I sat back down, glaring at Walt and rapping my knuckles on the desk. *Leverage, leverage, leverage, where was my leverage?*

"What are you in for, anyway? Possession? Distribution?"

"None of your beeswax."

Oh. Something worse, then.

My smile must have been a very special one, because Walt visibly flinched. He thought I was the dumb one? He may as well have said "restricted entry." I went back to the record room, found Fe–Fr, and returned to the desk. I opened Walt's file. "Drugs, drugs, drugs, boring, boring, boring — ah ha! Breach of computer security and online impersonation? That's interesting. Leo sure never mentioned that."

It wasn't easy to track his eyes, shadowed as they were, but I caught their brisk back-and-forth. I followed the line of his gaze to his bulky black laptop, which was still sitting on Billy's desk from earlier that day.

"Is that yours, Walt?"

His eyes dropped. "No."

"Nice try." I picked up the computer and hugged it to my chest. "Don't worry," I said. "I'm going to put this somewhere *very* safe — which is a particular skill of mine. It kind of runs in the family. And as long as you keep your mouth shut, I'll be happy to give it back when I'm ready to leave town."

"Like I'd believe you," he said.

I held up a middle finger. "Thieves' honor."

"Whatever, take it, see if I care — it's backed up and encrypted anyway."

Liar. I know how to tell when something's important to a person. If I didn't, how would I ever get anything done?

"Sorry, dude, I don't really have any other options, so I'm going to have to call your bluff."

His hand gripped the bars. I could see the white of his knuckles from across the room.

"I'm not going to be stuck here forever, you know."

"Yeah, well, getting out's not all it's cracked up to be."

CHAPTER TWENTY-SIX

A half hour later, I was sitting at the reception desk in the Prospect Inn, strangling my left hand with the telephone cord.

Jared Vincent's folder lay in front of me. Beneath the notes on the robbery and the mountain of paperwork generated by his long list of petty offenses, I'd found his last known address and phone number — from eleven years ago.

For so many reasons, I desperately hoped the address was still up to date.

I checked the time — seven o'clock. Surely someone would be answering by now.

I dialed the number. The phone rang. I swallowed and clutched the receiver.

"Custer County Jail, how may I help you?"

"I'd like to schedule a visit, please. For today, if possible."

"Today's visitation is for last names L through Z. If that's not what you're looking for, you'll have to come back tomorrow."

"No, that's fine."

"Who do you want to see?"

I forced my mouth to move. "Jared Vincent."

As I listened to the sound of keystrokes being entered, I wrapped the cord even more tightly around my wrist. My palm began to swell.

"Do you want to come at nine, nine-twenty, or nine-forty?" the clerk asked.

I opened my hand and let the blood flow back into my fingers.

"Nine, please."

I gave the clerk my details and let the handset fall back into the cradle. It didn't necessarily mean anything that Jared was still in jail, I told myself. He still could have killed my mother somehow — like maybe he had been out on parole or had the wrong kind of friends or commanded an army of demons. But I didn't want that to be true. I wanted him to have the alibi to end all alibis. If he turned out to be who I thought he was, I didn't want our first father-daughter talk to be about how he killed my mother.

I was going to need a ride to the prison, so I searched through the inn's registration book until I found Peter's name and room number, climbed up to his room, and rapped my knuckles against his door. When he answered he was dressed in plaid pajamas, and his hair was matted down on the crown of his head. His eyes were gloopy and confused.

"Rebecca?" I could tell that he wasn't so much asking if I was there as he was confirming that it was actually my name.

I held up Jared's folder and smiled.

"Told you I'd come through. What do you say to a field trip?"

The road to the jail was relatively smooth and straight, but Peter still flinched with every wobble of the wheels. His fingers were clenched together at the top of the steering wheel, and he was leaning so far forward his head was practically pressed against the windshield. The hair on the back of his neck was damp with perspiration. His sweat smelled like bay leaves.

New Yorkers. Useless.

I reached over and unlocked my door in case he took us off the side of a cliff and I needed to make a quick escape.

The part of me that wasn't contingency planning, though, was glad for the distraction. I rubbed at my chest. It was like fucking Mauna Loa in there.

"How'd you get Leo to give the file to

you?" Peter asked.

"I told him how important this story was to you." I paused. "Why *is* this story so important to you?"

"Are you kidding? A small town beauty gone bad? If we can find a picture to run with it, we're talking *Vanity Fair*–level stuff."

I hid my scowl. I hadn't made it into *Vanity Fair* until my trial, and the photos they'd selected hadn't exactly been editorial quality. The best of the bunch had been 1) a picture of me with a dusting of what everyone speculated was cocaine under my nose (like I'd be that tacky) and 2) a picture of me posing with a club promoter who was later busted for, basically, being a club promoter. Other than that it was just mug shots and sketches from the trial, when I'd barely been able to stand on my own two feet. We'd brought in a makeup artist, but even in colored pencil I wasn't remotely presentable.

I bet they'd only choose the most flattering pictures of my mother. That would just fucking figure.

"Are you going to tell me what's in there or not?" Peter asked, jerking his chin at the folder.

I opened Jared's file. "Okay, so, Jared Vincent, age nineteen, was arrested August

17, 1985, for the armed robbery of $13,128 from the Jenkins Savings and Loan. The day of the robbery, a white male entered the bank and asked to rent a safety deposit box. When the manager took him back to the vault, the man pulled out a gun and asked for whatever cash was on hand. Then the man shut the manager in the vault — the door was on a timer — and exited through a back door. By the time the manager was able to escape, the robber was long gone."

"Wasn't there anyone else working that day?"

"There was, but —" I scanned the next page. "Oh."

"Oh?"

"There was a fire on the other side of town, and the other teller was a volunteer fireman, so only the manager was left."

"That's awfully convenient," he said. "Does it say anything else about the fire?"

"It was a false alarm."

"Sounds about right. How'd they catch Vincent?"

I turned to the next page. "Um . . . there was a hidden camera in the vault. They distributed his picture, put out an APB, and he was stopped in North Dakota trying to cross into Canada."

"But he didn't have the money."

"He had *some* money — about fifty bucks. Looks like the DA suspected someone else was involved, but when they offered him a plea, he wouldn't talk. The police ransacked his stuff back in Ardelle and interviewed all his friends, but it never led anywhere."

"Did they interview Tessa Kanty?"

"She was already gone."

"The police didn't think that was suspicious?"

"They did." I flipped through a few more pages. "And it looks like everyone they interviewed did, too. 'Thief,' 'liar' — oh, 'tramp,' that's a good one."

Peter's eyes slid in my direction. "You're saying she wasn't any of those things?"

I kept my voice very la-di-da. "Well, when Chief La Plante wasn't looking I snuck a look at Tessa's folder. But there wasn't anything in there except a shoplifting report."

"That's strange — I could've sworn from the police blotter that she got into all sorts of trouble."

"Did the blotter mention her by name?"

"No."

"Maybe it was some other girl."

"Or maybe someone tampered with her records — like that brother of hers. I've talked to a lot of people, and everyone agrees that Tessa was bad news."

I fiddled with the edge of the folder. "Did you try talking to Eli?"

"He nearly ripped my head off when I mentioned Tessa's name. But I got an earful from . . . shit, what's her name. Ruby? Sapphire?"

"Crystal?"

"Yeah, Crystal. Met her at the Coyote Hole. She had a lot to say."

"Is there anything else —"

He swerved out of the way of a minivan whose turn signal had been on for a good half a mile. "Goddammit, can't anyone drive out here?"

The moment Peter's attention was back on the road, I reached into my bag and pulled out the report from the night Tessa had been picked up for solicitation. She had been spotted in the alley behind the Coyote Hole in the company of a man named Darren Cackett, and the officer had apparently witnessed some sort of cash exchange. Cackett claimed that he'd just been lending her money for cigarettes; Tessa hadn't said anything at all. Cackett had been released hours before Tessa. Neither had been charged.

Had Cackett been telling the truth?

Had my mother started as she meant to go

along, too?

I pushed the report back into my bag, zipped it, and tossed the bag under my feet. I settled my clunky boots on top of it and wished that I had the strength to push it right through the floor of the car and out onto the highway. I pictured everything inside being smashed and crushed and torn until all that was left were a few strips of dirty paper clinging to the novelty mud flap of a tractor trailer. I didn't want to think about any other men who might be my father. Not yet, anyway.

I turned to the window and traced one letter in the cold-fogged glass: J.

The county jail was an economy-sized limestone building that was one part turn-of-the-century stateliness and three parts 1970s brutalism. We parked next to a fountain that was scummed over with mildew. The stone surround was slightly warm and damp to the touch, like a diaper that needed changing.

It wasn't a pretty sight, but it felt an awful lot like coming home.

When we reached the door, Peter eyed the top of my head, which barely came to his collarbones. "Have you ever been to a jail before?" he asked.

"Have you?"

"Well, no," he said. "But I've seen — never mind. I just wanted to be sure you wanted to go in with me."

"I'm not scared," I said.

But, naturally, the first thing I did when we walked into the visiting area was gasp.

Peter put his hand on my back. "I know," he said. "It's not easy to be in a room like this."

Ha. Little did he know. The place was actually pretty nice — what offended *me* was its silence. We were the only visitors.

What *bullshit.*

Noah rarely missed a visit, but when he did, they'd usually had to double up on my Haldol. I thought of all those poor inmates L–Z who had probably gone to their windows as soon as they woke up to see what the weather was like, to estimate their chances of company that day, to predict whether or not love would outweigh the light drizzle.

I pictured my own little room, with its blue-sheeted bed and stainless-steel toilet and blessed lack of carpets, antiques, tapestries, and upholstery. No hints of lavender or rose — just the caustic scent of urine. I'd found I preferred it.

Each night before lights-out I had liked to

trail my fingers along the line between the floor and the wall, simultaneously dispirited and reassured by the reminder of my cell's structural integrity.

Sometimes I worried about bugs, that they would get in and get stuck with me. Not because I was afraid of bugs, but because I was scared that they'd serve as some sort of temptation to my splintering mind. Like maybe I'd name them and keep them as pets, and then, when they died, line them up in creepy-crawly funeral processions. Or eat them.

(Although, other times, deep down, I liked the idea that I might one day stop being that girl who killed her mother and instead become that girl who ate bugs — even though I knew that really I'd just become the girl who killed her mother *and* ate bugs.)

We were escorted to our little cubicle. Jared was waiting for us. He had rabbit teeth and black hair that was two inches past redneck; his skin was an ambivalent shade of tan that could just as likely have been caused by dirt as sun. The lines around his mouth were deeper than those on his forehead, like he smiled more than he frowned, which didn't make any sense.

His convict wear was olde-timey, a loose jumpsuit striped in white and gray. "County

Jail" was printed on his chest in Dior Rouge No. 9. I felt a moment's pique. This jumpsuit would've been way nicer with my complexion's undertones than the traffic-cone orange I'd been stuck wearing.

He was staring back at us with an expression I recognized: the wariness of the prisoner confronted with an unknown variable and no means of escape.

I shifted nervously in my chair, one hand moving to pull my hair in front of my face, the other hand moving to push it back. I wasn't sure if I wanted this man to be fooled — like, maybe I actually wanted more than anything for him to see past the pasty face and cracked lips and tired eyes all the way down to the DNA beneath. *Half of that is mine,* he'd say.

I could feel all the wrong words working their way up my throat like that last little bit of watery puke after you choke up a meal. The question was begging to be spat out: *Are you my father?*

"I was wondering if I could ask you a few questions," Peter was saying, introductions apparently having been dispensed with while I was quietly freaking out. I pulled my shirt away from my body, flapping the hem to cool the sweat that was pooling above the underwire of my bra.

Jared wiped his nose on his sleeve. "You a reporter?"

"Yes," Peter said.

"What do you want?"

"I'd like to ask you about the robbery."

Jared laughed. "I don't know what I can tell you that isn't already in the police files. Don't know why I would, either. I've got everything I need here. Peace. Quiet. My own crapper. If I can just keep adding years onto my sentence, I won't ever have to leave."

Peter was holding the phone slightly away from his ear so I could hear, and even though Jared was speaking normally, his words made their way to me in a whisper, as if what he was saying was for me alone.

"It's Tessa Kanty I want to know about," Peter said.

"I don't know any Tessa Kanty."

"I've come from Ardelle, Jared. I know you know her."

Jared crossed his arms, his fingers scratching his elbows. Then he pointed at me. "Who's she?" he asked.

Peter looked over and frowned. "My research assistant."

Only then did I remember to flip open the notepad he'd given me.

Jared sat back and tilted his head. His eyes

were milky blue, like cornflower soap that had been worked into a lather. They skimmed over my face, lingering on, of all places, my right ear. I pulled on it nervously. Then he leaned toward the glass and rubbed his thumb against the glass window, like he was smudging a charcoal drawing. His brow lifted; his eyes cleared. A slow smile spread across his face.

My heart tried for a triple axel and broke the shit out of its ankle.

He *knew* me.

"Yeah, okay," Jared said, still looking at me. "I'll tell you about Tessa."

"Was she your accomplice?" Peter asked.

Jared didn't answer right away.

"The statute of limitations ran out a long time ago," Peter said. "There's no need to protect her now."

Jared gave this great maybe–maybe not smile — a kind of smile I could appreciate, because I'd tried my damnedest to perfect it myself the first time I'd been interviewed on TV. "I'm not so sure about that," he said.

"Whose idea was the robbery?" Peter asked. "Hers or yours?"

"Hers. She picked the bank, rented the safety deposit box, cased the vault —"

"But you were the one who went in there, who took on all the risk," Peter said. "Why?"

Jared shifted in his seat and tugged at the neckline of his jumpsuit. "There wasn't much I wouldn't've done for Tessa," he said.

"Were you in love with her?" Peter asked.

I leaned forward.

"Tessa wasn't the kind of girl you fell in love with," he said. "There's probably some other word for what we were to each other, but I never knew what it was."

"But if you didn't love her, why'd you give her every cent?" Peter asked. "You only had fifty dollars on you when they picked you up. That's not much of a return."

He lifted a shoulder.

"Did she love you?" I blurted out.

Peter shot me an irritated look.

"No," Jared said, smiling again. "And I was glad for it. I always said Tessa's love must be a terrible thing."

(I recognized this new smile, too. It was the no-big-deal smile — another one I'd tried my damnedest to perfect. It only ever meant one thing: *This is actually a huge fucking deal.*)

I nodded, beginning to understand him now. "You would never have done anything to hurt her," I said.

His eyes went wide. "No, of course not."

It was at that moment that I really truly let myself wish I was his, and I rolled around in that wish like Scrooge McDuck in his money. I imagined taking Jared aside and buying him a decent sandwich and some cigarettes, and then we'd tell each other everything we knew about my mother in the hopes of piecing together a coherent whole. I understood things he couldn't — but maybe he understood things I couldn't. Maybe we would find something like comfort in the telling of it.

I stared at Jared, unable to help myself. I wanted to curl forward until my forehead was pressing against the window, leaving a sheen of sweat that wiped away all the fingerprints of all the inconsequential visitors who'd been there before.

"Do you know why she needed the money?" Peter asked.

No, no, no, wrong question!

Jared looked away from me long enough to roll his eyes, and I had a sudden sharp image of what he must have looked like as a teenager. Not so different from a young Marlon Brando, I realized.

Not bad, Mom.

Peter cleared his throat. "Okay, let me rephrase: Do you know why she needed to leave town?"

"Who *doesn't* need to leave that town?"

"In Ardelle they seem to think she left

because she was pregnant," Peter said.

I scribbled something on the notepad because I couldn't bear to look at Jared's face.

"Where'd you hear that?" Jared asked mildly.

"Tessa's friend" — Peter tapped my shoulder — "what did you say her name was again?"

"Crystal," I said, still keeping my eyes down. "Rhymes with pistol."

"Crystal was no friend of Tessa's," Jared said.

"Well, she said you were the father."

My pen careened off the page.

"If Tessa was pregnant," Jared said, very carefully, "I had nothing to do with it."

I looked up.

"Are you sure?" I whispered. "Are you absolutely sure?" There was no way my voice was loud enough for Jared to hear it over the phone, but he didn't need to hear me to know what I was saying.

"Like I said, it wasn't like that."

"Do you know who was?" I asked.

"I'm sorry," he said.

Me, too, I thought.

Fancy that.

Peter was watching me out of the corner of his eye, wincing slightly, presumably wondering how grim Jared's life must be that he would take notice of a creature as pitiful as myself. I sank lower into my chair. Let him think whatever.

"There's also the suggestion that Tessa was in the habit of —" Peter paused, delicately. "Charging for certain services."

"That's bullshit," Jared said without hesitation.

"Why would Crystal and everyone else lie?" Peter asked.

"Oh, they're not lying," he said.

Peter straightened. "You mean —"

"I mean, they *believe* it. Everyone believed the worst of Tessa — Crystal, Stanton Percy, her brother. She was fired from more jobs than most people've ever had. If merchandise went missing, Tessa was the one who'd lifted it. If the cash drawer was a nickel off, Tessa was the one who'd stolen it. Now don't get me wrong, Tessa was no angel. But it wouldn't have mattered if she was. She was a Kanty."

Peter sat back and crossed his arms. "It must have hurt like a son of a bitch when she hung you out to dry," he said.

Jared shrugged. "Like I said. It's not so bad in here."

"Do you know where she went?" Peter asked.

404

"No."

"Have you ever heard from her?"

"Yeah, she used to come by to see me every now and then."

My pen fell from my fingers. *She what?*

"When was the last time you saw her?" Peter asked, as oblivious to me as ever.

"A little more than ten years ago."

"Do you know where she was living at the time?"

Jared glanced at me. I shook my head slightly.

"No, I couldn't say."

Peter cocked his head, thinking. "Did you know it was the last time you were going to see her? I mean, did she say anything — unusual?"

Jared rubbed his sleeve over his nose again. "Well, there was this one thing: She wanted me to pass on a message, in case — *anyone* ever came looking for her." He looked directly at me.

"What did she say?" I whispered.

" 'Get the fuck out of here while you still can,' " he said. " 'And whatever you do, don't trust Eli.' "

JANIE JENKINS

BREAKING: GRAND THEFT AUTO

TMZ has again obtained exclusive information regarding the whereabouts of Janie Jenkins. . . . Yesterday it was reported that Jenkins likely spent the night in a motel in McCook, Nebraska. TMZ contacted Kayla Simmons, the employee who was on duty at the time. She told us that the guest was a "middle-aged woman" who was behaving strangely.

"I thought she was on drugs or something," says Simmons.

But wait — that's not all. Simmons's truck was also stolen that same night. It seems too convenient to have been a coincidence . . . which means that Janie Jenkins has probably added another crime to her rap sheet. If anyone has any information on a blue 1996 Ford F-150 with Nebraska plates 48-CTXU, possibly driven by a brown-haired woman, send us an email or contact us at our tip line!

CHAPTER TWENTY-SEVEN

Everyone has some idea about what separates us from every other animal, about what makes us humans so fucking special. God, language, cheese, that sort of thing. But you might not have heard of this one: What makes us different is the fact that we'll voluntarily step into a locked cage with a predator. Ladies, you know what I'm talking about. It's night. You're alone, in a parking garage. The elevator opens — there's a man inside. For whatever reason, your rapey Spidey sense is tingling.

What do you do?

You step into the elevator, of course. Because you don't want to judge him unfairly just because he's big or because he looks different or because he's wearing a chain wallet. You overrule the animal inside you that's screaming *danger danger danger* because you don't want to *feel bad*. You talk yourself out of your instincts because you want to feel empowered, because you want to feel noble.

But, truth: Never once when I've done this have I felt empowered. Never once have I felt noble. I've only ever felt lucky to still be there when the door opens again. Because you know who's the only kind of woman who doesn't *feel bad*? A dead one.

And yet, each and every time I step into that elevator. Otherwise I never would've come to Ardelle to begin with. Otherwise I never would've let Peter take me back that day.

While you still can? What the *fuck*. In our long history of shouldn'ts and don't-you-dares, none of my mother's demands had ever been for my benefit. I could maybe understand it if she'd just been trying to keep me from sticking my nose in her business — that was classic Mom — but this was . . . protective. The discordance shook me.

Or — had she known that there was nothing she could have said that would have sent me back to Ardelle so quickly? Had she *wanted* me to go there? Reverse psychology always was my kryptonite, and she'd always taken ruthless advantage of it.

For the first time in probably ever, I wished I could talk to her.

Anyway, my knees were shaking, and not just because of Peter's driving. We were nearly back to Ardelle.

"That went well," I said, breaking the silence.

"He didn't tell me a damn thing I hadn't already figured out."

"At least he confirmed it," I said. "Kind of."

The trees rushed by. I pretended to watch them.

"Do you really think she was pregnant?" I asked.

"Who knows?" he said. "Sounds like she was one of those girls who slept around just enough for everyone to think she slept with everybody."

I thought of the police report from the night with Darren Cackett. "Is there anyone else she was seriously involved with?"

"Crystal said something about Mitch Percy."

"But Mitchell doesn't start with J—"

Peter gave me a weird look. "I hope that's not your eureka moment."

Oh right. He doesn't know about the diary.

"Forget I said anything."

We passed the gas station on the outskirts of town, and I scanned automatically for the flash of a lens, the pale curve of a satellite, but no, all I saw were the orange festival banners flapping in the breeze. One had been blown off. It lay at the foot of the street lamp in a tattered heap, looking like I felt.

"Christ, I can't believe she actually talked some other sad sack into covering this thing."

My head snapped up. The inn had just come into view — and there was a TV truck out front.

They'd found me.

"Peter —" I said.

He groaned. "Poor schmucks. Cora told me she'd pitched the festival to some small-town news something or other. A story on the historical ball thing tomorrow. And they sent *two* reporters? Christ."

I broke out into a sweat. There was only one way out of this. I had to tell him — I had to tell Peter everything. I'd offer him an exclusive interview in exchange for a speedy escape to a remote location. He wouldn't want to give the story to anyone else. He'd do whatever I asked. I opened my mouth —

"Oh, thank god, they're packing up. There's nothing like local newscasters to make a journalist fear for his future."

I finally let myself look over. The correspondent, sure enough, was loosening his tie and reaching for his heavy coat. The expression on his face was the same as that of someone who'd just attended a staged reading of the *OED*. I exhaled. The reporter clearly hadn't found anything of interest. He hadn't found *me.*

Peter looked at his watch, utterly unaware that I was an irregular heartbeat away from asking for a defibrillator. "Shit, we're about to miss the historical society luncheon — my editor will kill me if I don't write it up. Are you coming or are you going to find some way to ditch this event, too?"

"Where's the lunch?" I asked.

"At the Percy house — that big place on the hill. It's on the national registry and everything, I guess. Which is apparently what the readers of my dumb magazine really care about."

All I wanted to do was go upstairs and crawl under my bed with a bottle of whiskey. But then I told myself that I probably only had a day or two left in Ardelle before the press really did find me — and that I could have a whole lifetime of whiskey if I could just figure out what had happened to my mother.

"Sure," I croaked out. "Let's go."

Peter jerked the steering wheel clumsily to the left and drove us to the end of Percy Street and up a steep, curved driveway. He squeezed the car between a rusty Corolla and a pickup truck, and we climbed out.

The house was three stories high and constructed of rough-hewn bricks of salmon-pink sandstone. My eyes followed the neat rows of terra-cotta tiles on the roof up to a central dome, which was topped with a silver finial. Was that a pineapple? An artichoke? I'll never understand the architectural obsession with produce.

We wiped our feet on a sisal mat and stepped into the foyer, a cavernous octagonal room that practically commanded visitors to look up and admire the fresco on the ceiling. In front of us, a circular table was dominated by a gratuitous arrangement of exotic flowers I wouldn't have thought would be available in South Dakota. I leaned in to smell them: They were fake. Good fakes — but still. I looked up at the ceiling again, wondering if the fresco was actually just really nice wallpaper.

"May I take your coats?"

I turned and found Crystal — in white gloves and catering blacks — holding out her hands. She flushed when she recognized

412

Peter and flushed some more when she recognized me.

Peter handed her his jacket, but I shook my head.

"I get chilly."

Peter moved on without another word, but I wasn't quite done with Crystal. I gave her a friendly, conspiratorial wink, and it mustn't have looked too clownish, because her shoulders settled. Then I uttered the words that have brought women together in a holy harmonious bond for centuries: "That guy's a dick."

She gave me a grateful smile, and when I walked away I felt the warm satisfaction of a mind well managed. When I approached her next it wouldn't be hard to get her to tell me what I needed to know.

Because let's be honest. I had a lot of questions for that mouthy bitch.

The luncheon was held in a spare but elegant buttermilk-yellow room that, had I not met Stanton, I would have assumed had been decorated by a woman. The windows were hung with shimmering Dupioni silk that would have flattered even the grayest of complexions — of which the room had plenty.

Another white-gloved worker bee led me

to a table laid with china and crystal and napkins twisted into improbable shapes — and also limp salads with chunky blue cheese dressing. Seated at the table were six local women dressed in what counted as Sunday best (i.e., floral-print suits), and when I sat down, they looked at me in unison, raised their eyebrows, then turned away. I couldn't blame them.

Stanton, Kelley, and Renee were sitting at the head table along with a woman I didn't recognize who was looking off to the side and picking at her cuticles. Cora was at the podium, reading what I guessed was the historical society's annual report.

Man, the gods sure weren't making it easy to keep from falling asleep. I bit down hard on my lip and tried to focus on Cora's speech, but her voice kept drifting in and out. And my eyelids were so heavy.

". . . pleased to announce that the Wednesday raffle raised $560 . . . our efforts to add Adeline to the state's roster of historic sites . . . this lovely house that Stanton has so generously . . . winner will be announced at the ball tomorrow . . . don't miss it. . . ."

My head listed to the left. I had that garbagey feeling in my stomach I always get after an all-nighter. I was so tired my body was all mixed up about the direction digestion was supposed to move in.

". . . and now I'll hand things over to Renee Fuller, who has an update on the status of the nature preserve . . ."

My eyes closed.

"Rise and shine, sweetheart."

I jerked awake. Leo was sitting next to me. He had flipped his chair around and was straddling it, his elbows on the table, a little crease in the middle of his cheek that I couldn't quite read. One of the women on the other side of the table gave him a disapproving look.

"I'm trying to pay attention," I said under my breath.

"And doing a great job of it," he said, popping a crouton into his mouth.

I ignored him and pretended to be engrossed in my place setting. Actually, now that I looked, there were too many forks and spoons for a luncheon. And they weren't arranged correctly: The fish fork was farther from the plate than the fish knife, and my soup spoon was much too close to the edge of the table. I gave the silverware a series of little nudges. When I was finished, Leo was still watching me, waiting me out.

"What do you want?" I asked.

"A few things went missing last night," he said.

"If you mean your brain, I'm afraid I can't help you."

A waiter swooped in and replaced our salads with clam chowder.

Seriously? Clams? In South Dakota?

"Where were you this morning?" Leo asked, apparently unperturbed. "I stopped by the inn for breakfast, but I didn't see you."

"A girl needs her beauty sleep."

"I knocked on your door."

"I mustn't have heard you."

"Nice try. I let myself into your room. It was empty."

I stiffened. "You broke into my room?"

"I was worried for your safety. You might've slipped in the shower or been knocked over by a light breeze."

"And did you find anything interesting?"

"Apart from clothes that could only be so ugly on purpose? No." He paused. "Which I'm guessing means that anything I might be looking for is in that bag you never let go of." He pointed to my purse. "Would you mind if I took a look?"

I shrugged. Like I'd be stupid enough to leave anything incriminating in my bag. I'm no amateur. "Go ahead. But if you need a tampon, all you have to do is ask."

While he rifled through the bag I attended

to my chowder. It was so gummy that when I pressed it with the flat of my spoon it jiggled.

"I don't know how anyone would expect to find anything in here," Leo muttered. "You seriously lug around a laptop all day?"

I scooped out a globule of chowder and touched my tongue to it before putting it in my mouth. I was beginning to miss my ramen.

Leo tossed the bag at my feet. "There's nothing here," he said.

Nope, because what you're looking for is tucked up in my coat pockets. "Sorry," I said.

He sighed. "Can I at least have my keys back? I walked here so I wouldn't have to ask Billy for the keys to the squad car."

"What makes you think I have your keys?"

"A bunch of your hair snagged on the doggie door when you crawled through."

I cringed. Maybe I was an amateur.

"I'll give them back to you on one condition," I said.

He rolled his eyes. "You and your conditions."

"Don't let Walt out of his cell," I said.

He peered at me, then nodded. "I can do that."

I blinked. "That was easier than I expected. Okay, then. Here you go. I pulled his keys out of my other pocket and dropped them in his soup. They didn't even break the surface.

"Didn't anyone ever tell you to grow up?"

"I'm just playing to my demographic."

He kicked the leg of my chair. I took another bite of soup to hide my smile.

"So who's the woman next to Kelley?" I asked.

He looked up at the front table. "That's Nora Freeman — Walt's mom."

"No wonder she looks so embarrassed." I wiped some condensation off the side of my water glass and pressed my hand to my neck. It was fucking hot in that coat. "She seems a weird choice for the board of the historical society," I said. "What with having spawned Walt and all."

"There's always someone from each of the five families on the board. They're like the UN Security Council, except the only thing they veto is what kind of cookies they serve at each meeting."

"Why these particular families?"

"Because they've been here the longest. And between them they still own all the land around here. Most of it's Stanton's, of course, but everyone else has some. Even Walt — even me."

I set my spoon on the side of a saucer,

thinking of the map I'd seen in Eli's study. "That land worth anything?"

"Not unless Cora can make something of it."

My shoulders slumped. "So *that's* why you're all so gung ho about this festival business, to keep Cora invested — and not just emotionally. Here I thought it was out of the goodness of your hearts."

"Frankly, I'm flattered you thought there was goodness to begin with."

I meant to say something cutting and juvenile, but the words died on my lips when I caught a glimpse of his expression. I'd never seen him look so serious. I pulled my coat more tightly around me.

"What?" I said.

He shook his head. "I can't quite decide if I should be throwing you in jail or running you out of town or —"

"Or?"

"I honestly don't know."

The meeting ended with a vote on, sure enough, what kind of cookies should be served at the next meeting. Then the historical society disappeared through a side door while everyone else scattered about for coffee and klatch. I took advantage of Leo's momentary preoccupation with dessert and slipped away. I tried to tell myself I should look for Crystal, but I found myself wandering the halls of the house instead. The place should have felt menacing — weren't mansions on hills supposed to be menacing? — but the hallways were so light and airy that I couldn't imagine anything was hiding behind a corner. I was almost tricked into believing there weren't even corners to hide behind.

Most of the doors were locked — my mother would have approved — but eventually I stumbled on a public room: a conservatory that had been converted into a breakfast room. Through the cloudy windows I could just make out the blurry shapes of a small formal garden, a parterre of rounded hedges and rosebushes that the weather had worn down to stems and prickles. Beyond that was a steep, forested slope. A thick mist sludged through the trees, steadily advancing on the house.

Okay, so maybe I was wrong about the absence of menace.

I moved on.

Upstairs was the ballroom, which was in the process of being transformed for what I assumed was the next night's costume ball. In the middle of the dance floor was a cluster of potted plants that had yet to be distributed throughout the room. I walked over and rubbed a leaf between my fingers. Also fake.

Then, through the open door came a muted arpeggio of happy laughter. I hesitated, but when I recognized Cora's voice, my feet carried me out of the room without asking for my permission. It seemed strange that Cora would abandon her hostessing duties. I headed down the hallway, following the sounds until I came to the door at the far end, all the way at the back of the house.

I opened it.

"Oh my god."

"It's lovely, isn't it?"

I heaved my head to the left. Cora was smiling at me, standing with Stanton in front of a roaring fire. She had let down her hair, and he had unbuttoned his cuffs. The distance between them verged on impropriety, and I tamped back the sensation of being their spinster chaperone.

"This is my favorite room in the house," Cora was saying.

"Your favorite room," I echoed.

She came forward and pulled me into the room. "Come, join us."

I hoped she didn't register the reluctance

in my muscles, which felt as if they'd been dropped in quick-dry concrete. I didn't want to go in. I *really* didn't want to go in. The room was rich and masculine, paneled in dark wood and laid with fine Persian carpets. A decorative Chinese screen stood in one corner, two leather club chairs flanked the fireplace. On one wall was a sideboard generously laden with crystal decanters; between two French doors was a Louis XV credenza. The well-polished billiards table was on the far side of the room, centered under a series of gilt-framed portraits.

Apart from the portraits, it was exactly like the billiard room in our house.

Right down to the shotgun hanging on the wall.

Stanton walked over to the table and began to pull out a set of billiard balls that looked an awful lot like genuine ivory. "Is billiards another of your accomplishments?" he asked.

"No, that's not what I used —" I stopped myself. "No," I said. "It isn't."

"Ah," he said. "In that case, Cora, would you indulge me?"

"You know I always lose," she said.

"Why do you think I take such pleasure in playing you?" The table apparently arranged to his satisfaction, he went to the sideboard. "Would you care for a drink?"

"Please," Cora said.

"No, thank you," I said. I needed to get out as soon as I could. I couldn't be in this room. I just couldn't. But how to leave politely?

Stanton poured a smooth, golden whiskey into two exquisite snifters. My hand itched, knowing how perfectly the glass would fit into my palm. We'd had the same ones, after all.

Stanton drank a third of his glass in one go before dabbing at his mouth with a handkerchief and picking up a cue. Cora was more circumspect, barely letting the liquid dampen her lips before setting the glass down.

I stationed myself near the fireplace. I tried to sling one arm casually across the mantel, but I was too short, so I settled for placing my hand on the carved frieze, all insouciance. I watched Cora and Stanton place themselves around the table. "Just three balls?" I said to break the silence and hurry things along.

"Eight-ball doesn't pair well with whiskey," Stanton said. "I prefer English billiards."

I took a small step back, needing the heat

of the fire even with my coat on. Cora lined up her first shot. Her stick glanced off the side of the cue ball, which spun in lazy circles before coming to a stop a few inches away.

At the same moment, my brain turned back on.

My mother has been in this room.

I cleared my throat. "Do you host events like this often?" I asked.

"Not for a number of years," Stanton said as he circled the table. "My wife was the one who enjoyed entertaining. I'm more of a solitary creature, I'm afraid."

There was a hint of melancholy in his tone, and I responded accordingly. "I'm so sorry," I said. "When did she pass?"

"Oh no, she's not dead — more's the pity."

Cora smacked his arm. "That's Mitch's mother you're talking about."

"And look how that turned out." He knocked the red ball off two sides of the table and into a corner pocket. "Mrs. Percy and I parted ways some years ago," he explained. "Ardelle isn't for everyone. It takes a rare creature like Cora to see its worth."

Cora took her turn, huffing out a ladylike curse as her stick slipped again. This time her cue ball didn't move at all. "I'm really not any good at this, Stanton."

"The most important thing, my dear, is patience. Don't rush your shot."

"That's what you say every time. And I never get any better."

I looked from Stanton to Cora and back again. They sure were friendly with one another in private. But if there was something to hide, why would they be acting like this in front of me? I must be imagining things.

"You play pool together often?" I asked.

"Billiards," Stanton said. "And yes."

"It's the only way I can get him to talk business," Cora said.

"You know I don't need convincing — it's always been our responsibility to look out for the town. I just wish I had more to give."

"We love you for more than your money, Stanton."

Stanton leaned over and knocked two balls into a side pocket with brisk efficiency. "And a good thing, too, because there's not much left."

That was it, I realized. Stanton was humoring Cora for the same reason everyone else was: for her money. I wondered how long his had been running out.

I hoped he didn't know about Trace Kessler's reward.

The door slammed open, and a man and a woman wrapped in an embrace stumbled in. They fell against a wall and knocked a sweet little still life to the floor.

Stanton pounded his cue on the ground. "I beg your pardon," he said.

They broke apart. I didn't recognize the woman, but something about the man —

My eyes fell to his beer gut, and I remembered. It was one of Mitch's buddies.

He flushed like a much younger man. "I'm sorry, Mr. Percy, but Mitch said —"

Stanton waved a hand. "Get out," he said.

He hung his head. "Yes, sir."

Cora said something soothing to Stanton, but I didn't hear what it was. I was too busy looking at the space where Mitch's friend had been.

Did all of Mitch's friends make a habit of bringing girls back to the billiard room?

And then I remembered something Rue had said:

Just another ex–prom king who still hangs out with all his buddies from high school.

Maybe I knew how to narrow down the search for J. after all.

CHAPTER TWENTY-EIGHT

"Where are the high school yearbooks?"

I'd barged into the back room of Kelley's store, hoping she'd retreated to her home base to recharge after the meeting. Sure enough, she and Renee were hunched over the coffee table, playing some board game and drinking wine. Kelley correctly interpreted my thirsty look.

"I buy more wine the week of the festival than I do the rest of the year combined," she said. "Would you like some?"

I stifled a groan. This whole town was a luscious piece of alcoholic fruit perpetually out of reach. "No thanks," I said.

"Why do you need a yearbook?" asked Renee.

"If I don't tell you, will you still show me where they are?"

"God, if I even can find them," Kelley said, rising to her feet. "Which one do you need?"

"Let's start with the class of '85."

"Why am I not surprised? Just a second." She disappeared behind one of the shelves, and I heard a rustling of box flaps.

Renee regarded me over the rim of her glass. "What in God's name are you wearing?"

I looked down. "I honestly don't even know."

"Do those jeans have a *drawstring?*"

Kelley came back and dropped a leatherette-bound book on the coffee table. I ignored their steady gazes and began paging through the yearbook.

"I'm going to say some names," I said, "and I'd like you guys to tell me the first thing that comes to mind."

I found the first name that started with J. "Jason Adams."

Kelley furrowed her brow. "I think he's in a fantasy league with my brother. Nice guy. Married to his high school sweetheart."

I struck a line through his name.

"Julius Lynch."

"Dead."

I paused.

"How long ago?" I asked.

"Right after college. Leukemia. We had a big fundraiser at the school to pay for his treatment. Didn't help."

(Of all the terrible things I've ever done, feeling good about being able to cross a name off a list because a kid died of cancer is pretty high up there. And yet.)

"Jake Olsen," I said.

"He's my accountant," Kelley said.

"And mine," Renee said.

"Married?"

"Gay."

I crossed him off, too. I moved to the next name.

"John Mitchell —" The words caught in my throat. "Mitch Percy's first name is John?"

"Ugh, rich people names," Renee said. "I bet he got into law school just because he had a first initial and a bunch of DUIs under his belt."

DUIs —

I pulled out *Jane Eyre* and did the math as quickly as I could. I turned to page 202: July 21, the date of the DUI I'd seen in the police blotter. A handful of words were scratched angrily in the margin. She must have been out of her mind — they weren't even in code.

Mitch was driving that goddamned car not me. God, what if we'd crashed. I could've lost everything.

429

Maybe Crystal was right — maybe my mother had been involved with Mitch.

Was Mitch J.?

And what had she been afraid to lose?

I looked up at Kelley. "Renee, can you cover your ears for a moment?"

"Why?"

"Oh, just do it," Kelley said.

"Was Tessa sleeping with Mitch Percy?" I asked.

Renee let out a snort of disgust. "Oh for god's sake, have you been talking to Crystal?"

"Real nice," Kelley said.

"Like I wasn't going to listen." She turned to me. "Crystal's been on this for years. Tessa this, Tessa that. The way she talks you'd think Tessa was Ursula the Sea Witch."

"But why would Crystal lie about Mitch?"

"Some high school shit, I bet, same as always in this place. Tessa probably stole her boyfriend or something. The rumors are like —" She thought for a moment. "Fleas. Just when you think you've gotten rid of them, another batch of eggs hatches."

"Yeah, but that's why we have flea bombs," Kelley said.

"It's not a perfect analogy, okay?"

It took me a moment to catch up with

430

them. "Didn't Crystal have a kid with some guy she and Tessa went to high school with?"

Kelley's nose wrinkled. "The only thing Crystal's ever done right is kick that guy to the curb. I think he runs a motorcycle bar outside Sturgis or something now."

"What's his name?"

"Darren Cackett," she said.

"Oh," I said stupidly.

The man who'd been found with Tessa the night she was nearly charged with solicitation.

"Maybe Crystal has more of a reason to talk about Tessa than you think," I said. "Do you know where I might be able to find her?"

"She'll be at the movie tonight."

"The what?"

"Cora screens *The Gold Rush* on the second-to-last night of the festival," Kelley said. "Even though — FYI — that movie is definitely not set in South Dakota." She reached out and put her hand on my leg, which I realized then had been quaking. "Rebecca, you said before that if I asked you'd tell me." Even when her voice was grave it was somehow still gentle. "Should I be asking?"

I looked at the two of them, sitting so close together, their bodies leaning unconsciously toward one another. I bet it was easy to believe in trust when it was something you lived with every day. I knew better. That's why the only person I'd ever trusted was Noah. (But then again, he was also the only person I'd ever a lot of things.) When I looked at Kelley's and Renee's faces, though, so open and shining and kind — and pretty, which I won't pretend didn't matter — and I thought that maybe —

No.

I turned away. "It's nothing important. I just don't like liars."

SGT. JOE SINCLAIR AND DETECTIVE QUENTIN HELY OF THE BEVERLY HILLS POLICE DEPARTMENT

INTERVIEW WITH Jane Jenkins (JJ)
Case 2938-A

Quentin Hely: Can you think of anyone who would have wanted to hurt your mother?

Jane Jenkins: What? (inaudible) I'm sorry, can you repeat that?

QH: Did your mother have any enemies? Anyone who might have been angry at her?

JJ: Apart from me? No, that was a joke. I didn't mean that. In fact, can we maybe pretend all of this is a joke? Can we all go home and have a good laugh and forget this ever happened?

QH: It's not a joke to us.

JJ: I can see that.

QH: Are you admitting that you might have wanted to hurt your mother?

JJ: Of course not.

QH: You never thought about it?

JJ: No.

QH: You never threatened your mother?

JJ: No, that was my youth, charm, and beauty that did that.

QH: Please answer the question.

JJ: I never threatened my mother.

QH: We have witnesses who say that last night you told your mother that you wished she was dead.

JJ: I didn't mean that.

QH: But you did say it?

JJ: I think I'd like to leave now.

QH: In that case, today's date is July 15, 2003, at 2140 hours. Jane Jenkins, you have the right to remain silent when questioned. Anything you say or do can and will be used against you in a court of law. You have the right to consult an attorney before speaking to the police and to have an attorney present during questioning now or in the future. If you cannot afford an attorney, one will be appointed for you before any questioning, if you wish. If you decide to answer any questions now, without an attorney present, you will still have the right to stop answering at any time until you talk to an attorney. Do you understand each of these rights I have explained to you? Having these rights in mind, do you wish to talk to us now?

JJ: I was afraid you were going to say that.

CHAPTER TWENTY-NINE

Onscreen, Charlie Chaplin was eating a shoe. And I couldn't possibly give less of a shit.

You'd think I would've been at least a little bit into the movie. It was my first time in a real movie theater, after all. I mean, sure, I'd been to movie premieres and everything, but at those things no one ever sticks around to see the show. When I'd actually watched movies, I'd watched them as I did anything I took real pleasure in: alone.

I was hunched low in my seat, half overwhelmed by the smell of stale popcorn and mildewed velvet. Renee and Kelley were on either side of me, like guardian lions. Every so often one would lean over to talk to the other . . . and I would hunch lower and lower to avoid the sound — the intimate goddamned timbre — of their conversation. I thought about getting out my hat and pulling it over my ears, but it had one of those dumb giant pompoms on top, and I didn't think the person behind me would appreciate the gesture.

Maybe if I slunk even lower —

"It's not working," Kelley whispered in my ear. "We can still see you."

I swatted her away, but not so quickly that I couldn't hear her low laugh. "Stop distracting me," I said.

But I was already distracted.

Everyone around me was having a great fucking time. They were laughing and cheering, whispering to their neighbors, holding each other's hands. They even seemed to like the popcorn. I didn't understand how such contentment could coexist with such self-awareness. I had yet to meet anyone who loved Ardelle blindly. No one pretended it wasn't small or isolated or decrepit or dull.

And yet, none of them seemed to want to leave.

Why had my mother been different? Had she left of her own accord or had she been driven out? Had she ever missed it?

Then I realized — to my surprise — that she had.

One summer — when I was fairly young, I think, probably seven or eight — my mother and I vacationed with a man named

Rémy Pasquier, on an estate that sprawled along the coastline of Brittany like a cat who was sunning its belly. Rémy was infatuated with my mother and kept her close, and because the estate was so isolated, I was allowed to spend my days running through the fields of flowers and herbs his family had been harvesting for centuries. It was an arrangement that, I thought, suited us all. But then, in late July, Rémy left to attend to a last bit of business in Paris. When we sat down to lunch the next day, just after my mother finished her third glass of muscadet, she looked over at me. She frowned at first, but then I remembered to sit up straight, and that single worry line between her eyebrows smoothed over. "Let's go somewhere," she said.

"Together?" I asked.

"Why not?" she said.

So she drove us out to Pointe du Raz, slaloming from one side of the road to the other, occasionally dropping below fifteen kilometers an hour before speeding back up again. When she got out of the car she left her door open. It took me a few seconds to steady myself enough to be able to close mine.

We walked along the cliffs, my mother stumbling when she wasn't throwing out her arms for balance. She skimmed her fingers along the wall surrounding the statue of the mother staring at her son (who was staring at the outstretched hand of a ship-wrecked sailor), but she didn't stop to look. We pressed on to the promontory, and there, finally, a stillness overtook her. We stood there together and listened to the ocean. We watched the sun set. We did all the things that normal tourists do. Then she grabbed at my arm with one hand and pointed out at the horizon with the other. "Look," she said, speaking for the first time in hours. "It's the end of the world."

This, too, should have felt like something normal tourists do.

"No," I said, because I still thought I knew everything. "It's not. Across the ocean is America, and after America is Asia, and if we kept going, after a while we'd come right back here."

My mother lifted her hand as if she was about to touch my hair, but she rerouted it to her own, picking the wind-blown pieces off her face and tucking them behind her ear. "It's not so easy," she said. "To come back."

"Then let's never leave," I said.

She swayed in the breeze. "You would say that."

I suppose she thought she knew every-thing, too.

I looked behind us, past the histrionic statue and past the precious little village, and on and on until I imagined I could see the spires of Quimper Cathedral in the distance. I'd seen a picture of it in a book once. I wondered if it looked the same up close.

It was dark when we finally left. By then my mother was barely able to shamble along beside me. Her chin kept dipping down to touch her chest; I had to tug her arm to startle her awake. I found a bristly-bearded souvenir seller who was just closing up shop and held up a wad of francs I'd taken from my mother's purse.

"Can you take us home?" I asked in my Swiss-accented French.

"Où est-ce que vous habitez?" he asked.
Where do you live?

Before I could answer, my mother's eyes rolled open. *"N'importe où,"* she said.
Anywhere.

The next thing I knew, the lights were up and Kelley was shaking my shoulder.

"What —"

"You fell asleep," she said.

"Oh." I tried to rub my eyes, but I forgot

that I was wearing glasses and I smashed the frames into my face instead.

Kelley smiled. "We'll be out in the lobby," she said. "Come find us when you're ready."

I might never be ready.

A few other members of the audience lingered in the theater, exchanging greetings, speculating on the food that was to come. I was the only one who was by herself. A couple looked over at me and whispered to each other. I turned awkwardly away and reached for my phone to give myself something to —

Crap. I'd forgotten; I'd killed it. No more sneering insinuations from Trace. No more news alerts. No more texts from Noah. I was flying blind.

I huffed hot breath onto my glasses and wiped the fingerprints off the lenses. That, at least, I could do.

The crowd in the lobby was concentrated near the concession stand, where a peach-fuzzed usher was serving bottled beer and wine in those fancy plastic cups that are shaped like real glasses. I spotted Eli, who had been waylaid by Peter and was looking none too happy about it. I took a step toward them before remembering Jared's warning. No, I wouldn't confront Eli yet. Not until I knew more.

A movement across the room caught my eye. Mitch was leaving the room with another of those pussy-eating grins on his face. *Oh, god, not again.* I searched the room for a fall of red-gold hair. Something putrid churned in my stomach. I went over to Cora and tugged on her sleeve. "Have you seen Rue?" I asked.

Cora looked around. "That's funny, I haven't. She was supposed to be —"

I was already peeling myself away. "Thanks," I said.

I went through the door I'd seen Mitch slip through and found myself in a dank hallway. A tangle of pipes ran overhead, clanking wildly under the strain of what I suspected was their busiest day of the year; something sticky coated the floor. At the end of the hall, I found a small door. Next to it was a wheeled yellow bucket and a mop. A utility closet.

I pulled the door open.

The first thing I saw was Mitch's back — I recognized the salmon-pink polo — being gripped by a pair of dainty, white-knuckled hands. I felt my gorge rise. Then the hands pulled Mitch forward and a face fake with pleasure appeared over his left shoulder.

My sigh of relief was the only honest sound in the room.

The woman in the closet wasn't Rue. It was Crystal.

Mitch's head turned. "Well, well, if it isn't the little busybody." He was so drunk he was swaying, pulling Crystal awkwardly along with him like they were middle-schoolers at a dance. He tilted his chin down to sneak what he thought would be a surreptitious look at my breasts. When he saw none, his brow crumpled, and his face spun through a fortune-wheel of expressions before settling on *oh why the fuck not.* "Care to join us?" he asked.

My relief curdled into disgust.

Would you still have asked if you knew I might be your daughter? I wondered.

But no — I didn't think I actually wanted the answer to that question.

"I think your wife's looking for you," is what I finally said.

Not the bravest of choices, perhaps, but at least it got him out of my sight.

Crystal stepped out of the darkened corner where she'd been hiding. Her face was resigned as she buttoned up her blouse. "Was his wife really looking for him?"

"I'm guessing his wife stopped looking for him a long time ago."

She pulled out a pack of cigarettes. "You don't mind if I smoke, do you?"

My lungs perked up for a moment, and I seriously considered bumming one, but then I saw what she was smoking. Kool Super Longs. I repressed a shudder.

"I don't see how any of this is your business," she said after a moment.

"It's not," I said. "I just can't help interfering. I think it's some sort of a, like, sisterhood thing? I don't know, it's kind of a new feeling. But that guy's a scumbag."

Crystal fidgeted with a ring on her right hand. "It's not like he has it easy," she said. "His father picked out his career, his house, his wife. Mitch could use a little comfort, a little warmth."

I surprised myself by putting my hand on her arm. "I don't think he's lacking for companionship, Crystal."

She pulled away. "Don't feel bad for me," she said. "I know I'm being stupid. And I don't buy his bullshit anyway. It just — makes things easier."

"You can do better."

"That's just something women say to each other to fill the silence. And why should I listen to what you say, anyway? You don't even know me."

"I don't." I played with the bristles of the broom. "But that doesn't necessarily mean anything, right? I mean, after all, that sure didn't stop you from saying all sorts of things about Tessa Kanty."

She barked out a laugh. "So *you're* the one who told Renee. She read me the riot act tonight. Renee's good people, but she never would hear a bad word against anyone she's related to." She took a breath. "So are you a reporter, too?"

"No," I said.

"Then why do you care so much?"

"If you'd prefer, I'm happy to go talk to Mitch's wife instead."

She tucked her hair behind her ears. "Fine. I guess I like you better than that Peter guy anyway. He looks at me like I'm a piggy bank. Go ahead. Ask away."

"Do you hate Tessa because she slept with your baby daddy?"

She put a hand on her chest. "God, you go straight for the jugular don't you?"

I pointed to my throat. "The jugular's up here, actually. And yeah."

Crystal chewed on her lip. "According to *Darren,* she cornered him at the bar, dragged him out back, and had her wicked way with him. I believed him at first." She looked away. "But I figured out soon enough that Darren never had to be dragged anywhere no matter who the girl was."

"Sound like anyone else you know?"

"Look, just because I know something is stupid doesn't mean I'm not going to do it."

"Yeah, I can see that. Next question: You told me Tessa was pregnant — you're absolutely sure about that?"

"I caught her puking her guts out in the bathroom at MacLean's one day. She begged me not to tell anyone, but. . . ." Her voice went soft. "Just a few months later, I got pregnant, too. Sometimes I think that was karma. Not that I'd ever wish I didn't have my Kenzie."

I snapped my fingers at her face. "Focus, Crystal. I don't care about your conflicted teen-mom bullshit. I need to know who . . . who the father of Tessa's kid was."

"*She* probably didn't know who the father was."

Seriously? Had no one in this town seen my mother for who she really was? My mother never even accepted a phone call without knowing who exactly was on the other end of the line.

"Then why did you tell Peter Strickland that it was Mitch?"

"An educated guess."

I threw up my hands. "Well, is there anyone else who might know? Anyone Tessa was close to? Any . . . friends?"

Crystal gave me a look like I was a bird who'd flown into a window. "Haven't you been paying attention? Tessa didn't have any friends."

So it turned out I had something in common with my mother after all: I didn't have any friends, either. Well, unless you count Marciela.

You can probably guess that I didn't spend much time around other kids when I was growing up, but before you start to feel sorry for me, let me assure you that even if my mother hadn't insisted on it, I wouldn't have had it any other way. I never understand it when parents talk about sending their kids to school to "socialize" them. Children aren't people. They're barely even animals. They're just suppurating wounds of emotion inflamed by too much positive reinforcement.

You can't be socialized by the unsocializable. That's like asking King Kong to teach tap dance.

I understood early on that it was the adults who were worth my time. Once, when I was five and we were still living in Geneva, I snuck out of the house while my mother was still sleeping things off and walked to a nearby playground.

446

There were a dozen kids there at least, most of them fighting for space on one of the various devices that move you back and forth between two static points like it's some kind of a life lesson. I watched a boy in a blue-striped shirt grab a handful of wood chips and smash them in his playmate's face. Another fell off a swing set and was then ignored by the other children, who ran to claim the empty seat. A little girl was crouching under a tree and shitting her pants.

I walked past them all, heading directly to the caregivers seated on the sidelines. I planted myself in front of the ugliest one, sweetened up my face with a Shirley Temple smile, and said, "You're the most beautiful mommy I've ever seen."

The woman gave me every single one of her kid's snacks.

That's socialization.

By the time my peers were rational enough to hold my interest, I was in prison — which is where I met Marciela. She was the prison's part-time librarian, and given how much time I spent in the library, she was probably the person I saw most frequently. But I didn't really get to know her until I got kicked out of vocational training for defending myself in a fight. Once I got out of the hole I was sent to work in the library.

When I walked in that first morning, I found Marciela waiting for me, tapping her foot.

"What took you so long?"

"Busy social calendar." (Translation: an encounter with a surly guard.)

Marciela took off her glasses before continuing, something I'd realize later was a sure sign she was about to feed me a fat line of bullshit. "Well, I have good news for you," she said. "You've been assigned to work here with me."

"What do you need me for?"

"The shelves are a mess." She gestured to the far corner of the room, disapproval deepening the hollow at the base of her chin. I craned my neck so I could see the shelf she was pointing to: PR 161 to PR 488. English Literature: Anglo-Saxon, Medieval, and Modern. It looked as pristine as always. Ours wasn't a large library, but even so, the only sections that saw any regular action were law and popular fiction, bibliothecal opiates of the hopeful and hopeless, respectively. There weren't many of us who could be tempted to try *Daniel Deronda,* myself included.

"What aren't you telling me?" I asked.

"The decision was made to remove you

from the standard vocational and occupational training programs. Again."

I didn't say anything, determined to preserve the outward appearance of equanimity.

She put her glasses back on, blinking rapidly as her eyes readjusted to the lenses. "You're lucky," Marciela said. "They could've just kept you in the SHU. Don't screw this up, stay out of trouble, and maybe you won't have to go back."

I thought of the tiny box where I'd been spending twenty-three hours of each day, of the voices that followed me in there.

"I'll try," I said. "Thank you."

"You're welcome."

Apart from my visits with Noah, it was the most amiable exchange I'd had in years.

Now this was not precisely the start to what I would call a beautiful friendship. We didn't swap secrets or braid each other's hair. She didn't see something "special" in me, something no one had ever seen before. She was probably just being cautious, operating under the false assumption that I would be kinder to those who were kind to me.

But it was a friendship nevertheless. I'd like to think we were happy to see each other, and even though we only talked about literature, we made each other laugh. When I was on my own for too long, it was her face that kept me from wearing out my memory of Noah's. And in the end, there was nothing I wanted from her except the assurance that I was making her life marginally better instead of infinitely worse, and doesn't that mean something?

Or maybe it doesn't. Maybe friendship is just something two people arbitrarily decide on together, like the right way to spell worshiper or when it's okay to say *cunt*. Maybe we just grab whatever raft's at hand.

When I got back to the lobby, I marched right up to Kelley and Renee.

"Can we get the fuck out of here?" I asked.

"Yes, please," they said.

I was utterly unable to hide my look of surprise — and pleasure.

CBS News — *Below is a transcript of the 48 Hours special report:* Janie Jenkins, Ten Years Later, *which aired on July 14, 2013, and was hosted by Monica Leahy. Guests included: Ainsley Butler, Det. Greg Johnson, and Marciela Rosales.*

LEAHY: Now, Ms. Rosales, you supervised Ms. Jenkins in the prison library for three years, from 2010 to 2013, is that correct?

ROSALES: On and off, yes.

LEAHY: What do you mean when you say "on and off"?

ROSALES: Jane had a habit of getting herself into trouble. Fighting, mouthing off, that sort of thing. She wasn't always allowed to spend time in the library.

LEAHY: So she wasn't exactly a model prisoner.

ROSALES: Far from it.

LEAHY: How would you describe Ms. Jenkins?

ROSALES: On her good days, she was pleasant. She was a bright girl, and she could work hard if she wanted to. She liked to read, which was a nice surprise.

LEAHY: And on her bad days?

ROSALES: Occasionally the world was a bit too much for her. Sometimes she would sit listlessly in a chair, sometimes I'd find her huddled in a corner. Other times she'd rearrange the books. She'd put them in reverse alphabetical order, chronological order, rainbow order. Usually I couldn't even figure out what her system was. But she always had a system, I can tell you that.

LEAHY: What was her favorite book, do you know?

ROSALES: I don't know if Jane can be said to have had a favorite anything, but she read widely — science, history, cosmetology.

LEAHY: And did she ever speak to you about her mother's murder?

ROSALES: No, of course not. We didn't talk about anything personal. I mean — it's not like we were friends.

CHAPTER THIRTY

The Coyote Hole was only half full, but when we sat down, Tanner wouldn't even look our way.

Renee smacked a hand on the bar. "Tanner. If you don't serve us right now, so help me God, I will tell your mother about the time you fingered Marcia Sinclair during Sunday service."

"Don't be like that, Renee. It was the Christian thing to do."

"You're a pig," she said. "Now give us whiskey. And don't let Kelley talk you out of it."

Tanner reached for the Jim Beam.

"No," I said.

"Excuse me?" he said slowly.

"We'll have what he's having." I pointed to an old man at the far end of the bar. He wore a clerical collar and had a Rudolph-red nose of broken capillaries.

Tanner's hand was still stretched toward

the Jim Beam, but when I refused to back down or even to break eye contact, he gave in and pulled down a bottle of something called Rittenhouse Rye.

Renee grinned. "Line 'em up, Chief. Neat."

"No way," Kelley said. "Rocks. Lots of rocks."

"Killjoy," Renee said.

He set three glasses out in front of us and left the bottle. Renee lifted her drink high in the air.

"To this week almost being over!"

I hurled the liquor down my throat. I had to put one hand on the bar for balance. The rye packed a wallop, and I'd forgotten how to roll with it.

Dutch Courage acquired, I turned to look at Kelley and Renee. "So I've decided we should be friends," I said. "How do we do that?"

Renee laughed. "You're asking the wrong person. I have one friend, and she's sitting right next to me."

"Don't listen to her. Renee likes to think she's a hard-ass, but she's a big softie."

I nodded, already feeling the warmth of the liquor. It lanced through me like one of Kelley's smiles. "Girl talk," I said. "That's where we should start, right?"

"Is that where we talk about sex and boys?" Renee said.

"Oh, I can totally do that!" Kelley said.

Renee raised her eyebrows.

"Like, okay," Kelley said, "so in *Buffy* season seven —"

Renee put her hand over Kelley's mouth. "Nope."

Kelley pulled Renee's hand away, giving it a little squeeze before letting go.

"Okay, so you guys are friends," I said. "What do you talk about when you're together?"

Renee smirked; Kelley smacked her. "We talk about other things too," she said. "Smart, important, smart things. Like . . . the news?"

I thought of all the news alerts my disabled phone hadn't been getting. "I've kind of fallen behind on that."

"Politics?" Renee said. "Movies? Benedict Cumberbatch?"

I shook my head. "Sorry."

"Stupid shit people said on the Internet?"

"I've got nothing," I said.

Kelley held up a finger, waiting until she had our full attention. "Our mothers," she said.

I finished off my drink and poured myself another.

"That," I said, "I think I can do."

Renee groaned. "Oh, god, do we have to?"

"I'll start, since I have the nice mom," Kelley said. "Last night my mother called to make sure I knew that the *New York Times* had published an article about a link between eating soy and a reduced risk of breast cancer, and that she'd send me a check if I would please go to the grocery story and stock up on soy milk. Please note that before she moved to Florida she'd never even heard of soy milk."

"I have the strict mom," said Renee. "The last time she came over, she went through my closet and pulled out all the clothes she thought were 'inappropriate' for a woman of my 'professional stature.' Then she told me that she couldn't believe someone my age still hadn't learned how to use an iron."

They looked at me expectantly. What was I supposed to say that wouldn't ruin the conversation? That once my mother locked herself in her room for a week because she'd actually tried cooking dinner and I'd refused to eat the haricots verts? That once my mother drank a fifth of whiskey and told me that she wished she'd never met my father, and when I'd reminded her that then I would never have been born, she'd waved me off and said, "Of course you'd think it's all about you." That once my mother kept me confined for three years to a drafty house in Neuchâtel, with nothing to keep me company but a parade of priggish tutors and the nineteenth-century pornography collection the house's previous owner had left behind. She hadn't even let me have a —

"My mother wouldn't let me have a TV," I said. "And we never, ever went to the movies. So I didn't know anything about anything other than decorative arts and etiquette until I was, like, fifteen. I basically lived in an Edith Wharton novel."

"Did you get to wear bustles?" Kelley asked.

"I bet she didn't let you have potato chips or sugar cereal, either," Renee said.

"I did have to eat a lot of muesli." I took a drink. "It was kind of a strange childhood — but yours must have been, too, right? I mean, growing up here?"

"It was different for those of us who were over in Adeline," Renee said. "That place really is just such a shit hole. But, for better or for worse, it's *our* shit hole."

Kelley cleared her throat.

"Okay, fine, it's our *stolen* shit hole. But either way . . . it has a hold on us, I guess. Like, it's not a house or a car or something that can go away, you know? There's some *there* there." She took a drink. "Oh what the fuck do I know, maybe it's some dumb cultural thing we've been tricked into, like high heels. It was just constantly drummed into us as kids, like 'This is your legacy, show some respect!' "

"If that was your legacy why'd you move to Ardelle?"

Renee smiled. "They shut off the utilities."

I fiddled with my cocktail stirrer. "The longest I ever lived in one place was —" I pulled up, frowned. "Ten years."

"That's long enough to miss a place."

I thought of that morning with Jared at the county jail, how as soon as I stepped through the door I'd felt like I was swimming in saline instead of chlorine. Back inside those walls, my body floated with so much less effort. "Yes," I said. "Sometimes I miss it."

"Oh, for fuck's sake," Renee said.

For a moment, I was almost offended — but then I saw that Leo was walking toward us.

"Tanner called," he said. "Said you girls were getting into some kind of trouble."

Kelley rolled her eyes. "If you're going to blame someone, blame Renee."

Renee pointed at me. "For once I'm not

the bad influence — she is."

"Should've known," he said.

I raised my glass in his direction, drained it.

"Can you two get each other home?" he said. "It's too cold to be stumbling around on your own."

Renee scowled. "We've had like two drinks, dickhead."

"Ignore her," Kelley said. "We'll be fine. Why don't you take Rebecca back to the inn."

I barely had time to shoot Kelley a dirty look before Leo grabbed me by my upper arm. He dragged me outside and sat me down on a bench. While I was putting on my coat, he spun around and went back inside.

"Wait, where are you going?"

He emerged just a few moments later; he had something in his hand. He came over, pulled back the collar of my sweater, and dumped a fistful of ice down my back.

I shot to my feet. "What the fuck!"

"Still seeing double?" he asked.

"Two of you? I shudder to think."

He wiped his ice-cold hand across my face.

I pushed him away. "Enough! Jesus. I didn't even have that much to drink."

"Just making sure. You're unpredictable enough when you're sober."

He tugged me to my feet and began to pull me down the street without another word.

The temperature was dropping. The wind rushed up through the couloir and sliced into my back, my neck, that crease between your ear and your skull, that fold of skin that's as delicate as a bat's wing. Soon the cold crept over the entire surface of my skull, and a distant part of me wondered how to calculate the distribution. Something to do with pi, surely. When I was eight my math tutor made me memorize as many digits of pi as I could — I stopped at twenty, but only because I was bored.

Once, during an interview with *Extra,* I pretended not to know the product of seven and eight.

I stumbled on the uneven pavement. Leo's hand cupped my elbow.

"Careful," he said.

When I looked up at him, I felt such a curious lack of exasperation that I wondered for the first time if maybe I actually was drunk. Slightly stunned, I let him drag me behind him, for once not feeling the need to guide our planchette to any particular letter on the Ouija board.

The inn appeared in front of us, and Leo pulled me up the stairs and through the door. I absently noted the lines and planes of Cora's elegant furniture. I thought of my room upstairs, with its chiffonier and its escritoire and I clenched my jaw. There was too much pretty here. And that didn't include me.

The radiator hissed; I slipped off my coat and let it slither to the ground.

Leo took the hint. He tugged at my sweater and I tumbled into him, my back against his chest, pressing the two of us against the door. His chest wasn't that warm solid wall of teenage daydreams but more like that of a CPR dummy. It creaked a little as it compressed.

It had been ten years since I'd been so close to someone.

Something inside me shook loose. His proximity had started some sort of chemical reaction that was eating away at my better judgment. And so it was Leo's fault, I told myself, that I decided not to step away, that when my hand fell from his shoulder it landed on his thigh and exerted just the slightest hint of pressure with my blunt, bitten nails. The denim of his jeans was rougher than I'd expected. Probably a cowboy sort of thing. Protection against

461

tumbleweeds and accusations of metrosexuality.

The space between us gave me pause. For one crazy moment I wondered if I was a magnet that was about to be flipped, but then I remembered that I don't believe in attraction — just utility. And Leo was as useful as anyone else in that town. I combed my fingers into his hair.

He set his lips next to my ear. "What are you doing?"

"Nothing smart," I said.

His hand snaked around my waist, slipping under my sweater but over my shirt. I settled my head back against his shoulder.

He turned me around and backed me up against the front door, and I felt a moment of self-consciousness. The protruding edges of the door dug into the back of my pelvis, and when I kicked a leg up around his hip, my back didn't arch so much as it did hinge. I watched his face for any of the signs of distaste that I, in another life, had so often exhibited, but the set of his mouth was inscrutable.

His forehead pressed against mine. His skin reminded me of those hot towels they begrudgingly give you in coach — not the soft cotton of business or first class, the rough terry cloth kind. But if you've been flying long enough, any heat is welcome, and you can always put the cloth over your eyes and pretend you're somewhere else.

My eyes closed, my toes flexed, and maybe my lips were about to do something too.

A throat cleared. *Shit* — another guest in the salon. I hid my face behind Leo's shoulder.

"Go away," Leo snapped.

"You first."

I put my hands on Leo's shoulders and shoved him to the side. Then my arms dropped. And my heart stopped.

"Hello, Noah," I said.

CHAPTER THIRTY-ONE

Noah stood in the doorway to the salon, rumpled as ever, his shirt sleeves shoved up haphazardly and his collar loosened. I was just as rumpled, I realized. I tugged down the hem of my shirt and jabbed Leo with a sharp elbow.

"Do you think we could have a minute?" I said to Leo.

"I don't think so," Leo said. "This is just getting interesting."

I looked back at him, despite myself. "*Just* getting interesting?"

His eyes flicked down to my mouth and up again, and behind his curiosity, I could've sworn I saw something like triumph. I put my hand to my face — he'd tricked a true smile out of me. For a long time Noah was the only person who could make me do that.

The smile faded.

When I turned around to face Noah again, I could barely swallow my mouth was so dry. The expression on his face was like the last ripple of a rock as it sunk into a pond.

"I'm not talking to you while he's here," Noah said, and I flinched at his tone. It was something I hadn't heard before. "Come on. That vicious little redhead set me up with some tea. As for you, Mr. —"

"Leo."

"I assume you can let yourself out."

When Noah looked at me his eyes didn't move even the slightest bit in Leo's direction, and when Noah didn't see something, it ceased to exist.

I followed Noah into the kitchen, wiping my mouth with the back of my hand, almost forgetting Leo had ever even been there to begin with. I didn't like what that said about me.

Noah set the kettle to boil and leaned against the counter. "So. Janie Jenkins. Back and better than ever."

I ran a hand through the tangles in my hair — tangles that Noah knew had been put there by someone else. When I opened my mouth, I didn't know what to say.

So once again I checked my Magic 8 Ball: *Sorry, sweetheart, not even I can help with this one.*

The kettle whistled. Noah dropped his

teabag in his cup with a messy splash. For someone with such an elegant mind he had surprisingly clumsy hands. He wiped up the spill with a dish towel much more thoroughly than was required.

"You always drink tea?" I asked.

"Of course I do," he said.

"How did I not know that?"

"They don't exactly keep Earl Grey on hand at the Santa Bonita Women's Center."

"Aren't you going to ask me if I want any?"

"No."

I hugged my arms to my chest.

"So," he said, setting his mug on the table. "Are you going to explain why you felt the need to lie to me?"

I summoned up some cheek. "Any chance you could narrow it down a bit?"

"Let's start with why you let me think you were going to Wisconsin."

"I knew you'd tell me not to come here. But you were wrong — I know you never thought this would come to anything, but it *has* —"

"You mean you've found the person who killed your mother?"

"No, but —" My mouth snapped shut.

He waited patiently, knowing as well as I did that I didn't have a satisfactory answer.

But it wasn't like I hadn't accomplished anything at all, dammit.

"Look," I said, "this is where my mother was from. And — I think it's where my father's from, too."

"That makes you not guilty?"

I jerked back. "No," I said, weakly. "The court ruling makes me not guilty." It felt like my ribs were collapsing in on themselves one by one.

"You should leave," he said. "You should let it go."

I swiped at my eyes. "You don't understand —"

"Shit," he said, crossing the room and jerking me into his arms, tucking my head under his chin. I could have sworn his lips ghosted across my forehead, but it was possible the sensation was nothing more than an echo of a million pathetic daydreams.

"It's good to see you," I whispered.

"It's good to see you, too."

I closed my eyes and breathed him in.

Wait —

My hands came up and flexed against his chest. "How did you know I was here?"

"I figured it out when the press picked up on that truck you stole from that motel."

I tilted my head back and looked up at him. Why did I get the sense that he hadn't answered my question? "But that was three hundred miles away," I said.

Before he could answer, the front door banged open. We pulled away from each other.

"Mr. Adams!" Cora said, her face lit up like one of her stupid fucking repro gaslight lamps. "Rue told me you'd checked in, and I just had to stop by and make sure you were all settled in."

Noah inclined his head. "I am, thank you."

She looked at his mug. "I'm glad you found the tea. I made sure to pick up the kind you liked so much the last time you were here."

I put my hands on the counter behind me to keep from falling to the floor.

"Oh, Rebecca," she said. "I didn't see you there. You've met Mr. Adams, I see — he's one of my favorite guests. I bet he could tell you more about the town than I could!"

I leveled my gaze on Noah. "Is that so?"

(Did you know that if you throw water out into space it boils first and then skips straight to ice? From gas to solid in seconds.)

Cora took a step back, her smile uncertain. "Well, then, you two have — fun now. I hope to see you both tomorrow night!" Cora backed out of the room. The door

468

slammed behind her.

"Mr. *Adams*?" I said.

"I didn't think Van Buren was gonna fly."

He took a step toward me.

"Don't even."

His hands curled around something invisible.

"How long have you known about this place?" I asked.

"A few years," he said.

"Why didn't you tell me?"

(Why. *God.* What a thankless fucking word.)

"At the time? I wanted you to find some — I don't know, peace?" he said.

"How did you find out?"

"I had access to something you didn't: the Internet."

My mouth dropped open. "Are you fucking kidding me? It was that easy?"

"Well, not quite. I had to take a few trips, do some digging. But it didn't take long to figure out that 'Tessa' was your mother — certain people around here sure were happy to tell me all about her." He paused. "I didn't know your father was from here too."

I stared at him. His eyes — they were such a deep brown and so enormously expressive. I'd always thought they belonged on someone else. A philosopher or a painter.

One of those dancers who flexes his feet instead of pointing them. Anything but a lawyer. But that was my weakness when it came to Noah. I always wanted him to be something transcendent.

"How could you not tell me?" I asked.

"The last time you went through this, you almost didn't make it. I didn't want to risk that again."

"That wasn't your choice to make."

"Well I'm giving you the choice now. I'm leaving tomorrow. Come with me."

"No. I'm not finished."

His expression hardened. "If you need additional incentive, I can always call the press."

"You wouldn't."

"Why would you think that?"

Because ever since my mother died, you're the only one who ever wanted me to think I was innocent.

Or so I thought.

I looked down at my hands. "Tell me the truth, Noah. Why did you really keep this from me?"

"Because you won't find what you're looking for."

"Is that what you believe or what you know?"

He didn't respond.

"Noah —"

"It's what I used to think I knew," he said. "But that was before I realized that you could lie to me, too."

I could tell you what happened next, but a million poets have already come up with a billion ways to describe a broken heart. Why bother rehashing it here.

I KNEEL IN THE NIGHTS BEFORE TIGERS
Written by
Mary Gallagher & Petra Mahoney

Current Revisions by
Allen Kraft

March 3, 2004

Int. Prison Visiting Room — Day

Janie sits alone in an empty room. Confusion etched in every line of her body. Her spine curls into the curve of a question mark. Orange isn't a good color on her.

She stares off into the distance and clings to her CIGARETTE as if it's her last.

And it might be.

A GUARD opens the door. He ushers in NOAH WASHINGTON (early 30s, Southern accent, a fresh face but tired eyes). His expression is serious. Not to be trifled with.

He sits down.

> NOAH
>
> Miss Jenkins.

> JANIE
>
> (sardonic)
> Mister Lawyer.

Noah, in the act of opening his BRIEFCASE, pauses.

> NOAH
>
> You know they tried you as an adult, right?

473

                    JANIE

Yeah? So what?

                    NOAH

So maybe you should act like one.

Janie takes a nervous drag on her cigarette.

                    JANIE

It's a defense mechanism. You do understand that word, right? "Defense"?

                    NOAH
        (lazily)
Oh, that's great. Keep going. Get it all out.

                    JANIE

I beg your pardon.

                    NOAH

Get it out — the ironic looks, the snide
remarks. Do it here, with me, right now,
but then get over it. Because every time
you do it in court you lose another heart,
another mind, another appeal.

Janie is silent.

                NOAH (cont'd)
Everyone in America has known someone
like you. At my high school it was Tamara

                    474

Peterson. So beautiful she made you believe in a higher power. Until she opened her mouth. Then you realized she had a soul like a sling blade, that she was just biding her time till she could cut you down.
  (beat)
Beautiful women — they think they can get away with anything.

                    JANIE
Not this time, though.

She's asking a question. Noah gives her the answer.

                    NOAH
No — not this time.

                    JANIE
Well.
  (beat)
At least you think I'm beautiful.

CHAPTER THIRTY-TWO

I didn't think, I just ran. Down the stairs, down the sidewalk, around one corner and another and another, until there I was, knocking on Leo's door.

He didn't do anything so dramatic as pulling me in or dipping me in his arms or sweeping me off my feet, even though I'm sure that as soon as he saw me standing on his doorstop, he knew why I was there. He just stepped to the side and took a swig of his beer.

"Want a drink?" he asked.

"No."

"Something to eat?"

"No."

"You here to watch the game?"

"There's a game?"

He moved toward me. I tried to tell myself that his lean, weathered face was ugly up close, but we all know that isn't true.

He reached over and pushed my bangs to

the side. "This is one awful haircut," he said.

I curled my arms around my stomach but stuck out my chin. "I can't begin to imagine why Renee left you."

He took my glasses off and examined my face. Then he put my glasses back on. "I think I like you better this way," he said. "The glasses hide the big black circles under your eyes."

"Stop, I'm blushing."

We looked at each other, our chests rising and falling. Not too much, not in some frantic, fish-mouthed, passionate way. Just like normal people breathe: in and out. But in unison.

Leo set his beer down on the nearest flat surface and put his hands — one warm and dry, the other chilled and damp — on either side of my face. I won't call what happened next a kiss, but the fundamental mechanism was the same. And when he went upstairs it didn't take too much to make myself go after him.

All in all, it wasn't nearly as unpleasant as I'd remembered.

"You know why I became a cop?"

I held the sheet to my chest with one hand and plucked the cigarette from Leo's lips with the other. "I have a feeling you're going to tell me."

"I was just out of college —"

"You went to college?"

He snatched back the cigarette before I could take a puff. "You can't have this, it's my last one. Now let me tell the story."

"I wasn't —"

"You were." He held up a finger. "Now. I was just out of college, and —"

"What was your major?"

"Irrelevant."

"Absolutely relevant."

"No, I mean irrelevant to the job market. I was a music major."

"God, why?"

"I thought I was the next Jeff Beck."

"I have no idea who that is."

"Then you're part of the problem. Can I continue?"

"Please."

He took another drag. "So I was driving back home in this shit heap of a car I'd bought from my cousin on Pine Ridge — and I went to college in Indiana, so it wasn't just a long drive but a boring-as-shit drive — so somewhere around Sioux Falls I was like, fuck it, this bag of weed isn't going to smoke itself. Then, not ten minutes after I kill a bowl, there's this cruiser in my rear-view mirror. Now, I'm not an idiot, I'm sticking to the speed limit. And, yeah, okay, maybe the tranny on that thing was about to fall out at any second, but you'd better believe those taillights were working just fine. I knew what was what.

"Problem is, I'd never bothered changing the license plates, and as soon as the cop sees it's a car from the reservation, what do you know, those sirens come on. Now, I got lucky. My record was clean. But if it hadn't been, if I'd even ever had a parking ticket, I probably would've gone away for — I don't know, a year?"

"So, what, you decided to join the force to, like, right a wrong? To make some kind of a difference?"

He exhaled a plume of smoke. "No, so I'd never get pulled over again."

"Why are you telling me this?"

He rolled to his side and tapped his cigarette in the ashtray. Then he pulled back to look at me. "I'm telling you so you don't confuse me for someone who's on anyone's side but my own."

Normally I would have taken him at his word, but after the day I'd had, I decided, perversely, to err on the side of optimism.

"I don't believe you," I said. "I think this is just your way of getting out of making breakfast tomorrow morning."

He rolled onto his back, a smile tugging at his lips.

"What?" I asked.

"I didn't think it was possible to literally fuck someone's brains out."

I went to punch him, but my stupid hand forgot to make a fist and ended up instead curling around his neck with the sort of tenderness you'd expect from a little girl who didn't know any better.

And I suppose I didn't.

My hand was wet. My hand was warm and it was wet. Blood. Again. I opened my eyes.

Oh God, Jesus, it's everywhere.

A scream threatened to fight its way out of my throat.

Then there was a whimper and the nudge of a nose against my palm.

Leo's bed, I remembered. I was in Leo's bed. I was clinging to the edge of Leo's bed, and my arm was hanging off the side and his dog was licking my hand. The scream subsided. I wasn't covered in blood. Just . . . slobber.

I covered my face with my hands and let out a half-choked half laugh that was maybe also a half sob.

That's what I get for thinking I could sleep in a bed.

When my pulse settled I peeked through my fingers at the pillow next to me. Leo was sleeping heavily, one knee drawn up to his stomach. I ran a tentative finger down the knobby length of his spine. I wondered if the bones beneath *my* skin could ever mean anything to someone else.

He sighed in his sleep, throwing one arm out toward me, reaching for what his body knew was supposed to have been his side of the bed. It landed just shy of my cheek. I almost moved to meet it. But instead I grabbed the dog and pulled him up onto the bed with me. He nestled his head under my chin.

Dangerous indulgence, all of it, no different than what I'd been doing for ten years or maybe more: disappearing off into some fantasy whenever the world didn't suit me. Except now it wasn't just a conversation I was losing track of. It was my whole reason for being here. And instead of doing anything about it, I was in bed with a guy I'd just met. I mean, I hadn't even checked the news. Trace Kessler could be outside Leo's bedroom window for all I knew.

Well, that, at least, I could do something about. I set Bones on the floor, opened the drawer to Leo's nightstand, and dug out the phone I'd seen there the other night. My

481

conscience spasmed a bit, but I ignored it. It's not like I was going to read the man's email.

Not right away, anyway.

I clicked the little button at the top of the phone. The screen lit up. And — *wham* — I was hit with a sense memory from twenty years before.

I was seven years old, and that night the cook had served me grouper. Unfortunately, it turned out that this particular grouper had eaten a fish that had eaten some seaweed that had been covered in something called a dinoflagellate. My body did not react well. Headaches, nausea, vomiting, gastrointestinal everything, paresthesia. Hallucinations, too. It was the most physically excruciating and repulsive experience of my life. It took me six weeks to recover.

This moment, though, was indescribably worse.

Because on Leo's phone was a picture of my mother. But this time it wasn't of Tessa. It was of Marion.

Chapter Thirty-Three

I swiped through the phone's photos, the sick in my stomach frothing up higher with each one. There were dozens of pictures of my mother: from charity events, from gala openings, from black-tie balls. Leo must have trawled every single society column on the Internet. He was obsessed.

Which meant he had to know who I was. He'd probably always known who I was. That's why he hadn't arrested me. He wanted me for himself — for God only knows what.

I leaped out of the bed and groped around on the floor for my clothes — ugly sweater, ugly pants, ugly bra, and ugly boots, one of which I had to pry out of the dog's mouth. As soon as the last bootlace was free, Bones let out a yip of delight and jumped up on my leg to ask for more. I gave him a vigorous scratch behind his ears and thought about taking him with me. I picked him up and held his face very close to mine.

"Do me a solid, sweet doggie, and just shit all over *everything.*"

I grabbed my coat and hurried downstairs and out into the frigid night.

First I went to the inn. The lights were still on. Was Noah still in there? Was he sitting on that couch, waiting for me to return? Was he doing that thing he always did when he was anxious, rubbing his thumb and forefinger down from the corners of his mouth in memory of some ill-considered beard from his past? Sometimes his fingers would get distracted from their purpose and pull together instead, pinching his lower lip so hard it would blanch from lack of blood. Which I knew because for years I'd cataloged his every word and gesture, storing up his details in my memory like butterflies in a jar. Like an idiot.

No, I couldn't ask him for help now. I wouldn't give him the satisfaction.

I kept walking.

I paused again at the corner of Percy and Main. To my right was Kelley's store — I'd figured out that she and Renee lived above it. They would let me in, I knew. But once Leo woke up and saw that I'd taken his phone, it was one of the first places he'd come to look. And who was Kelley going to believe, anyway? Me, who she'd met four days ago? Or her big brother?

I continued on until I came to end of the road, to the Kanty house. But here I didn't even consider stopping. Not with Eli inside.

I rewrapped my scarf around my face and used Leo's phone as a flashlight. I was heading for the pass.

Finding out, I'd decided, was much worse than not knowing. It was time to leave.

When I started down the trail to Adeline, I never expected to find a party on the other end. But when I emerged from the forest, that's what I found: the old Kanty house, throbbing with music, overrun with teenagers. The first-floor windows flickered with the intermittent glow of battery-powered light; in the front yard, a fire burned in a metal trash barrel.

I found myself moving toward the fire, hands held out in front of me to catch its warmth.

"Rebeccaaaaaah," came a voice over the wind.

("Mrs. Danvers?" I almost whispered back.)

Rue emerged from behind a sagging column at the rear of the porch, a red Solo cup in her hand. Her face was flushed in two perfect circles, like a china doll who'd had her blush airbrushed on. I'm not going to lie: Her boots were pretty cute.

"What are you doing here?" she asked.

"Taking in the sights."

"You are so weird."

I looked over her shoulder. Three boys were chucking beer bottles into the fire while their girlfriends cheered them on. "So this is what you do for fun in Ardelle?"

"I know, right? But the more you drink the less it sucks."

I glanced down the street toward the barn where I'd hidden Kayla's truck. I coughed and stamped my feet, stalling, hoping that when I looked back Rue's attention would have been redirected elsewhere. But no, she was still standing there, watching me avidly, like I was a jack-in-the-box with a bomb inside.

Her eyes lit up then. "Oh my gosh, I have the best idea! You should totally come meet my friends."

Oh, hell *no.*

"Rue, I can't —"

She pulled at my sleeve. Again, I marveled: for such a little thing she was surprisingly strong.

And also freakishly hard to say no to.

The house stank of liquored-up Kool-Aid

and delusions of invincibility. I turned in a slow circle and took it all in. A girl in a tank top and leggings was grinding her ass up against a guy whose feet were far too big for his frame. Her face was the picture of determination; he was just looking around the room with a stupefied *are-you-guys-seeing-this* expression. At the coffee table were two dudes way more into their arm-wrestling match than either of them was probably willing to admit. A couple that wasn't nearly old enough to have their hands so far down each other's pants was starting up the stairs.

"Hey!" Rue shouted, reminding me for the first time of her father. "How many times do I have to tell you? Stay the fuck downstairs. The floor up there could collapse at like any minute!"

The boy's salute was 100 percent irony free. "Yes, Ma'am," he said.

Rue winked at me. Or she tried to, anyway — she was drunk enough that she had to do a sort of Bell's palsy thing to make it happen. But I admired her dedication.

We passed a flock of boys whose T-shirts displayed muscles that would soon give way to boozy those-were-the-days mush. One slung an arm around Rue's shoulders and tried to steer her toward him. She plucked his sleeve between two fingers and lifted his arm off.

"I don't even want to know where that hand's been," she said.

Eventually we came to a group of girls who were practically dripping with ennui.

"Rebecca? My friends. My friends? Rebecca."

There was a ripple of laughter as they took me in. I sighed. *Plus ça change.*

A girl I recognized from the potluck dinner stepped forward. "Rue, if I'd known you were looking for a rescue dog I could've given you directions to a shelter."

Ten years earlier I might have taken a moment to appreciate such a neat bit of honeyed menace. Hell, I might have even done so ten *days* earlier. But that night I was just so totally over it.

I turned and left the room.

"No, you guys, you guys, you guys," Rue was saying behind me, "you don't understand. Rebecca is my — wait!"

She caught up to me on the porch. "Where are you going?"

"I'm leaving. Have a nice life."

She clutched at my sleeve. "Take me with you."

I brushed her off. "Go back inside, Rue.

I'm not some ticket to a better life. I'm not Tessa."

"Good."

I stopped. "What?"

She stumbled, and I caught her by the elbow. She looked up at me. "Tessa would never say yes. She's kind of mean, isn't she? And you're . . . slightly less mean."

I ran a hand over my face. *Shit.*

"Okay, fine," I said. "Come on."

I'd figure out what to do with her later. Maybe when she was sober I could drop her at a rest stop or a McDonald's or an insane asylum.

We weren't even halfway to the truck when she started whining.

"Rebecca," she said, "my hands are cold."

I gave her my gloves. "Here."

Twenty feet later: "The rest of me's cold, too."

"Jesus," I muttered. "Fine, take my coat." I began to unzip it, then stopped, remembering the police files I'd stashed in the coat pockets. I reached to pull them out, and —

"Fuck!"

Rue giggled. "Has anyone ever told you that you have kind of an anger management problem?"

"Shut up." The files were gone. The only time I'd been away from my coat was when

I'd fallen asleep — briefly and apparently unwisely — in Leo's bed. That sack of shit. I was such a fool.

I yanked my arms out of the coat and stuffed Rue's arms in. She snuggled into it with a sigh. "Where are we going?" she asked.

"To my underground lair."

She giggled again.

By the time we got to the barn, my teeth were chattering, and I'd lost feeling in half my fingers. My lips even *felt* blue. It took me three tries to slide open the door, my feet struggling to get a grip on the cold ground. I pulled Rue in after me.

She ran a finger over the hood of the truck. "Sweet ride."

"Bite me."

I opened up my bag and fumbled with my shaking hands and clumsy fingers for the keys to the truck. Eventually I got a grip on something that felt like a car key and pulled it out. The light from the phone wasn't much, but I managed to get the key into the lock, and — it didn't fit. It didn't fucking fit. My mother had lied to me and Noah had lied to me and Leo had lied to me and, God, even *I* was probably lying to me. Was it too much to ask for a single goddamn thing to go my way?

I spun and hurled the keys against the wall. They ricocheted off a rack of rusty tools and disappeared into the darkness.

Why must everything suck so hard all at once?

I sat down and let my head fall forward. I rubbed my shins with my hands to keep them from going as numb as the rest of me, but then I thought, *Fuck it. Let 'em fall off.*

A tap on my shoulder. I looked up. Rue was holding the keys in her gloved hand. She shifted uncomfortably. "I'm sorry," she said.

I was about to say the same thing back when the keys swung into the light of the phone, and something flashed gold. I grabbed the keys and looked at them, really looked at them. They weren't Kayla-the-hotel-girl's keys. They were my mother's — the ones I'd found in her closet the night she died. And there, among house keys and car keys and all the keys that probably opened the locks to a hundred different secret doors, was a small, worn gold key with a number on it.

It was a safe deposit box key.

And there was no doubt in my mind where that safe deposit box was.

491

JANIE JENKINS

CAUGHT ON TAPE!

BREAKING: A car matching the description of the one stolen from a motel in Mc-Cook, NE earlier this week . . . and suspected to have been stolen by Janie Jenkins . . . was caught on a traffic camera located on I-385 near the South Dakota–Nebraska border at 4:32 p.m. CST on Monday, November 4th.

Although this would have put Jenkins on a direct path to the Canadian border, there is no sign that she crossed over into Saskatchewan . . . and she hasn't been spotted anywhere else in the Great Plains. However, TMZ can exclusively report that just yesterday, Noah Washington, Janie's lawyer, was spotted boarding a plane to Rapid City, South Dakota.

This can be no coincidence . . . have the two arranged a secret meeting somewhere in South Dakota? TMZ will keep you up to

date on every new development as we
finally close in on Janie Jenkins.

CHAPTER THIRTY-FOUR

It was 4:00 in the morning by the time we got to Custer. I figured the bank wouldn't open until nine at the earliest, so I found a parking garage where we could inconspicuously spend the rest of the night. Rue had fallen asleep as soon as I'd snapped her into her seatbelt. She was snoring.

I kept the truck's engine idling as long as it took me to feel really warm, then I pulled myself up into a ball, tucked my hands between my legs, and waited. The truck was warm and moist, the windows fogged over from our breath. As usual, I was afraid to go to sleep, although this time I had a good reason to worry that someone might sneak up on me. I kept pinching myself awake, little nips on my face and my neck and the undersides of my forearms. I sang the alphabet backwards. I counted to a thousand in French. I recited the creative directors of Dior in chronological order — but then I got stuck on Galliano. God, I didn't even know if Galliano was still there. I didn't know *anything*.

Which brought me back to Leo. I picked through our every interaction, trying to figure out what I'd missed, but every time I saw the same thing: a guy who was kind of a jerk and kind of a know-it-all, but also kind of decent. There was nothing about him that said, "I like to hoard pictures of dead women and then also fuck their emotionally vulnerable daughters."

(But don't get the wrong impression — I wasn't upset that I'd slept with him. I was upset that I'd *liked* him.)

Rue shifted in her seat, mumbling something incoherent. In profile, I realized, I could see the family resemblance. Her coloring was totally different, but the slope of her nose, its upturned tip — just like my mother's. Before the rhinoplasty, of course. Rue's lashes were so long they lay heavy on her cheek, the shadows they cast rippling along with her dreams. I reached over and tugged up the collar of her coat — of *my* coat. I smoothed back a stray piece of her hair.

I watched her for a long time before I finally curled back into my ball.

■ ■ ■ ■

The Jenkins Savings and Loan was about what you would expect. A square brick building, a rectangular sign. A freestanding ATM like you'd find in the back of a shitty bar. Inside was shabby industrial-grade carpeting, two desks — one for a loan officer, one for the manager — and two tellers. A velvet rope as thick as my thigh and redder than a maraschino cherry marked out the waiting area. A little bit of L.A. in South Dakota.

"Can I help you?"

A pillowy woman with rosacea and a trapezoidal haircut approached me with a smile. I held out my key.

"I'd like to access box 117," I said. She told me to take a seat while she found the key and signature card. I wiped the sweat from my face with the back of my hand. I hoped they didn't ask for ID; I hoped my mother's handwriting hadn't changed over the years.

Five minutes later the woman's head popped up from behind a filing cabinet. "Oh! You're Miss Kanty!"

I tried to smile. "You know who I am?"

She emerged with the register, which she

laid on the desk. "Of course I do," she said. "A few years ago when the lease was up I spent *ages* trying to track you down. But I couldn't find hide nor hair!"

"I live a very private life," I said, hoping that would be the end of it.

I ran my pen down along the entries: My mother had accessed the box several times before the robbery, once five years later, and then one last time, just three months before her murder. I signed the book and handed it back.

The woman glanced down at my signature — a perfect replica of my mother's, as it should be after all those account withdrawals I forged in high school — and nodded her approval.

"Looks good to me!" she said. "Let's head on back!"

I followed her mutely, too nervous to speak.

"You might not know this," the manager was saying, "but since we couldn't find you, we eventually got in touch with your brother — he's actually the one who's been paying the rent on the box these past years, you know. He must be so happy to have you back."

I just barely managed to keep my balance. Eli knew about the safe deposit box? Did he think Tessa was still alive?

"You mean you haven't been to see him yet?" she asked, misinterpreting my silence.

"It's my next stop," I said, tightly.

Depending on what I'm about to find, anyway.

The manager turned her key in the door to box 117 and left the room with some sort of disproportionately affectionate valediction. I turned my own key, opened the door, and pulled out the drawer, heaving it up onto the table. It was one of the largest boxes in the vault, deeper than it was wide, about the size of a cooler you might take for a long day on the beach. I set my hand on the lid and closed my eyes.

"Please be a detailed and complete explanation of everything that has happened," I said. "It would also be cool if there was an apology for that time Mom threw out my spike-studded Viv Westwood platforms."

I opened the lid. Inside I found:

A stack of bills.
A piece of paper.
An engraved card.
A letter.

My hand went first to the letter, but I chickened out and picked up the card instead. It was thick and expensive, printed on cream-colored linen stock and engraved in Edwardian script: *Many Thanks*. If I hadn't already known whose box this was, the card would have removed all doubt. An actual thing my mother once said to me: "Unengraved stationery is like a fat girl without a bra." I always thought that if my mother were going to come back from the dead for any reason other than revenge, it would be to chastise me for never having written a thank-you note for some birthday present I don't even remember.

I opened the card. There, in my mother's handwriting, was a single sentence:

If you weren't such fucking pricks, I wouldn't have had to take this in the first place.

The manager popped her head back in. "Is everything okay?"

It wasn't until she asked that I realized I was laughing. I wiped the corner of my eye. "Yeah, no, it's fine, thanks. I'll just be a few more minutes."

She left. Still sniffling, I tried to eyeball the number of bills in the box, but I could guess how much was there: $13,128 — plus, probably, interest. My mother never liked to leave her debts unpaid, and apparently that applied to theft, as well. The sheet of paper, a legal document transferring possession of the money to the bank, confirmed this.

It was such a tiny sum, considering. I wondered what she'd bought with it. A new wardrobe? Her first surgeries? Prenatal vitamins? Or maybe a Swiss midwife who didn't mind falsifying a birth certificate.

Finally I picked up the letter. The envelope was addressed simply: Jane. I opened it.

Dear Daughter,

Took you long enough.

Don't tell me you really thought I'd let you find anything I didn't want you to find? Get real, kiddo. You were meant to have this key. What were you looking for when you found it, I wonder. Earrings? A necklace? Class?

You always were so predictable. Does it bother you, to know that?

I thought we were going to work out at first, I really did. You were a beautiful baby from the start, with peachy skin and bright blue eyes whose whole reason for being open was to track the movement of my face. You smiled when you were just a week old. Sometimes I would wake you up just because I missed you. Oh, I thought we had something special, little girl.

Now I know you just wanted my milk.

Are you sorry that I'm dead? Yes, I know I'm dead. Inheriting the deed to the land in Adeline is the only thing that could have led you to this box. I'm not stupid, Jane. When I really want to keep something from you, I send it to my lawyers.

(What did you think of Jared, by the way? If you see him again, please thank him for passing on my message.)

Now, as I've always said, living well is the best revenge, and so far I've managed this brilliantly. And when I die, I hope to be very old and wearing Givenchy. But in case I have instead come to an exceedingly premature end, I need you to finish the job.

I'm assuming you've met my brother by now, and I'm assuming you know what he thinks of me. The bastard. I gave him everything I had, but he wouldn't lift a finger when I needed something from him. Sound like anyone else you know?

I heard he has a daughter now. I want you to find her. And I want you to make her exactly like you. It's only fair.

(That reminds me: Has your father introduced himself yet? If not, you should find him. I think you'll be entertained. And now that you have all my money, you no longer pose a threat to him. Another thing you can thank me for.)

Despite it all, I've always tried to do right by you. For once do the same for me. Unless, of course, you were the one who killed me, in which case I suppose all bets are off.

Although really, Schätzli, why split hairs? It doesn't matter how I died. You killed me the moment you were conceived.

All my love,
Tessa

I returned everything to the box except the letter. I locked the lid and removed the key. Then I reached into my bag and pulled out the matchbook. There was one match left. I lit the letter on fire and watched it burn.

I was staggering out the door when the manager called out to me.

"Oh, Ms. Kanty, hold on! I have your brother on the phone — he asked us to call him, you know, if you ever came in, and I was just so excited that I wanted to do it while you were still here!"

502

My hands were as numb as they'd been the night before. I took the receiver.

"Who is this?" Eli asked.

I didn't answer.

"Is anyone there?"

I still didn't answer. I had to pull the receiver from my ear at the force of his exhalation.

"Speak, dammit."

"Meet me at the old house," I said finally. "In an hour."

FROM THE DIARY OF TESSA KANTY

March 23, 1985
If only I'd been born first, none of this would have happened.

CHAPTER THIRTY-FIVE

Rue was still asleep in the seat next to me when I pulled up to the inn. I shook her shoulder.

"Rise and shine, kid."

Her eyelids fluttered open — and immediately slammed shut. "No. Sun bad."

I pressed my room key into her still-unresponsive hand. "Go inside and sleep it off. Don't even think about trying to face your parents until you've rested."

"Oh man," she groaned. "Why'd you bring me back here? My dad's going to kill me."

"If it makes you feel any better," I said, "I'm guessing he has bigger things to worry about today."

She bolted upright, blinking rapidly against the light. "What happened?"

"Nothing that concerns you," I said.

"But it concerns my dad?"

"Well —"

"Don't lie to me."

"He and I, we're just going to have a little talk, that's all."

"Is it about Tessa?"

I hesitated, and whatever I was doing with my face clearly gave her the answer I was trying to withhold.

"I'm coming with you," she said.

I shook my head. "Absolutely not."

She smacked her hands against the dash. "If it involves my family, then I deserve to hear it as much as anyone."

"Rue, there are things you don't understand —"

"That's not your choice to make."

Now I was the one who was blinking against the light. "You just had to put it that way, didn't you?" I checked the clock on the dashboard. I didn't have much time. "Fine," I said. "You can come with me. Just stay out of sight, okay?" I paused, considering Eli's size, his bulk, his discipline. "Unless I scream. Then run for help, okay?"

"Why would you scream?"

"I guess we're going to find out."

I hid Rue in the kitchen of the old Kanty house and planted myself on the beer-stained couch. Less than ten minutes later, the front door creaked open behind me.

"Over here," I said.

Eli came into the living room, stopping dead center in a dingy shaft of light. "You" was the only thing he seemed able to say.

I sighed. "Can't anyone ever be happy to see me?"

"I'm — confused."

"You don't recognize me, do you?"

"Of course I recognize you."

"That's not what I mean." I pushed back my hair, took off my glasses, and gave him my best paparazzi smile. "Look again."

He took a step toward me, his face screwed up in concentration.

"You're not even *trying,*" I said, horrified by the whine that had worked its way into my voice. But why couldn't he see me?

He shook his head again. "I don't know —"

I slapped my hands against my thighs. "For fuck's sake, I'm Tessa's daughter. I'm your *niece.*"

Eli crossed the room in three efficient strides. I scrambled back on the couch, but he got to me before I could dodge his grasp and jerked me up onto my feet. "What the hell are you talking about?"

I struggled against him. "Look, I'm no happier about it than you are."

"How old are you?"

"That's kind of an indiscreet question —"

He shook me. "How old are you?"

"Twenty-seven."

He dropped me. "Jesus Christ. She actually did it."

The backs of my knees hit the sofa, and I collapsed onto it, my hands pressing into the cushions on either side of me. Even though the sofa seemed sturdy enough beneath me, I still felt ready to tip over.

"She actually did *what*?" I whispered.

He sat down on the stained and scarred coffee table, lost in some fog I couldn't see my way through. We sat in silence for what felt like eons before he spoke again.

"It was my fault," he said. "I can see that now. Dad always told us there was gold out there. When Tessa and I were kids he'd give us a colander and a chisel and send us out into the woods. 'Treasure hunting,' he called it. It never occurred to me that it was just a game.

"And when he died, well — I suppose a part of me was glad that I'd finally get my chance to go out and find that gold for real. I used the money they left us to hire surveyors. When that money ran out and they still hadn't found anything, we sold everything we could. We got jobs. And when that didn't work out, I went to the bank for a loan."

"The Jenkins Savings and Loan," I said.

He nodded. "They gave us the loan and took the house as collateral. But I wasn't making much money, and Tessa couldn't hold down a job, so we fell behind on our payments pretty fast. The bank was going to take the house. I went to them, I asked them to give us more time, but they wouldn't. So —"

"What?"

He looked up at me. "I came up with another plan. I just never thought she'd take it so far."

I clenched my hands in my lap to keep them from shaking. "Explain it to me. Use small words."

"You have to understand, she was just so beautiful — and I'd seen the way Mitch looked at her."

I glanced at the half-rotted kitchen door, wondering how much Rue could hear, wondering if I should stop Eli before he went any further.

But I'm a selfish bitch, so I didn't.

"It seemed like it would be easy enough," Eli was saying. "All she had to do was get — was come up with a good reason for him to marry her. Then we'd never have to worry about money again."

I'd been right. It *was* possible to fall even

when sitting on solid ground.

"Did she volunteer for this?" I managed to ask.

He put his face in his hands. "I told her she wouldn't be welcome in our home if she didn't."

Now, I've said plenty of staggeringly dopey things in my time, but each and every one of them was on purpose. Or at least they were until this:

"That is *so* uncool."

His head came up. "You couldn't possibly understand what it was like for us. We didn't have *any* money — we'd already lost the house in Ardelle. Sometimes Tessa had to steal from work just to feed us. We had to burn our furniture for firewood, for God's sake. We were desperate."

I looked up at the ceiling, wondering if maybe I could just stare at it for the rest of my life. Sure, it was water-stained and on the verge of collapse, but it was so much better than the alternative.

"What about the land?" I asked. "The land you owned. You could've sold that."

"No," he snapped. "That's Kanty land."

"There had to have been other options."

"Look, it's not like it was anything she hadn't done before."

I crossed my arms. "So she fucks a person

once, she'll fuck anyone anytime, is that it?"

He swallowed. "I wasn't thinking, I'm sorry. I didn't mean it like that. I'm sorry about everything, really — will you . . . will you tell her I said that?"

I stared at him in abject horror. He didn't really think my mother was still alive, did he?

"Will you tell her?" he asked again.

I watched him very carefully. "She died ten years ago," I said.

It was then that I had the dubious pleasure of seeing a man's composure collapse in excruciating detail right before my eyes. His face went slack first, then his shoulders, then his knees, a puppet whose strings had been cut.

I looked back up at the ceiling and pressed a hand to my mouth.

He hadn't known.

"What happened?" he asked.

"Oh, you know, the usual. Shot in the chest with a twelve-gauge Winchester."

"Jesus."

"No, I don't think it was him."

His laugh was bitter. "That sounds like something Tessa would have said."

I sat up. "No, you don't get to say that."

"I'm sorry."

"Words."

511

He drew in a breath. "Look, I don't know what Tessa left you with — if anything — but I have plenty of money now if you need it."

"Because you just executed another variation of your plan. Mitch, Cora, same diff, right?"

"My marriage is nothing like that," he said tightly.

"Yeah? Then why don't you have a job?"

He pushed himself to his feet and straightened his jacket, tugging at its hem until the shoulders smoothed out. "The offer stands. Think about it. I'm sure Tessa would have wanted you to be taken care of."

I settled back onto the sofa and threw my arm over my face. "You don't know anything."

"Something else Tessa would've said."

As soon as Eli left, the door to the kitchen creaked open.

"I'm sorry you had to hear that," I said.

Rue slumped on the other end of the sofa and stared at the wall. "It's okay," she said. "Probably better to hear it now."

I made a noise of agreement.

"On the plus side," she said, "I'm pretty sure I never want to see Mitch again."

"Don't be so hasty. If he leaves his wife

for you, you could be my stepmom."

Rue chewed on a thumbnail. "Were you telling the truth? Tessa's dead?"

"Yup."

She laughed, then clapped her hand over her mouth.

"What?"

" 'She likes to give back to the earth.' You're fucking sick."

"I like to think so."

I propped my boots on the table. She followed suit. Our feet, I noticed, were the same size.

Rue looked at me expectantly. "So what now, cuz?"

I hesitated. Should I really let her be a part of this? She could take it. She could stand to find out if Leo or Mitch had done it. It might even do her good.

But what if I *had* done it? How would she look at me then? And why did I care so much?

If I *was* guilty, though, I might never see her again.

I tapped her toe with mine. "What would you say to solving a mystery?"

CHAPTER THIRTY-SIX

I had to bang on Leo's door for a good ten minutes before the son of a bitch finally opened it.

"I didn't think you were coming back," he said.

"I sure wasn't planning on it," I said.

Rue poked her head out from behind me and waved impishly. "Hi, Leo."

"What's she doing here?" Leo asked.

"She's my bodyguard, so no sudden moves." I held up the phone I'd taken from his nightstand. "Recognize this?"

He leaned against the doorframe and crossed his arms. "I think it's called a cell-phone."

"Let's try again." I switched on the phone and navigated to a picture of my mother at the Vienna Opera Ball. "Recognize *this*?"

He held up his hands. "Hold on now —"
At the Russian Ball in Biarritz.
"Or this?"

"Jane —"

At the Geneva Charity Ball.

"What about this? I mean, I'm not saying I was dumb enough to trust you or anything, but — dude, this is seriously fucked up."

"Jane." He grabbed my wrists. "Listen to me. That's not my phone — it's Walt's."

I was so busy hearing the first name I barely registered the second.

"What did you just call me?"

"What did you just call her?" echoed Rue.

Leo didn't say anything. That was something I realized I liked about him. He was willing to wait for me to figure things out.

"But . . . if this isn't yours, then how did you know?" I asked.

"As soon as that truck was flagged as stolen, pretty much. That along with the news coverage . . ."

I lifted my chin. "Did it live up to the hype?"

"What?"

"Fucking Janie Jenkins."

A choking noise from behind me.

"You can't possibly think I'm going to answer that," Leo said.

Rue shoved us apart. "Would anyone like to explain what's going on here? Did you just say you're —"

"Wait," I said, finally rewinding the con-

515

versation and playing it back in my head. "This is *Walt's* phone?"

Leo hesitated. "Look, we both need coffee. You too, squirt. Why don't you guys come on in."

"Hurry up," I said to Leo.

He made a soothing noise as he operated the French press. "You can't rush greatness, Jane."

"Just because you know my real name now doesn't mean you have to use it all the time," I said.

I was standing as far away from Leo as I could. Rue was over in the corner, looking a little lost and a little pissed. Bones, meanwhile, was rummaging happily through a bowl of kibble at my feet, oblivious to it all.

Rue opened her mouth. I held up a finger. "Leo first."

He took a breath. "The day we met — on the highway — I was not, as you guessed, planning on arresting Walt. The two of us, we had kind of a deal. Sometimes he'd do a little work for me; sometimes I'd do a little work for him. He's kind of like a snitch, but one who gets all his information by hacking into other people's email accounts."

He paused to pour the coffee.

"I guess he'd been staying with a buddy

of his over in Pine Ridge — I hadn't seen him in so long I was beginning to hope he might never come back. But then one day he called me up and told me he was stuck on something and asked if he could use the station's computers to finish it off. I said sure, but he had to tell me what the job was first — that's my idea of due diligence, I guess."

"And he told you he was looking for me."

"That's a nice way to put it."

"Did he tell you why? Was it for the reward money?"

Leo hesitated. "I didn't get that impression. That's why I put him in jail when I figured out who you were the next morning."

"What, to protect me or something?"

"I value my life too much to do that. But with him asking about you and you asking about Tessa Kanty — I mean, I *am* a cop. I wasn't *not* going to be curious."

"So you were just controlling one of your variables."

"Well, I knew I wouldn't be able to control you."

Rue held up her hand. "Can I ask a question now?"

I steeled myself. "Shoot."

"You're Janie Jenkins?"

"Thanks for starting with an easy one. Yes."

"Which means that Tessa was Marion Elsinger?"

"Yes."

Leo set down his mug. "Wait, what?"

"Tessa's her mom," Rue explained. "The one she was supposed to have killed."

I frowned into my coffee. "If we're going to get into details we should probably ask Kelley and Renee over, too. I don't want to have to explain this a second time."

Rue came over to stand next to me. "I never believed you did it," she said.

"That makes one of us." I tapped my foot in an anxious rhythm, trying to think things through. "Okay, but here's the fucked-up part. Those pictures on Walt's phone — those are all pictures of my mother — Tessa, Marion, whatever you want to call her."

Leo let out a long, low whistle. "I knew Walt had a thing for Tessa, but Jesus."

"Does that mean Walt knew who your mother was all along?" Rue asked.

"It means we need to go talk to Walt." I threw back the last of my coffee. "And we're going to need a hammer."

When we walked into the police station, Billy was making a paper airplane out of a blank incident report. In his cell, Walt shot to his feet.

"Hi, Billy," I said.

"Good morning, Miss Parker — uh, hey there, Chief. Rue."

"If you fold the paper at the front a few more times you'll concentrate the center of gravity and make it more stable," Leo said.

"I have no idea what you might be referring to, Chief."

Leo's smile was short-lived. "Billy, would you mind giving us a minute?"

"Oh, sure, of course —"

I put my hand on Billy's shoulder and pressed him back into his seat.

"Actually, Leo, if you don't mind, I'd like to ask Billy a question or two."

Leo shrugged. "Go for it."

I perched on the edge of Billy's desk. "How well did you know Tessa Kanty?"

Billy glanced at Walt. "Uh, well, that was a long time ago —"

"She was your babysitter, right?"

"Yeah, but —"

"And *so* beautiful, I heard. I doubt a little boy could forget that."

"If it's Tessa you're interested in, you should probably ask Walt. I mean, he was the one who —"

Walt slammed a hand against the bars.

"Shut up, Billy."

"He was the one who *what*?" I prompted.

Billy swallowed. "He had a crush, that's all."

"Oh, Walt," I said. "So you *do* have a heart."

Walt pressed his face against the bars. "I'll show you a heart, you —"

"Billy," Leo broke in, "I think you can leave now."

"Copy that."

As soon as Billy stepped outside, I walked over to the desk nearest Walt's cell and set my bag on top. I pulled out the phone, the laptop, and the hammer, arranging them as neatly as I had Stanton's sterling place settings.

Leo was keeping a close eye on Walt; he pulled Rue behind him, shielding her with his body.

I stroked the top of Walt's computer. "You were the one who helped Tessa disappear last time, weren't you?" I said. "That's how you knew who she was — how you knew who I was."

"No. I knew who you were because I know a bitch when I see one."

Leo took a step toward Walt; I waved him off.

"Forging a new identity is an impressive

feat for a twelve-year-old boy, genius or no," I said. "I didn't even realize they had computers back then."

"Flattery will get you nowhere."

I picked up the hammer, weighed it in my hand. "Well, there are other ways." I tapped the cover of Walt's laptop once, twice, three times. With each tap, Walt's mouth tightened.

"Like I said, everything on there's backed up."

"Oh, okay, then you won't mind if I do this." I lifted the hammer —

He threw himself against the cell door. "No!"

I kept the hammer poised over the computer. "Why do you have so many pictures of my mother on your phone?"

Walt swung around to face Leo. "Don't you know what she is? She's a murderer. She killed Tessa — are you going to let her just get away with that?"

I rapped the desk with my knuckles. "Eyes on me, asshole. I want answers. Were you stalking her? Were you obsessed with her? If you helped her get away, then you were the only one who knew how to find her — was it you I heard in her closet that night?"

"I don't know what you're talking about."

"Where were you the night of her murder?

I mean, I'm sure Leo could find out for me, but it would be too late for your computer here. And don't try to bullshit me. I've spent hundreds of hours in interrogation rooms. I *will* know if you're lying."

"You never give up, do you? Ten years later, and you're still claiming you're innocent."

"That actually kind of depends on your answer."

"No, it doesn't. There is *no question* who killed your mother. Face facts, *Janie.* I have a 180 IQ, and even I can't see how anyone else could have done it."

I set down the hammer. "I beg your pardon?"

"I *said* —"

"No, that was actually more a figure of speech, I totally heard what you said — because you've said it before, haven't you? Or written it, anyway."

His mouth snapped shut.

I stomped my foot. "Oh my *god,* I should've fucking *known* that was a fake name. I mean, a crime blogger called *Trace*? I am *such* an idiot."

"That's what I've been saying all along."

I swept the hammer off the desk so I couldn't throw it at Walt's head.

"You want to explain what's going on

here?" Leo asked.

"This guy's been harassing me for years," I said. "In fact, I'm pretty sure there's no one on earth who hates me more — and considering Oliver Lawson's still alive, that's really saying something."

"So he didn't kill Tessa?" Rue asked.

I recoiled, the full implications only just hitting me. I'd known this man for ten years: His rage wasn't the kind you could fake. He truly believed I was responsible for my mother's murder, and he truly believed I deserved to be punished for it.

"No, he didn't kill her," I said as soon as I could tolerate the agony of acknowledging it. "Not unless he has an even worse memory than mine."

Walt snorted. I looked over at him. I'd be damned if I didn't at least get some useful information out of him. "How'd you raise all that reward money? I know that it didn't come from you."

"Anonymous donations. You'd be surprised how far people are willing to go to make your life miserable."

"It would be hard for anything to surprise me after this week." I leaned across the desk and peered at Walt, running my fingers along the edge of the laptop. His eye twitched. "What's on this computer, anyway?" I asked.

"It was a present from your mother. She sent it to me when she heard I got kicked out of college."

"Bad news, buddy: She gave presents to all sorts of men she didn't care for."

He shook his head. "Forget it. I'm not listening to you. Everything that comes out of your mouth is a lie."

I took the two steps to his cell and grabbed ahold of the bars. "Why are you so sure I killed her?"

"Were you not listening at your own trial? You had motive, you had opportunity, you said — in public — that you wished she were dead. There was gunpowder on your hands. Your fingerprints were on the gun. Your fucking DNA is under her *fingernails.*"

"No," I said, "it wasn't. The crime lab — that evidence was mishandled. Those results were falsified."

"They weren't falsified, they were *exaggerated.* I hacked into the original chemist's files and managed to restore the lost data, and you know what? It was still a partial match. Do you even understand what that means? I mean, I suppose I *could* explain how alleles and genotypes work — if I thought you could understand it — but the logline is this: *You did it.*"

A scream and a yell, and I don't know who was responsible for either. All I know is that Leo picked me up and threw me over his shoulder, and even after we closed the door behind us, even after we were halfway down the block, I could still hear Walt's voice trailing after me.

"You did it."

Leo and Rue took me straight to the bookstore. As soon as we got there, Kelley wrapped me in a blanket and brought me a glass of water, while Leo and Renee conferred in a corner. Rue was sitting next to me on the couch.

"Walt's full of shit," she whispered.

I squeezed her hand.

"Do you think Leo's telling them who you are?" she asked.

"I don't know," I said. I summoned up the memory of one of Kelley's smiles just in case I wouldn't be seeing it again.

"I can hear you guys," Renee said. "And no, Leo's not telling us who you are, because he didn't have to."

"Jesus Christ," I burst out. "Is there anyone who doesn't know?"

Renee gave me an arch look. "Frankly, you're lucky you came at a time when everyone's pretty drunk."

I pulled the blanket around my shoulders. "How did you know it was me?"

"Obviously we knew right away that you weren't who you said you were — even academics have nicer clothes than you do. But it was Kelley who figured it out."

"When we were looking through the police blotters," Kelley said. "You took off your glasses and pushed back your hair. And . . . well . . . I'd just seen a picture of you on one of those celebrities-without-makeup blogs."

"That fucking picture from St. Barts," I muttered.

"If it means anything," Kelley said, "I think you look better without makeup."

"I think you could do with a little blush," Renee said.

"But why didn't you tell anybody?" I asked.

Renee reached over and flicked me on the forehead. "Dummy. It wasn't our secret to share."

I shuffled my feet on the floor, trying to ground myself against the unfamiliar sensations that were buffeting my insides. "In that case, there's one more thing I suppose I should tell you," I said. "Tell you *and* Leo, actually."

"That sounds ominous," Kelley said.

"Just you wait," Rue said.

"It's only like the thirtieth worst thing about me. I think they can take it."

Renee and Kelley and Leo waited expectantly.

"I think Mitch Percy is my father."

Three jaws dropped.

Renee recovered first. "Yeah, no, Rue's right, that's pretty fucking bad. I mean that in a highly supportive way, of course."

"How did you find out?" Leo asked.

"Tessa kept a diary," I said. "She doesn't come right out and say who it is, but it's pretty clear."

Kelley was frowning at me.

"What?" I asked.

"I can't believe I didn't see it before," she said. "Do you still have that book I gave you?"

I pointed at my bag on the other side of the room. "Yeah, it's in my purse."

"Save some time and just get another copy," Leo said. "It's a jungle in there."

Kelley slapped his arm and grabbed the book out of my bag. She opened it up and came over to sit with me and Rue. She pointed at a sepia photograph of a small, unsmiling woman.

"Here," she said.

The woman's nose was narrow and sharp,

her eyes turned up at the corners. Her hair was pulled back into what looked like a chignon, but I could guess what it would have looked like if it was down — it would have looked a lot like mine. Take away the hairdo and the dress, and we could have been twins.

"I'm sorry," Kelley said. "If anyone else had ever bothered to read my book, we might've figured this out sooner."

"Who is this?" I asked.

"Abiah Percy — Mitch's great-grandmother."

I handed back the book and leaned against the sofa. "Well, that settles that."

So now I knew: Mitch was my father.

If someone had written just those words on a piece of paper and sent it to me in jail, I might have welcomed the information. But this knowledge was part of a package deal. I couldn't pretend I hadn't seen the kind of man my father was.

No wonder I'd turned out like I did.

Leo cleared his throat. "This might sound a little bit crazy —"

Renee laughed. "In this crowd?"

"— but Walt said that the DNA under your mother's fingernails was a partial match, right?"

"Thanks for the reminder," I said.

"But you know what that means, don't you?"

Renee made a face. "Just spit it out, Columbo."

"It means," Leo said, "that the DNA might have been from a member of your immediate family."

At this, even Renee had to sit down. "You won't hear me say this often," she said, "but Leo — you might've just had an idea that isn't totally stupid."

I wrapped my arms around my legs and tried to squeeze back the hope that was bubbling up inside me.

"Is there any way we can know for sure it was him?" Kelley asked.

Leo rubbed his forehead. "I don't know. But if he did kill Tessa, he had to have known about Jane. He could be looking for her now, for all we know. And with all the press coverage — he has to know that she's coming here."

"Do you think she's in any danger?" Kelley asked.

"Possibly," Leo said.

"Have they tracked me all the way here yet?" I asked.

"It's just a matter of time," he said.

I rested my head on my knees. "But he doesn't think anyone knows about *him*," I said slowly. "He doesn't think *I* know about him."

"What are you thinking?" Leo asked.

"Hold on, I'm working through a whole 'all men are Greeks' thing."

I closed my eyes.

If Mitch killed my mother, he knows Janie Jenkins is his daughter.

If Mitch knows Janie Jenkins is his daughter, does that mean he killed my mother?

If Mitch killed my mother, will he try to kill Janie Jenkins, too?

And then, for the second time in my life, everything I'd learned crystallized into a perfect, glittering plan.

I turned to Rue. "Remember that girl you mentioned who's just 'magic with hair'? I think it's time we give her a call."

CHAPTER THIRTY-SEVEN

In the late autumn gloaming, framed by a forest that melted into fog, the Percy mansion loomed large and imposing, its lights less a beacon than a declaration: We can afford obscenely high electric bills. I hiked up my petticoats and picked my way across the cobblestone drive. Kelley and Renee were close behind me, Rue and Leo behind them. None of us said a word.

We handed our coats to a liveried footman (who I was pretty sure was a guy I'd seen at the Coyote Hole) and climbed the stairs to the ballroom. I stepped through the door . . . and was confronted with a sea of ill-fitting pantaloons and overflowing bodices. Everyone in Ardelle was there — as well as at least a few dozen others, if I counted correctly. In one corner, a quartet of surprisingly passable adolescent musicians played Mozart relatively inoffensively. An athletic young couple with beautiful hair gamboled past. The girl looked like she knew her way around a deep-conditioning treatment.

I plucked sourly at my skirts. Puce: the final indignity.

"Don't look at me," Kelley said. "You're the one who waited until the last minute to pick out a dress."

I pointed an accusing finger at Renee, who was wearing a white petticoat gown with a red ribbon around the waist. "That's not even from the right time period," I said. "Or state."

"Fiddle-dee-fucking-dee," Renee said, but I'd already pushed past her to survey the crowd.

"Is everyone here?" I asked.

Kelley nodded. "We're probably the last to arrive. No one wants to miss the hors d'oeuvres."

I located the pieces on the board. Peter was by the bar, attempting to extract information from Billy. Cora and Stanton were laughing at something together up on the dais. Mitch was dancing with a cool blonde who was too old to be anything other than his wife.

"Where's Eli?" I asked.

Kelley pointed to a small seating area by the balcony doors. "He's over there." She leaned forward, squinting. "Who's he talking to?"

I followed the direction of her gaze. "Oh," I said, wishing I had my old hair back so I could flick it back over my shoulders in a breezy I-don't-give-a-shit sort of manner. "That's no one — just my lawyer."

"Are you planning on needing one?"

I didn't answer.

Rue nosed between us, a garment bag slung over her arm. "I'm going to go hang this up while I still can," she said. "As soon as my mom sees me I'm gonna get roped into doing something dumb."

Renee tugged at Kelley's elbow. "And we should go see Cora about the raffle."

Kelley hesitated, but Leo waved her forward.

"Go ahead," he said. "We'll be fine."

"You'll let us know if anything changes?" Kelley asked.

"Of course," I said.

The three of them fanned out, twisting and squeezing their voluminous skirts through the crowd. Leo and I eased back to the periphery of the room.

"There are only three doors to the ballroom," he said in a low voice. "The girls will each be watching one; I'll be watching Mitch. But if I lose him — promise me you won't confront him on your own."

"Don't lose him, and I won't have to."

"Deal."

Cora waved from across the room. I smiled brightly and raised my hand.

"Don't lay it on too thick," Leo said.

"She's a hundred feet away. I'm playing to the rafters."

We came to a column not far from the balcony doors and settled into its shadow.

"So he's your lawyer, huh?"

I looked over at Noah. He was dressed in jeans and a poorly ironed blazer. His hair was bronzed by the candlelight.

"*A* lawyer," I said. "I fired him."

Leo gave me a sidelong glance. "Didn't look that way last night."

"Stop fishing," I said.

Noah's head came up at the sound of Leo's laughter. He frowned at us.

"Do you think he's going to be a problem?" Leo asked.

"Yeah," I said, rubbing absently at my sternum. "I do."

I tapped Eli on the shoulder. "I'm sorry to interrupt, but I was wondering if I could talk to your friend here."

Eli glanced at Noah. "You two know each other?" he asked.

"Not really," I said.

It might have been Eli I was looking at, but it was Noah I was watching. I'm sure he thought his face was expressionless and smooth, but I'd picked apart the pieces of all the things he said and did for so long that I could fit them back together without even thinking about it, a career assassin assembling her sniper rifle. And I wasn't so out of practice I couldn't still score a hit.

"Can it wait?" Eli asked. "Because actually I was hoping I could talk to you."

I shook my head. "Let's just enjoy the party for now, shall we?"

"Tomorrow, then?"

"Take a hint, Eli."

His eyes darted between the two of us. Then he ducked his chin and walked away.

Noah was watching me warily. "Am I supposed to ask you to dance?"

"No, because that would be really fucking weird. Let's walk instead."

Noah's smile was too thin for my tastes — I was no longer acclimated to his altitude. "Where to?" he asked.

"N'importe où."

I tucked my arm into his, and we walked together around the perimeter of the room. His sleeve grazed my bare arm. A week ago it would have been all I could think about.

535

Now I hardly noticed.

"I didn't call the press," he said.

"It doesn't matter that you didn't; it matters that you threatened to."

"Your inability to forgive has always been your most ironic character trait." He hugged my arm closer to soothe the sting of his words. "So what comes next?"

"I'm staying here. For the moment."

"And then?"

"We sort of have to wait and see."

He turned sharply. "What are you planning?"

"Nothing smart — as usual."

"Why are the smartest people I've ever known also the stupidest?"

"Is that an apology?"

"More like an acquittal."

I pulled up so I could watch the dancers as they passed. Were I anyone else I would have been delighted by the costumes. I saw a poodle skirt, a flapper dress, something that Eleanor of Aquitaine would have worn — was that a *wimple*? And no matter what the costume, everyone in the room seemed to be brimming over with joy. Everyone else, that is.

I looked at Noah, at the dear, sad slope of his cheek.

"So what are you dressed as?" I asked.

"I haven't decided," he said. "But I was leaning toward repentant lawyer."

"It doesn't work if it's just a costume, Noah."

He pulled me around to face him. My skirts ballooned out, wrapping around his legs.

"What happens now?" he asked.

"Now," I said, "you do me one more favor."

"Anything."

I laughed. "You never did stop to think what you were getting into with me." I let my hand go to his jaw, the sort of sentimental gesture that wasn't at all like me but that suddenly seemed not just appropriate but necessary, if only to give him the illusion that what I'd done was reparable. "But this one's easy: All you have to do is leave."

He didn't look particularly surprised. "Does this have something to do with whatever it is you're planning?"

"Yes," I said. "But I'd be asking you to go anyway. I don't want you to get into any more trouble because of me."

"You wouldn't listen when I asked you to leave. So why should I?"

"I'm not doing this for you, I'm doing it for me. I can't have you getting in the way.

I can't worry about you worrying about me."

He tipped up my chin and looked into my eyes. "We're just not made for the outside world, are we?"

"No." I slipped my arms around his waist, pulled him close, and whispered in his ear: "But next time I go to jail, you'll be the first person I call."

Then I let go.

"And now, if I could have your attention please, it is at last time to pick the winners of this year's Ardelle Women's Historical Society raffle!"

I watched from a safe distance as Cora spun the raffle drum with a flourish, to polite applause.

"Our third-place prize, dinner for two at the Coyote Hole, generously donated by Tanner Boyce, goes to — Kelley, if you would?"

Kelley handed Cora a name from the drum.

"Charlie Rodriguez!"

A lanky dude in skinny jeans and a tuxedo shirt hopped up onstage as the smokers on the balcony shouted their approval. Renee winked at me from her position near the rear door just a few feet away.

"Our second-place prize, two free nights at the Prospect Inn, breakfast included, donated by Rue, Eli, and myself, goes to . . . Rufus Blanchard!"

One of the footmen briefly abandoned his station and ran over to Cora.

I looked to my right. By the side door, Rue was shaking off her skirts.

"And now, our grand prize, a bottle of twenty-one-year-old Lagavulin, *very* generously donated by our host for this evening, goes to — drum roll please!"

Leo's eyes met mine. I nodded. Kelley handed Cora the card.

"Jane . . . Jenkins?"

A hush fell over the room.

Cora laughed nervously. "Well, I'm sure it's not *that* Jane Jenkins."

Everywhere heads turned, waiting to see who would approach the stage. I paid close attention to the crowd, but apart from Peter — whose face was lit with hope, poor guy — no one looked particularly angry or anxious. Merely curious. Mitch hadn't even moved from his chair.

"Jane?" Cora said. "Jane Jenkins? Are you here?"

Nothing but whispers. I tried to tell myself this didn't mean anything.

Cora, finally, rediscovered her smile.

"Well, everyone needs to go the ladies' room sometime, I suppose."

CHAPTER THIRTY-EIGHT

As soon as the music restarted and conversation resumed, I slipped out the side exit — Rue gave me an unconvincingly optimistic thumbs-up — and made my way upstairs to the billiard room. Rue had already done as I'd asked: The lights were dimmed and the curtains were closed; the fire was banked. The garment bag was behind the ornamental screen. I made one important additional adjustment to the décor and settled in to wait.

If Mitch was looking for me, eventually he'd have to come here.

I thought of his reaction back in the ballroom — or, rather, his lack thereof. God, what if I was wrong?

Please, please come find me. I don't want to play this game anymore.

I paced across the room a few times before heading to the billiard table. I pulled a ball from a corner pocket and rolled it between the palms of my hands as I examined the four portraits on the wall in front of me. They progressed in chronological order from left to right. I gazed at the oldest — the town founder, I supposed. You'd think someone who was such a stickler for propriety would have done a better job grooming his ear hair. My gaze dropped to the brass nameplate: John Tesmond Percy.

My breath caught in my throat. I walked down the length of the wall, my fingers leaping from nameplate to nameplate.

John Tesmond Percy
John Gibson Percy
John Stanton Percy
John Mitchell Percy

Behind me, the door opened.

Stanton's head appeared around the door. "Oh, Miss Parker." He pulled out a handkerchief and blotted his forehead. "I'm sorry to disturb you, I was just looking for someone."

I glanced over his shoulder. He was alone. "No need to apologize," I said carefully. "Who are you looking for? Maybe I can help."

"I don't know if you were in the ballroom for the raffle drawing, but we're still trying to track down the grand-prize winner." He gave a rueful twist of his lips. "I was hoping I might convince her to share."

"There was a girl in here just a few minutes ago, could that have been her? Skinny, blond — *very* pretty."

His lips pressed together before they remembered to smile. "That sounds about right. Did she say where she was going?"

"She's going to be right back," I said. I held up the billiard ball. "She challenged me to a game."

"Well, thank you, dear." He lowered himself into one of the chairs next to the fire. "I think I'll just wait here, then."

"I could go find her for you," I said.

"No, I'll be fine here. You go back to the party — no need to keep an old man company. I hear Cora's about to bring out the pie."

"Well," I said, "I do love pie." But I didn't move.

He leaned back in the chair and crossed his legs. He scratched his eyebrow, dislodging a flake of skin from the white wiry hairs. It fell to the lapel of his jacket. He looked at it with distaste before flicking it off. I watched it float to the ground.

"Was there something else you needed?" he asked.

There were so many ways to answer this: Valium. A better bra. A crystal ball. Over the past week my uncertainty had expanded to fill the infinite space I had given it. I didn't know if I was doing the right thing, if I had the right man — if I was the right woman. What if Janie wasn't even in there anymore?

But, then again, this might be my only chance to find out.

I steadied my breath. "You wouldn't be interested in a game, would you?"

"Some other time, my dear."

"I think I have something that might convince you." I held up a finger. "Would you excuse me for just one minute?"

"I —"

"Great. Back in a jiff."

I slipped behind the screen and pulled off the mobcap and wig.

"Miss Parker —"

I unbuttoned my dress, unhooked my corset, stepped out of my petticoats. Pulled off the glasses and popped out the color contacts.

"Just a second," I sang.

I peeled off my stockings and tugged up the little black dress Rue had lent me. I stepped into shoes that actually fit. I put my fist to my forehead and recited all the words

I knew that had anything to do with benevolent divinities.

Showtime.

I stepped out from behind the screen.

"Miss Parker. I hate to have to put it like this, but I am tired, and this is my house, and I would really just like —" Stanton finally looked over. He clutched the arm of his chair. "Mother of God."

My hand fluttered to my head. "Is it the hair? I know it's a little Princess Di, but it was the best we could do with these bangs."

I walked over to the cloudy mirror that hung on the wall between the balcony doors and fluffed my newly ashy-blond waves. "Clairol," I said. "Who knew?" I heaved my purse up onto the credenza and dumped out a pile of cosmetics. I picked up a thin, angled brush and a pot of gel liner. I pulled my left eyelid taut and began to trace a thick black line. Then I winged it out at the corners, because that's what Rue told me the kids were doing. Let me tell you, it's not an easy look to do when your hands would rather be shaking.

I paused, checking behind me in the mirror. Stanton was still frozen in place. "You know," I said, "they say that the eyes are the windows to the soul — I've always thought that's why I'm so fond of false lashes." I finished the left eye and moved to the right. "In case you were wondering? I prefer Shu Uemura, but Urban Decay totally works in a pinch."

I layered on mascara until my eyelids had to strain to stay open.

I checked the mirror again. Stanton had risen to his feet. I reminded myself to breathe.

I twisted the mascara shut and set it on the credenza. I looked at the makeup I had left. Once I did one of those little mini-interview things for a women's magazine where they ask you about, like, what's in your purse and stuff, and one of the questions was, "If you were stranded on a desert island, which one beauty product would you want with you?" Of course I *should* have said sunscreen, but my answer was, "Dior Addict in Diorissime." They hadn't had it at the drugstore I'd sent Kelley to, of course, but I still had the old tube I'd brought with me to prison. So what if it was a little gummy?

I pressed it into my lips and took one last look in the mirror.

Was this how a killer smiled?

Time to find out. I turned around.

Stanton was ten feet in front of me, a gun in his hands.

My knees gave out.

I didn't do it. Oh god, I didn't do it.

My face was in my hands, and one or both of them or maybe all of me was trembling, like the filament of a lightbulb just after it's burned out. I ground my back teeth together to keep my face from doing something even less dignified. Mostly because I didn't want to fuck up my makeup.

Eventually I managed to look up at Stanton and his neat little pistol. "I have to admit, I was hoping you'd pick the Winchester."

"For old times' sake?"

"No, because before you got here I took out its shells."

He inclined his head in a way I might have interpreted as admiration if I weren't so attuned to bullshit.

"It's astonishing, really, how much you resemble my grandmother," he said.

"Is that how you found us?"

He rolled a shoulder apologetically. "The price of fame."

I tried to keep my eyes from darting over to the door, but Stanton read the intention nevertheless. He walked over, locked it, and pocketed the key.

I swallowed back a mouthful of bile. This had seemed a lot less stupid when I'd thought Leo would be on the other side of that door. I grabbed at the credenza and pulled myself up.

"Hands where I can see them."

I huffed and set them on my hips, trying for bravado. "What do you think I'm going to do, kill you with lip gloss?"

"I prefer not to test the limits of your resourcefulness. Away from the credenza, please."

"If you're so worried, you should've just shot me in the back in the first place."

"Just what kind of man do you think I am? I can't shoot you in the back — then it wouldn't look like self-defense."

I waved my empty hands in the air. "Defense against what?"

"You think Janie Jenkins really needs a weapon to be considered a threat? Reasonable grounds are a given, my dear."

He cocked the gun. I spun on my heel, flung the curtains to the side, and threw open the French doors.

"Don't tell me you're going to jump," Stanton said.

"Not like you think —" I leaped out.

An explosion of light and sound, of flash

flares and exhortations. A phalanx of reporters charged toward the balcony; five satel-
lites perked up toward the sky. I braced
myself against the balcony rail.

"Janie, where have you —"

"Janie, what have you —"

"Janie, who have you —"

"Hello, boys. Miss me?" I looked over my
shoulder at Stanton. "I thought it might be
a good idea to bring some witnesses. There
are *some* benefits to a bad reputation."

He took a step back; I watched him
closely. I had to walk a fine line — I didn't
want to scare him off. I just had to keep
him from killing me long enough to find
out what happened. Needing to know *who*
wasn't enough anymore. I needed to know
why. And I knew just how to get Stanton to
tell me: I'd attack his pride.

"She was supposed to go after Mitch, you
know. That was the original plan. I wonder
— did she decide you were the easier mark?"

His expression hardened. "Do you honestly believe I didn't know exactly what she
was doing? Who do you think made sure
the bank wouldn't give them another loan?"

"That's a long way to go to get laid," I
said. "But then — she was just *so* beautiful,
wasn't she? Did you ever pretend, when she
was with you? That she actually wanted to

be there? Or did you get off on the reality?"

Stanton's hand tightened on the gun.

The crowd below was growing louder. I gave a pageant-queen wave and blew them a kiss.

"Tell me this," I said. "If you knew exactly what she was doing, how'd she manage to get pregnant?"

"I'll admit, I underestimated her commitment — and her ingenuity."

"I don't know, those sound like pretty good traits in a wife."

"I'm not a Fuller. I don't give my name to trash just because it happens to be within arm's reach — your mother knew that as well as I. She didn't come to me with a proposal; she came to me with a demand."

"Blackmail," I said.

"Of the simplest kind. I would pay her — and she would destroy the . . . incriminating evidence."

"Janie, what are you wearing?"

"It's off-the-rack!" I yelled. "Let's never speak of it again."

Stanton was looking at me like I was that flake of loose skin. "Would it have been so bad?" I asked. "If people knew?"

"Fucking her was one thing. Letting her win was another."

"You couldn't have just paid her off?"

550

"But I did," he said, easily. "I was rather generous, really. I gave her — oh — about two hundred dollars, if I remember correctly. I told her she could either use the money to take care of it herself, or she could keep the money, and I'd take care of it for her."

"What do you know, I'm not the only one whose memory sucks." I strode back through the door and over to the credenza, ignoring the way the barrel of the gun tracked me. I dug the money I'd found in Tessa's closet out of my purse and tossed it at Stanton's feet. "It was a *hundred* dollars," I said. "And she didn't touch a cent of it."

If the gun wavered, I couldn't tell. He swept the money to the side with his foot.

"Janie, come back!" Light flooded in through the windows behind me. They must be setting up for live shots.

"So was that it?" I asked. "You killed her because you're a sore fucking loser? You held a grudge for eighteen years?"

"Don't be ridiculous. It was a crime of practicality. A cost-benefit analysis."

"What was the benefit?"

"Apart from the look on her face? The gold, of course."

"The *what*?" I shook myself. "You've got

to be fucking kidding me. Does Eli know?"

"It's not on his land, just Tessa's. Eli's no luckier than his great-grandfather. A few years after Eli left town I found an old field journal of my grandfather's. He'd known where the gold was all along — he was just waiting the Kantys out. He neglected to take into account the resilience of roaches."

"That's when you started looking for Tessa."

He nodded. "She did a good job disappearing, I'll give her that. I would never have thought to look in such rarefied circles. But I was patient."

My hand reached out and grabbed the doorframe. "And then you saw my pictures."

"Even I go to the grocery store."

I looked at the gun in his hands. It was unnervingly steady. I glanced at the door. It was unnervingly silent.

"Janie, say something!"

"Why didn't you just buy it from her? She didn't need that land — she had more money than even I could ever spend."

"She wouldn't sell to me any more than you would." He paused. "You wouldn't, would you?"

"Fuck you."

He inclined his head in acknowledgment. "Fair enough. By the time I found her, Tessa was immune to extortion. When I threatened to expose her, she just laughed and said — I'll always remember this — 'You can get away with anything if you wear great clothes, throw great parties, and —' "

"Give money to kids with cleft palates. Yeah, that was one of my favorites. I probably should've taken it more seriously." I wiped my forehead with the back of my hand. "But how would killing her help — oh, *shit*. You didn't have any ties to Tessa. But you had ties to me."

He smiled. "Yes, Jane: It really is all about you. Does it feel as good as you'd hoped?"

"You killed her to get to me."

"Well, yes. If you'd died at the same time, the land would have gone to whomever else she'd named in her will. I think it was that last husband of hers? But you were still a minor so you didn't have a will yet, did you? Just a long-lost father — who was going to be utterly devastated when he tracked you down only *after* your own tragic death."

"How were you going to do it?"

"I was thinking an overdose." His smile faded. "But then you just had to go and get yourself arrested, didn't you?"

The piece I hadn't even realized was missing fell into place.

JANE.

My mother's last act had been a fuck you, all right. It just hadn't been directed at me.

"You couldn't get to me in prison," I said. "That's why she set me up. So you couldn't get to me."

Outside, tires crunched over gravel. The smooth, round tones of on-air locution drifted up into the room. This time I didn't bother to try to hide my glance at the hall door. *Wasn't anyone coming?*

"I should go outside right now and tell them everything," I said.

"You *could*," he said. "But who would believe you?"

"Leo would. And Kelley and Rue and Renee."

"None of those people would speak against me. Not in my town. This place would crumble without me."

I shook my head. "But it isn't your town — not anymore. It's Cora's."

His face twisted. "Enough." He lifted the gun —

"So how about that local sports team?"

He pulled up. "What?"

"We could also talk about the weather," I said.

"What are you — ?"

"Stupid shit people said on the Internet?"

"This is ridiculous," he said. He aimed.

554

And then finally — *finally* — the doorknob rattled.

"Oh thank God," I said. "I really suck at small talk."

"Jane! Are you in there?"

"It's Stanton!" I yelled. "It's not Mitch, it's Stanton!"

The door thudded with the impact of a foot.

"It's over, Stanton. Kill me now and you're just making it worse for yourself."

Stanton curled his lip, tilted his head. "But can you really kill something that should never have been born?"

He pulled the trigger.

I shouldn't have been able to hear it. Not over the crack of the gunshot or the pounding at the door. Not over the frantic chorus of inquiries from outside. But still it was there, louder, somehow, than anything else in the room: the slow gurgle of blood from a wound. I looked at my left shoulder.

"Shit," I breathed. "Red is so not my color."

Movement, out of the corner of my eye. Stanton lifted the gun to take another shot, and adrenaline coursed through me, numbing my arm, lighting up my legs.

Thank God I can run in heels.

I slammed into Stanton, clawing at his

wrists, forcing the gun up and away. A bullet shot into the ceiling. He freed his right hand and thrust it at my chest, shoving me back. Then he let out a roar of fury, grabbed me by my shoulders, and slung me at the fireplace. I twisted around and crashed into the wrought-iron screen. He fisted his hand in my hair, wrenching back my head before ramming it forward into the marble edge of the mantel.

Through the door: *"Jane, hold on! Billy, get over here and help me —"*

Stanton's arm came around my waist. I reared back, kicking my feet up against the screen. He stumbled, pulling me with him, then spun me around and threw me into the credenza. My hand shot out and scrabbled across the tabletop for my purse.

"On three, Billy —"

A thump. The door buckled, but held.

My fingers wrapped around the purse strap, and I hurled the bag at Stanton's head. It caught him in the face; the gun fell to the ground. I blocked the swing of his fist with my good arm and drove my hip into his side. I kicked at the gun, just barely catching it with my toe, and it skittered across the floor. I lunged for it.

"Does anyone here have a gun?"

Stanton kicked out his leg, knocking me

to the floor. My hand clipped the grip of the gun and sent it sliding. It disappeared under the settee. Stanton put a knee on my back.

I tried to wriggle free, but he was too heavy. I twisted beneath him and managed to flip over. I squeezed my fingertips together and jammed them at his wild eyes. He howled and drew away. I scrambled out from under him and staggered to my feet, my chest heaving. Stanton started to come at me again — then saw something that changed his mind.

I followed his gaze. The contents of my purse had spilled out onto the floor. And amid the scrap and rubble of my belongings, there was a glint of silver.

Stanton's head came up. Our eyes met. My scissors.

And he was closer.

A shot exploded through the door, just missing the lock. Another series of slams and kicks. The door shuddered but still wouldn't open. *They're not going to get through in time.*

I ran for the balcony. Stanton grabbed the scissors and ran for me.

He caught me just as my fingertips grazed the railing. I screamed, and every single camera lens lifted toward me.

I spat. "You fuckers —"

Then, all of a sudden, the metal railing was digging into my spine, and Stanton's fingers were digging into my collarbone. The scissors I had sharpened to such a fine point were aimed at my heart, and in Stanton's eyes was the absolute certainty that This Was It for me — and sure enough, I was still expecting that miracle cure, that second wind, that call from the governor. That last-minute rescue by the cop who was at that very moment trying to break down the door.

No, that's not right — I wasn't expecting it. I was *wishing* for it.

I bared my teeth.

Fuck wishes.

I grabbed the scissors and wrenched them around.

Inside, another gunshot. The sound of splintering wood.

Stanton snarled and tried to regain control of the scissors, but I fought him off. My arms were trembling, on the verge of giving out.

Leo appeared in the door, Kelley and Renee right behind him —

With the last bit strength I had left, I drove the scissors forward and shoved them up into Stanton's chest.

We fell to the balcony floor together. A

bloom of blood pushed past Stanton's lips like a flower emerging from a bud. He choked, and beneath us pooled the sticky murk of our comingled blood.

Leo tried to pull me off Stanton, but I held tight, kept close, and looked into my father's face as the life left it. I had his eyes.

My mother's voice whispered through me: *Took you long enough.*

Kelley and Renee were carrying me back inside. They laid me on the settee and pressed something against the hole in my shoulder. Their hands pushed back my hair and stroked my brow. It hurts worse than it looks, Kelly said. Next to me, Rue was ripping off strips of her dress to use as makeshift bandages. Renee said she shouldn't be here. Rue told her to fuck off. I thanked God there wasn't room inside me to feel anything more.

"Call Hill City for backup," Leo was saying — to Billy? "We'll need paramedics, too. That lawyer guy said he'd deal with the press."

A crowd jostled at the door. "Move, goddammit," someone shouted.

Mitch forced his way through. He saw me first. "Jesus Christ."

I held up a hand. I didn't have the strength

to curl it into a fist, but he'd just have to deal. "Hey, bro. Up top."

Mouth hanging open, he turned and looked out at the balcony. He staggered over to the door; his hand clutched at the curtain. His words floated over to me — or maybe I just imagined them — or maybe I was remembering them.

"I should feel more than this."

More noise, more commotion. Peter and Eli had managed to push their way to the front of the crowd. When Peter's eyes landed on me, the recognition that flickered there was insufficient. He only saw Jane. Eli, though —

Eli turned and shouldered back the crowd. "Out," he ordered. He cast me one last glance over his shoulder, his eyes doing something I hadn't seen them do before. They weren't softening, but there was a sign perhaps of a slight easing of his inner regulations — like maybe, just this once, he would forgive his trousers a wrinkle or two.

The door closed behind him.

Something brushed against my arm. Leo was crouching down next to me. "You're a fucking idiot," he said.

"You don't know the half of it. Now give me a goddamned cigarette already."

He pulled a pack out of his shirt pocket

— then frowned. "Are you sure you should?"

"Way sure."

He tapped out a cigarette and put it between my lips. He lit it and held it while I inhaled. The smoke slipped into my lungs; relief rolled out through my veins. I leaned into Kelley's shoulder and closed my eyes. No one said anything. Not even Renee.

And as the rest of the world erupted around us, we sat, letting everything else fade away until the only sound was my breath, the sizzle of the cigarette, the infinitesimal hastening of my own demise.

That's the thing about smoking. Even when everything else is out of your control, awful and random and bleak and unfair, for a few moments a day, at least, you can control the velocity of your life.

Also it helps keep you thin.

From: CNN Breaking News
   <BreakingNews@mail.cnn.com>
Subject: CNN Breaking News
Date: Jan 14, 2014 2:43:29 PM EST
To: textbreakingnews@ema3lsv06.turner
  .com

A South Dakota jury has found Jane Jenkins guilty of grand theft auto, possession of stolen property, and second-degree murder.

Jenkins was convicted in 2003 of the murder of her mother and was imprisoned for ten years before the ruling was overturned. Eight weeks after her release, despite the objections of the police in charge of the investigation, Jenkins was indicted for the murder of her father, Stanton Percy. She maintains that she was acting in self-defense.

Noah Washington, Jenkins's defense attorney, told CNN today that he was already preparing an appeal.

WITHOUT A TRACE
Published 1.14.14

Trace here.

Karma's a bitch.

And so's Janie Jenkins.

No one who knew Rebecca Parker would have believed she was capable of murder.

And, despite the conclusions of the prosecutors, most commentators, and a jury of her peers, I still don't.

— Peter Strickland,
The Murderess & Me:
Five Days with Janie Jenkins

ACKNOWLEDGMENTS

I am deeply indebted to Clare Ferraro, Allison Lorentzen, and everyone else at Viking and Penguin Random House, particularly Hal Fessenden, Nicholas Bromley, Holly Watson, Angela Messina, Carolyn Coleburn, Nancy Sheppard, Paul Lamb, and Winnie De Moya.

My heartfelt gratitude as well (and as usual) to Kate Garrick and DeFiore and Company, to Shari Smiley and Resolution, and to everyone else who supported me and/or inspired me, wittingly or otherwise: Alison Hennessey, Annabel Oakes, Lane Shadgett, Megan Crane, Scott Korb, David Gates, Annie Ronan, Sara Burningham, Alison Cherry, Liz Lawson, and Ellen Amato.

And, of course, none of this would have been possible without my very beloved family.

(Which reminds me . . . Mom, please

repeat after me: *This is a work of fiction.*)
  Thank you.

The employees of Thorndike Press hope you have enjoyed this Large Print book. All our Thorndike, Wheeler, and Kennebec Large Print titles are designed for easy reading, and all our books are made to last. Other Thorndike Press Large Print books are available at your library, through selected bookstores, or directly from us.

For information about titles, please call:
  (800) 223-1244

or visit our Web site at:
  http://gale.cengage.com/thorndike

To share your comments, please write:
  Publisher
  Thorndike Press
  10 Water St., Suite 310
  Waterville, ME 04901